Seeking
a Perfect World

JOHN VITO PALLO

Visjonær Press

Published by

Visjonær Press
111 Doc Mac Dr.
Boscobel, WI 53805

ISBN-10: 0984959890
ISBN-13: 978-0-9849598-9-1

ACKNOWLEDGMENTS

Since this is my first attempt at writing, I have to acknowledge several people who stubbornly pushed me onward.

My wife Clara: She helped carry our bulky tower computer on our winter trips to Arizona and Florida. And she was brutally frank in her criticism of the actions and scenes portrayed in my story. I needed that. (Oh–we did finally get a laptop.)

My brother: Again a frank critic. Among other things, he corrected several geographic areas and even paid me a compliment which he is not prone to do. For example, "How did you imagine that stuff?"

And finally Tim–the main man–and his wife Lisa: Since Tim is a writer, I casually asked him to read my manuscript. His reading was anything but casual. He went through all 400+ pages with a microscope and still held on to his day job. His thoroughness is gratefully appreciated.

Seeking
a Perfect World

PROLOGUE

In 12167 N, Sogan, the Chinese dictator and the Premier Commander of Earth, declared the world "perfect."

In AD 1787, Alexander Tyler, a Scottish history professor at the University of Edinburgh, said:

> *A democracy is always temporary in nature; it simply cannot exist as a permanent form of government. A democracy will continue to exist up until the time that voters discover they can vote themselves generous gifts from the public treasury. From that moment on, the majority always votes for the candidates who promise the most benefits from the public treasury, with the result that every democracy will finally collapse due to loose fiscal policy, which is always followed by a dictatorship.*

The year is 12206 N (Neolithic). This corresponds to the old dating system of AD 2206. Instead of using the BC/AD form of dating invented by a monk Dionysius Exiguus in AD 525, it was decided to use Neolithic Age since that is when humankind most resembled modern humans. The dictator Sogan decreed there is no god and Christ is only a legend. Therefore AD and BC are meaningless.

Due to the preponderance of greedy, self-serving and corrupt politicians in the United States, as well the voting population, the country collapsed into complete gridlock and stagnation. Finally, with the lawlessness in Mexico and the bickering of a divided Canada, the three countries found they couldn't survive independently. In 12046 N (AD 2046) the United States, Mexico, and Canada joined as one nation and called themselves the Provinces of North Americus. Even so, by 12050 N (AD 2050), the Provinces of North Americus became second to the China Republic. Other nations also combined but still China was the major power. By 12051 N, there were only six nations. The China Republic (China, Asia and the whole Far East) became the major power in GNP, defense, production, physics and engineering technologies. They also led in energy consumption and had the greatest population. China was followed by the Provinces of North Americus, the Lands of Europe (Russia, the rest of continental Europe, England, Near East, Middle East and the Arabian Peninsula), South Americus, Africa United, and the nation of Australia. The uniting of the many nations resulted in many small pockets of bloodshed and ethnic fighting until the year of 12056 N.

A great worldwide electronic processing crisis occurred in 12055 N. Due to a supercomputer virus, all electronic funds disappeared. Every citizen, business, industry, municipality and nation was suddenly penniless. While the general Chinese population was insolvent too, the rulers and military of China still possessed electronic credit. Remote and primitive peoples had no knowledge of the problem and were completely untouched and unconcerned. They didn't even understand what had transpired.

Communication satellites mysteriously ceased to work. Sogan had decided that there were too many personal communication devices, and the proliferation of radio waves passing through the body were permanently damaging human DNA repair capabilities. Nearly every person in the civilized world had two or three communicating devices, and when all bandwidths were accessed, Sogan ended their rampant and invasive growth. Disposing of lithium batteries became a problem and the advent of long-life silicon batteries became the standard.

The printed word continued as a means of limited communication although highly censored. Writing by hand disappeared. The All Communication System, or ACS, became the primary means. Thought-communication was available, but it was not popular. Motion detecting communication devices failed to attract users and were viewed as ridiculous.

Sogan also initiated massive power outages, thus bringing the civilized world to its knees. Militaries, except Chinese, ceased functioning due to lack of fuel, ammunition and weapons of war. And, most assuredly, the lack of compensation removed the will to fight. Soldiers left their commands and returned to their homes. The only currency anyone possessed was that which they physically held on their person. Many of the wealthy committed suicide. The poor thought it comical.

In 12056 N, China stepped in and ended the crisis by selectively restoring electrical power and allotting everyone an equal amount of electronic credit. For years the world watched and suspected the Arabic countries of precipitating some kind of calamity. All the while, China had been preparing and planning such an event. When the communication and economic systems collapsed, China dispatched their soldiers to key cities throughout the world to maintain order and prevent the complete failure of a country's infrastructure. China then implemented its own limited communication system called ACS. It, too, was greatly censored. Due to the speed of computers, encryption became virtually impossible. Government eavesdropping became the norm.

In 12060 N, to prevent mutual annihilation, Sogan directed all nations to eliminate weapons of death and destruction. Nations had no choice but to comply. Since the majority of the world's armies were unpaid and unequipped, no nation attempted to repel the Chinese soldiers.

The citizens had food, shelter, clothing and several forms of entertainment so they became completely apathetic. Remote areas of the world were ignored.

The massive deployment of China's armies left the country nearly defenseless, but no one knew or cared. The strategic placement of soldiers ended all fighting and skirmishes. China also confiscated all precious metal reserves as well as the ownership of all residences, businesses, factories and financial institutions, rendering title to property worthless. Citizens were allowed to live in their current homes but were told they did not own them. Employees were told to remain at their place of work until replaced by robots. The wealthy were humbled at being made equal to the middle class. By establishing equal credit to all, the poor were also now raised to middle class levels.

No country took credit or blame for the calamity but, since China was unaffected, it was blamed. A few pockets of citizens rioted but were quickly quelled. The Chinese leadership knew quite well how to give the rioters small victories while all along they were being subdued. It was easily accomplished since no one was hungry or cold. Indifference reigned supreme.

Consistently and surreptitiously China had been secretly infiltrating governments and replacing officials with Chinese zealots and sympathizers. The conquest was accomplished in 12057 N with minimal bloodshed or resistance. North Americus' Congress, and even the Supreme Court, was disbanded. For a short time, Sogan allowed the President to be the supreme ruler of North Americus.

The takeover was so insidious that no one knew for many months what transpired until China demonstrated its control by eliminating all elections in the civilized world. This occurred in the year of 12060 N. In addition, insurgents mysteriously disappeared and ethnic violence suddenly was nonexistent. No faction could afford a conflict.

By 12065 N, all known weapons were destroyed other than in China, which maintained a complete arsenal. Although China denied it, there were rebels in remote areas of the world and they most assuredly had a hidden cache of small weapons.

By 12151 N due to genetic engineering, most abnormal behavior and illnesses had been gradually eliminated. While not yet complete, over three billion units of the human genetic code had been identified and cataloged. If a tendency toward diabetes or cancer was exhibited in a person's genes, it was corrected. If a tendency toward aggressiveness or untruthfulness was revealed, it too was repaired.

Nanotechnology (machines a thousand times smaller than the human hair), otherwise known as molecular manufacturing, had been successfully developed. These miniature machines would seek out and kill diseases after being injected into the bloodstream. There was practically no lying, stealing, and cheating, and seldom any murder, rape or disputes of any kind.

Arguments had been reduced to discussions. There was little need for politicians, lawyers and soldiers but an increasing need for police (now known as Sentinels). Since illness and disease were no longer threats to life, pandemics were unheard of. Doctors or nurses were only needed as medics in cases of injury until a person could be transported to a robotic hospital.

Teachers and schools had been declared useless since the All Level Education and Knowledge Center (ALEKC) taught in the home whatever it thought was necessary. There was definitely no need for religion or religious ministers since belief in god was discouraged as a futile exercise.

There were only two classes: the authorities and the middle class. Slowly the population had become peaceful, docile and content. No one saw a need to covet another country's land or possessions. More and more professions and industries had been replaced by robots. In addition, most robot repairs were being performed by other robots. Soon humans would have nothing to do. Each adult had an allotted amount of credit in their account.

A perfect form of socialism had been gradually taking shape. The government decided what luxuries a person may have and, if he or she had enough credit, they could requisition an item. All electronic income was equal. As robots took over industries and factories, humans had less to do. The government paid all medical expenses and, as genetic repair became commonplace during gestation, less medical needs existed.

In 12166 N, all humans had to submit to be "chipped." A small electronic/bionic chip, about five millimeters square, was implanted at birth by robots at the back of the neck at the base of the skull. The chip held a code for each person. Genetic information was encoded, as was a unique identification number. The chip transmitted its information and location at all times. At any gathering, whether it be a meeting, social event, theater or sporting event, the visitor and/or participant would be scanned at the entrance. The scanning was quite unobtrusive and the chip could transmit and receive data even through clothing. There were also many portable scanners operated by the All Comprehensive Director (ACD) Sentinels. Also, hidden scanners were placed in a surreptitious manner in many locations. Humans could be unknowingly and randomly scanned at any time or place. If a person's chip missed a random scan or did not transmit a signal for ten seconds, immediately an alarm was sent to all Sentinels to ascertain the reason.

Sogan felt the scanning and transmission ability of the chip provided double-control of his subjects, and insect-sized spy drones were no longer needed. While destroying other nations' satellites, China positioned its own dedicated satellites to visibly track any warm-blooded being. They could not, however, scan a chip. If a person died, the lack of life signs was immediately transmitted to ACD.

Sogan, the Premier Commander of Earth, appointed Vice Premiers in each nation. The Vice Premiers had a limited amount of authority. The Premier Commander had his residence in an undisclosed location in China, and he was the supreme ruler. Sogan, however, received his orders from the ACD. The ACD was a highly complex, trained virus/bionic/electronic computer capable of tracking the six billion inhabitants of Earth by means of their chip. ACD had the power of reason and imagination. People surmised that ACD was located on the Moon and, since one side of the Moon always faced Earth, the computer was in constant contact with earth-bound relay receivers. All disputes were handled first by a chamberperson and next by a Vice Premier. If not resolved at those levels, the dispute escalated to the Premier Commander. If still unresolved, the Premier could relay the problem to ACD. ACD decisions could not be questioned. Lawsuits were terminated 150 years previous to this time. A few in the population suspected ACD was all-knowing and all-seeing and could even control the actions of all humans by means of their implanted chip. This theory had not been confirmed or even tested. Since peace and contentment were evident all over the known earth, no one seemed to be concerned by these alarmists. Discipline, if needed, was handled by Sentinels. Although vehemently denied, in extremely remote lands, some humans remained unchipped, living in poverty and completely oblivious to the condition of world.

There was no currency; all fund transfers were processed electronically. Gold, silver and other precious metals had been confiscated. These metals were publicly declared worthless and, after several generations and the market being flooded with these metals, no one cared to save or acquire them. Bartering persisted for a while until it was realized it was unnecessary. There was no need for trading since desired items were available by ordering them and debiting an account. A large item, such as a yacht or mansion, was not allowed since individual citizens could not own these items.

Only a minimum of employment was still needed and it was mainly accomplished from the home. The Premier Commander stated that by 12230 N all employment, except by officials and Sentinels, would be unnecessary since all work would soon be performed by robots. All credit dispersal amounts were determined by ACD, and compensation levels were public knowledge. ACD set the maximum and minimum compensation amount. All mechanical assembly was performed perfectly by robots in manufacturing complexes. Replacing failed home equipment was accomplished by a robot delivery system. Computer-guided robots brought the item to a home, removed the defective item and installed the new. Smaller items were simply delivered to the home by the same robot delivery system. All computer functions had gone from the magnetic core computer to trained virus/bionic methods.

Communication could now be accomplished by a personal thought system, but it was not well accepted. Two probes had to be in placed on the scalp. The thoughts of the person, such as thinking of another's name, established a communication connection, but only if the other person was wearing his or her probes. Since the device was powered by body heat and there were no relay towers for this system, its range was quite limited. Also, because the personal thought communication system required the two terminals to be in contact with a very small shaved area of the scalp, most preferred the old tried-and-true earpiece and mini-microphone. In addition, the personal thought system required some intense mental discipline, especially if the caller knew two or more people of the same name or if the other person was in communication with someone else.

Vision screens grew smaller and smaller until they went out of favor. Larger screens again became the norm. Touch screens also faded from use as users grew tired of constantly raising their arm and the screens becoming dirty and scratched. Eyewear that contained a small monitor built into the glass was unpopular, since people felt the glasses were cumbersome and unattractive.

With thought probes connected to the scalp, a person could virtually put themselves into a scene of a game. While it was only a mental picture, it proved too dangerous, as some programmed themselves flying through the air or jumping off a cliff. When they hit the ground, even though only a mental picture, the participant was traumatized so dramatically that he or she died. The same was true of fight events; if the operator lost a battle, they actually died. In addition, some became addicted to pleasure scenes. Few realized that memory and imagination died. They were not needed.

Voice command of devices returned as the easiest and simplest method. The keyboard and even the archaic mouse resurged as another interface of choice. As employment became less and less necessary, and the population became more and more unconcerned with the affairs of the world, instant communication also became unnecessary. Writing by hand and the need for memorizing disappeared completely. As previously stated, the government at one time dispatched small insect-sized spy drones, but since the people became so apathetic and non-threatening, drones were deemed unnecessary. People were kept in check by fostering a rumor that the chips transmitted all thoughts to ACD, although this was untrue.

Any partial body organ failure could be repaired and rebuilt into a healthy organ, but a complete failure could not be salvaged. Robotic surgery still could not attach every nerve fiber in event of a severed limb but it was predicted that soon a loss of a finger or leg could be regenerated as easily as hair regrows when cut. Stem cell repairs remained problematic due to some cases of uncontrolled cancerous cell reproduction and occasionally grotesque results. There were no birth defects, no unwanted births or out-of-wedlock births. By means of gene modification, addictive and compulsive behavior had been removed from all humans.

The only two classes of people were the ruling class and the middle class. There was no lower class. The maximum population of the world had been declared to be six billion, reduced by attrition from ten billion years earlier. And except for a few outlaws in remote areas who were unchipped, population remained constant. Some argued there were almost one billion unchipped people, but it was impossible to verify. Bounty hunters of all nations were searching for these unfit beings with orders to "erase" them.

Aging had been slowed considerably. All humans died at 150 years. Some very useful individuals were allowed to live to a maximum of 200 years, but people did not understand why or who determined the age of death. How death occurred was even more mysterious.

ACD rigidly controlled all human reproduction by neutering children at birth. When ACD determined the population was falling below the six billion limit, it allowed additional births. After the age of twenty, if a man and woman wanted to marry, ACD allowed a marriage. But no child would be allowed unless a couple requested permission and ACD issued a permit. Then, a robotic operation reversed the neutering, and a boy or girl would be permitted to gestate in the womb or birthing lab, whichever the couple desired. ACD decided whether a female or male was needed. ACD then forced both parents to be neutered again. Couples were allowed a maximum of two children. Two humans of the same sex could also ask for a marriage permit. The pair could ask to raise a child and, if permitted, a fetus would be propagated in the birthing lab. The fetus would have chromosomes from each parent. Sexual activity had become purely recreational.

Ninety-nine percent of birth defects had been eliminated because of genetic engineering and repair. A defective gene could be located and repaired in the womb or birthing lab or even after birth, although it was more difficult in later years and was not foolproof. If a fetus or adult was determined to have a missing or extra gene or even a broken code in the gene, it would be repaired. For example, if a person exhibited the genetic code for diabetes, a tendency toward extreme anger, illness tendencies, or any unacceptable behavior, it would be corrected to ACD parameters.

The maximum height decreed for men and women was 1.87 meters. The maximum weight was 455.5 kilograms. The maximum IQ allowed was 150 and, not surprisingly, all parents chose it. Most couples chose the maximums for males and, due to old traditions, chose a lesser height and weight for females. The parents could request certain hair color, eye color, etc.— even ethnic features—and the requests were usually granted.

Gene engineering and repair had been functioning for fifty-six years. Therefore, anyone over fifty-five years old would still be part of a motley mix in terms of skin and hair color, features and size. Allegedly, all human frailties in older humans had been genetically repaired, although such repairs were difficult and not always successful, sometimes even regressing. Occasionally, a few "perfect" humans displayed unorthodox behavior or an illness later in life. It was assumed that a cosmic ray collision caused a scattering of gamma particles, thus damaging a perfect gene. Usually, the defect was repaired quickly. Cloning had been determined unreliable and only a short-term fix. Therefore it had been declared illegal.

Massive, electrified walls surrounded all metropolitan areas. Citizens could leave their city with approval but were cautioned about danger from outlaws.

Old residential buildings from the 2000s had been demolished or allowed to rot and crumble. New housing took the form of football-shaped structures lying horizontally, half of which was below ground. They were called domes and consisted of single, duplex or quadraplex units. They were constructed of an almost indestructible and impenetrable blue material called Plaztec, which needed no maintenance. Domes shielded occupants from weather and even from gamma rays. No housing was permitted in flood or major earthquake zones.

A cold fusion powered reclaim unit serviced each dome. The unit supplied temperature control, electricity, communication needs and waste removal. The only supply needed by a dome was a rationed amount of water to replace evaporation. A robotic vehicle gathered waste from each done once every six months. Waste was transformed into a 20-centimeter cube of rock.

Local travel was accomplished by cambris. These four-wheeled, four-passenger vehicles were powered by forced electron batteries and had a top speed of 80 km/h with a range of 150 km. Any fuel-burning vehicle was expressly forbidden. ACD controlled vehicles to the occupants' desired destinations. No local control of the cambri was required, but the operator had the option to override ACD. Letting ACD control the vehicle assured no accidents, but some of the elder citizens preferred to do their own operating. After securing an imaging headset, merely the thought of a desired location entered it in the mobile computer, and the cambri traveled to the requested location. The location could also be entered by voice. Removing the headset was the means to override ACD's control.

Nationwide long-distance travel, except over large areas of water, was accomplished by trams (monorail vehicle ferries). Cambris and individuals were loaded on these trams for travel to distant cities. The top speed of a tram was 500 km/h. The old highway system between cities had been allowed to deteriorate.

Forced electron battery hovercrafts accomplished a limited amount of short distance air travel for the general population. The hovercraft could ferry only four pedestrians. It could reach speeds of 300 km/h over smooth land or water but their range was approximately 200 km. VIPs had their own means of travel. All air travel for sub-premiers or any VIP was supplied by long distance, hot-fusion engine, vertical takeoff and landing (VTOL) hover vehicles. These vehicles were much faster than battery hovercrafts and were capable of 600 km/h and had a range of 2100 km. They had a capacity of ten occupants. The average citizen was not allowed in one of these hover vehicles and there was a limited amount of them in existence. Since ACD controlled the airspace, the proliferation of these air vehicles would, as Sogan said, cause radio wave gridlock. Surface cambris seemed to cause no problem.

Previously, travel to the Moon was by hydrogen/oxygen fueled rockets and left only moisture as waste in its combustion. Burning of any material that produced ash, carbon monoxide or carbon dioxide was prohibited in 12090 N. In the past, proton ejection engines and Medusa propulsion systems accomplished travel to distant planets and beyond, but outer space journeys were ended many years previously. ACD deemed such travel useless and a waste of energy. Protection from cosmic rays and sun flares also proved to be a vexing problem. ACD also had reasoned Earth beings were the only living entities in the universe. It asserted that the planets, and galaxies contained nothing of use. A rumor persisted that one or two rebel colonies existed on Mars and possibly a moon of Saturn.

Sentinels were not considered to be police. Allegedly, ACD chose a person to serve as a Sentinel because he or she exhibited completely benevolent characteristics.

It was advantageous to a person to allow scanning of the chip as he or she moved about. Since few humans did anything illegal, there seemed to be no reason to avoid being scanned by ACD. In a more suspicious time, a person might worry that these chips knew one's every thought and controlled life and death. By design, unauthorized removal of the chip caused death.

A well-known disease was creeping into this perfect society. Dr. Roland Davidson was not aware of it, but the disease of boredom had infected him and others.

He contemplated whether his existence was the result of intelligent design or random mutations and natural selection and also whether some greater or supernatural being existed. Dr. Davidson had an unusual and dangerous hypothesis that led him to wonder whether he'd discovered a means to redesign life or even create life. He wrestled with the thought of whether this was the responsibility solely of a greater being.

In 12167 N, the Premier Commander declared that the world simply needed a kind and just king. He claimed to be that king and the world was now "perfect." But Dr. Roland Davidson was one of a growing number of anomalies.

JOHN PALLO

PART I

WE LIVE HERE

CHAPTER ONE

"Dad. Did they really used to burn oil?" Fifteen-year-old Risa Davidson was reading her ancient history school program on the All Communication System (ACS). She twisted sideways on her shiny, Plaztec chair, slightly slouching. She was linked to the All Level Education and Knowledge Center (ALECK) channel. She took off her brain wave receptor and its tiny scalp sensors, pulled some of her blond, tangled hair from it, and looked at her dad.

"Sure did," Dr. Roland Davidson replied. "I think around the late 1980s and early 2000s nations began showing concern about the soot, ash and carbon dioxide emitted by burning fossil or mineral fuels. Eventually burning anything was prohibited except, for a time, as fuel for ground vehicles. They didn't have forced electron battery cambris as we have now. The vehicles were called automobiles, and they all required a refined version of oil or ethanol distilled from plant matter as their energy source. Finally the automobile was replaced by forced electron battery cambris.

"The governments of most nations began trying to cut back on the pollution caused by burning," Dr. Davidson explained. "I think it was about fifty to hundred years later all burning was prohibited. Except for air vehicles, everything was electric-powered. All power plants were fission fueled. It's amazing but it was about the time most world scientists agreed cold or hot fusion was a hoax or at least a foolish dream."

Risa laughed, "You mean they thought the fusion powered reclaim unit we have in the lower level of our dome couldn't be built?"

"Yep. And now every dome has a fusion reclaim unit purring away. Your program should tell you the date most civilized countries decided to outlaw all burning without a deviation permit. I think it was about 12090 N or 2090 AD as they called it then, wasn't it?"

Risa concurred, "Yeah. It says here in 12090 N all burning was prohibited except by the government granting a deviational proclamation."

Dr. Davidson walked over to the bright screen of Risa's All Com System and looked at her study work assignment. Every residence had one or two All Communication Systems. Risa was logged on to the ALEKC channel. Six days a week, five hour a day, all students were required to be connected to the interactive portion of the ALEKC. A brain wave and scalp sensor provided most of the interaction between the student and the bright, flashing monitor. Students were no longer taught how to write, since all lessons were transmitted by brain waves and a limited amount of vision displays. They were, however, taught to read the printed word in their native language and Chinese, even though their ACS could easily translate any language to any other language. If a person needed to make a note or reminder, they could simply enter it in the memo-minder of their ACS. There were extremely few occasions when a hand-written note needed to be made.

To be certain each student's time was properly recorded, their workstation was located under one of the many scanners in a home, or dome as they're called. The scanner read and received transmissions from the personal chip implanted at birth at the back of every human's neck at the base of the skull. Each student could spend as much extra time as desired disconnected from the ALEKC but still use the library extension channel. The All Comprehensive Director (ACD), a supercomputer located on the Moon, determined their major field of study by what was needed in the world and assigned it to a student. This contradicted the statement that soon robots would accomplish all services and manufacturing.

At times Roland wished he could have lived in the early 2000s or even earlier when the United States was the greatest superpower. By 12050 N, the United States was second to China and deeply in debt to them. At that time, 99 percent of the United States population didn't bother to vote and the government had completely collapsed into stagnation, corruption and total gridlock. China had embedded their zealots and sympathizers in all governments of the world. The last election was held in 12060 N and the supposed winners were completely unknown individuals. The Great Monetary Disappearance of 12055 N precipitated the final and complete demise of the United States' world influence. By some means, all electronic monies disappeared. The only money anyone had was what they had on their person. Massive power failures brought the country to their knees. Strangely, China stepped in to rescue the United States.

"Gosh, that was after 12046 N when Canada and Mexico joined into one nation with the United States. We were still second to China, weren't we?"

Risa's father agreed. "Yes. United States national pride suffered a great defeat then. Now, nobody seems to care where they were born or what nationality they were. We're just citizens of Earth."

Risa's feelings were just the opposite of her father's desire to return to simpler times.

"It also says terrorists threatened the world around the early 12000s. I'm sure glad we didn't live then. What did terrorists do anyway?"

Leaning against the curved wall of their dome, Roland looked out the window, staring at the artificial, green grass under a cloudy sky.

"They would set off bombs in populated areas. They were intent on destroying anything connected to the United States. They had an intense hatred of us because of our constant attempts to implant our way of life into their societies. They saw us as big bullies who assumed our way of life was the only way. I believe the terrorism period peaked around 2025 AD or 12025 N. As the United States, also known as the Great Satan, lost its influence in the world, the terrorists lost their cause."

Risa contentedly replied, "I'm glad our great Premier Commander Sogan is so kind. He doesn't force his will on anyone. From what I've studied so far, socialism is such a wonderful way of life."

Risa didn't see her father frown. "Yeah, I suppose so." Roland had growing doubts about the Premier. "At one time he was a great benefactor but lately...." Roland let his words trail off as he continued gazing out the window.

Risa was still looking at the ACS screen. "How'd everyone travel in the old days, you know, with all those borders to cross and stuff?"

"It wasn't until 12166 the 'chip on the ol' neck' was instigated and it pretty much solved the travel problem. The people had to have a driver's license and a passport before they could travel."

"That sounds so silly," said Risa.

"Now the chip takes care of that." again referring to the implanting at birth of a computer chip in all human beings, the removal of which supposedly caused immediate death.

"Dad, it says here about 12060 N, the people of North Americus stopped voting. Is that the election you were talking about when the winners were unknown names?"

"Yep." Roland appeared thoughtful. "The way I heard the stories from my great grandparents, citizens could vote for their leaders. But the people grew so apathetic about the corruption of officials, they gave up being concerned. The Chinese had cultivated so many Caucasian converts to their way of life; they embedded these fanatics into our government and other governments around the world. The affluent population had all the luxuries they wanted, and the poor were kept out of sight, so the rich didn't care who was in office. One day, they found out. It was China. Still nobody cared."

Risa was bored with this part of her school session and was glad to digress with her father about earlier times. Even though occupations were becoming more scarce and unnecessary due to the prevalence of robots, schooling was required. She had to continue. After all, her father was a doctor of something scientific, something to do with genes. Maybe she would be forced to enter a scientific field too. He could never explain to her the complete nature of his profession. She did know he was experimenting with something and it was all very secretive. Except for scientific studies and experimentation, robots were performing just about all mechanical labor and services.

Risa was expected to finish formal training by age sixteen, and her sixteenth birthday was in six months. Then the government would do a quick and usually haphazard interview and assign her to a vocation dependent on availability. After four years of apprenticeship, the student would be granted some leeway as to what branch of work could finally be chosen.

With more and more occupations being performed by robots and computers, it was becoming increasingly difficult to find an available position. Most people were content to do nothing all day except watch roundball games or vision discs, or simply travel. Risa was just like her father: she had to be doing something worthwhile. Since her father was a fairly famous scientist, she would be expected to follow in his footsteps. Roland didn't want her to follow him into his field of gene structure analysis.

Most known diseases had been eliminated by 12150 due to humans having perfect DNA structure. Some DNA repairs were performed on humans born before 12150, albeit more difficult and the repairs seemed to fail after several years. Molecular nano-machines injected into the bloodstream eliminated molecular diseases. Most body organ failures could be corrected by sequential stem cell replacement. Hence the edict of 12167 N that "The Earth is now perfect." However, not many advances had been made in treating mental diseases.

Risa looked up at her father. "When do you have to go to Lower California?"

"Next week. I'll be there only one day but it'll take two days' travel. It'll take about ten hours each way on the Tram. I'll take the red cambri. You and Mom can use the blue one if you need to go somewhere."

"Dad, can I tell you something?"

"Sure, Sweetie."

Risa almost whispered, "I want to grow plants. I want to work in the plant growth industries."

"Oh Risa," Roland replied with a bit of exasperation in his voice.

"I don't want to be a scientist, Dad. I don't mean anything against what you do, whatever it is. I just want to watch food products grow. People are getting tired of eating chemical cenes. A lot of people want cenes like they had in the old days, and I want to be a part of that. I love listening to great-grandfather's stories about his grandparents growing food on his father's farm."

Growing food was almost a lost art. All nourishment was available in the cene bars. They were provided in many flavors and colors. They reminded Dr. Davidson of a very old vision disc story in which dead bodies were ground up and cooked. The human remains were then reconstituted as cenes, called food in the old days. Fortunately, unlike in the old vision disc, today's cene bars were not dead body parts. Water and liquid soy were the only beverages available, flavored, colored or plain. Alcohol was expressly forbidden, but it did turn up now and then. Any intoxication of any kind was not permitted or tolerated. Mind-altering drugs still turned up every so often.

What Risa said was not treasonable, but it was highly unusual. It was like going back two hundred years. But there was a growing segment of the population wanting earth-grown cenes.

"We'll have to see about it, Risa. We'll have to see what the government assigns you as a vocation."

"Dad! You know I don't have much choice. Don't you have some pull with the state? Can't you put in a word for me with the chamberpersons? You know, in four years there may not be any work positions available. It wouldn't be easy to get into the food growth industries then."

Risa's father looked at her All Com System screen as it announced rudely, "Risa Davidson, I am waiting for your next input! Please reposition your brain wave receptor!" It was flashing and waiting for a response from Risa.

"Maybe," he said, "but you know ACD decides what professions are needed. Have you looked into this field at all? Is it crowded? Have any of your student friends inquired about this study?"

"No. And I'm afraid they'll laugh at me if I ask them or even talk about it." Risa looked bored and wistful. "I don't like science and that's all there is to it."

"What about your study of the Chinese language? Don't forget your practice with the translator." Roland was trying to change the subject.

Risa plopped her elbows on her desk and looked out the curved window, not looking at anything in particular, "Why do I have to practice? We have the ACS."

The ACS was becoming impatient, waiting for a reply from Risa. It blurted out, "Do you want to continue lesson forty, switch to your Chinese lesson or terminate for today? If you choose to terminate, you will have completed only three hours of the required five hours."

"Continue lesson forty," she said grumpily. "This brain wave receptor sure messes up my hair."

Risa's father wasn't angry at his daughter since he didn't like his chosen vocation either. He had a great, delicate and definitely dangerous decision to make. His true reason for his trip to Lower California could be quite treasonous and its purpose was definitely illegal. His life and that of his family could be put in a terribly disadvantageous position and possibly in great harm. There was no stopping him though. He had to go. He wondered how he'd be able to bypass the scanners at the Genome Conference and go to the meeting of fellow malcontents. How would he be able to fool the scanners? And most important, he didn't want to draw any attention to himself by talking to a chamberperson about a favor for his daughter. None of the thirteen chamberpersons in his district owed him any favors.

"I'll see if there's anything I can do, Sweetie."

Roland stroked his daughter's long, blond hair sticking out from under the brain wave receptor. She had fine features; long eyelashes and a cute dimple her left cheek. Risa was quick to smile just like her mother. He was glad he and his wife chose blond hair and blue eyes for his daughter. Her light blue utility coveralls and white blouse contrasted nicely with her hair. They designed Risa to be tall and athletic.

Melody, Roland's wife, designed Risa to be about three to four centimeters taller than herself for no particular reason. I always wished I was a little taller, Melody would say.

JOHN PALLO

CHAPTER TWO

Roland went to the upper level of their dome and began preparing for his trip. The tan Plaztec fiber carpeting crunched lightly as he climbed the stairs. He noticed for the first time several changes and additions Melody had made to the décor of their dome. Several artificial flowers and pictures were added to brighten up the dull interior of their home. The wall and ceiling color of the Plaztec dome material was light beige, which was unusual since the normal color of Plaztec was blue. The color didn't bother Roland much but he could see where the atmosphere would dampen her spirits. Melody was insistent regarding the interior wall colors. She wanted any color as long as it wasn't blue. Somehow she got her way. The Plaztec furniture left no color choice. It was all blue. Even the cene warmer and cooler appliances were blue. Also, the human waste and personal cleaning room was blue, thought Roland. Since the amount of light passing through a window could be controlled, curtains were a thing of the past.

Dr. Davidson was assigned the vocation of cytogeneticist gene structure analysis. For many years he had been working on further slowing of the aging process of genes, cells and telomere length. His true mission to California, though, had nothing to do with gene aging. He was sure the real reason he was invited to the Genome Conference had nothing to do with the conference as such. By an extremely devious method he was invited to the conference as a ruse. Once in California he would somehow leave the conference and attend a secret meeting of underworld scientists. He was positive it had something to do with his recent writing of the feasibility of disassembly and reassembly of molecules and, most assuredly, the addendum.

Roland had written an article published on the ACS about his accidental discovery of a theory, or more correctly, a hypothesis of molecular construction and reconstruction. A hypothesis is simply an unproven theory. But he was convinced the real reason for his invitation to the clandestine meeting in California had to do with his addendum to the paper. The subject of the addendum catching everyone's attention was the additional possibility of disassembly and reassembly of atoms. Molecular reconstruction meant an orange could be changed into an apple with addition, subtraction or rearrangement of a molecule or two. But by atomic reconstruction, changing the number of electrons, neutrons and protons in the atom, meant lead could be changed into gold. Transmutation could change a neutron into a proton. Since every object on Earth consists primarily of empty space, rearranging the atoms means it could be changed into something that doesn't now exist. What scared Roland, and yet fascinated him, was this secret underground group had also noted the addendum. The atom rearrangement was a proposition Roland felt sure he could prove and even perform given enough energy and an extremely powerful computer.

Several extremely powerful computers have been built but they required the energy of medium sized city. These computers could now make human-like decisions, for example; is this a dog or cat?

But what was their interest? Who are these people and what do they do? Roland didn't know the name of this group but they contacted Roland by a strange courier. The message was hand delivered by a young and attractive, blond haired woman. The message was sealed in a special envelope. It contained a flyer announcing an upcoming roundball tournament in South York's main stadium. The woman told Roland to read the back side. On the back was a message inviting him to their meeting in California. The message stated all secrecy and security would be handled, including the by-passing of scanners. After reading the note, Roland looked up to question the woman further. She was gone. Within fifteen minutes, the note disintegrated just as the woman courier appeared to have done. He looked around as if someone might be watching him, although he knew this was unlikely.

Roland's primary fear was Sogan, the Premier Commander. The Premier too was most interested in the addendum. He commanded Roland to give him an update on his progress in six months. Roland dreaded the fact he even added the addendum to his paper. By official encoded messaging the Premier asked if, just in theory, a human could be changed into a different life form. And he asked if the reverse could be accomplished too. The ramifications were horrendous. Roland took the questions one step farther. Could the modified being think, talk, write as before? Would it still have the same human emotions? Could an ape be changed into a human? He didn't know. The most difficult operation would be the reconstruction of the cell. The DNA would have to be redesigned so the item or creature would look or act properly. If a chromosome was improperly positioned, the being may have an extra eye or a leg appearing on its stomach. Roland shivered as he thought about what he had proposed. He originally hypothesized only inert material could be changed but not living organisms. Once again he pondered the existence of a god. What would this god think of his tinkering with life? This is why he had to go to the meeting of fellow radicals. He needed help and he needed cohorts. He cautiously wanted to trust these unknown fellow scientists because he had to trust someone. Hopefully they could sort through choices he had. He had been stalling his results of the experiments on molecular reconstruction for a year now, and the Premier Commander was getting impatient. Atomic reconstruction was the next step. The Earth is humming along smoothly. Why is there so much importance to his hypothesis? Dr. Roland Davidson had been given an order to present his progress report to the Premier six months from today, the month of his daughter's graduation and birthday.

Roland looked in his mirror and pondered his life. His hair was still pure black, just as his parents ordered when his genes were chosen. He had dark eyes, a prominent chin and no age spots or wrinkles. His skin was slightly tan and smooth, a result of his parents wanting to pass on their Italian origin. ACD did allow the choosing of ethnic appearances. His height was 1.87 meters and weight 455.5 kilograms. He was 44 years old and his wife, Melody, was 45. She was given a Norwegian appearance which, like her daughter, included blond hair and blue eyes. This too was chosen by her parents. Melody was slim and appeared at first to be quite delicate. She was, however, in very good physical shape. She exercised regularly on the synthetic resistance game and had very visible muscle tone. Roland, while not maintaining muscle tone as well as his growing ten year old son, was in good health. Young Brooke also exercised regularly on the synthetic resistance game. He was designed to look like his father as was Risa designed to look like her mother. Even at age ten Brooke was beginning to express his individualism. He preferred to keep his head shaved causing Roland to wonder why they included thick, black hair in his genetic structure. Darker eyes and heavier eyebrows were also integrated into Brooke's makeup. In designing an offspring, some thought had to be put into the outcome. It would be very easy to create apparent twins of different age or possibly a clone. He was maturing nicely with an interest in roundball sports but he also had a keen curiosity in things mechanical. This was somewhat unusual because most mechanical equipment was repaired by robots.

Roland and Melody had been married for twenty years. Since he had been born well after the DNA correction programs had begun, he wondered why he had such feelings of discontentment. Did these fellow scientists at the upcoming secret meeting have some of the same feelings? Roland had noted a common thread running through a few of the populace; discontentment. Maybe a stray gamma ray damaged a gene in his makeup, causing him to be discontented. Could he now easily lie or cheat or steal? Years ago in his ethics class he learned a human could not, without difficulty, exhibit these human frailties. Would he have to lie at the gene structure meeting, telling the organizers he couldn't wait to hear their speeches while knowing he was going to duck out to a secret meeting? His wife, Melody, hadn't asked him specifically about attending the meeting but would he, or could he, tell her a bold lie? Many humans told small, insignificant, lies but his reason for the California trip would be a great distortion of the truth.

Roland was thoroughly confused but at the same time excited.

And on top of all these questions was the presence of ACD. Was ACD monitoring all his thoughts by means of his chip? Was ACD letting him and his fellow traitors plod along to their demise? Would his family be punished or persecuted or would Melody be simply told Dr. Davidson's time on earth had ended? Melody would receive a short, state epistle on her ACS recommending she remarry. ACD seemed to like humans living in pairs, whether male and female, male and male or female and female.

Roland remembered reading in an old friend's hidden Bible about Adam and Eve. They were supposedly perfect with no weaknesses or illnesses. Roland knew it was all fantasy but what if is wasn't. Why did Eve tempt Adam? Why did Eve even want to try the apple, or whatever fruit it was? Legend says she wanted to have the knowledge of God. She ate the apple and gave some to Adam to eat. As the old Bible story continues, their minds were darkened. Did that event cause their chromosomes to be damaged? Is that why Adam and Eve felt shame? Is that why their child, Cain, could now feel jealousy and hatred? Hatred enough to kill his brother? It seems as if from that time on humans could feel anger, hatred, jealousy and all human frailties.

"Dad!" Roland's son Brooke brought him back to reality. His shaved head was wet with sweat. "Our coach Mr. Leeger collapsed at roundball practice! He was running with us and just fell down. He looked terrible. He looked all blue. I think he died. I thought it wasn't supposed to happen like that anymore."

Mr. Leeger was a long time chamberperson and seemed to be held in high esteem by the Premier Commander. He was also part-time roundball coach. He was 168 years old and due to his high position was being allowed to live beyond the mandated 150-year life span to 200 years. He was born over a hundred years before DNA repair was initiated. Forty or fifty years ago he had 'died' of heart failure but miraculously recovered. It was assumed gene repair had performed the miracle but due to Mr. Leeger's age Roland had his doubts. The rest of his body had the appearance of a 168-year-old man yet he was able to run with the kids, that is, until today. If Leeger has truly died, there will be an immediate appointment of a new chamberperson. Anyone older than forty years of age could be appointed and there was no refusing the selection. Five years of service were demanded after which the chamberperson could resign. Strangely enough, almost everyone stated they would resign after five years but no one ever did. Gene correction or not, humans still loved power and control.

Roland and his son ran to the roundball field. It was about three hundred meters to the field from their dome. The roundball field was similar to the soccer fields of years ago but with designed mounds placed in various locations. On their way, Roland saw a yellow and green Sentinel's bug-shaped cambri driving away. Sentinels were allegedly docile, unarmed enforcers of the laws. He tried to wave it down but the Sentinels didn't notice him.

At the field a group of roundball players and spectators stood in a large circle. They were all straining to see into the middle of the circle. They separated as Roland and Brooke ran up. Mr. Leeger was lying face up on the ground. His eyes were open and his face had a bluish hue. He didn't seem to be breathing.

"Has anyone called a Sentinel?" Roland asked out of breath.

The crowd looked at each other but no one answered.

"We didn't know what to do, Dad. A couple of Sentinels were here watching us practice but after Mr. Leeger collapsed we didn't see them anymore."

Roland could understand their confusion. Death was seldom ever witnessed. One morning a person would just not show up. A curious wife, husband or associate would enter their name and ID number in the ACS and receive an unknown entry display. That was it. Confirmation of termination would be when the spouse or employer received a remarry or rehire suggestion.

Not bringing his bothersome thought communicator Roland had to use his Personal Communicator System to call a Sentinel. The Sentinels didn't move too quickly so he knew it would take them at least a half an hour to arrive. Maybe the two Brooke saw were still nearby. He then called Melody to tell her.

"Melody, I believe Mr. Leeger just died here at…"

Melody interrupted him, "Roland. I was just going to call you! I just got a call on my PCS from an assistant vice premier! I've been appointed to replace Mr. Leeger! I'm a chamberperson!"

A chamberperson was at the bottom of the chain of command. ACD is the top of the chain with the Premier, Sogan, next. Following the Premier are several Vice Premier and then a multitude of chamberpersons. Sentinels were simply around for security.

"What?" The hair on the back of Roland's neck rose. "How did you…? How did they know?"

"Roland, where are you?"

Roland shivered and wondered how ACD knew of Leeger's death so quickly.

"I'm at the ball field with Brooke. This is where Leeger died. It just happened. When did you get the notice?"

Melody voice was shaking. "I got the notice about five minutes ago. I went numb and then I called you. Roland, I don't want to be a chamberperson."

"Just relax, honey. Just relax."

"Roland, what do I do? Where do I go?"

Roland tried to calm his wife. He was shaking too but he hid his quivering voice from his wife.

"I'm sure someone will contact you soon," Roland said reassuringly. "I'll be home soon."

Roland kept thinking over and over, how did ACD know so quickly? Does the chip actually transmit everything to ACD? It was only a rumor, a kind of folk lore, that the chip transmits everything to ACD. Can the chip read our minds? Can the chip terminate life? Roland felt nauseous.

Mr. Leeger was lying face up on the green Plaztec grass. His shirt was partially unbuttoned. Roland noticed the top of what seemed to be a scar on Leeger's chest.

"Please people, stand back! A Sentinel will be here soon."

Dr. Davidson was a known professional scientist. Reluctantly the crowd backed up at his request. Still, they were eager to see death. The majority had never seen death and all were curious about it.

Mr. Leeger didn't wear the usual pale brown coverall type clothing of his generation. He was wearing an old fashion khaki button down shirt and pants. Hiding his actions as much as possible, Roland unbuttoned one or two more buttons. It was definitely a scar. It ran from below the neck vertically down almost to the navel. It reminded him of pictures of humans having a heart transplant common years ago. He also noted another long horizontal scar beneath the ribcage. Mr.

Leeger was a thin man and Roland noticed a small lump in the upper part of his chest. It didn't seem to belong there either. To further confuse things, if the dead man had a transplant, he showed no external signs of rejection. Transplants had long ago been deemed unnecessary, illegal and, with older humans, successful for only short periods. Rejection was a problem never quite solved but Leeger exhibited none of the signs.

Two Sentinels drove up in their yellow and green cambri. Their crisp, clean coveralls were also yellow and green and crackled as they walked up. Roland was amazed at how quickly they were on the scene. The crowd gave them a path and both looked down at the body.

Roland asked his son, "Is that the two here earlier?"

"No, they were older."

"Is he dead?" one of them asked.

"I think so." said Roland. "There's no pulse or breathing."

The Sentinels were quite young and didn't seem to know what to do either. They crudely turned him over onto his stomach and ran their portable scanner over his neck chip. The chips are powered by changes in body temperature. As the body loses heat in death, the chip loses its power to transmit a signal. A portable scanner in close proximity to the chip may still be able to read some data.

"It's not transmitting any vital life signs so I guess he's dead," the other Sentinel said.

"How about his ID?"

"Yes, it's transmitting his ID number. I can barely read it. Record it and let's put him in the back of the cambri."

The first Sentinel said, "Look at the ID number! It's..." The second Sentinel quickly hushed the first man.

They picked up Leeger's remains and carted him off like so much trash. Throwing him into the back of the cambri, they drove off leaving Roland and the crowd staring at the disappearing cambri.

"Let's go home," Roland said to Brooke. He knew it would be difficult to determine Leeger's state of health and previous medical procedures. Roland was a renowned cytogeneticist but it would be difficult to use his official position to examine the body. Dead bodies were cremated quite quickly. The first problem, though, would be finding where the body would be taken.

Melody met the pair at the door. She stood in doorway wringing her hands.

"Roland, I don't want to be a chamberperson." She had long, blond hair like her daughter and it was in some disarray. Roland could see fear in her blue eyes.

"Mom! You're going to be a chamberperson?" Brooke yelled. "Wow!"

"Roland, I don't want to be a chamberperson," she repeated.

Risa ran up to the group. "Dad. Isn't this great? Mom can get me into the food growth industries."

Brooke added to the melee. "You want to grow stuff?" he said to Risa. "Dumb!"

Roland gestured for all to settle down and be quiet.

"Melody. Don't worry about it. Not much will change. And you know you don't have a choice. It's just for five years."

"Mom," said Risa. "Can you call tomorrow?"

"Kids. Leave your mother and me alone. We have to talk." Roland and Melody walked to the rear of the dome and sat outside on soft, blue Plaztec material chairs.

"Roland, what can I do? What do I do?" Melody had finally stopped shaking.

Roland held Melody's hands. "Don't worry. All decisions are made by ACD, and the Premier," he added. "All you do is send any questions or problems to an assistant vice premier and they take it from there, even to ACD if necessary. You don't carry a weapon, deleter or portable scanner like the Sentinels."

"That's a lot of help," said Melody.

"Yeah, eventually you'll relay the decisions back to us common folk."

"Don't be funny Roland."

"You don't even have to enforce the decisions. Most people don't question any decisions and if they do, you just call a Sentinel."

"Roland, you don't understand my dilemma. Every person I know becoming a chamberperson doesn't quit after five years. They stay on and what's worse, they change. They aren't the same person. Look how Samuel changed. He doesn't visit us anymore. He ignores us on the street. He doesn't go to the theater or roundball games. And his poor wife. She ought to get a marriage termination. Samuel spends his nights at what's her name, Shelia's. It'll wreck our marriage and our lives too. I hate this!"

Roland knew Melody was right. Every one appointed to chamberperson changed. Every one became a loner, aloof and detached from the common person. They almost became an extension of ACD. They became ACD's finger on earth, not mean or vindictive but stern and rigid although seemingly fair dispensers of regulations. They also now had a chance to be appointed to assistant vice premier. This is probably the reason no one quits the position of chamberperson.

Melody's PCS began flashing red, beeping and vibrating. It was a level three call. All three attention modes meant an extremely important message waiting. No face appeared, just the yellow and green striped ACD logo in the lower right corner of the small screen.

Melody jumped up. "Roland! What's all this?"

"My dear," Roland said in an all knowing voice, "ACD is contacting you. You'll have to wear your personal thought communicator more often. You must be receiving your first assignment."

"Roland, no! Don't I get training or something?"

"You're getting it now. Better answer it."

Melody sat down again almost crying.

Roland moved closer to her. "Don't worry. We'll change the pattern. We'll stay the same. Chamberperson or not we'll stay together. Now, you better answer it."

Melody spoke into her communicator, "Yes?" she said weakly.

"Why aren't you wearing your thought communicator?" Then not waiting for an answer it continued, "A death has occurred in your area. Place yourself at the holding area immediately. Activate the automatic direction system for driving coordinates to the holding area, number 10229. The death is Mr. Ramford Leeger, ID number 4605766853. Enter or answer 'confirm' to acknowledge receipt of this message."

Melody entered "Confirm."

"Roland, help me."

"Help you?" he said. "I'm going with you."

This was the perfect chance to check into Leeger's death. Melody told Brooke and Risa to have dinner without them.

Risa yelled to her parents, "I'm staying at Roalf's tonight. I'll see you in the morning."

Roland opened the door of the cambri for Melody. "Sometimes I think all that girl thinks about is sex."

Melody countered, "Did you forget about us in our youth?"

"Yeah."

Melody added wistfully," Me, too."

CHAPTER THREE

Melody entered the coordinates flashing on the screen. Then she punched in her ID number 4732996020. Immediately, the cambri silently began to move. It seemed to travel at an unusually fast speed. Other cambris stopped and let Melody and Roland whiz past them. The steering and speed mechanism moved as if being controlled by an invisible hand. Roland and Melody sat strapped in their seats leaving the steering and speed to ACD.

"I didn't know these things could go this fast. I always thought chamberperson's cambris traveled a lot faster than the rest of us, and they surely do."

"Roland, this is weird. I don't like it." Melody was getting nauseous. "Where in the world are we going?"

"We'll soon find out. I've never been in this part of York. Wow! I love how the other vehicles get out of our way. ACD must take over their cambris, too."

The cambri suddenly came to an abrupt stop near a very large dome. Twenty or thirty Sentinels were milling about; some playing cards, some reading and some throwing dice. The cambri began slowly parking itself in a row of other multi-colored vehicles. The next row had eight or ten yellow and green Sentinel cambris neatly parked. To their left was a large dome of Plaztec blue with several doors. Three of the doors were quite large, large enough for big cargo cambris. The other three doors were for pedestrian traffic. The last door on the right was boldly marked "Chamberpersons Only." Another door was marked "Sentinels Only."

"Roland…," Melody cowered at the size of the building and all the Sentinels. The Sentinels seemed to not notice these two citizens as they walked between them.

"Let's go in," Roland said half confidently.

As they walked through the doorway into a dimly lit foyer like area, a scanner chirped from behind and above them acknowledging their presence to somebody.

A voice from above startled them. "Proceed through door C."

Melody and Roland walked from the foyer into an empty room, except for a white sheet covering something on a table in front of them. In comparison to the foyer, this room was brightly illuminated. They immediately knew the sheet covered the body of Mr. Leeger.

Roland was wondering if someone would question his presence but no one so far even noticed him.

They both noticed at about the same time, something approximately five millimeters square covered with dried blood lying next to Leeger. Roland recognized it as Leeger's chip. Melody had never seen one. It was apparently removed from Leeger's neck and laid beside him. Another bloody item was located next to the chip. It confirmed Roland's suspicion. It was a pacemaker.

Again the voice from above, "We will begin the examination. Please stand clear of the remains."

Two robotic arms came down from the ceiling and removed the sheet, revealing the naked, blue and pasty body of Mr. Leeger. They began to move some electrical device over the cold corpse. It chirped and buzzed for several minutes. The odor of death immediately caused Melody to gasp as the arms retracted into the ceiling. They returned, one with a surgical steel knife in its grasp and the other with a kind of claw or gripper.

Melody and Roland were near vomiting. "I'm getting out of here!" yelled Melody.

"Me too,"

They both raced through the door and stood outside, gagging. It was a long time since lunch so they were only visited with dry heaves.

They stood outside the door for about fifteen or twenty minutes expecting someone or some voice to tell to get back inside, but no one did.

Finally Roland said, "I'm going to take a look. I'm very curious about Leeger's death."

"You go right ahead."

Roland peeked into the room slowly. The arms were not moving. Amazingly, Leeger's body parts were neatly arrayed on the table. He could see his brain, heart, lungs, liver, intestines, kidneys and all Leeger's organs neatly arranged as though a medical class was being prepared. Big cavities were evident in Leeger's body where the organs had been removed. Even though Leeger had been dead for less than an hour, there was no blood splatter anywhere. The knife was perfectly clean, the table and floor had no signs of bones or skin or any debris. It looked completely antiseptic.

Slowly Roland approached the table. He had to get a good look at Leeger's heart. A machine behind him began embedding data on a permanent holographic film sleeve. The sleeve is almost completely indestructible and made of quartz. It requires a sleeve reader to translate. The sleeve can contain mountains of data.

"Deposit the report in the ACD import channel through door B," the voice from above again. "Thank you for your service."

Service? We didn't do anything, thought Roland. He tried to take the film sleeve but a voice announced, "Improper ID!"

He then looked at the heart. It definitely was a transplant. He could clearly see fairly crude stitches. They were not the nearly invisible stitches of a robotic surgeon. Why the transplant? Had his original heart completely failed? This heart looked in extremely good shape. It showed no signs of rejection. He had to find a sleeve reader. Roland left the room and joined his wife.

"It's unbelievable," he said. "I don't understand it. He's had a heart transplant. There were absolutely no signs of rejection. I've got to find out what he died of."

"What do we do now?" she asked.

"You'll have to get the sleeve. You're supposed to put this sleeve in one of the import channels through door B, but I wish I could find a reader." He looked around for a film reader. There was none.

"You know what else is strange?" Roland added, "No one or no thing even questioned the fact I was in there and not you. It wouldn't give me the sleeve but thanked me for my service."

He stuck his head back into the room where Leeger's body lay. He looked up and tried to find a scanner. There was none.

With a gasp he looked at the table. Leeger's body was gone and the table was completely empty and sterile. Melody grabbed the sleeve and she and Roland left the room.

"Roland, my PCS is flashing and vibrating. It's a level two call."

"So, answer it."

Again no face appeared on the screen, just the yellow and green stripped ACD logo.

"Melody Davidson, ID number 4732996020, go to room B for orders. Place the sleeve in an import channel and receive instructions from export channel 4. For positive ID, please firmly grip the identification rod at the red mark with the right hand while inserting. Enter 'confirm' to acknowledge receipt of orders."

"Roland! I got to fix dinner for the kids. I want to run away. I hate this stuff. Help me."

"Enter 'confirm'!" the voice rudely announced again.

"Confirm!" Melody almost yelled.

"The kids are fixing their own cenes," Roland said. I'll stay with you." He wondered how much she'd be asked to do while he would be in lower California. "Let's see what's in the export channel."

They entered door B and found several import and export channels. Roland didn't want Melody to let go of the film sleeve just yet. He wanted to see what Melody's next orders were. Each channel had a scanner above it and Melody picked the first one. As Melody stood in front of the import channel, she was scanned and then told to insert the sleeve.

"Wait!" yelled Roland. Too late. Melody had already inserted the sleeve. An information packet was ejected from the export channel slot.

Roland couldn't help but wonder what would happen if

Melody disobeyed her orders. Like the rest of the population her genes were corrected to be amiable, honest and follow most orders without question. Roland did know some of the perfect beings did question authority almost approaching revolt. It seemed boredom was a growing dilemma, too. Actually, Roland thought, isn't this exactly what he himself is doing by going to a secret meeting? The courier inviting him to the meeting told him it would be extremely eye opening. He wanted to go more than ever.

Melody opened the packet. It read:

Melody Davidson ID #4732996020

Within one week go to the dome housing of Mr. Leeger ID #4605766853.

Present yourself to Mrs. Dorma Leeger ID #4721356141.

Inform Mrs. Leeger you are the chamberperson investigating Mr. Leeger's death.

Inform Mrs. Leeger she will co-operate with you completely.

Inform Mrs. Leeger of the fact that Mr. Leeger had numerous illegal heart and liver transplants.

Inquire where it was performed and by whom and when.

Inquire if Mr. Leeger mentioned anyone he noticed at the location.

Mrs. Leeger will have no choice but to answer honestly and completely.

Inform Mrs. Leeger ACD will not tolerate lies or vagueness.

Any prolonged hesitation on her part will result in a visit by two Sentinels.

Enter your results of the interview on your personal sleeve dispatcher.

Roland was stunned and speechless. He took the packet from his wife and began skimming through it. At the end of the first page, listed as cause of death: *PACEMAKER FAILURE.*

Roland leaned against a wall. Were it not for the failure of his pacemaker, he'd still be alive. Why did he have those transplants? Maybe his original heart and liver was too damaged to be regenerated. But where did he get the organs? They seemed to be a perfect match, almost like a donor from a clone of Leeger, but cloning is illegal. And it was very perplexing that the pacemaker failed. Electronic failures were almost unheard of now days with the perfection of robotic assembly. Usually only a strong signal from outside the pacemaker causes a failure.

Roland looked further in the report for chemicals in the blood stream. None! This too is truly amazing and odd. If he remembered correctly, Asmazone B was the alleged wonder drug used many years ago to retard rejection. As in previous anti-rejection drugs, it too proved to be faulty after continued long term use and possessed too many side effects.

"Roland, I want to go home." Melody pulled his attention from the report.

"Okay. I'm getting my appetite back."

As they walked through the foyer, another man entered. He wore the chamberperson's official outfit of dark red coveralls. Melody assumed she'd receive her outfit soon.

"Hello," said Melody. "Have you been a chamberperson long?"

The man completely ignored her.

"See, Roland. He completely ignored me."

47

Roland answered, "Yeah." He was still transfixed by Leeger's report.

They climbed into their cambri and waited for the invisible driver to take them home. Nothing happened.

"I guess we have to enter our own coordinates now," Roland said. "I assume Mrs. Leeger's coordinates will take us to her dome. They're here in the report."

Roland spoke the coordinates of their dome. The cambri began to move but more slowly than their drive here.

"Do we have to go to Mrs. Leeger now?" Melody asked.

"No. We can go tomorrow."

Melody asked, "Have you ever met her?"

"No, I've only seen Ramford at the games. I never got to know him. I never saw his wife."

"Roland, can you skip your meeting next week?"

"No," he said. There was no way he was going to miss the meeting. "I have to go."

"Can you go with me to see Mrs. Leeger?"

"Yeah," he said. "If we go before I leave."

"Roland, what's your meeting about?" Melody asked.

"Just technical stuff."

"Are they going to have women for you men?"

Roland was glad Melody wasn't asking more detailed questions about the meeting content.

"Yeah, they'll have the usual women for us and some men for the women attendees. I probably won't have too much time for the women though. I'm only going to be there two nights."

Melody seemed somewhat concerned. "You know, Jules got too attached to his woman at his water conservation meeting and then got a marriage termination. Poor Lois was devastated."

"That won't happen, dear," Roland said assuredly. "I love you way too much."

"Sean said he'd come over for me while you're gone," Melody said. "I wish he'd use your brand of cologne."

"So, tell him to spray some of mine on himself."

"I will," Melody said pretending to pout. "I told him he's a better lover than you. That really excites him."

"Is he?" Now Roland showed a little more interest.

"No. He has no imagination. And he's always in a hurry. His wife always wants him to come home as soon as we're finished. I miss having someone to cuddle afterwards."

Roland seemed satisfied. "I'll come home as quickly as I can."

"Good." Melody leaned on Roland's shoulder. "I can't imagine life without you, Roland. Don't ever leave me, even if the chamberperson duties change me. I'll quit after five years, I promise."

"I'll hold you to that."

The late summer sun was setting as they arrived home. Risa had already left for Roalf's. Brooke was playing the synthetic physical resistance game on the All Com System and had worked up quite a sweat.

"Risa said she'd do her 'ECKK' lesson at Roalf's tomorrow," yelled Brooke.

"I hope so," said Roland.

"I'm tired, Roland," said Melody. "I'm going to grab a cene to eat and then shower and go to bed. Let's try to see Mrs. Leeger first thing tomorrow."

"Aren't you supposed to use the antiseptic body pads until Sunday? We don't want to use up our water allotment already."

Melody seemed completely exhausted, "I know," she said, "but I need to feel the warm water on me for a while."

"Okay. I've got some preparation work to do. I'm going to eat first and then use the ACS in the lower level since Brooke is so engrossed in his game. See you in the morning."

Melody looked somewhat dejected. "I hope I'm not too tired to sleep."

CHAPTER FOUR

Even though there was an automatic lift between the three levels of the dome, Roland chose to use the cushioned stairs down to the lower level. Again he smiled at Melody's decorating work. Even some of the artificial flowers emitted a mild, sweet fragrance. He wanted to finish some work ahead of time since he'd be gone three days next week. Roland wasn't as curious about the secret group's interest in his work as he was about the Premier's interest. He could understand this radical scientist gathering and their interest in anything out of the ordinary. But the Premier? Why was there an interest at his level? Or her? Few have ever met the Premier and those that did were very tight lipped. Roland wasn't sure if he would even have a face to face meeting with Sogan. He put on his brain wave receptor and chuckled to himself. We're getting so many gadgets to put on our heads we'll soon need two heads.

"Work paper, Chapter Seven, fourteenth paragraph, third sentence." Roland announced to the ACS. He thought about Brooke, he smiled slightly. He wondered if ALEKC would still recognize Brooke's voice after he reached puberty and his voice changed.

ALEKC immediately came on line and displayed the half-finished chapter seven of his document studying the reoccurring failure of the anti-aging SIR2 gene and its relation to Alzheimer's. He had a personal interest in the disease. Roland's mother and grandmother suffered from the disease. He was having difficulty determining why repairing the gene and the nano injections didn't halt brain damage in every case. If he could just get the mRNA to change its instructions he would feel some kind of satisfaction. No matter what ACD said, Roland didn't feel the human genetic code was correctly mapped. Everyone is not perfect yet. And the human genome is extremely resistant to modification. Injecting healthy genes into defective genes has shown only limited triumphs. Gene therapy seems to only work with somatic genes, which aren't inherited.

Roland continued dwelling on his parent's plight. They were into their late sixties and both still volunteered to work in the electronic funds transfer department. His mother, though, contributed little due to her disease. She and his father could both work a few more years before they could convert to rest years. It was an option. His mother and especially his grandmother may not even be allowed to reach the 150 year limit. If they desired they could work until death or play thought games on their ACS or just do nothing. Like most older citizens, they wouldn't be content sitting around and watching vision discs as do the younger, lazy populous. The women were in failing health but they still had to feel needed. They were born before gene repair became common place. Their disease could be slowed but not stopped. Roland began the year determined to find a direction of cure regarding this phenomenon. His latest work had been telomere length although other scientists had declared telomere length irrelevant. Some studies indicated Alzheimer patients had shorter telomeres but his studies didn't indicate which came first; short telomeres brought on Alzheimer's or Alzheimer's brought on short telomeres. His grandmother was ninety-six and her quality of life was as bad as his mother's. The two women didn't respond like most other humans to the gene repair procedures. If their lives continued as it did, he knew one day soon their time on earth would end before they even got close to the age of 150. ACS would display brightly, almost happily, 'Unknown Entry'. People born after genetic engineering of the fetus easily lived a complete life to at least 150. Scientists are able to screen for over 5000 disorders. Roland's father and grandfather seemed to be doing okay, though. Melody's parents and grandparents died simultaneously in a freak lightning strike while picnicking. There were not enough remains to even try to reassemble their bodies. Their nerve endings were completely destroyed.

A news flash superimposed itself over Roland's work. Someone went running through a children's exercise area wielding a club. He was yelling something about not letting more children grow up in this boring, stoic world. As usual, two young Sentinels stood watching, not knowing what to do. An older, experienced Sentinel jumped the man and used their deleter to paralyze him. Roland hoped he wouldn't be called in to examine the chromosomes of the deranged man to determine what caused the erratic behavior. Not surprisingly the report added the man later died.

"Boredom!" Roland suddenly allowed the thought to be formed into words. He was bored. This is what is beginning to emerge around the country, and the world. This is what's sporadically occurring to cause the human race to do unreasonable actions with disastrous results. This is why he is so anxious to go to the secret meeting. Everyone here acts the same. Everyone buys the same product. Everyone almost looks the same. We're all the same height, the same weight. Nearly every roundball game ends in a tie. The athletes are so equal in ability. Except for a few optional ethnic differences, we all look the same. I hope this meeting gives me something exciting to do, Roland thought.

"I'm goddam bored!" he yelled.

"What'd you say, Dad?" Brooke called down from upstairs.

Roland realized he had voiced his feelings a little too loudly. "Oh nothing," he said to Brooke.

Boredom is the problem with the country, the continent, the world. Everything is planned, organized and determined by ACD. Other than worrying about a few outlaws outside city walls, there is nothing to concern us. The Premier, and ACD, takes care of everything. We don't even have to work. Tornados or hurricanes or blizzards can't hurt us. At first the world was overjoyed with the thought of labor, disease, wars and famine being eliminated. Water use was strictly controlled and redistributed by means of large, underground pipes. In doing so it made droughts or floods a thing of the past. Next, complacency set in, and now it's boredom. And somewhere in his life, laziness became Roland's trait. He didn't actually have to work. The only reason he worked at this moment was to find a cure for his mother. If a family needed a communicator, or a cene heater, or an ALEKC viewer, they just gave a voice message to their local assembly plant and one was immediately delivered to their dome by a robotic cambri. They could even put on their personal communicator and think about what they wanted and it would be delivered the next day. The value was deducted from their account. If someone broke an arm, the medical bill was deducted from their account. And there was always enough in their account. The world was running on automatic pilot, piloted by computers and robots. Roland's daughter was feeling boredom at her young age. The world is not perfect.

A cold chill crept up Roland's back. Was ACD monitoring his thoughts? Exactly what do these damned chips do? Roland finished his work for the night and went upstairs to join Melody. Neither Roland nor Melody slept well.

The morning sun was just beginning to shine through the clearform window. Roland opened his eyes to see Melody sitting on the edge of the bed. She was already dressed in her pale blue, two piece coveralls. She didn't like the one piece style coveralls. Soon she would have to wear the dark red chamberperson coveralls.

"Anxious to get started?" he asked.

"Yeah. I'm not hungry but I guess I'll eat something."

"Go on downstairs. I'll be down shortly."

Roland quickly wiped himself down with an antiseptic body pad, shaved and got dressed. He wore pale blue coveralls as usual of people his age. Although not mandated, citizens of Roland's age wore pale blue, those from 51 years to 100 wore pale green and those from 101 to 150 wore pale yellow. Those from 151 to 200 wore pale brown and were somewhat proud of the fact that they were allowed to live longer than the usually mandated 150 years. Teenagers wore just about anything and bright hues of any color were worn by officials. Chamberpersons wore red. As he finished shaving, Roland again wished his parents would have picked no facial hair when they picked his genetic structure. He hated shaving. The daily news was superimposed on his mirror but he decided he had no interest in it. He switched it back to 'mirror only'.

Downstairs Roland found Melody staring at her cene floating in a bowl of reconstituted liquid soy. The cene began to sink as it soaked up more of the liquid. There were no clouds today. The sun lit up their dining room but it didn't change the mood of the couple.

"Did you make any coffee?" asked Roland. Coffee was on the restricted list.

"No, we're about out," Melody said as her cene finally sank. "Roland, let's go right now."

"Honey, I doubt if she'll be awake yet."

"I'll contact her." Melody spoke to her PCS. "Mrs. Dorman Leeger."

A computer generated voice answered, "There are twelve Dorman Leegers. What city?"

"York," Melody said to her communicator.

After a short wait, a tired sounding voice answered, "Yes." An old, haggard woman appeared on the screen.

"Mrs. Leeger. This is chamberperson Melody Davidson. I have been instructed to interview you as soon as possible. How soon can you receive us?"

"Us? There are two of you?"

"Yes. My husband is coming also."

"I have been advised I have no choice in the matter so you can come now if you want." Mrs. Leeger seemed resigned.

Melody answered, "We'll leave in about ten minutes."

"Good bye," Mrs. Leeger answered.

"She doesn't sound well, Roland. And she said she had already been advised I am coming."

"You know," said Roland, "sometimes I feel as if we are

on a big vision screen, being observed by someone. Sogan tried that for several years but he found us uninteresting and our chip kept good track of us. He didn't need to see us."

"I don't like to think about stuff like that. It scares me."

"Let me finish eating so we can go." Roland preferred his cene dry and drank some juice purchased by his son.

"This is a good drink but I think I'd like it hot. Where did Brooke get it?"

"I don't know where," she said.

Melody finally ate her cene. "I think he saw it on the vision screen and ordered it."

"Let's go and get this over with."

Roland and Melody headed to the cambris. The vehicles were housed in the back of the dome. "I see Risa took the red cambri. I hope the blue cambri is connected to the charging circuit."

He saw that it was charged. "Good girl."

In the corner of the vehicle storage area Roland saw a telescope. "My God," said Roland. "Where did that come from? They are not allowed."

"It's Brooke's. He got it from Risa's friend Roalf. Roalf said it didn't focus properly so he gave it to Brooke. You know Brooke. He can fix anything."

"Let's hope no Sentinel sees him using it. Anyway, let's go."

They drove off in the bright sun with just a touch of slight morning haze, past dome after dome, each an exact copy of the next one. Each one was Plaztec blue. Only by the address could a person locate their dome. The streets were as straight as a chess board, no curves. ACD deemed curves a waste of energy. Every dome had the same green, artificial Plaztec lawn. No wonder I'm so bored, thought Roland. There's no variety in anything. Roland noticed none of their neighbors was out this morning. He thought why should they be? They've nowhere to go.

Once outside, Melody voiced the coordinates of Mrs. Leeger's residence. The cambri immediately began to move, although not as fast as yesterday. Again, other cambris let them pass. A driver of a cambri never has complete control of their vehicle. ACD can take over anytime it deems necessary. Since any human reaching the age of reason could sit at the controls and think of their desired destination, or enter the coordinates, billions of cambris populated the world. How it can control all those constantly amazed Roland. Even so, it was not foolproof and accidents still occurred.

CHAPTER FIVE

The trip took about fifteen minutes and they finally arrived at Mrs. Leeger's two residence dome. Even though Plaztec is supposed to be indestructible the dome looked faded and dirty. There were bits of trash and even uneaten cenes on the artificial lawn. The windows of Mrs. Leeger's dome were dialed to complete light blockage.

"Hey, I like this being married to a chamberperson. That was a quick trip."

"Roland, quit it," Melody didn't see any humor in Roland's remark.

"Look! Did you see that?" asked Roland.

"Yes, it looked like two people running out the back door of Mrs. Leeger's section."

As they pulled up on the entrance driveway, they saw someone standing in the doorway of the right half of the two unit dome. They assumed it was Mrs. Leeger. She wore a loosely fitted white but extremely dirty and tattered robe. The robe was a type usually worn to dressy occasions.

Melody got out of the cambri and headed toward the door.

"Mrs. Leeger?" she asked.

Roland followed behind Melody.

"Yes, I am," the old lady answered. "Come in."

Mrs. Leeger looked as old as Mr. Leeger. She was terribly hump backed, quite thin and walked with an extreme limp, leaning heavily on her cane. She had many age spots, wrinkled skin and dirty, gray hair. One of the lenses in her glasses was cracked. Since they were both born before gene engineering, skin aging could not be prevented as it is today. It was strange, though, Mr. Leeger could run with the kids even though he looked quite old.

Mrs. Leeger's house was extremely dirty. Due to the light blockage setting of her window controls, the room was extremely dark. The built-in Plaztec ceiling lighting system was quite dim. There were no 3D vision boxes anywhere and very little furnishings. Her old ACS was covered with dust showing it wasn't used very often. Roland noticed it was the old style with the small vision screen. The populace had long since abandoned the smaller screens and returned once again to larger, more visible monitors. Half eaten cenes were lying around, some drawing flies. Mrs. Leeger kept looking toward the kitchen area but invited Roland and Melody to sit down. With just two Plaztec chairs, Roland volunteered to stand. Mrs. Leeger abruptly sat on the floor and told Roland to take the other chair.

"Is your communicator set on 'record'?" Mrs. Leeger asked.

"Oh! I didn't think about that. I guess I should record everything." Melody switched to 'record'. She wondered how the old lady knew she was supposed to record the conversation but she herself didn't know it. Roland wondered why the conversation had to be recorded at all if ACD knew everything. It was very confusing. Sometimes it seemed as if ACD knew everything and sometimes is seemed as if it didn't.

Melody began, "Mrs. Leeger, I'm supposed to ask you about your husband's transplant. I know he's had several."

Mrs. Leeger didn't seem to hear. "I'm 180 years old. Yes, I am older than my husband. I was allowed to live past the 150 year limit because of my husband. They didn't want him to live alone. I have been informed I will be allowed to live thirty more days. I will be allowed to get my affairs in order. Then I will cease to exist. I am no longer needed."

Melody mouth dropped. Roland felt the same chill he felt yesterday at the roundball field.

"Ramford was the first chamberperson in the Provinces of Northern Americus," she began. "In those days the Northern Americus Premier – called the president - was allowed to appoint chamberpersons. Then, the Americus Premier had some authority, not like today, and he appointed Ramford. Ramford and the Northern Americus Premier were good friends. Ramford was the president of a very large chemical company. Our Premier Commander in China is such a wonderful and kind leader and has all the proper authority needed to care for us."

To Roland, it sounded like she was reading a script.

"As you probably know, Ramford and I were born before your wonderful system of gene correction was instigated. We both had serious artery clogging problems – I forget what you call it."

"Arteriosclerosis," Roland volunteered.

"Yes, that's it. Anyway we've had to struggle with that disease all our lives. At first we had stents, two on me and Ramford three."

"What kind of disease is that, Roland?" asked Melody.

"I'll tell you later."

"You children don't know what life was like 200 or even 150 years ago," Mrs. Leeger started to reminisce. "My mother used to tell me stories about it. We didn't have wonderful, healthful cenes to eat. Ramford and I didn't eat properly so we were told. We ate too much animal flesh and drank too much alcohol. And we had other worldly problems, too; small revolts, small wars and terrorist bombings, sickness and epidemics. Extreme wealth and extreme poverty were visible from every direction. There was no middle."

Roland wanted to get to the transplant question but felt it rude to interrupt the old lady.

"Our politicians, that are what we called you chamberpersons then, were so afraid to do anything that would cause them to lose their position that they did nothing. They kept spending our tax money – do you kids know what taxes are? Anyway, they were afraid to legislate, so nothing was accomplished by those useless slugs."

Roland tried to change the direction of the conversation. "Yes, Mrs. Leeger, but what about…?"

Mrs. Leeger interrupted Roland's attempt. "I suppose the thing that crushed us completely was the great monetary disappearance of 2055, or what you now so ridiculously call 12055. Can you imagine waking up one morning and finding out your bank account, your savings, your retirement funds have disappeared?"

"No, I can't," said Melody.

"Have you ever heard about the stock market?"

"No," said Melody.

"It had nothing. All the pretty printouts and computer screens showed absolutely nothing. All you saw were zeroes."

Roland knew some things in history were not recorded in their entirety either by accident or by design.

"The only money you had was what you had in your purse or wallet."

Melody asked, "What happened to it?"

"No one knew but there was a lot of finger pointing and a lot of guessing but no one knew for sure. No one took credit for it or even took the blame although some thought an Arabian country created a computer virus."

"How did everyone live?" asked Melody.

"The wonderful people of China gave each and everyone one of us a set amount of credit. With Ramford's job we had once been among the very rich. It was quite humbling seeing us now living on the same amount of credit as poor people.

"You know?" Mrs. Leeger continued, "as if on cue, the great monetary disappearance happened about a week after China directed all governments in the world to declare all income to be directed to them. They said they would then dole out to all citizens what was necessary to live. It was like being nationalized. Nobody argued with China. They were too powerful, militarily and monetarily. They confiscated all of our incomes. Not just us but everyone in the world. They said they were losing so much money because of cheats. They just took all income. That's when the Army — not China's - and other branches revolted. But there was no shooting, they just walked away from their commanding officers and went home to their families."

Roland figured he should let her talk. "Yes, I read about that and my great grandparents told me about it, too."

"Luckily for us, several soldiers lived in our neighborhood. They kept their weapons and protected us from looters and robbers. Each little neighborhood banded together for their mutual protection until China's troops were fully mobilized."

Again, another look toward the eating room. "Everyone was broke, except for the money in their wallet. I suppose it was worse than the depression in 1929 AD. Every one from paupers to billionaires had no money in their electronic accounts. The banks were broke, corporations were broke, company presidents had nothing but their big houses, financial institutions had zero dollars on their beautiful printout balance sheets. Their pathetic little computers were completely devoid of any dollar amount. If you lived in a dome, or house as they use to call it, you could stay there but you just didn't own it. If you had something of value to sell, no one wanted it. They couldn't buy it anyway. Trading became very popular. No one knew where this electronic money went. It just didn't show up anywhere. That's when illustrious and great China gave us our credit amount."

Melody asked, "What about gold and silver?"

"That's the first place the Chinese soldiers went to confiscate or 'protect' as they called it. I think the Chinese had advance knowledge of the coming monetary crisis. They were strategically ready to deploy soldiers at all precious metal reserves in the world."

Roland again tried to speak. "Mrs. Leeger, I…," Again, Mrs. Leeger kept talking.

"It was as if some great loan shark – you don't know what a loan shark is –demanded full payment from everybody. The United States and the entire world was broke. You talk about panic. There were a lot of suicides."

Mrs. Leeger looked quite tired. Roland was afraid she would collapse before they got any answers.

"We were so lucky again. China sent a large mass of troops to restore order. Once everyone realized they'd have enough credit to buy food and keep warm, we all settled into acceptance of our fate. The country realized they let this happen to themselves. You know, it had always been said the United States will be conquered without a shot being fired. And that's exactly what happened. The great country of China took us over and we are so much better. And you know what else? It was many months before most of the United States citizens even knew what happened."

Roland had wondered about some of the happenings of years ago and had to ask a question, "How did China's troops maintain order and control over so many people in the United States? And other countries, too?"

"In the water," she whispered, again looking to the rear of the dome.

"In the water?" he asked.

"Yes, and Ramford was party to it."

Now Roland was getting more interested. "Party to what?"

"Ramford was a chemical engineer. He was ordered to secretly add a chemical to the water supplies to stupefy or placate or whatever, to make everyone quite docile. He worked for a very large chemical company – world wide – and he was put in charge of many trusted employees and soldiers. They had orders to add the chemical to all water supplies throughout the world. It was supposedly fluoride but it was not. The vice-premiers ordered it to be done so they wouldn't have a bloody revolt. All it did was make it easy for China to take over. Everyone became like lambs, except for a few people on private wells in the countryside. You call them outlaws."

"Mrs. Leeger," Roland stood up. "I don't believe your cockamamie story."

"I don't care if you do or don't," she said grumpily, "but it is true."

She spoke more forcefully now, "You people have been running around fat and sassy, thinking you know everything about your wonderful world, but Ramford and I knew differently. Why do you think they…," now she began whispering again, "allowed us to live from transplant to transplant? But for some reason they - ACD - decided we had lived long enough. Maybe his drinking of that alcohol stuff he made was making him talk too freely. I bet that's what ACD was afraid of."

Roland was puzzled, "What's this about transplants?"

Mrs. Leeger looked around now a little like a crazy person; extremely paranoid.

"Transplants, you ask?" speaking more loudly now, "Ramford had his first transplant sixty years ago. He was 108 years old. I was 120 when I had my first. He kept telling me his company would find a cure but it never happened. We kept having heart attacks, one after another. Ramford told me not to worry. He was working on something that would solve our disease. We took our medicine, waiting for the cure. I kept thinking he was talking about a new medicine."

Mrs. Leeger kept glancing toward the back room, toward the eating area. She seemed quite nervous. Roland surmised anyone knowing death was coming in thirty days would be very nervous. He wondered about the two figures he and Melody saw leaving the rear of the dome.

"One day Ramford came home quite enthusiastic about something," Mrs. Leeger continued. "Dorma, they're ready. They're ready for us. We have to go right now. Get in the auto. We didn't have cambris then."

"I asked Ramford about stents. I thought we couldn't get any more stents. He said no. This is the ultimate cure."

With another glance toward the rear, Mrs. Leeger continued again. "We drove to the flying vehicle pad. A man ushered us in the vehicle, I think they called them helicopters, and off we went. We were blindfolded and strapped in. We must have flown for three or four hours before we landed. Our blindfolds were removed and we seemed to be on an island. I'd never been on an island. It was beautiful and warm. I had never seen ocean waves. The white foam on the blue water was gorgeous. There was a warm, gentle breeze. We were then transported to a large underground building, not a dome, and taken to a small room. I was told to lie on a small table and that is all I remember about our first visit."

Another furtive glance to the back room.

"That's all you can remember?" asked Roland.

"When I awoke, I was back on the vehicle, flying to our home. And I can tell you I felt great. My heart was beating so strongly I could hear it in my ears."

"You said this was your first trip. How many trips did you take?" Melody was getting into the spirit of the interrogation.

"We went about once every ten years. That is until now. It's been about twelve years and I could tell Ramford was getting depressed."

"What about?" Mrs. Leeger.

Mrs. Leeger turned to Roland. "First, let me ask you this, Dr. Davidson, noted scientist. What do you think was done to Ramford and me?"

"Transplants."

"Exactly. We each had a heart transplant. Try as they may, they couldn't get our genes repaired. We kept getting arte... whatever you call it. After ten years, we would need another heart, then another and so on. Last time Ramford needed a liver, too. He has some kind of thing in the lower level he used to make his alcoholic drink. Like I said, he drinks, or should I say, drank quite a bit. Anyway, you can imagine my shock when I looked at the scars on my chest. I nearly screamed. Ramford explained it was the only way. Illegal or not, it was the only way we could live until our assigned 200 years. Ramford's position was important enough to live to 200 and I was allowed to live because he needed companionship."

Roland was almost afraid to ask the next question. "Where did you get the organs? I saw no signs of rejection."

Mrs. Leeger looked toward the back room and then lowered her head. "Here comes the sad and terrible part of my story." She again looked toward the rear of the dome.

"Donors."

"Donors?"

"Yes, donors."

Roland sat up straight in his chair. "But there was no rejection. Where did you get a perfect genetic match? Have you found an anti-rejection drug?"

"We received our organs from clones."

Roland now stood up. "Clones? Where, or how? You must have gone to your special island five or six times."

"Six times." Mrs. Leeger spoke quietly now. "I had five clones and Ramford had six clones."

"This can't be! It's been declared illegal. And what about the clones? What happened to them?"

"Dr. Davidson." Mrs. Leeger now looked Roland straight in the eye. "A person can't live without a heart, you should know that."

"You mean they died. They were killed so you could get your heart. You and your husband had eleven donors - people - killed so you could live a little longer? God Almighty!"

"Dr. Davidson, you know there is no god."

"Don't play semantics with me!" Roland was getting angry now. Melody sat speechless on her chair.

Mrs. Leeger slowly turned to look toward the eating area of her dome. Roland thought he heard a noise but was too entranced by his thoughts of Mrs. Leeger's story.

"ACD eventually found out about his – our – escapades, I guess. ACD found out but didn't do anything until now. I don't know why. And that's it."

"And what?"

"That's all I am supposed to say."

Roland was still very angry. "What do you mean, who said that's all you're supposed to say?"

Mrs. Leeger seemed to be pleading now. "Let me live my thirty days. Let me live in peace, please. They told me I will not be punished if I cooperated. I think I have told you too much already."

"No! You can't leave us like this. What else is there?" Roland was almost yelling. "Who's going to punish you? We don't punish people anymore."

"No, I can't say anymore. Please. I've cooperated. All you are supposed to do is tell the world two people using transplants from clones were properly punished for their crime. You can tell them I didn't know the location of the site. That's only reason they wanted you here, Mrs. Davidson."

Roland was still yelling, "But you've been chipped. Why didn't ACD know about your travel to the distant island?"

"Hah! Even you Dr. Smartman don't know. Ever heard of proxies?"

"Proxies. What's a proxy?"

"I've told you enough. I can say no more." Mrs. Leeger suddenly became very calm.

"Yes you can! You can tell us more!" Roland face was turning red.

Now Mrs. Leeger began getting excited again and started screaming, "Ramford saw someone on the island he wasn't supposed to see. He saw...! Suddenly Mrs. Leeger began stammering. She couldn't talk.

Roland was sure he heard an almost inaudible, ultra high frequency tone. From her seated position on the floor, Mrs. Leeger suddenly fell over in a heap. Now Roland saw a figure run out the back entrance. The man joined another man in a cambri and the two quickly drove away. Roland saw it was a yellow and green cambri.

"Roland, what happened? What's happening?

Roland rushed to Mrs. Leeger. She was lying face down on the floor. He felt for a pulse and there was none. "I think she's dead," he said. "She must have had a stroke or something."

"Roland, I don't like what's happening." Melody hated her chamberperson duty even more. "Ever since I have been a chamberperson, I have felt sick. I'm not going to do it. I quit."

Roland bent over to look at Mrs. Leeger's chest. "You can't quit, Melody."

"Just watch me. Let's go home and let someone else find her body."

Opening her robe, Roland found similar scar and stitch marks on Mrs. Leeger's chest just like Mr. Leeger's marks.

Melody stood up, screaming. "Roland! What are you doing?"

"Look! She has similar scars on her chest just like Ramford, but they are not clean or precise stitches the way the robot surgeons do."

Roland was beginning to get a feeling that ACD didn't have the perfect control over earth beings the way everyone thought it did. He remembered a speech by the vice Premier of North Americus alluded to that very fact. That was before he became completely powerless and only a figurehead.

"Let's get out of here," yelled Melody.

The visitor chime rang. "Too late," said Roland.

JOHN PALLO

CHAPTER SIX

"Who in the world is that?" asked Roland.

Through the window he saw it was two Sentinels. "They sure work fast. I guess we should answer it." He wondered if it was the same two he saw leaving from behind the dome.

He opened the door and let them in without questioning their purpose.

"There's been a death here," an extremely old Sentinel stated as a matter of fact.

"Yes, she's over there."

"How did she die?" the old one asked.

"Stroke or something. My wife is a chamberperson and was given the assignment to interrogate her. The lady got very excited about something and collapsed."

"Do you know what excited her?" Again the old one. The young Sentinel just stood in the doorway.

"Yes, evidently she and her husband had several illegal heart transplants. My wife and I were trying to find how and where these were performed and file a report. Mrs. Leeger got quite angry and began yelling. Suddenly she collapsed."

"Did she tell you where she got the transplants?"

"No," said Roland. "Just on some island."

"Did she tell you about anything or anyone she saw on the island?"

"Just it was warm and beautiful."

"Did she tell you she was to terminate in thirty days?"

"Yes, she did. That's why we were so surprised when she suddenly died."

The young Sentinel was entering the complete conversation in his communicator.

"How do you know she is dead?"

"There is no pulse."

"Oh. And that is all she said?"

"Yes, that's all she said." Roland didn't want to tell much more, especially about her unfinished sentence and the two figures in the back of the dome. They may in fact be the very two Sentinels now standing in front of Roland and Melody...

For the first time ever, Roland felt the Sentinels were not the docile, helpers of humankind they portrayed.

"Did you see anyone else here?" The old Sentinel seemed to be driving at something.

"No," Roland lied.

The old Sentinel turned to Melody. "You don't say much for a chamberperson."

"I'm new at this — not even twenty-four hours. My husband is a professional scientist. He's used to this kind of stuff." Melody seemed quite self-assured now, surprising Roland.

Roland made another chilling observation he never noticed before. The Sentinels each had some kind of hand-held restrainers half hidden in their yellow and green jackets. Do they have weapons, too? Usually weapons were carried only if the situation seemed to warrant a need.

Suddenly, the two Sentinels seemed satisfied with Roland and Melody's answers.

"Okay, we'll take the body." They moved toward the dead Mrs. Leeger.

"Wait, she has to file a report on the info holographic film sleeve."

The old Sentinel was clearly in charge. "No she won't. This case had been reassigned to another chamberperson. You can go now and I advise you to speak nothing of this incident!"

Roland and Melody were all too eager to leave. They hurriedly and silently headed home. They arrived at their dome just before lunch. Risa arrived at the same time as her parents. She looked completely terrified.

"Dad! Mom! Roalf said some kind of world catastrophe is going to happen soon. He and some of the guys heard about it from someone who heard it from some outlaw who lives outside the city walls. It scared me."

Roland and Melody were not truly hearing what Risa was saying.

"Uh, what did you say, Risa?" asked Roland, totally absorbed in his thoughts about the morning's events.

"Roalf said these men, and some women, have a large stash of ancient weapons and are planning a revolt. They say we have to leave Earth."

Melody tried to calm Risa down. "Oh, honey, we can't leave Earth. ACD is watching out for us. There can be no catastrophe. ACD has had all possible dangers eliminated. And there aren't enough outlaws to revolt about anything."

Roland added, "She's right, Risa. There have always been rumors like that."

"But Dad, Roalf wants to join them. He's all excited about it. It was all he could talk about. We didn't even have sex!"

"Wow!" said Roland.

"Dad. Here's the strange thing. He said - the outlaws say - that ACD cannot read your mind at all. All the chip does is transmit your identification number, your location and if the being is alive or dead. And it can only terminate life with an outside signal transmitted from nearby!"

Roland said, "Honey, we all know it can terminate life."

"Yeah, Dad, but they say it cannot transmit thoughts. Remember one day you said you wondered if it could?"

Risa was correct. He did wonder out loud about the possibility of the chip transmitting thoughts. That question again entered his mind regarding the upcoming meeting in Lower California.

"Mom! He wants me to go with him. He said they have a vehicle ready to launch."

"Oh, sweetie. That's ridiculous. ACD isn't going to allow the outlaws to build a craft for space travel." Melody hoped Risa wasn't serious.

"So, when's he leaving?" Roland was making light of the situation.

"Dad, he's serious. He won't tell me when he's leaving but it's soon."

Melody began trying to grasp the seriousness of Risa's possible decision.

"Risa, in just six months you'll be finished with your schooling. You'll get a vocation assignment and you and Roalf can plan your marriage and …"

Risa interrupted Melody. "Mom, you don't understand. Roalf is serious."

"I know, Risa," said Roland.

"No. You don't understand," Risa said. "I don't want to leave the Earth or even the city but I'm scared. It sounds like the world will blow up or something. If Roalf goes I want to go with him. He says there'll be revolts and stuff. There'll be riots and wars."

"No, no, no," said Roland. "The Earth is going to be around for quite a while and everyone is too complacent for riots."

"Dad, don't go to lower California. Stay here with us. It's supposed to happen soon."

Roland mind was racing with possibilities, "How soon?"

"He doesn't know for sure," Risa said. "I tried to get that out of him. Either he doesn't know or won't tell me."

Roland again longed to be back in the twenty-first century. He and his family could easily put up with corrupt politicians and dishonest business leaders and even minor wars. Even as late as five years ago Roland felt he was in Paradise. Now things seemed to be getting out of control. He used to feel so knowledgeable, now he was feeling quite ignorant and helpless. He didn't feel he could protect his family. But I still have to go to California next week, he thought.

Roland tried to calm his daughter. "Honey, every generation feels like the world is coming to an end. And somehow we always get through it. And then another crisis pops up and we get through that one too."

Roland hugged his daughter. "Now go and do some more of your school work – and don't forget your Chinese language study."

"Okay, but I don't feel good. I don't feel safe."

Melody hugged her daughter too. "It's okay, honey."

Risa left them and went inside their dome.

"Roland, I don't feel secure either. You're so anxious to go to your meeting. Does it have anything to do with these happenings?"

Roland wondered how much he should say and how much he should lie about. He could not be a pathological liar; that genetic fault was purged from his genes while still a fetus. But he felt he had to be vague and lie by omission.

"It's just a genetic engineering meeting, honey. That's all."

"I don't believe you're telling me the whole story, Roland," Melody said, "but I trust you. Just don't leave us behind. If something's going to happen, revolt or whatever, I want to be with you. And I'm sure the kids do, too."

Roland was deep in thought. "You know, Melody. Before this morning I fairly believed ACD read our thoughts. But I think those two Sentinels were listening to Mrs. Leeger. As soon as they felt she was going to give away some big secret, they transmitted the death signal. If ACD knew all thoughts, it wouldn't need two eavesdroppers."

Melody added to Roland's suspicions, "Yes, and those two Sentinels who happened to drop by just as Mrs. Leeger died sure questioned us thoroughly. I wonder if they believed us."

"I don't know if they did but they sure arrived quite quickly. I still wonder if they were the same ones I saw leaving out the back door."

"Roland! If they were there in the back room, then they know we lied."

"I know. I thought of that when they suddenly stopped questioning us."

Roland sat down at the eating table. "You know, Melody. I'm not afraid to say this now but if we could remove this damned chip, I think I'd like to leave the city and live with the outlaws. And they aren't truly outlaws. That's what ACD likes to call them. They chose not to be chipped. I think they're smart."

Melody took some cold cenes out of the cooling cabinet. "Do you want yours heated?" she asked.

"No.

"What are you going to do this afternoon?" Melody asked.

"Work on my Alzheimer project. I feel the solution is so close but I can't grasp it."

Melody poured some more of Brooke's drink for the both of them. This time it was pink. "As bad as your mother is – and your grandmother – I have often wondered why ACD hasn't terminated them."

"I have, too."

Melody hesitated but then again asked the question. "Roland, what's your meeting about?"

"Melody, you said you trusted me. Keep trusting me."

"Okay, Roland. I do. But please don't leave me behind."

Roland got up and put his arms around his wife. "I don't know enough to tell you anything now but if and when I do, I will tell you everything I know. I promise."

Risa yelled down from the upper level of the dome. "Dad, there was a tram wreck up in the Canadian section. ACD published it was sabotaged by outlaws."

"I guess if I asked you not to go, you'd still go," Melody answered her own question.

JOHN PALLO

CHAPTER SEVEN

Monday arrived all too quickly for Melody and all too slowly for Roland. Even though there was enough daylight, the cambri front lights came on. He unplugged the charging cord and threw his luggage bag in the back seat. Melody stood in the doorway.

"I don't know why this meeting isn't a visual conference meeting on the ACS like your other meetings."

"I don't know either. They just want us there in person."

"So I won't see you until Wednesday evening, right?" Melody said.

"Yeah." Roland looked up at some birds flying overhead. For some reason he remembered about the dogs people use to have as pets.

"Isn't it strange how people use to keep dogs as pets," he said. "Then the dog flu hit and nearly all dogs died. I think Sogan knew what he was doing prohibiting pets. They were a waste of food when we humans needed it so much."

"What in the world made you think of dogs?" asked Melody, leaning on the door sill.

"Oh, I guess just looking at the birds in the morning sky. The birds made it through their flu episode in 12008 but the dogs didn't make it through their flu years ago."

"Hurry back," Melody pleaded.

"I will, I promise. Tell Brooke to keep that telescope hidden. Even though it's a hand-held scope, Sogan doesn't like them."

With that he climbed into the cambri, spoke the code for the York tram station, engaged the transit lever, and drove off. Roland's neighbor waved at him but he was concentrating so much about the meeting, he didn't see him. The cambri moved along almost silently on the smooth Plaztec and concrete combination roadway. With the surface able to contract and expand with the temperature, it didn't exhibit any cracks or irregularities. Allegedly, once the road surface was built, it would last forever. Increasing daylight caused the front cambri lights to switch off as he turned the corner. His cambri clock stated 11:00 GMT. I think that is one good thing Sogan did, he thought. He eliminated the old time zone business. Let's see, that would probably be 6:00 AM in the old time system.

Monday morning traffic seemed unusually light as he neared the center of the city and the tram station. As he traveled through the lower city area he saw several more old skyscrapers being demolished and replaced with rounded shaped buildings. Sogan stated the old square shaped were ugly and not very durable. He decreed all housing shapes shall be of dome design. The Plaztec building material was indestructible and more pleasing to the eye. Less office space was needed since most work was done from the home. As robots and computers did the work, there soon would be no need for downtown offices. I wonder if Sogan thought of that, mused Roland.

There are ten east-west tram rails across the country and eighteen north-south rails. The trams carried pedestrians toward the front of each car, cambris at the middle and cargo cambris and loose cargo toward the rear. Dining and entertainment cars were toward the front. Roland was taking the number three tram. At Chi-Louis, the number three tram heads more southwest whereas number two tram branches northwest. More rails were supposed to be built but the construction by the robot teams had been halted for some reason.

There was the usual line at the scanning station. Several bold signs stated to keep hands and feet off your cambri controls. ACD will safely operate your vehicle to its parking location. It looked like at least ten to fifteen cambris were ahead of him, all anxious to get somewhere in a hurry. After a wait of about twenty minutes, it was Roland's turn to be loaded on the tram.

"Good morning, sir," the attendant greeted Roland. "Where to today?"

"Going to lower California. Station 2100." Roland leaned forward slightly so the scanner could read behind his neck.

"Okay," the attendant said. "Open your rear door so I can look in." Roland opened the rear door, lowered the seatback exposing the storage bin.

"Okay, sir. We gotcha entered. Scanner says you're approved for travel. Do you want an electric charge hook-up too?"

"Sure do," answered Roland.

"How about eating? Will you be dining in our dining facility?"

"Yes, sir," Roland answered. "Big load today?"

"Yes, we do. For some reason a lot of Sentinels are being

moved to the Mississippi River area, around the Chi-Louis region. Don't know why, though."

The attendant looked behind Roland's cambri, "Next!" he yelled.

Roland's ticket said space fifty-four, level one on tramcar seven. There were two rows and three levels of cambri parking. Each cambri lock down area was clearly marked above and below its spotting space. He was automatically transported through six trams until he reached his tram, number seven. At his assigned space the wheels of his cambri were unceremoniously plopped into depressions. He felt the four locking clamps grab each wheel. There would be no way he could move his vehicle until reaching Lower California, Station 2100. Another cambri rolled in behind him. Somehow the assigned spaces always worked out so that no one was blocked in no matter where they disembarked. Roland guessed ACD was figuring it all out. Once again he wondered how much ACD controlled life on earth.

Roland adjusted his seat to the recline position and closed his eyes. He tried to imagine what he was going to learn at the secret meeting. He also wondered how he'd be able to hide from the ACD scanners. What did Mrs. Leeger mean by proxies? He looked at the cambri behind him. It was occupied by two women. They couldn't possibly move unless Roland moved first. Maybe they're going to the secret meeting, too. He hoped Melody didn't get any more assignments until he returned.

After a ten minute wait, without any lurch, the tram began to move. He could barely see the tops of the many domes sliding by. Within a few minutes the tram began to climb upward as the monorail rose over the city's protective walls. Soon the landscape became a whizzing, five hundred kilometer per hour blur. Roland's plant loving daughter had only traveled by tram a few times and the high speed made it impossible to look at real trees and shrubs. Several times she wished the tram would stop so she could look closely at the vegetation. Inside city walls, only artificial plants were allowed. Roland dozed off thinking about Risa's outlaw stories.

Roland slept off and on until about 16 GMT. He was continually amazed at how smoothly a particular, individual tram car could be unhitched from the middle of the tram and switched to its particular destination.

At the Toledo-Detroit terminal, a single tram, with its passengers and cambris, was switched off at the station. The single Toledo tram would be completely unhitched front and rear. Without any slowing of speed the Toledo tram continued to run along at almost the same speed as the rest of the tram but completely under its own power. Roland could tell the Toledo tram had switched from the left wheels on the left rails to the right set of wheels rolling on the right rails. He could see it slowly moving to the right on the right rails. As it moved right he watched it descend. From there he could see it slow down as it approached its terminal. Then, almost effortlessly the rear half of the tram sped up slightly to re-couple with the main body of the complete tram.

At the Indinapa station, a double tram was added exactly in reverse of the Toledo-Detroit procedure. The number of trams dropped off and picked up at each station depended on the volume of passengers, cambris and cargo. Each tram had a seating area towards the front for passengers and a parking area near the middle for cambris. At the rear of each tram was the freight area. Cargo cambris parked in the rear as well as loose cargo. The left side of each tram was the walking area for pedestrians to move about to the rest rooms or to the dining and entertainment tram.

An observation tram was located toward the front near the dining area. Roland thought he would walk up to the dining tram and spend some time in the observation tram until lunch time. As he walked through one tram after another, he noticed quite a few Sentinel cambris bunched in groups of four. As he got to the observation tram, he noticed it was very crowded but unusually quiet for so many people. He then noticed the crowd was made up of Sentinels, and they were armed! Roland had never seen that before except for the two Sentinels at Mrs. Leeger's. His mind flashed back to Risa's outlaw story. He also remembered the sabotage event up in the Canada province. Maybe the Sentinels knew something or had some kind of warning.

Roland had always believed the descriptions concerning the Sentinels. They were docile, helpers of humankind, but now he began to wonder if he was being naive.

Roland looked more closely at the older Sentinels, some of whom were wearing glasses. One even had a flesh-colored thing in his ear. They were born before fetal gene perfection which meant their genetic imperfections had to be modified after birth. It was a common concern among scientists if gene correction after birth was as reliable as fetal gene correction. Roland had read several papers with facts demonstrating that it was not as good. Also it was noted that the results were not always stable – regressive was the term used. ACD and the Premier repeatedly denounced these heretics, stating pre-birth fetal correction was as reliable as after-birth genetic correction. Roland recalled Mr. Leeger was one hundred and sixty eight years old, born well before fetal gene modification.

Roland had to admit to himself, the world of Camelot seemed to be changing. And the change was not toward the better. Chaos seemed more fitting.

The Sentinels didn't seem to be talking much. The few civilians arriving in the observation tram hardly looked out the windows. They looked at all the Sentinels and quickly left. The Sentinels appeared to assemble in groups of five to ten. At the center of each group was one or two quite old Sentinels. It was so strange and abnormal. Roland felt as if he was drawing attention to himself so he decided to go to the dining tram. Here there were no Sentinels. At least he could relax and eat his cenes. The robot arm serving his cene and drink also scanned his chip in order to debit his account.

Roland glanced out the window of the dining tram. He wondered if he had crossed the Mississippi River yet. At this speed, he might have missed it. They passed through several rain showers which might have obscured his vision. The tram rails average ten to fifty meters above the ground depending on the terrain. The earth would rise up closer to the tram as they crossed a hill and then fall away as they traversed a valley. In the mountains farther west the rails rise more noticeably and it's easily perceivable when the tram climbs. Curves are almost unnoticeable.

Roland finished his meal and decided to return to his cambri. As he returned he noticed most of the Sentinels were gone. They must have departed at the Chi-Louis station as he ate.

Roland thought he'd look at his Alzheimer's retardation work, although he knew he'd be just looking at the pages, not reading a word. His mind was fully on the expected meeting. He hoped it would not be disappointing. Climbing into his cambri, he again noticed the two women in the cambri behind him. He reclined the seat, put the paperwork on his lap, and immediately dozed off.

A knock on the window abruptly awoke him from his nap. The two women from the cambri behind him were tapping on his right window.

Roland opened the window.

"Dr. Roland Davidson?" the brown haired one asked.

"Yes," he answered.

"May we speak with you for a moment?"

Roland didn't quite know what to say. After all, the trams are secure as far as he knew, so why not.

"Sure. What about?"

"May we get in?" the blond woman asked.

"Sure."

The women appeared to be about forty and were quite attractive. The dark haired woman got in the front seat and the blond climbed into the rear.

"What do you want?" asked Roland.

"You're going to the Genome conference, right?" The dark haired woman seemed to be the leader.

"Yes."

"And then what?" she asked.

Roland now got a little suspicious. "That's it," he lied.

"What if I told you we know exactly where you're going?"

Along with suspicion Roland was getting annoyed, "I told you where I'm going. Maybe you should get out before I call a tram controller."

"Dr. Davidson, we know the Genome Conference is only a cover. You're going to, let's say, another meeting."

Now Roland was annoyed and angry. He was preparing to get out of his cambri and push the emergency call button.

"Please wait!" yelled the blond woman. "We mean you no

harm. We're here to help. We're on your side."

Roland hesitated, "I'm listening."

Now the blond woman talked. "I'm Char Blancho, she's Lynn Paget.

"Okay," said Roland, half in and half out of his cambri.

"We read your paper on ACS regarding molecular and atomic disassembly and reassembly. We know the Premier is very interested in your hypothesis. Do you want to know why he's interested?"

"Go on," said Roland.

"Would you please get back in your cambri?"

"Okay. Now, go on."

"He wants to know if you can truly disassemble an old, sickly and dying human being and then reassemble this being into a young, healthy human being."

"Yes?" Roland was not sure if the women were serious.

"You don't believe us, do you?"

"Actually, no," he said.

"The Premier wants you to give him a firsthand account of the discussions and the meeting," Char said.

"Sure. The Genome meeting synopsis will be common knowledge anyway. It'll be on all ACS's. And ACD knows all. What's there for me to tell?"

"Dr. Davidson. You know very well you aren't going to the Genome Conference," said Lynn slightly perturbed.

"Please get out. I've heard enough. Get out of my cambri, now!"

"Dr. Davidson, we're prepared to offer you triple credit balance for the next twelve months and unlimited favors and travel for you and your family," Lynn said in a slightly louder tone. "And," she added, "think of the plant growth industries for Risa or complete machinery training for Brooke, even relinquishing Melody's chamber- person responsibilities."

"I'm calling for help, now." Roland began exiting his cambri.

"Think of your family's future!" yelled Char.

"What? What did you say?"

"Dr. Davidson – Roland - we were dispatched here to ask for your help but I see we got off on the wrong foot. We were told to offer you a great credit value for your summary of the meeting, offer you the great gratitude and indebtedness of Sogan, and the future success of your wife and children. That's all. No threats. It's simply an offer."

Roland calmed down a bit. "It sure didn't sound like it. It sounded more like a threat."

"We are also supposed to offer you our company this evening, if you'd like," the blond Char said.

"I'd like company this evening but certainly not from either of you two."

"We can understand that," said Lynn. "So you won't help us help Sogan?"

"I don't know what you are talking about," said Roland, "but I'll publish my report and the Premier can read it and discuss it with me when I see him in six months. And I'll be rushing to complete the results by then anyway. He'll have to wait."

Char said, "So, you won't help the Premier and you don't want our company. Is that it?'

"Under different conditions I might like your company, and I might like to help the Premier, but something doesn't seem right with you two." Roland still sat in his cambri but with the door open. "I think you ought to leave."

Char said, "Sogan won't like hearing you refused him but I'll try to soften my report to him."

"If Sogan, and ACD, are so 'all knowing', they already know my reply."

Lynn replied, "I think the committee made a good choice inviting you to the, ah, meeting."

"Good bye," said Roland.

The two women left Roland's cambri and headed toward the rear.

The blond turned around and yelled, "Did you enjoy the roundball tournament in South York?"

Roland sat in his cambri a minute, going over the conversations with the women. They surely knew of his secret meeting. Why didn't they just come out a say it? And as far as the Premier, if ACD knows all, why give a report to the Premier and ACD. It didn't make any sense.

Suddenly he realized what the blond woman said. The South York roundball tournament? She was the blond messenger back in York. He jumped out of his cambri and looked to the cambri behind him. A man was sitting in the driver's seat. Roland rushed back to the man and asked him about the two women.

"Yeah. I saw two women get out of your cambri. They ran to the rear. One was a lady who asked to drive my cambri onto the tram. Why do you ask?"

"Do you know them?"

"No," the man said. "The blond said she was a tram official. She said she had to drive my cambri on to the tram because of a defect in the computer placement program. She said I could get back in once we were under way."

Roland began running toward the rear of the tram. At the coupling of the tram to the following tramcar, the door was in the process of locking. Evidently the next tram was preparing to uncouple and terminate at the Omaha station. He'd have to wait until the tram was recoupled or another tram inserted. Maybe the women are taking the uncoupling tram and terminating or maybe they went on through to the next tram and continuing to California. He wondered what their purpose could be. He concluded that if he sees them at the secret meeting, he'll have to be very careful what he says. He walked back to his cambri trying to deicide whose side they could be on. He wondered whether he should skip the clandestine meeting and just attend the Genome Conference after all.

As he sat back down in his cambri, his PCS began a class one call. It was Melody.

"Hi, what's up?" he asked. Roland was glad to see Melody's smiling face.

"How come you're not wearing your thought communicator?" she asked. "I've been thinking of you."

"I'm sure it's out of range. They don't work well on moving vehicles."

"Oh. I thought I'd just let you know, I've been assigned my fifteen Sentinels."

"How did you find out?"

"They just appeared at our door. They said they are my personal Sentinels and completely at my disposal."

"Wow. I didn't know they did that. I guess that makes it official. How do you contact them? They aren't going to live in our lower level, are they?"

"No, but they're supposed to be able to get here within twenty minutes," she said.

Roland laughed, "I don't believe that, but it is nice to know you have them available."

"Maybe I won't need Sean tonight, huh?" Melody chided.

"Do they do that service, too," Roland asked with a little more interest.

"I don't know. Most of them are pretty ugly and old."

Roland wondered out loud, "I wonder why there aren't any female Sentinels?"

"I was waiting for you to ask," Melody asked with a laugh in her voice. "Actually two of them are females."

"I'll be darned," said Roland. "There were quite a lot of Sentinels on the tram, too, but they got off at Chi-Louis. I don't know what's going on but something may be brewing."

Melody answered, "I don't know either but I'm worried about Risa. She seems distant and detached. Do you believe her that she's not interested in Roalf's plan to leave? I feel she wants to join the outlaws with Roalf."

Roland tried to calm Melody, "Honey, it'd be hard to do. With the chip, she couldn't hide."

"That's what worries me, Roland. There are so few scanners outside city walls and the satellites aren't too reliable. And she says the outlaws have a way to remove chips."

"Now Melody, we've heard that many times and every time someone tries it, the person dies."

Melody was still worried, "That's what worries me, Roland. The person always dies when removal is attempted."

Roland again tried to comfort Melody, "So, keep an eye on her and her trips to Roalf's. Maybe you can talk to Roalf's parents."

"He has no parents. He just lives with a guardian."

"So keep up a dialogue with her until I get home. Also, watch her travel bag. If she starts packing, or if it's not in its usual place, let me know. I'll come home by air vehicle."

"Okay, Roland." Melody said, "Come home as soon as you can. I love you."

"Sure thing. Love you too."

CHAPTER EIGHT

Roland had about all the naps he could take so he decided to walk up to the dining tram where a reading and ACS room was located. The reading room had about twenty ACS public terminals available for travelers to use at a small fee. These terminals were more convenient and private than using a personal ACS. Someone could be looking over your shoulder and a personal ACS signal can be quite intermittent on moving vehicles. Also, the screens were much larger. Roland thought he might check the news line and see in any more information was available regarding the sabotage in the Canadian territory. The latest news said the derailment was most likely caused by sabotage. There was also an underground channel that posted rumors. The citizens were discouraged by the Premier from viewing it but since each ACS terminal was shielded from view by passing pedestrians, Roland thought he would be unnoticed.

It flatly stated, contrary to ACD statements, the tram accident was caused by robot error. A large contingent of Sentinels was being sent north, though, just in case of outlaw involvement. That explained the many Sentinels he saw earlier on the tram. Nothing else of interest caught his eye, until the city of York was mentioned. Evidently an underground tunnel was found under the northwest wall. His dome was in the northwest section of the city. Sentinels had left the tunnel open for several days to catch anyone using it but only two young men were caught. Roland was glad neither one was named Roalf. Yesterday they cemented it shut.

As Roland got up to leave, he saw Char Blancho heading toward a vacant ACS terminal. He quickly ducked into another vacant terminal and avoided her. He sat there until he assumed she was entered on line. She didn't notice him as he walked behind her. Roland would have loved to peek into her booth to see who or what she was doing but there was no way to look without being observed. He picked up a drink and headed back to his cambri.

Roland had to get a quick dinner in the dining tram. His tram had to be uncoupled at Francisco terminal and coupled onto a south bound tram to Lower California. The transfer would be taking place in about twenty minutes. There are only two warnings about the transfer. If you miss your tram, you're out of luck.

Roland had just got seated in his cambri when he noticed his tram was moving away from the main tram. The tram began descending and slowing. He was told there'd be a ten minute wait until his tram began moving again and speeding up to couple to the south bound tram. He got out of his cambri and stood in the pedestrian walkway as the tram began moving again. It accelerated quite quickly and began to ascend, the rushing air blowing some dust in his eyes. He again was amazed how his tram rose and placed itself in the passing south bound tram. The tram moved into the open space created in the passing tram and as their speeds equalized, his tram moved into the space. Smoothly they all coupled together and headed south. The evening air was quite pleasant except for the wind blowing in his ears. As he looked out to desert with the setting sun behind him he wondered why he chose to live in the crowded east when there is so much open space here. Roland had seldom been to the West and he thought it was very stark but beautiful.

He checked his timepiece and realized he'd be arriving at his destination in one hour. Glancing at his information sheet, he saw he'd be staying at the Diego Inn. The conference was being held at the Diego Inn's Saturn Room at 15:00 GMT Tuesday morning. Roland was still ambivalent about attending the underground meeting. The old saying is still true; curiosity killed the cat.

Roland returned to his cambri as the tram ascended over the city's wall and then descended. It came to a gradual stop at station 2100. Roland heard his wheel clamps release and the charging cable eject but had to wait until the cambri ahead of him moved before he would move. The white cambri began moving and his cambri began moving forward too. He was navigated through eight trams until he reached the exit ramp. There he voiced the coordinates of the Diego Inn and let the auto drive take him there. He could have traversed manually but it was so much easier and convenient to let the auto drive do the steering, especially through the traffic. He saw one traffic accident and wondered why some people insist on doing the steering. With the automatic computer driving, accidents rarely occur.

At the Diego Inn Roland got out and let the parking computer take his cambri and park it somewhere below ground. The clerk assigned him room 303 and handed him his entrance card. She also handed him a note. It said to please call room 305 when he arrived. No name was given.

"Sir, do you want to eat your cenes in your room eating area or do want to use our dining room?" the clerk asked.

"I don't know yet," Roland answered. "Let me decide later."

"Fine, sir. Your cooling and heating units are stocked however for your convenience."

Roland headed for the elevator and then for his room. It overlooked the city; simply row after row of rounded, Plaztec rooftops. He remembered reading that just like the city of York there used to be many tall buildings but Sogan outlawed any structure over four stories high and had anything taller demolished. Too many earthquakes. His thoughts returned to Melody. He thought about her and hoped no crisis had erupted. He sat down to give her a call.

He looked about the room. The view of the Pacific Ocean was captivating. As usual, everything was made of Plaztec although of different colors. Even the bedding material was made of a woven Plaztec thread. At least no germs or insects can flourish on it. He pictured his dome and was grateful for Melody's attempts to add some variety to the décor. The sun finally sunk in the west, its golden glow shinning on the ocean.

Melody didn't answer so Roland left a message.

"Honey, I'm here. I'm in room 303 at the Diego Inn. Talk to you later."

Melody's answering device immediately picked up his call on her mobile relay PCS. "Hi, Roland. I love seeing your face. I miss you. Anyway, I'm on my way to an altercation at the robot repair depot. Roland. It seems as if people are getting more impatient and less tolerant. I don't know what I'm supposed to do there but I hope some other chamberperson it there, too."

"Yeah, I wonder if there is anything in what Risa is saying. I read about the tunnel located near our dome on the underground channel."

Melody said, "I know. I'm just glad Roalf wasn't involved. Risa said he hasn't decided yet what to do. Also Risa said she wasn't supposed to tell us about his plans. She had to tell him that she hadn't told us yet. Please don't let on that we know."

"Okay. I hope I learn something from this meeting tomorrow. I'm anxious to see what's going on in the world."

"I thought you said you weren't too eager to hear the same old stuff rehashed again."

Roland realized he didn't mean to let on his excitement about the secret meeting.

"Oh, you never know. There's always a chance something new will show up." He hoped he satisfied Melody.

"Honey, don't forget your promise," Melody said.

"I won't. I'll call you tomorrow after the meeting. Oh, did Brooke tell you what he plans to do with the telescope?"

"Yes. He said Roalf told him if he fixes it to let him know. They've heard there's a meteor heading for Earth and they want to look for it. I told him it's a bunch of nonsense."

"Well, who knows? At least it'll keep them busy," said Roland. "See you soon. Love you."

"Love you, too."

JOHN PALLO

CHAPTER NINE

Roland woke before his timepiece sounded its alarm. It was 14:00 GMT. Back in York it would be 11:00 GMT.

Looking up his third story window he saw the familiar smog hanging over the city. When all burning was halted, the smog was supposed to be eliminated. While it did improve the air, it didn't completely disappear. It seems to be a natural phenomenon. He commenced shaving and cleaned himself with the antiseptic pads furnished by the hotel.

He finished breakfast early and headed for the lobby. Just like every other hotel lobby it was furnished with plush Plaztec sofas and chairs. Artificial green plants were spaced here and there. A weird mixture of music was emitted from hidden sound sources. He mused that, except for the plants, almost everything was the same, boring Plaztec blue. As usual the hotel guests were dressed in a motely mixture of coveralls while the employees wore a varied assortment of clothing, name tags and badges.

He just remembered he never called room 305 last night. He called but there was no answer. He decided against leaving a message. No one but Melody knew he was here anyway. It couldn't have been too important or they would have called him. Now the big question; how would he be notified about the 'other' meeting. A lot of people were milling around just like Roland, looking for their particular meeting destination. Most attendees wore pale green but some under fifty as Roland wore the pale blue coveralls. There were a few wearing pale yellow and even fewer wearing the pale brown coveralls. He checked with the bulletin display of meetings. Only three meetings were listed. A Sentinel meeting in the Mars Room, a cene manufacturing meeting in the Saturn Room and the Genome Meeting in the Galaxy Room were the only ones listed. He didn't expect there'd be a signboard saying "Secret Meeting in the Moon Room." Roland thought he should head to the Galaxy Room.

So far he hadn't seen any familiar faces and didn't expect to. Several men and women were standing outside the room talking and munching on breakfast cenes and drinking a hot soy liquid. A large billboard called attention to the sign-up table. He walked over to it and wrote his name. He should have printed it since reading and writing cursive was a lost art. The woman at the desk couldn't read Roland's handwriting so she told him to pick out his name tag. Roland's name tag wasn't on the table with the majority of tags, but he found it on a separate table with a few other tags. As soon as he picked his tag, another woman told him to follow her to a side door. They went into a small room where she had a portable scanner. She scanned his chip.

"Welcome, Dr. Davidson. We're very glad you came. Now you know there can be scanners anywhere and they're usually well hidden. I am sure there's one in this room but I scanned you anyway. We want to make sure ACD knows you're here.

Please stay here for a moment. I'll be right back."

"Sure, but who are you?"

"I'm Sandy. Just a minute, please."

She soon returned with a man about Roland's age. He was wearing a scarf. It wasn't that cold in Lower California so it seemed a little odd.

"This, Dr. Davidson, is your proxy. We'll call him George."

"Hello, George."

"Hi," said George.

"Now here's how we do this. Timing is very critical."

"Do what?"

"I want you and George to stand back to back as close as possible. I have to slip this scarf from George's neck to yours. If we do it in less than ten seconds, ACD won't lose the transmission and we don't want ACD to get double signals. The material in the scarf completely scrambles your chip signal and ACD will immediately pick up George's chip. His chip has all your information in it and will transmit it to ACD. He'll sit in the meeting for you. ACD will think you are there all day. This evening we'll reverse the process."

"But what about George's chip?" asked Roland.

"George doesn't have an internal chip."

"How can that be?"

"He's wearing an external chip. He, Dr. Davidson, is what you call an outlaw."

"Yeah?" said Roland not fully believing Sandy.

"After the exchanging of the scarf again tonight, George will destroy his external chip. He'll deposit it in the hotel fusion reclaim unit."

George and Sandy watched Roland carefully to see his reaction.

"If you don't want to go through with this, just tell us, and George and I will disappear and you can resume going to the Genome meeting."

Roland stood silently for several seconds, absorbing what was happening. Since before he could remember, ACD kept track of him by means of the chip. It was like suddenly losing an arm or hand, or more accurately, a cancerous tumor. His mind raced. He could run away and never be found. He'd be free of the Premier and all the Sentinels. Then he thought of Melody and Risa and Brooke.

"I'm ready," he said.

"Good. Now, stand back to back, as close as possible. I would like to add, George is being compensated handsomely for his effort. You, on the other hand, risk death if a Sentinel gets word from ACD that your chip was muted for a time."

Sandy stood close to Roland, face to face. She put her arms on Roland's shoulders and reached behind him grasping George's scarf.

"Keep your hands down and out of the way. On three, I'll yank George's scarf off his neck and slap it down on the back of your neck. That will then mute your chip and George's eternal chip will be exposed and begin transmitting your chip information."

"What if ACD should happen to get two signals of me?"

"We don't know what ACD would do if it gets a double signal. Let's don't find out."

Roland tried to think of Melody and the kids. Her perfume distracted him somewhat. Also distracting him were her buttons on her pale green coveralls. He imagined them aligning perfectly with the nipples on her breasts. Sandy's voice brought him back to reality.

"Dr. Davidson, you know an alarm sounds when Sentinels

go after someone tampering with a chip. They'll have your coordinates and rush into this room. Are you still ready?"

"Let 'er rip."

"One, two, three." On three she grabbed George's scarf and quite violently thrust it on Roland's neck. They waited for the sound of an alarm. There was none.

"Okay. We did it."

Roland suddenly realized he was sweating. "Wow!"

"Now you can follow me to the meeting."

George left to go to the Genome meeting and Roland followed Sandy through another door in the small room. He still had a bit of giddiness knowing he was 'free.' Over forty years he had been tracked, watched and maybe even had his thoughts exposed. The scarf was ugly but he loved it.

Sandy led him to a door leading outside. She opened it to see two Sentinels with portable scanners. They were standing near a cambri.

"Darn. That's our cambri. Do you want to walk to it as if we were just going someplace, or do you want to wait and see if they leave?"

"How much time do we have?" Roland asked.

"Not much."

"Let's go. I don't want to miss any part of the meeting. "

"I knew they picked the right man, Doctor. Okay, let's go slowly."

"I hope they don't question why I'm wearing a scarf."

Slowly they walked to the cambri. "Look into my eyes," she said.

As they started, Sandy put her arm around Roland they gazed into each other's eyes like two kids experiencing their first love.

"Hi," said Roland to one of the Sentinels. The Sentinel

said nothing. Roland saw these two were wearing restrainers and deleters. Sandy grabbed the scarf, pulled Roland closely and kissed him. The love birds got into the cambri, unchallenged.

She entered several coordinates. The cambri only went about two hundred meters, out of sight of the Sentinels.

"Okay, let's get out."

"We could have walked," said Roland.

"That would have attracted more attention. Follow me."

They entered a large dome. Several abandoned cambris were strewn about. Sandy entered the dome through an unmarked door and Roland followed. Once inside, Roland saw a smaller dome. They entered it. Inside, a man scanned both of them but Roland didn't hear the usual chirps. He motioned the both of them inside another door. Inside the third smaller dome was a compact auditorium with several men and women sitting and quietly speaking. It was dimly lit with heavy burgundy curtains draped, floor to ceiling, wall to wall. Where's the Plaztec, thought Roland?

Another man entered escorted by another woman. He had a similar scarf around his neck. Roland looked at the other attendees and noticed they were all wearing a scrambler scarf. That makes sense, he thought.

A voice came through the loudspeaker system. "If anyone wants a cene or drink, please feel free to grab one before we begin. We'll start in about five minutes."

Roland turned and noticed Sandy was no longer in sight. He took a seat near the center. It looked like the room had seating for about twenty-five people. Almost all seats were now taken and an old man sat next to Roland on his right. On his left, a very old woman groaned as she sat down.

"Hello," she said.

"Hi," said Roland.

Roland saw that most of the audience was quite old but a few were probably Roland's age.

Again the voice from the speakers, "Please turn off all PCS's. And your thought communicators are shielded so they are inoperable. And by all means, don't remove your scarves. That would be the end for all of us."

Everyone checked to see that their scarves were secure.

"And now, here's our speaker, Dr. Sam Winston."

No one applauded. The audience didn't know if they should or should not. No one seemed to know Dr. Winston. Most assuredly Roland had never heard of him. Even though well advanced in years, he was quite short and stood upright and straight. He had long grey hair and brown piercing eyes. Noticing his long mustache he was definitely Asian. He was not wearing the usual coveralls but some sort of motley colored Oriental gown.

"Good morning, ladies and gentlemen. I am Dr. Sam Winston, professor at York University."

Roland thought he's from York, too, but I wonder why I've never heard of Dr. Winston? He was definitely born before the fetal gene repair. Roland thought the guy appeared eighty years old.

"Thank you all for coming. Whether you know it or not, you all were thoroughly screened before and after being invited. I hope our screeners did a good job. I doubt you noticed our screeners unless you met them on the tram to our meeting. They have been screening you for the last year. You most likely would like to meet them officially now. Screeners, won't you please come out on stage."

A small group of men and women walked out on stage. Dr. Winston introduced them one by one. Roland didn't pay much attention until he heard, "Lynn Paget and Char Blancho."

I'll be damned, he thought. They were screening me. I guess I passed. I wonder what would have happened if I said I'd take one for the night.

"Okay, we've a lot to cover. I am going to begin by stating some of the facts a few of you may already know. So please bear with me as I get all of us up to speed. And ladies and gentlemen, I'm going to tell you a lot of things that are to be kept very secret for the time being. Things are heading for a change; in a year, in two years, definitely in three years. This program is strictly voluntary. If you don't want to be a part of it, that is fine. We do feel we can trust you, though, to not disseminate any of what you hear today."

Dr. Winston paused to let his words sink in, and to raise everyone's curiosity.

"Now, just so you all know, this is the twenty-fifth meeting like this we have held. We had hoped to have more participants and more meetings in other parts of the world but here in North Americus we've had the most success. This is our smallest gathering. Usually we have up to fifty in attendance. The outlaws have made our lives very difficult. The citizens are afraid of the outlaws and since we are different, they are afraid of us and call us outlaws, too. We are not outlaws; we like to call ourselves Reformers. We have screened many people in different countries and we have found a few like yourselves. We keep searching and when we have enough, we hold similar meetings such as this in their country. We just cannot find many citizens interested in change.

"Contrary to the proclamation of 12167 N, the world is not perfect. Even though we have gene correction and repair, there is much discontentment. No matter what All

Comprehensive Director tells us, the human genome is still not accurately mapped and may never be. There are too many situations where an extra chromosome works in conjunction with another to cause an entirely unexpected result. The same is true with a missing chromosome. So far we know of over 3 billion combinations to record. We're finding out things about human nature we didn't know were necessary to our fulfillment. For one thing the human species seems to possess something, let's say invisible or intangible or spiritual. Human nature needs to be challenged. We also need variety. We need purpose, goals and we need a feeling of accomplishment. We need to use our imagination. So, while the world may seem perfect, it isn't. Our higher human needs are not being met. Sorrowfully, throughout the world, there are not many like you sitting here who feel as you do."

Dr. Winston paused again.

"The majority of the world's population seems to have forgotten something. The human mind needs to wake up in the morning knowing something needs to be accomplished today. Have you noticed how few people really care who wins a roundball tournament? Other than accidents here and there, there is no use for doctors or nurses as we had we were young. Robots perform all our surgeries. Robots operate the fiber farms and make cenes and liquids for us to consume. Robots make our cambris. Robots operate our communication and fulfill financial needs. We put on our brain wave receptor and think of something we need and a robot delivers it. Robots debit and credit our accounts. Robots build and repair our trams and tram rails. A robot team builds all our housing needs. And what was the last insult to human kind, robots repairing robots."

Another pause while Dr. Winston took a drink of water.

"You people here are the only ones with an actual purpose. This is why you were invited and why you came. You are all scientists and you are all curious. You are working in the last frontier as they say. Do any of the other humans on earth have to get up in the morning and do something? Would anyone miss them or would any pertinent work not get performed if they didn't sit down at their ACS each day? The answer is an emphatic no. But we, all of us here, rise each day because we have a purpose that we created ourselves. We are scientists. We are pushing ourselves to find an answer to something. One of us in this audience is studying using trained viruses co-joined to iron molecules for even faster computers with an extraordinary feature; it has an imagination. One of us here is continuing to map the human genome. Nanotechnology is going to manufacture the strongest metal yet.

"Another has a beautiful hypothesis regarding the disassembly and reassembly of the molecule and even the atom. Another is so very close to creating a gravitation shield, bringing a perpetual motion machine into reality. And how about the work being done bending light rays, making an object seem invisible? A woman working with him feels she is on the verge of being able to align atoms so that light rays pass through a solid mass as light rays pass through glass. There is also a man in here today who feels sure he has received an intelligent signal from outside of our galaxy. He admits, I might add, traveling at the speed of light it would take us 300 years to reach that particular system, but he does feel we can accomplish traveling any distance as fast as we can think it. The mechanism to do that is right at your feet. A very young scientist in here has a hypothesis about traveling through space on magnetic waves, needing no more power than that which powers your chip.

"And finally, may I say, one of us has complete knowledge of the internal workings of the chip you all have in you. An example of her work is the scarf you are all wearing. Please note. I am not wearing a scarf. We, ladies and gentlemen, are unique."

Roland felt a little uneasy. Dr. Winston had included his work in his examples.

Dr. Winston looked around.

"The world has always dreamed of Utopia," Dr. Winston continued, "or Nirvana. It's here. And you know what? We're not happy. We are lazy, careless, discontented and bored out of our sanity."

Roland remembered his outburst last week regarding boredom.

"Let me digress for a minute," Dr. Winston said. "Do you know how many so called outlaws exist today?"

The group looked around. Someone said, "They say about one or two thousand, worldwide."

"Yes, that's what Sogan says. In truth, there are approximately one million."

Another murmur through the audience.

"Yes, that's what they want you to believe, a few thousand. If you think about it, two thousand is quite ridiculous. No matter what ACD tells us, the world is too big to be controlled. And I might add, the Chinese population is the least chipped of all. But we are not outlaws, we call ourselves Reformers. And there are approximately five thousand of us. Our biggest hindrance to growing larger is communication. You may have noticed a cord or wire extending from my microphone. We can't use radio waves as they would be picked up by ACD. It makes it very difficult to talk and enlist new Reformers without long distance conversations. Everything has to be communicated by landlines, wires or couriers. Don't laugh. We have had to send some messages by couriers to other countries. It was most difficult to get approval for international travel across borders. Years ago everyone was so naïve assuming wireless communication could be safely and securely encrypted that no one would be able to decipher messages. New and more powerful computers could break codes so easily nothing was secure."

Dr. Winston paused again.

"We've all been told over and over again how the great benefactor, the Premier of China, came over and took us all under his wing, not forcefully I might add, but what I call friendly 'terror.' Since China was so big and powerful, we believed they could annihilate us all if we didn't subject ourselves to their will, especially after they dismantled all our satellites and replaced them with their own. But those of us over one hundred years old know full well how China brutally controlled those Arabic and African countries, and all countries with internal strife, until the will to resist was quelled. I leave it to your imagination when I use the word 'controlled.' There is even a rumor that the world water supplies were treated with some sort of tranquilizer or sedative. A lot of fallacies exist, and ACD and the Premier perpetuate them. Today, I am going to burst many fallacies. ACD can be easily confused and it is so simple. Unless I tell you differently, everything I say today a tested truth.

"What we are doing today is continuing a movement already started by what we call outlaws. The outlaws are little pockets of uncontrolled groups, hiding from the Sentinels and refusing to be chipped. We Reformers were all once chipped and came to the conclusion we didn't want to be led like sheep. Instead of joining the outlaw's actions of violently and haphazardly disrupting the world, we formed a more peaceful environment for our citizens. And as I said, there are definitely many outlaws out there, maybe more than one million. But I am talking about chipped outlaws turning Reformers if you will. We are a small group of outlaws who have decided to call ourselves Reformers. The outlaws are a violent group. We broke away. We decided we want change but not change just to cause chaos. We want a change for the better.

"We are, and will remain, non-violent if at all possible. We have a peaceful and purposeful mandate. We want a perfect world, this is true, but we want this perfect world to be our choice, not dictated to us. And the big difference between us and the outlaws is we have a chain of command. We have elected leaders. The outlaws have no leaders. They subscribe to mob rule. These mobs even fight amongst each other. And so far, they have no idea we 'Reformers' exist. And I am also proud to say, we have scientists, engineers, philosophers, artists, horticulturists, doctors, educators and many other highly educated people in our group. They, the outlaws, have only rabble rousers.

"I want you here, and your families, to join the Reformers. I will tell you how."

Someone in the group spoke up, "Doctor! Aren't you forgetting about the chips? We're not free to do this reforming. We're not even supposed to leave the city's walls without permission. We shouldn't even be here. The outlaws don't have chips so they are free to move wherever they want."

Dr. Winston turned to look toward the right wing of the stage. "Dr. Wang, maybe it's time for you to come out here."

An elderly Chinese woman briskly walked out onto the stage and up to the podium. She stood tall and straight, at least ten centimeters taller than Dr. Winston. Her hair was black with many strands of grey. Roland was amazed at her skin. There were no age spots or wrinkles and her eyes sparkled and seemed truly excited as she glanced at the audience. She wore a colorful, flowing type of kimono.

In halting English, the woman spoke. "I was the chief engineer designing the chip. When I completed my work, ACD and the Premier tried to have me killed. They were afraid I knew too much. I escaped but they believe I am dead. I tell you I am not dead. My chip told them I was dead but how that can be I will relate to you."

A nervous laughter went through the assembly.

"The chip does not read your mind. If it did, all of here now would have been terminated while en route to this meeting. Second, it does not by itself terminate life. To end life it needs a signal from a transmitter no more than twenty meters away. Third, removing it can be done without causing death, albeit a delicate procedure. Fourth, truly it does transmit your coordinates to ACD. It takes a series of scanners and satellites to constantly update your location to ACD and there are a diminishing number of blind locations in the world but I can make you disappear or even appear dead. Last, I can make duplicates of any chip in one minute. Your proxies are an example of that. I made your duplicates when you first were scanned entering the small changing room."

Now the murmuring among the audience was a little louder. Roland wanted to believe his ears but it sounded too good to be true.

Dr. Winston spoke up, "Let me add something here about the diminishing number of blind locations Dr. Wang spoke of.

You've noticed the robots have ceased building tram rails throughout the country. They are instead installing more and more scanners outside of city walls. A time may come when even outside our cities scanners will be everywhere transmitting our location to ACD."

Roland raised his hand. "Dr. Wang. You say these are tested facts? I have been burdened with this damned chip all my life. It would be like receiving a new life."

"Yes, it is true. Dr. Winston will talk more about the chips later."

"Yes, about an hour before lunch," Dr. Winston interjected. "I'll answer all your questions about the chip. And I know what the first question will be."

Roland's head was spinning. It was a tremendous increase of the feeling of freedom he had when he first put on the scarf.

He turned to the man next to him, "Do you believe this?"

"I do. I want to and I do. I have to believe it."

Dr. Winston began talking again. "First, contrary to popular belief, The Premier, in conjunction with ACD, is not the kind and just ruler we're led to believe. Yes, Sogan was in the past, but power is addictive and all consuming."

Tell me something I don't know, thought Roland. Roland again questioned why the Premier wanted to see him.

"He has become like any other tyrant. He has a purpose and goal. Like any other tyrant, he needs more and more power. And he is not chipped!"

The statement brought a slight murmur from the audience.

"He is one hundred and ninety years old. He has not had any gene repair. Another fallacy; after birth gene repair is not foolproof. Unless performed before birth, genes seem to have an internal clock and no matter how we try, the clock is always ticking toward mutation, old age and death. We can slow it down but we can't stop the clock. The Premier knows this fact. In order to stay alive, he has had many, many transplants of most of his organs. He has several clones on an island where he harvests whatever organ he needs. We know, as does the Premier, using a cell to create a clone, creates a young person with cells as old as the donor. But the Premier doesn't care. His one hundred and ninety year old cells are creating one hundred and ninety year old seemingly young clones. Just as in after-birth gene repair, the organs he obtains from clones are lasting shorter and shorter periods. Now he is running out of identical clones so he is using any being he can. He is telling us one thing and doing another. The transplants are illegal for us and okay for him. After-birth gene repair is not one hundred percent foolproof and it looks like it will never be. And it is a very difficult task mapping the human genome much less correcting its mistakes. So many genes do not do their work individually. Many work in conjunction with other genes."

Roland thought this man seemed to know quite a bit.

Dr. Winston looked down at his notes. "The Premier knows cloning and gene repair won't give him eternal life. My sources tell me he has a new plan for life eternal but they don't know what it is. I dread what it might be."

Roland tried to picture life without the chip. He thought of Risa growing food like in the old days. His family would have perfect genes and live freely like Adam and Eve. Only this time they wouldn't eat of the forbidden fruit.

"Now, each of you has a reason to be here. Each of you will be interviewed by a member of our group. We will discuss what we can do for you and what we expect from you. As I call out your name, you will go to the member signaling you. They will explain everything. If you want a report of other attendee's discussions, we will make that available to you at a later date.

But remember, time is of the essence. Changes are coming, quite quickly I might add. I believe, and I'm positive you will also agree, the changes coming are wonderful, awesome and almost unbelievable. I know the Bible is an outlawed piece of literature and I doubt if any of you have one, but I don't believe the changes will be destructive as Armageddon in the New Testament of the Bible, such as Revelations 16, verses 15-21. I do mean, however, the end of our world as we know it."

He added, "Let's take a break and then you can meet with your interviewer."

JOHN PALLO

CHAPTER TEN

Roland sat silently, awed by what he had heard so far. He wondered if maybe they were trying to do too much in one day. So much information and it's only two hours into the meeting. He wondered if his friend still had an old copy of the Bible.

He didn't pay much attention to the names being called out until he heard his name.

"Dr. Roland Davidson." Roland looked around and saw Char and Lynn waving at him. Oh, no, he thought. Not those two. He began making his way toward them.

"Hello, Doctor," said Char. "I believe we have met."

"We sure have," said Roland. "Now what?"

"Follow us."

Roland did as he was told. They walked into a small room with a table and three chairs.

"Doctor Davidson," said Lynn. "Do you completely trust us? We have to know?"

Roland shook his head. "I don't know. I don't quite know what to think about you two. I don't know what to think about

Dr. Winston. I just don't know whom to trust."

"We don't blame you," said Char. "Let's see if we can put your mind at ease."

Lynn began. "We know you have a hypothesis about the molecule and about the atom. You believe you can disassemble them and re-assemble them, correct?"

"Yes, that's common knowledge since I wrote that fool paper. I now wish I hadn't."

Lynn said, "Doctor, I don't think you mean that."

"No, I guess not. But what's your concern?"

"We want to offer you unlimited means and facilities to continue your experiments. We can't even imagine of all the good that can come from successfully completing your hypothesis. And even if it proves to be impossible, I think you'd like to know that too."

"Yes, I'd like to know if it can or cannot be done. The problem I have is I need so much…"

Char interrupted. "Energy, is than not correct?"

"Yes, that's the problem. I need so much energy to do this. I need a large amount of energy to hold the molecule in suspension. And to hold the atomic particles, I need a hundred times the energy. Getting the atom rebuilt and then the genes back to the proper location, or new location, on the chromosome is my biggest obstacle."

"We can supply it," said Lynn matter of fact.

"Sure. Where is this place? On the sun?" Roland asked in disbelief.

"We can supply it," Lynn repeated.

Roland looked at the two women. They seemed to believe in what they were saying. They seemed to believe in Roland.

"Where?" he asked again.

"We can have an underwater facility ready for you in one

month. It's already been five years in planning and construction. We don't feel we should tell you its location yet. We want to feel you're completely on board with us."

"How could you have started it five years ago? I only came upon this idea a year ago."

Lynn said, "Another scientist, Doctor Guitarez, had preceded you about this hypothesis. The Premier tricked him into coming to his chamber to give a report. For some reason the doctor decided he didn't want to live any longer and he bit his poison pill. He died right there in the Premier's chamber."

Another chill down Roland's back. "Do you know Sogan has ordered me to meet with him?"

"Yes, we know. We're not sure of his purpose but we know he wants to see you just as he wanted to see Dr. Guitarez," said Lynn.

Roland leaned back in his chair. "Do you people realize how much information you are throwing at us? It's so much and so fast I can hardly keep up with you. Some sounds too good to be true and some sounds terrible. I want to believe but just can't yet."

"We understand your hesitation," said Char. "Tell us your concerns."

"Let me think. My family. What about my family?"

"You tell us, Dr. Davidson," said Lynn. "If you want them with you at the site, it will be done. We'll remove their chips also. If you'd rather not have them with you, we'll arrange to have it appear as if you are on an extended genome study. You'll be able to visit them once a month."

"What about my parents and grandparents?"

"At this time we cannot include any of your relatives, just your immediate family. Doctor, if we succeed, they will all be better off and can then join you."

Roland asked, "With either choice, will they be safe?"

Lynn spoke up, "Dr. Davidson – may I call you Roland?"

"Sure."

"Roland, to be honest, as with any choice there are dangers. There are dangers in everyday living. Remember the meteor that fell in Africa last year, killing a hundred people. Since the Premier ordered all ground-based telescopes destroyed years ago, no one saw it coming. Even so, meteors are very hard to find – not that much could have been done about it. A robot went berserk in Canada last week causing a tram wreck. By the way, ACD and the Premier wanted everyone to believe it was sabotaged by outlaws. It wasn't. The truth leaked out before ACD could contain it.'

"Yeah, I read that."

"Guess who made sure it was leaked?"

"I guess it was the outlaws, or should I say, the Reformers."

"Right."

"And you can't assure my safety or that of my family's."

"True, we cannot but the possibility of danger is quite remote."

"How long before I have to make a decision?"

"Roland, we can give you a week. We don't have a lot of time. Things are moving so swiftly. Even we can hardly keep up."

Roland thought for a moment. "My wife knew this was a different kind of meeting. She sensed something was going on. She told me to not leave her out of it."

"While we were screening you, we couldn't help but notice you wife. She's an intelligent woman and she is learning all the pitfalls of being a chamberperson. We can relieve her of that duty."

"Now my children, that's another matter," said Roland. "They are in those troublesome years. Brooke is up for anything contradicting ACD. He hates his chip. I know he's really interested in anything mechanical. Now Risa, she a little contrary. She's emotional, easily excitable and says and does things spur of the moment. I guess you could call her spontaneous."

Char said, "This is perfect chance for her to grow food, and as for as your son, we desperately need mechanical technicians."

"You guys do know a lot about my family and me."

"It's our job," said Lynn. "Now, can you give us an answer in a week?"

"You are assuring me that my family and I will disappear from ACD's sight?"

"That's correct," said Char.

"But doesn't ACD have to get a continuous signal that we are alive or receive a termination signal? We can't just disappear."

Chat said, "We know that. At that time we'll decide exactly what signal to send to ACD."

"And most likely we'll never be able to return to York?"

"That's right. But you will be given another place to live with the same names but no ID number or chip. Roland, your name will be in the new world or, if we fail, in this world. We would reinstall your chip and old ID number. Things will have either changed for the better or there will be no change at all if we fail."

"How much time do I have to prove my hypothesis?"

Char said, "The Premier wants his report in six months. Can you have your proof by then?"

"If you give me the power."

"Okay, we will need to see your proof before you show it to the Premier," said Char.

"Where is this super lab?"

"We'll tell you when we get your answer," said Lynn. "Now, it's time for you to get your answers regarding the chip. You can go back to the auditorium."

"Okay"

"One other thing, Roland," said Lynn, "We asked you once before, do you want to see one of us this evening? We've seen the women they have for you gentlemen to choose for the night. We didn't have enough time to find many attractive Reformer women we can trust. Not that we're bragging but they're not too pleasant looking."

Roland had to admit, Char and Lynn were quite attractive.

"Sure, why don't both of you come," he said. "We can have dinner first."

"Sounds good, Roland," said Lynn. "But remember, we cannot talk about any of today's happenings tonight at dinner. We can't be sure there are no scanners or sound pickup devices in your room or in the dining room."

"Okay. How about six?"

"Fine."

The women left through a back door and Roland headed to the auditorium.

CHAPTER ELEVEN

As Roland returned to his seat, others were just returning to their seats. This time he was seated between a very young black man and older man. The young man seemed lean but didn't look frail. In fact, he looked to be in great athletic shape like a long distance runner. He couldn't imagine this youngster doing anything scientific.

Roland spoke to the young man. "What's your field?"

"Actually, no field," he said. "I've been assigned to be a sort of assistant if you choose to join us. Char and Lynn are to help you with any logistics. I'm here to help you with any technical problems you may encounter. I'm well-schooled in physics, chemistry, nuclear studies and electronics. Dr. Winston hopes if you and I get acquainted, you might be more inclined to join our group. My name is Chantel Joyce." He stuck out his hand for a handshake.

"Hello, but I'm not sure I'm in with you all yet." Roland shook hands with the man.

"We know, but we can hope."

"I just don't understand at all why you people are so

interested in me and my hypothesis. How will that help your Reformers cause?"

"I'm not sure either," said Chantel, "but I have an idea. I've listened to some of their discussions. It has something to do with God."

"God?" said Roland. "Are you people a bunch of religious fanatics? I don't believe in a god, or Jesus, or anything like that. If you people are, then I'm gone. I'm not joining a bunch of Jesus freaks."

"No, Dr. Davidson." said Chantel, "I don't know if I believe in a god either. But I do believe in the Reformers cause. I don't like Sogan or Sentinels or scanners or any of that stuff. But I do know a lot of Reformers want to bring religion back into their life."

"I just don't know what to believe about you people."

The older man on Roland's left spoke up. "I know what the young man is talking about."

"So, tell me," said Roland.

"The young Reformers want to start a colony of perfect beings somewhere; perfect genes, perfect chromosomes, no defects. And most assuredly, no chips or scanners."

"What about people born before gene correction like you? What will they do with you?"

"A limited number of us would be taken along and quarantined. We would not be allowed to reproduce or associate with the perfect generation. They'd allow us to live until we died naturally, not when ACD dictated."

Roland ran his fingers through his hair which he was sure it was graying quickly now. "I don't think I can comprehend all I'm hearing. It sounds like you all are going someplace."

The old man continued, "I don't know if we're going someplace or not, but the way I understand it, it's like the

Garden of Eden all over again. Only instead of one Adam and one Eve it would consist of all of the perfect generations. It would consist of all those born after fetal correction began. I'm sure, sir, you'd be one of them. I, on the other hand, would not."

"You people are dreamers," said Roland, "You're out of you minds. I'm staying just long enough to learn how to get rid of this chip for me and my family and then I'm out of here."

Chantel turned to Roland, "I think you'll stay for the whole program, Dr. Davidson, and you and your family will join us."

"Don't count on it."

Roland folded his arms and sat back in his chair. Dr. Winston walked back to the podium.

"Ladies and gentlemen, this will be short. There are two dangers. One, we can remove the chip in a thirty minute operation. A special robot has been programmed by Dr. Wang to perform this operation. The robot surgeons provided in our hospitals by ACD are programmed to install a chip but not remove one. ACD foresaw no reason to ever remove a chip. Yes, there is some risk. There's a one half of one per cent chance you will be paralyzed for the rest of your life. There is a one half of one half of one percent chance you will die. It is an entirely optional operation and we definitely are not pressuring anyone to have a chip removed.

"Now, here is the other danger. If you are unchipped, the scanners will not acquire a reading from you. If a public scanner is above you, it will simply do nothing. If an official or Sentinel scans you with a portable scanner, they too will read nothing. Younger Sentinels will simply not know what to do and will assuredly do nothing except shrug their shoulders and move on. Older Sentinels will definitely sound the alarm and identify you as an outlaw. We have been told outlaws are forcibly chipped but we know this is not always true. ACD terminates anyone who seems to be a threat. If a chip has been removed, an internal scar is quite obvious to a robot and that person is seen as a threat. It is most difficult to reconnect the nerve endings and reinstall another chip. Once the robot 'sees' an internal scar, it has been programmed to identify the person as a threat and will terminate life at that moment. Any questions so far?"

Some raised their hand. "What about these scarves?" Can we keep them?"

Dr. Winston shook his head. "No. Two reasons. One, you'll be quite obvious wearing a scarf in summer, especially if more and more scarves start showing up around the world. Second, the scarf contains some very sophisticated electronics. We don't want this to be discovered by ACD. And it will leave a trail leading to the fact that Dr. Wang is still alive."

Roland raised his hand. "When would this operation be done?"

"We will commence tomorrow morning 12:00 GMT."

This would require Roland staying another day. He'd have to get approval for a second day out of his city. He didn't like that thought.

As if reading Roland's thoughts, Dr. Winston said, "We can easily get permission for you to remain here a second day. Ladies and gentlemen, again, contrary to what the Premier likes you to think, fooling ACD is quite easy. Everyone believes what they are told, that it is impossible to fool ACD. This is simply not true."

Dr. Winston looked at his time indicator. "Any other questions? If not, let's go to lunch. And I think we have quite a surprise for you."

Another attendee asked a question. "What do we do this afternoon?"

"This afternoon is open for discussion. We'll discuss anything you would like."

With that everyone broke for lunch.

The group walked to the rear of the small auditorium where tables had been set up for lunch. Roland noticed something was different. Usually, at the center of the table, a stack of cenes would be placed. Instead of cenes, plates, bowls and eating utensils were placed at each setting. As usual, drinking glasses were placed beside the plates.

Char, Lynn and other screeners began bringing out containers of a green leafy material, items completely unfamiliar to Roland. He had an idea what was going to be served; food from the 2000's. Roland had never eaten anything grown out of the ground. He also had never eaten animal flesh. If flesh would be served, he doubted he could eat it.

"Ladies and gentlemen, as you can guess, we're serving some of the foods, or cenes, from the twenty-first century." Dr. Winston stood near the center of the tables.

"I realize the younger of our participants may have never eaten these items. If you feel you'd rather not partake, we also have the customary cenes available. Just tell your server you'd rather have them. We will not be offended. The foods have quite a different taste and smell. We would like you to at least try one or two items. Enjoy your meal."

With that Dr. Winston and the attendees sat down and began to eat. Roland sat next to two older men. They had graying beards and thick glasses. They were both somewhat balding and slightly overweight. Their clothing was similar to what he saw in old pictures of his grandparents.

Roland glanced at each of them, He asked, "Why didn't either of you gentlemen have your eyes corrected? It's so easy today."

"I'll tell you, young man," said the man on Roland's left, "It's too much trouble. I've had my genes worked on so many times I feel like a lab specimen. It just won't last."

"Yes," said the other gentleman, "For anyone our age — I'm one hundred and forty and Simon there is one hundred and forty two — the correction won't last. Our genes are old and I guess they want to stay that way. Stem cell treatment didn't work either. So we wear glasses."

Roland had to agree. "Yes, I understand. I'm currently working on the aging of genes. It's been an elusive pursuit."

The man on Roland's right said, "I'm Dean Cornish and he's Simon Wilson. What's your field, young man?"

Roland answered, "My name's Roland Davidson. Gene repair is my field. I'm currently working on gene aging. What about you gentlemen?" Roland still wasn't too sure to whom he would want to reveal his real interest. All Dr. Winston had told the audience was that someone in the room was working on atom disassembly.

"We're into the gravitational field," said Simon. "We're trying to bend or deform the lines of gravity."

Dean spoke, "Do you believe all Dr. Winston is telling us? It sounds too good to be true. I've had this damned chip for almost fifty years. I feel as if someone is always watching me."

"I know what you mean," said Roland. "I'd have it removed tomorrow, risks or not, but I have my family to worry about. And there is that slight personal danger."

"We have no family," said Simon, "so we're having it done as soon as we can. We'll take our chances with scanners."

"I know this is a knife," said Roland, "but what are these two other metal things used for?"

"They are a fork and spoon. You use them to eat with," said Simon. "You don't eat these foods with your fingers like you do with cenes."

Roland took a bite of his 'food. "What is this?"

"That, young man, is lettuce, carrots and onions," said Dean. "I don't know what kind of topping they put on it, though. What do you think of it?"

"It's different. I just bit into something that's making my eyes water."

"It's probably an onion," said Simon. "I loved them. I haven't had one in years."

"This is strange," said Roland. "First they serve us this green and orange stuff and now I see another meal being served."

"That's the way it was done in the old days," said Dean. "This was called a salad and I believe they are now serving the main course."

Roland was fascinated. "What are these?"

"Potatoes, green beans and corn. I don't see any meat or animal flesh as you call it."

Roland seemed to find the food fairly tasty. "I don't think I could eat any flesh."

"Most people stopped eating flesh a long time ago. Too much arteriosclerosis. Do you know what that is?"

Roland remembered Mrs. Leeger. "Yes, I do. Now, what's this? It looks like a cene but doesn't taste like one."

"That's bread."

Roland thought of his daughter, Risa. "My daughter wants to get into the food growth industry. I wish she could be here and taste the food she wants to grow."

Dean looked around. "Who knows?"

Once again Roland thought of the dangers to his family if he joins this group. If he were a single man, he'd join in an instant. When he returns home, he'll have to carefully sound out each one of his family.

Roland finished eating and thanked his two friends for their conversation. He returned to the seating area of the auditorium. During lunch Roland had turned off his PCS. He turned it back on and it began sounding a level one call. It was Melody. This time Melody she had the picture portion muted. He missed seeing as he called it, her cute upside down smile. She had a beautiful smile but the corners of her mouth turned downward slightly when she smiled.

"Roland," Melody's voice wasn't as cheerful as usual. "When are you coming home?"

"I was going to call you. There's been a delay. I won't be leaving here until Wednesday afternoon."

"Oh, why Roland?"

"There's been a little addition to the program. Is something wrong with Risa?"

"Not Risa. My Sentinels."

"What about your Sentinels?' asked Roland.

"Roland. I can't say much over the communicator. I have to see you in person."

"Melody, it sounds serious. Is it?" Roland asked.

"I believe so. Please come home."

"I can't until Wednesday. I'll travel straight through. I'll be home early in the morning."

"Please hurry. I love you."

"Love you, too," Said Roland.

What is going on, thought Roland. I have to decide if I

want my chip removed and I have to get home as soon as possible. Something's wrong at home and Melody sounded terribly worried. Everything was fine until I wrote that stupid article.

JOHN PALLO

CHAPTER TWELVE

The afternoon was spent by the attendees asking many useless and repetitive questions. Even with five thousand Reformers as they like to call themselves, how would they ever be able to take back the world from ACD and the Premier? Roland didn't care. He wanted the chip removed. He wouldn't tell his family until he knew how they felt. He would then let them decide. His main worry, though, was Melody. What was wrong at home? He had to get home as soon as the chip was removed. Roland had heard enough to know what he was going to do.

He looked around wondering who or how the arrangements would be set up. Dr. Winston was busy answering questions. These are supposedly intelligent, scientists. Why do they keep asking the same question only in different ways? He saw Char coming in through a side door. Roland got up and made his way over to her.

"Char. I want to talk to you."

"Sure, Roland," she said. "How'd you like lunch?"

"Great or least it was okay. But I want to know about tomorrow. How do I arrange it?"

"You just give me the word."

"How will I get on the tram? It scans me to see if I am registered?"

"You'll get an external chip. You'll have to tape it on your neck in places where scanning is necessary."

Roland asked, "This external chip, it has all my information on it?"

"It has your complete identification information but not your actual vital life signs. It just transmits typical life signs of a living being."

"And the scanners will be satisfied with that?"

"Dr. Wang has been wearing hers for several years. And so have many other people."

"How about you?" Roland asked Char.

"Not yet. I have to move around this world too much yet. You on the other hand, will be fairly stationary in your lab. I predict in three years at the most, chips will be a thing of the past."

"Okay. Do it."

Char looked him straight in the eyes. "Roland, are you committed?"

"Yes."

"Are you committed one hundred percent?"

"Yes."

"How about your family?"

"I don't know about them. When I get home I'm going to talk to them individually. I'm going to feel them out and see where they stand. I'm most confident my wife will go along willingly."

"Roland," said Char. "I'm not talking about the chip removal. We won't do it unless we can count on you to continue your work on atom reassembly in our facilities. Chip removal is of minor concern for us."

Roland sat on a nearby chair. "Char, I don't know how they'll feel about moving to some secret lab. I can't even tell them where it is."

"I can tell you this much, Roland. You and your family won't be isolated. There will be other families nearby. It'll be like a very small village."

"Where is it, damn it!"

"Roland, believe me. It's not in your or our best interest to reveal the location yet."

"I could just lie to you and tell you I'm going along with your scheme and then change my mind."

Char sat down next to him. "Roland, we screened you quite thoroughly. You've too much integrity. You won't lie to us."

"You're right. Okay. How about this scenario? I agree to do my work for you but my children refuse to go along with it. Then what?"

"We would trust you that you tried your best. Then the decision you have to make is will you and your wife go with us and leave your children in the care of ACD's guardians?"

Roland buried his head in his hands. "God." Then, as if correcting himself, "I know, there is no god."

"There are those who would debate that."

Roland stood up and looked at all the other people around the room. They were all talking in low tones to their screeners or Dr. Winston. Even Dr. Wang mingled through the audience.

Char stood up too. "Roland, let me prepare approval for you to stay tomorrow until noon. You'll have to let me know by six this evening. If it's a go, then we're set. If not, so be it.

We won't transmit your delay approval."

"Okay. I'm staying. I'll stay for the operation."

"Not just the operation, you'll join us to continue your experiments."

"Yes," said Roland emphatically.

"I have to hear you say it, Roland."

"Yes! I'll join you to perform my atom experiments. But what if my hypothesis doesn't hold up?"

"We'll trust you gave it your best effort," said Char as she walked away. "I'll call you in a minute after we get delay approval."

Roland sat down again, trying to comprehend what he had just done. He almost forgot about Melody's problem, whatever it was. The chip was like an Albatross. He couldn't imagine life without it. There would be tricky times getting around and not being recognized on the many scanners throughout the world. He'd gladly chance it.

He wished he could get the operation completed now and take a night tram home. What was wrong at home? Why was Melody so upset? Why couldn't she tell me over the communicator? She did say it was not about Risa. That at least is some good news.

"Roland!" Char and Lynn came almost running up to him.

"Roland," said Lynn. "There's some kind of problem. We can't get you the time extension."

"Why?"

"We don't know," said Char. "It's never failed before."

"Something is overriding our program. ACD won't let us do it. We've always been able to fool ACD."

Lynn said, "It's almost like you're in too high of a position. It acts like you're a vice premier or something. You aren't a vice premier, are you?"

Roland almost laughed. "Not that I know of. But my wife is a chamberperson."

"No," said Char. "There's a lock on your status identification that we cannot open."

Roland said, "What do I do now?"

"Do you still want to join us?"

"Yes."

"Okay," said Lynn. "Dr. Wang said she'll do your operation tonight, if you're willing?"

"Do it now, for all I care."

"No," said Lynn. "Tonight. You're supposed to be at the Genome meeting and then meet George about five. We'll stay with that plan."

"Okay." Roland was slightly bewildered by all the happenings. Why is his ID locked? Why is Melody upset? Why? Why? Why?

Char said, "I guess this means our evening is off. Darn."

"We can still have dinner," said Lynn. "Then we'll watch Dr. Wang do the operation. You shouldn't feel any after effects. Maybe you'll want to see us then?"

"I can't think of anything right now except getting this damned chip off and then see what's wrong at home."

"How do you know something is wrong at home?" asked Lynn.

"Something is wrong but she couldn't tell me on the communicator."

"Do you want us to check for you?" said Char. "Maybe it has to do with your ID being locked."

"Can you do that?" asked Roland.

"Roland, we're small but not that small. We have very many cohorts."

"That'd be great."

"We'll let you know tonight," said Char. "See you then."

Lynn said, "Here comes Sandy. She'll escort you back to the Genome meeting."

Sandy brought Roland back to the same little room at the main meeting room as before. George met them and they reversed their routine, quickly switching the scarf again without causing any alarm. For most of Roland's life he lived with the chip and gave it little thought. Now, for the first time, he felt as if he were under ACD's microscope. Having the freedom of life without the chip made him feel like an escaped prisoner. Now he was back in prison; the virtual prisoner of the chip. He knew he had to get rid of it. He hoped Melody would feel the same way.

The meeting ended and Roland headed for his room. It was quite a day and he needed time to comprehend all that transpired. Did he actually attend a secret meeting of Reformers? Is he really going to get his chip removed? The danger of being paralyzed or even death didn't even faze him. He wanted the chip removed. Damn the chances of failure. He was going for it.

Later that day, Roland left his room and descended the stairs to the eating area. He thought about his lunch. It was good and, except for a few strange belches, he enjoyed the 'real food.' Now, back to the ordinary. Laid out buffet style were the many cene choices. Roland grabbed a few cenes and some orange colored drink. He wasn't sure how or when Lynn and Char would contact him.

He picked a table near a window where he had a good view of the whole room. Listening to the murmur of the people in the dining room he wondered how many were in the Reformer meeting. He finished his first cene and began munching on the second. Three cenes were the recommended amount for a male unless involved in hard labor.

Roland saw the two women walk in. They were dressed in typical evening attire; white knee length robes with a cinch like belt attached above the waist. He had to admit they were very attractive but not as attractive as Melody.

"What? No work uniform?" said Roland.

"No, officially we're off work. How are you? Been thinking much?" asked Char.

"I would say so, and mostly about my wife. I am sure worried about her."

Lynn put her hand over her mouth and answered in a muffled voice, "Don't worry about her. You're the one. Tell you more later."

Roland knew better than to try to answer but he did feel somewhat relieved. He felt sure he could handle himself as long as he didn't have to worry about his family.

They quickly finished their meal with little conversation. As they drank their drink, Lynn motioned they should leave. "Follow me," she said.

Roland followed the two women back to the Genome meeting area and into the same little room where he received his scarf.

"Here's how we'll do this. Your new external chip is wrapped in this scarf. You'll take this with you to Dr. Wang. She will first direct her robot to remove your chip and delete it. On her command I'll uncover your external chip. The scanner will pick up your new external chip. Remember, unless ACD gets a death signal, it has to pick up your chip signal from somewhere constantly. Of course it becomes a moot point if you die during the operation."

"You guys are sure blunt," said Roland.

"We have to be, Roland. This is not a game."

In a most serious tone, Lynn said, "Roland, now I want you to understand this. It's true ACD has to get a chip signal at all times from every human or at least, an official reason why the signal was interrupted. You could just leave your external chip on your pillow at home and ACD would be happy. That is, as long as there is enough residual heat to keep it transmitting. Don't forget the chip needs your body heat to function. It will function only about four hours at room temperature. Now, if someone would try to scan you somewhere and you had no signal, they'd immediately assume you to be a threat. You would be terminated on the spot. The Sentinels can terminate life by sending a coded tone to the chip but if you had no chip, they'd use a more crude method. Let's just say it would hurt terribly. Do you understand?"

Roland looked at Char and Lynn. "Yes I do."

"Okay," said Char. "Let's head out to the cambri."

"Once again Roland followed the women. The parking lot was now lit with low intensity low reflection area lights. They headed out to a cambri parked outside the rear door. And once again, Sentinels were standing around the cambri.

"Now what?" asked Roland.

"Put your arms around our waists," said Char. "Act happy."

The trio walked out to the cambri cheerfully laughing and talking.

"Hey!" yelled a young Sentinel. The three stopped instantly but Lynn kept laughing.

"Yeah?" said Char laughing too.

"Aren't you the same guy I saw walking with a dark haired lady this morning?" asked the Sentinel to Roland.

"Uh, yeah," said Roland trying to fake a smile.

"How do you do it, Buddy?" said the Sentinel. "One woman this morning and two this evening. You must be quite a man."

"He sure is," said Char faking a swoon.

"Wow!" said the other Sentinel. "Good luck."

A third Sentinel said, "If you need help, give us a call."

"I think I'll be okay if they don't rush me," said Roland.

With that the Sentinels shook their heads a walked away. Char, Lynn and Roland now gave a genuine laugh and continued to walk to the cambri.

"That scared me," said Roland.

"Roland," said Char, "This is the world you're entering. Fifty percent joy and fifty percent pure panic. Are you up to it?"

"You bet. Lead on." With that, they headed on to the old building.

They entered the building and walked up onto the stage. They walked to a room at the rear of the stage. It had an extremely thick door and a strange brown material on the walls. Two robot arms were attached to a large metal chassis on the ceiling. Dr. Wang stood behind a glass window in an adjoining room. She had many controls at her fingertips. For the first time, Roland felt a little queasy and apprehensive. Did he truly want to do this?

"Are you ready, Dr. Davidson?" said Dr. Wang.

Roland hesitated answering. "Yes, I am."

"Okay, lie on the table, face down. Ms. Paget will administer the anesthesia. Just breathe the air from the tube."

"Breath this, sweetie," said Lynn smiling.

Again Roland hesitated and then grabbed the tube willingly. Almost immediately he was asleep. Dreaming, he dreamt about hospitals of many years ago. He saw pictures of many people wearing masks, covered in green gowns. There were many machines all around the patient and a varied assortment of tools within one main operator's reach. He saw blood and gauze material all around and heard a hissing sound. Everyone wore gloves, not like present times when germs pose no problems. Suddenly he saw the patient. It was Mr. Leeger. With that he suddenly awoke.

"You okay?" asked Lynn.

"I think so. Are you finished?" he asked.

"Yep, and you're still alive," said Char. "Ready for us tonight?"

"Can I turn over?"

"You can get up if you want," said Lynn.

Roland carefully turned over and sat up. He gently felt the back of his neck. No pain. This is great, he thought.

"Am I truly free?" Roland asked.

"Yes you are," said Dr. Wang.

"Don't forget, Dr. Davidson, "said Lynn, "You owe us your soul."

Roland looked directly at Lynn, "I do owe you my soul and I won't forget my promise. Tell me what I should do next."

"We have bad news," said Char. "We won't be spending the night together. Our sources have found out what is concerning your wife. It seems the Premier wants to see you as soon as possible. He knows you were supposedly at the Genome Meeting today. You are to leave tonight. He wants you to see him at his chamber as fast as trams and air vehicles can get you there. You can stop by your home and then continue on to the China Republic. It has nothing to do with what has happened here this evening."

"What's this have to do with my wife?" asked Roland.

"It seems the Sentinels aren't at her disposal. She is a sort of prisoner until you see the Premier."

"Prisoner?"

"Evidently the Premier wants to make sure you get there as soon as possible."

"God damn it, and yes, I know there is no god!" said Roland. "And you swear it has nothing to do with this chip removal."

Lynn answered, "I assure you neither the Premier, nor ACD, has any idea of your chip removal. It seems you were going to see him in six months. He has decided he wants to see you now."

"Why wasn't I notified by my PCS?"

Char answered, "A PCS signal goes to where your chip is located. It was with George in the Genome Meeting."

"Shit!" said Roland.

"What?" Lynn asked.

"It's an old slang word. My kids found an old book on ancient slang words. It's the new fad kids are using now."

"If questioned, the best excuse you can use is that you forgot your PCS in your room this morning. I think that'll work," said Char.

"I gotta get back to my room and check out. I got to go."

"Roland," said Lynn, "Don't forget your external chip."

"Okay, explain my procedures again."

"As you leave this room, we will hand you your external chip. It's transmitting your location now. Some people tape it, or use Type Three skin adhesion to glue it to the back of their neck but if you don't expect any close scanning you can shave a small spot on the back of your neck. Use the skin glue to secure it to your scalp and cover in with hair. You're lucky you have a full head of hair."

"I've got to go," said Roland. He looked at the people around him. "Thank you, Dr. Wang. Thank you, Char and Lynn. How will I contact you?"

"You're welcome, and we'll contact you in two weeks. I don't think you'll have time to discuss our program in one week after spending time in the China Republic."

"I will truly miss our night together," said Char.

"Me too," said Lynn. "We'll see you again, soon."

"Okay, now get me back to my room."

Roland taped the chip on the back of his neck and covered it with his collar.

"Is there a scar?" he asked.

"No external scar."

"Great. I'm going home."

Roland hoped his return trip to York would be without incident. So far all scanners seemed satisfied with his transmissions. The tram attendant seemed satisfied with his identification and cleared him to York.

"Wow!" said the Francisco attendant at his transfer. "It says here you're continuing on to the China Republic. I wish I could travel like some people do. Have a nice trip."

Poor man, thought Roland. He's soon to be replaced with a robot attendant. I wonder why it's taken so long.

The tram passed through several thunderstorms on his return trip but Roland never noticed. All he could think about was the chip. He was free. He wanted Melody and the kids to be free, too. He wondered, too, about the location of the village of the reformers. Would Melody accept the change? Would his children accept the change? Would Roland Davidson continue to accept the change?

CHAPTER THIRTEEN

Except for the storms, Roland's return trip to York proved fairly uneventful. He called Melody and told her he was returning and everything was okay. She was only half convinced but she told Roland to wake her as soon as he got home. She also said she told Sean she didn't feel like seeing him. Risa seemed calm for the moment.

Roland stood on the walkway as the tram raced through the night nearing the east coast. He was unable to sleep most of the night and could hear the muffled roar of the wind as the tram sped through the night air. Staring out into the darkness he was sure he saw small lights here and there far from the city lights. It was probably an outlaw camp, or rabble rousers as Dr. Winston called them. Every so often he would pass a metropolitan area and a maze of dimly lit, low reflection, low-power-consumption lights would catch him for a moment. Then the tram would be over darkness again. Finally he saw the lights of York.

"We'll be arriving at York in ten minutes," said the tram announcer.

Since the tram terminated at York, there'd be no disconnecting of trams. The whole unit would stop and all passengers would disembark. Roland tried to imagine what the overseas trip would be like. This would be a first for him.

He returned to his cambri and drove off the tram. He set his coordinates for home and settled back as his cambri weaved and bobbed through the darkness. He arrived at his dome Wednesday morning at about the same time he left Monday. Melody must have been waiting up for him because she ran out to his cambri to greet him.

"Roland, I'm so glad to see you. What's happening? Why do you now have to go to China?"

"I don't know," said Roland hugging his wife. "Sogan wants to see me as soon as possible. I have no idea what for."

"Roland, I don't think the Sentinels are here at my disposal. I feel like I'm in protective custody."

"I know," said Roland.

"How do you know?" asked Melody.

"I'll tell you but it is such a long story it may have to wait until I get back from China."

Melody grabbed Roland and looked up at him. "Roland, you promised you'd tell me all that's happening!"

"I will, and I think you will think it's great."

"What, Roland? What?"

"Come with me outside to the back of our dome." He took her hand and led her to the rear of their dome. The sky was just beginning to glow.

"I think we are outside of the listening devices in the dome. Melody," he said in a low voice. "How would you like to get rid of your chip?"

"Oh Roland. Are you serious?"

"Dead serious," he replied.

"Roland, how?"

"I can't tell you now. But we can do it." Roland didn't think it wise to tell Melody he had already had his chip removed. He had to be sure she didn't see the chip taped on the back of his neck.

A movement near the rear door of their dome startled them. It was two Sentinels leaning against their dome, half hidden by shadows.

"Oh," said one of them. "We didn't mean to scare you. Did you have a nice trip, Dr. Davidson?"

"Oh, yes. I learned a little but most of it was repetitious."

Roland felt panicky. Had they heard any of his conversation?

As calmly as possible, Roland said, "Honey, I have to pack again for China. I don't know how long this trip will take."

A Sentinel spoke up, "We're here to assist chamberperson Melody Davidson in any way needed. You can travel secure in the knowledge we'll be at her side."

"That's very comforting," lied Roland.

Another Sentinel spoke, "Wow! That's going to take you about thirty-five to forty hours flying time if you go by air vehicle."

"I know," said Roland. "And it will mean ten or eleven recharging stops. It'll take me two days to get there if the Premier wants me to go by air or five days by watercraft."

"Roland," said Melody. "Take us with you. The kids can study on the ALEKC anywhere as long as they're scanned."

"I don't think I can get you travel approval in time," said Roland.

"I can get your approval immediately," said an old Sentinel listening nearby.

"What?" Roland asked.

"I can get approval right now, if you want them to go."

"Roland, please," begged Melody. "Think of the kids, especially Risa."

Roland knew why Melody mentioned Risa.

"Okay," he said.

The old Sentinel said, "Start packing and head out to the tram station. I'm not sure by what means you'll be traveling but you will all be able to go. Approval will be obtained by the time you get to the station."

Roland wasn't sure what this meant. Citizens just don't decide to go to China or anywhere overseas without days spent obtaining approval, and then at the last minute, getting approval for a whole family. Something just didn't seem right. He thought about Char and Lynn's words; it had nothing to do with his chip removal.

Roland and Melody ran into the dome.

"Wake up kids," said Melody. "We're all going to China."

"What?" Risa and Brooke asked simultaneously.

"We're all going to China. Come on. Get moving!" yelled Roland.

"No!" said Risa.

"Yes!" said Brooke. It took Brooke mere seconds to get dressed. "Why?"

"Dad's got work there," said Melody. "Come on, Risa."

"I'm not going!" yelled Risa.

"Yes you are," said Melody. "The Sentinels are going to close and lock up our dome. You'll have no place to live."

"I'll go and live with Roalf."

Roland reminded her, "Don't forget what you said last week. Roalf may not be living here for long."

Risa looked at the Sentinels standing nearby. "So?" she said defiantly.

"And you want a favor, too. Remember? Food industry? We just might see someone who can help you."

"Yeah, I remember," Risa said slightly pouting. "Who are we going to see?"

"I don't know about you but I have an appointment with the Premier," said Roland.

"The Premier Commander?" she said.

"That's right."

"Can I tell Roalf?"

"You can call him from the cambri after we're on our way."

Risa began dressing but not as fast as Brooke. They stuffed their clothes in baggage containers along with a month's supply of cleaning solution. The four travelers climbed in the cambri and Roland voiced the coordinates for the York station. He assumed approval, directions and mode of travel would be ready and waiting.

They arrived at the York Transportation Station and everything was in order. They were told they'd be traveling by air vehicle. Brooke was ecstatic. Risa was too but she tried not to show it. Many official type travelers were standing around waiting to board the air vehicle. Roland's motely dressed family stood out from the other passengers.

"Roland," said Melody, "I can't believe this. Why are we getting such attention?"

"I don't know," he said, "but whatever happens, I don't think we have a choice."

Completely mystifying Roland was the fact that they were ushered to a separate vehicle with no other passengers. They boarded in utter silence and awe. Roland and Melody sat back, not quite sure if they should enjoy the trip. The children raced to a window. The interior of the aircraft was again Plaztec but in a shade of pink. Two heating and cooling appliances were place along the wall. By gestures the attendants motioned that they should feel free to partake of anything they contained. Several couch-like seats were located along the wall, too, with three bedrooms to the rear, two small beds and one larger.

The children were ecstatic. Brooke and Risa sat glued to the air vehicle's window and didn't move unless they were eating. Each refueling stop was a new adventure for the family whether it would be on land or on a floating, robot tended island. They marveled at the blueness of the ocean. A large iceberg held them speechless. No other aircraft or floating ship was observed. Risa forgot completely about calling Roalf. Attendants were constantly asking if they needed anything. This vehicle even had humans piloting the craft instead of the usual robots. Roland's enjoyment was tempered by a lingering doubt. Why was the Premier giving him and his family such royal attention? He knew the Premier wasn't just a kind philanthropist. If the Premier gave something to someone, that someone was going to have to give the Premier something in return. And it usually wasn't an even trade.

As the time came for sleeping, they were shown their sumptuous bedroom quarters toward the rear of the craft.

"Roland, why is this happening to us? What did you do in Lower California to deserve this?"

"I told you, nothing in California is causing this. I was supposed to see the Premier in six months but he, or she, moved it up a bit."

Melody stretched out in the beautifully decorated bed. "I'm afraid to enjoy this. When can you tell me about your meeting?"

Roland was sure any conversation was being monitored. He pointed all around and then to his ears, hoping Melody would understand that he couldn't tell her now.

"The meeting was the usual stuff," he said. "Very repetitive."

"Okay," she said. "Good night then."

With the forward reading scanners, any weather turbulence was detected and the aircraft compensated its flight path. The result was an extremely smooth flight.

The total flight lasted forty-seven hours. After several landings in the Lands of Europe, they landed in a seemingly remote location they assumed to be China. They were greeted by two Chinese gentlemen. Their English was fairly easy to understand but they spoke slowly.

"This way, please." one of them said.

They were shown the way to a large vehicle, not at all like a cambri. It was quite high with extremely high ground clearance. Roland couldn't believe it but the large, knobby tires seemed to be filled with air. He could tell by the valve stems. Pneumatic tires were long ago discarded in North Americus. It had a rather noisy engine that emitted terrible smelling fumes.

They had to climb up three steps to get into the large vehicle. The inside was not too luxurious but it was clean and functional. As it began to move, they realized its ride was a little rough. Roland assumed it was made for rough terrain travel.

"How far do we have to go?" asked Roland.

The drivers just looked at them and smiled.

As they traveled, Roland saw a few domes here and there but there were many more of the old style huts he'd seen in history books about early China. He saw even fewer cambris. Roland was surprised to see poverty. He and his children hardly heard the word much less witnessed it. All they ever heard was that the world is perfect. It surely isn't perfect here in China. Is it possible some of these people aren't chipped? Roland and his family were even more amazed to see animal drawn carts as they reached farther into the city.

"Dad. How does that animal know to pull that cart?" asked Brooke.

"I guess they teach it somehow."

Another fallacy revealed. ACD led the population to believe the whole world was the same; all peoples live in domes, everyone has one or two cambris, nearly all animals were extinct. The country just looked plain and simply backward. Risa was thrilled to see rice growing in paddies. The people seemed happy and waved as they passed. As Roland thought about it, there wasn't a lot of smiling back in York.

The driver made a sharp, left turn into a large building. It was not illuminated very well but they could see they were descending. They seemed to be driving into a large cave toward the rear of the building. Roland could see the building was just a front to the cave. As they descended farther into the cave, the lighting improved, but there was still nothing to see except gray walls.

Twice they stopped at inspection gates to be scanned. Each time Roland froze, hoping his taped chip would register properly. Each time it did. Thank goodness, he thought. Finally they came to a brightly lit area. It was a very large open area with the bright light at first seeming like the sun. As they looked more closely, they realized it was an artificial sun.

Risa yelled out, "Look, Dad! They're growing things! It's beautiful."

"Yes it is." Roland felt like their dome in York was light years away. Would they ever return?

The vehicle stopped and they were politely asked to disembark. The men pointed to a dome. It seemed it was especially made for the Davidson family. It appeared out of place but was very much like their dome back in York. It appeared to be in the middle of a field of green plants. They were about a meter high and had large green leaves on them.

When they entered the dome, they group stood in awe. It was furnished exactly like their dome. Everything was exactly like home.

All Melody could say was, "Roland!"

The kids checked their clothing containers and found the exact same clothes just as they had left them in York. Roland and Melody found the same. There were three dimension vision boxes and ACS machines just like at home. The cooling unit was well stocked just like home and the heating unit was in operating order too.

"Roland, tell me what's going on?" asked Melody.

"Melody, I'm speechless. I have no idea why the Premier is treating us this way. And I'm afraid to find out."

A voice startled them. "The Premier will give you twelve hours to accustom yourself to the time change. At that time, a vehicle will pick up your family for an audience with the Premier. We hope everything is satisfactory. If not, please call us on your ACS. Good evening."

"Gosh, dad," said Risa. "We're all going? Wow!"

"I guess so," he said. Roland didn't want anything to happen to his family. He was fairly certain his meeting in California wasn't the cause of this meeting. It was planned well before he went to the Genome Conference. But there was a certain element of doubt.

The kids went out of the dome and began exploring. No one stopped them or even questioned them. It seemed they could go wherever they desired. Risa was entranced by the growing crops and Brooke examined the strange ground transportation vehicles. After an hour, they became aware they were extremely sleepy. As their excited brains relaxed, they retired and slept quite well.

Roland checked his time indicator. Ten hours had passed since they arrived. In two hours a vehicle would be sent to pick them up. Roland wondered if they'd all see the Premier or just Roland by himself.

CHAPTER FOURTEEN

At precisely 18:00 GMT, a smaller vehicle arrived at their front door. It too had squishy, pneumatic tires that just completely fascinated Brooke. This engine was not as noisy as the other vehicle but it emitted fumes too. The ride, however, was a lot smoother.

Roland couldn't believe how big this 'cave' was. He couldn't tell if it was a natural cave or manmade. Many green plants were growing all around them and they even saw small creeks and rivers. Giant fans created gentle winds but there was a slight musty smell.

"Awesome!" said Brooke.

Their vehicle slowed near a large palace type building. That figures, thought Roland. The Premier probably lives here. Damn! Why did I write that article?

The vehicle stopped and they were again politely asked to disembark. They did as they were told. The man motioned the group to follow him up several stairs. They walked through several ornate halls and rooms and finally stopped at a small theater type room. It contained only ten or twelve seats and they all faced a large vision screen. They were asked to be seated which the family did. Standing at the rear of the room were two women and two men.

"Five minutes," the man said in perfect English.

"Thank you," said Roland.

The Davidson family sat in utter disbelief and astonishment. They didn't know what to say or expect. They just sat there, saying nothing. The five minutes seemed to take fifty minutes. Finally, the screen illuminated. The face of an approximately forty year old Chinese man appeared on the screen. He was a very handsome man. This didn't seem right. Roland knew the Premier was supposed to be one hundred and fifty to two hundred years old. The Premier had a large, white cat on his lap and he constantly stroked it.

"Hello," he said in perfect English. "I hope my Chinese to English translator is causing me to be understood."

Roland didn't know if he should answer or not.

The man said, "You can answer. I will hear you."

Roland spoke. "Yes, your Excellency."

"I hope your accommodations are good for you. We attempt to make it much like your home place as be possible."

"They are perfect, your Excellency," Roland said.

"Good. I am joyed by your remark."

Roland realized his translator needed some refinement.

The Premier continued, "Let me greet each children of you and wife. First, Risa. Is it proper pronunciation?"

Risa cowered down in her seat. "Yes, sir. Oh! I mean, your Excellency."

"Do not be distressed about my title. I am not easily detracted ..., I mean, offended."

Risa sat up a little.

"I understand you want to work in the food growth industry, is that correct?"

"Yes, uh, your Excellency."

"What did you think of our..." there was a slight pause, "farms?"

"I loved them, they are beautiful," Risa said.

"Have you ever digested," another slight pause, "eaten earth grown foods?"

"No."

"So, if desired, you may digest such foods at your next meal."

"Thank you, your Excellency."

"For now, you may roam our fields and talk to any of the farmers you may wish. They all have translators at their disposal. If you decide that is the field of endeavor you want to enter, it will be assigned to you."

Rise sat up straight now and smiled at her Dad.

"Now. Brooke. Is that correct pronunciation?"

"Yes," said Brooke in a weak voice.

"What is your interest?"

"I guess how things work and, oh, Roundball, sir, I mean, your Excellency."

"Great. I was a fair Roundball player in my day."

Roland was concerned about the Premier's last statement. He looks like a young, healthy and muscular man. What could he mean by 'in my day'?

"If you would like you can watch our great national Chinese Roundball team practice. They will even let you practice with them if you like. Would you like to combine with them?"

"Wow! Yes, your Excellency."

"Great. I love to see the exuberance of youth, don't you

Dr. Davidson?"

"Yes I do," said Roland.

"Risa, in a several minutes, you can combine with the young woman in the back of the room. She'll take you wherever you want to go. Brooke, at that time, you can combine with the young man. He'll do likewise."

Brooke said, "Dad, does he mean join?"

"I'm sure he does, Brooke," said Roland.

The Premier spoke, "I am positive my translator does not translate perfectly to your language. I hope you can bear with me and understand some of everything."

"It's okay, your Excellency," said Roland.

"Okay," said the Premier. "I love very much that English word 'okay'."

The Premier continued, "What do you children think of me?"

Risa and Brooke didn't know what to say.

"Your children and your…" a slight pause, "playpartners. Ah, playmates is the word I choose."

Risa answered, "We think you're okay."

"Ah, that word again. I favor it. Thank you"

The Premier took on a more serious look. "Do you discuss all the good and great things I, and ACD, have done?"

"Yes we do, your Excellency."

"I have simplified your country and the world so much. Isn't Socialism such a wonderful thing? There is no rich, no poor; we're all equal. No one owns anything. Everything is there for us to use whenever we want. There's no crime and if a criminal exists, he is immediately punished. No, ah…lawyer can get a criminal released on frivolous reasons. Your politicians are relinquished of their ridiculous duties. There's no one too rich or too poor. Medical repair is all supported at no debit to you. No one has to labor at an occupation not desired. I have tried to do what is right and easy for all people."

"Yes, your Excellency," said Risa.

"As you can observe, I and ACD are still working very hard in China. I have to admit we have great…ah…resistance here in my country. I don't comprehend the reason. I reason it is because we have such many numbers of people."

.Roland was concerned about the some of the apparent poverty they observed upon entering the city.

The Premier continued his speech. "Your country and all the major countries have robots taking complete care of all your needs. The Lands of Europe and Southern Americus seemed to welcome our efforts. I wanted to help your world before I attempted to simplify China. I feel it was the unselfish way to do these things. As the prophets say, one is not appreciated in his own country as he is in other countries. But I will try to continue my efforts."

Roland began to wonder if the Premier is possibly the kind and gentle ruler he's alleged to be.

The Premier raised his hand. "Children, you may combine with your assigned guiding person at the rear of the room."

Melody shot a concerned look at Roland.

"Don't worry, mother. You will all return here at eating time."

"Now. Melody. A beautiful name. You're not happy being a chamberperson. Do you want to be relieved of that duty?"

"I don't know. I'm not sure. It seems so overwhelming to me. It seems to disrupt families."

"You state your concerns very succinctly. I understand, but we need good people for chamberpersons. Why don't you go with the older gentlewoman and she'll give you a special lesson on chambering. If you do not like it, I will relinquish your duties immediately. If you want to try it for a period of time, you can do that also. You may end your assignment any time at a later date without waiting the required five years. Does that sound interesting?"

"I think so, maybe. What do you think, Roland?"

"I guess it sounds okay. Just try it."

"Yes, thank you, your Excellency."

"Great. Combine with the gentlewoman at the rear of the room. Dr. Davidson, I'll speak to you privately."

With that, the screen went blank. Melody and the kids left the room. Roland was left with one elderly man, standing in the back of the room.

"Come with me," said the man. Roland noticed for the first time the man was a Caucasian.

Roland got up and followed the man to a door at the side of the small auditorium. They walked for a short distance, going through several doors. At the last door, a Sentinel scanned both of them and showed them through. It was the first Sentinel Roland had seen since leaving York. As they went through the door, they were scanned again by another Sentinel. Roland noticed several more Sentinels around the hallway, all visibly and heavily armed. They seemed to make sure Roland noticed the weapons. Roland wasn't familiar with weapons but he could tell these were large and powerful weapons. He quickly surmised he was approaching the Premier's quarters. He wondered just how deep he was in the cave. Finally he reached a medium sized room with one chair in the center. At the front of the room was a closed double door. The Sentinels placed themselves in a semi-circle around the chair.

"Please be seated," said a man.

The double doors opened slowly. Roland could see nothing. There was no light behind the doors. Slowly the room brightened. Roland began to make out a figure reclined on a couch. As the room brightened, he saw an extremely old man. As the lighting improved, he could see the man was horribly disfigured. His face was distorted, almost grotesque. One eye was blue and the other was brown and inflamed. One arm was obviously shorter than the other and deformed. It was even a different color of skin. He seemed to have no legs. A terrible stench reached Roland's nostrils as the doors opened completely. He was transfixed by the ugliness of the man. He couldn't look away. The same white cat sat on the Premier's lap.

An attendant put a translator near the Premier's mouth. There seemed to be blood on his lips.

"Surprised?" came the voice.

Roland didn't know what to say.

The Premier spoke, "I had my attendants compose a pleasant figure for your family to see. I didn't want them to see my actual self. Even my halting English translations were staged just for your family."

"Yes, your Excellency," was all Roland could say.

"This is my most trusted assistant, Morgo." The Premier motioned to a menacingly large and well-muscled man standing next to him. He was definitely taller than Roland and completely devoid of hair. "Hand him the picture."

Morgo stepped down and walked over to Roland.

"Look at the picture!" Sogan said. It was more like a command.

The man handed Roland a picture of a striking young Chinese male. It was the same man he and Roland's family saw on the vision screen back in the auditorium.

The Premier tried to move slightly and Roland could see it caused him a lot of pain.

"I read over and over again your thesis regarding the disassembly and reassembly of atoms. Can it be accomplished?"

"I believe so, your Excellency, but it's only a hypothesis. I have yet to prove it."

"What are your impediments?"

"I need a laboratory with a large amount of power," said Roland.

"That's all?"

"No, your Excellency. Practically speaking, I need powerful magnetic generating equipment, large magnetic line benders, heat and electrical insulators, inert gas generators, super- conductors and many other items I'm not even aware of yet. And yes, I need well trained assistants."

"How long will this take?"

"Your Excellency," said Roland. "I'm not sure how long it will take and I'm not sure it will even be possible to do."

The Premier seemed to be pondering. Then he spoke. "Look at the picture closely again?"

"Yes, your Excellency."

"I am told I have less than a year to live. I have used up all my clones and, as you can plainly see, some beings that are not clones. I know you must be thinking of your Mr. Leeger. I could never understand but he and his wife chose to live in poverty. Your Mr. Leeger was becoming an inebriated fool. And, since he saw me at the island of clones, his loose tongue worried me. It became time for his and his wife's, termination.

Roland wasn't surprised by the Premier's callousness. Realizing his disregard for the lives of his clones, the termination of the Leegers made perfect sense.

"Even your genetic repair cannot help me. As you can laughingly see, I can't even obtain matching body parts."

"I'm not laughing, your Excellence."

"No, you are too concerned about your family's welfare to laugh at me. I can assure you, they are safe for the moment. ACD wanted to terminate your mother and grandmother this year. I intervened for now."

Roland for the first time was shocked with fear for his family. 'For the moment'. What did the Premier mean by that?

"For the moment, I am requesting of you. I do not want to have to command you. I am requesting you to disassemble me and reassemble me to the likes of the man in that picture. You must do it before it is too late."

Roland was stunned and speechless. The group of Reformers in Lower California wanted him to prove his hypothesis. Now the Premier wants – no, demands - he prove his hypothesis. And he wants it performed on himself. A cold wave of fear crept over Roland. He wasn't afraid for himself. He wanted his family out of this place. He wanted them safely back at York. But then Roland realized York was no safer since he wrote the article.

"What are you thinking, Doctor Davidson?"

Roland tried to be honest. "My mind is racing, your Excellency. I haven't proved it can be done or cannot be done. I won't know until I try it."

"Until I read your article, I was resigned to let my attendants terminate me. I have no chip. ACD would then assign a new Premier, most likely my great grandson. I read your article and a ray of hope shed its light on me. Do you understand my feelings, Doctor?"

"Yes I most certainly do, your Excellency." Roland could truly understand the Premier's desire to be rebuilt, seeing his decrepit condition. "But what if my hypothesis proves unattainable? What then?"

The Premier again seemed to be pondering. He tried to move again and grimaced in pain. Another attendant tried to assist him and the Premier angrily pushed his hand away.

"I'm very tired," the Premier said. "Except for Morgo, I don't know whom to trust. I don't know if you would give me your best effort to save me. I know you don't like me. You don't like your chip. You hate ACD constantly monitoring you. You are bored. You want to live back in the 2000's. Am I not correct?"

Roland once again wondered if his chip was transmitting his inner feelings. Of course now, he has no inner chip.

He assumed he had better be as honest as necessary. "I have longed for simpler times, your Excellency. But we do have so many improvements in our lives. My wife and I were able to design our children to be beautiful and extremely intelligent."

The Premier spoke, "I must leave you now. You can return to York whenever you desire. I will give you six days to give me an answer. I am very uncomfortable in saying this but you must think of your family. I am sure you want them to succeed in their endeavors. You want your wife to be contented. You don't want any of them to suffer pain. If I could be the man in the picture, I could live forever. Your machine could keep rebuilding me as I aged. I would be immortal. You and your family would be allowed to live anywhere in the world without the chip. We are even debating the possibility of enhancing the colony on Mars. You could live there if so desired. Leave your machine with me and nothing more would ever be asked of you. After your machine remade me, I would allow you and your family exclusive use of it to remake yourselves and even your sickly mother and grandmother into whatever you wanted."

Roland couldn't think of a proper response.

"How does that sound?" asked the Premier.

Roland still couldn't speak. It was clear now. His family was being threatened.

"Six days! And I trust that you want to protect your family so I know you will tell no one of my terrible condition."

Roland wanted to leave China immediately.

The Premier continued, "Oh, I have received some disturbing news from my California Sentinels. They said ACD noted some unusual transmissions from your chip while there. They couldn't explain it. Do you have any explanations?"

"No, your Excellency." Roland tried to think of a reason. "There was a tremendous rain storm. Maybe it caused some interruptions."

"There was no rainstorm," said Sogan.

The Premier's room began to darken and the doors closed. Roland sat in his chair. He was sick to his stomach; near vomiting.

A man approached Roland. "What would you like to do, sir?"

Roland mustered up a voice, "Go home, immediately."

"Do you wish a meal before you leave?" he asked.

Roland thought of the kids. He would like them to taste real food. A thought was forming in Roland's mind; a thought of joining the Reformers and taking his family away from this world. Away from ACD. Away from the Premier. He had to get in touch with the Reformers. He had to get in touch with Lynn or Char.

Roland answered, "Yes, we'll have a meal. And then we want to go home."

"Fine, sir. I'll see to it." The man left.

Another man entered the room and motioned for Roland to follow him. Roland did as he was directed. He knew he couldn't eat but he wanted his kids to see what the outside world could offer.

CHAPTER FIFTEEN

The aircraft began rising vertically and slowly started its forward motion.

"Roland, why didn't you eat anything?" asked Melody.

"I wasn't hungry."

"Gee, Dad," said Brooke. "Wasn't the Premier great? I got to kick two goals in a practice roundball game. I know they let me kick it, though, but it was really neat."

"And Dad," said Risa almost yelling, "We ate some of the things I saw growing. Why didn't you eat anything? I saw the things we ate growing right up out of the ground. I don't understand how that can happen. Are there robots underground making the plants move up? It's unreal."

"I know, honey," said Roland.

"Dad, isn't that how great-great-grandmother and great-great-grandfather did things? How did they know putting that little thing in the ground would make something grow?"

"It's called a seed, Risa." Roland was still nauseous and just couldn't get caught up in their conversation. "You plant a seed and it grows. Just add water and sun."

"Gosh, it is just unbelievable," she said. "The Premier is such a great person, Dad, and gosh, he's so good looking."

Melody knew something was wrong.

"What's wrong, Roland?"

Roland found a piece of writing material and a manual line maker. Writing notes was no longer common place and finding material wasn't always easy. He printed a note telling her he'd explain everything to her when he was sure they were out of a vision scanner's sight and out of a sound device's range.

Roland put his hand over his mouth and mumbled to Melody, "We've got problems."

"I knew it," said Melody.

Little was said by Roland and Melody on the return trip. They watched the excitement of the children and listened to their ravings about the wonderful Premier. What worried Roland and Melody the most was the kid's anticipation of telling their friends the wonders of China and the Premier.

The children finally wore themselves out and slept most of the forty-hour trip home. Roland and Melody slept very little.

Roland opened the garaging door and drove their blue cambri in next to their red one. He connected the charging cable and unpacked their luggage. The kids didn't know if they wanted to sleep or go see their friends. They chose to go tell their friends about the trip. Roland hoped the Sentinels hadn't seen the telescope.

"Risa," Roland said. "You know how much Roalf hates the Premier. I'd go easy telling him how wonderful the Premier is."

"Oh, I know, Dad. I doubt I'll even go see him. Roalf is a foolish young man. The Premier won't let the world blow up.

I'm going over to Ariel's now. Then we'll go over to Lynn's dome."

The name 'Lynn' caught Roland's attention. He's got to contact those women. He only had four days left. Also he wondered how the Premier would contact him to receive his answer.

Melody restarted their ACS to check for any messages received since she last checked on the aircraft. There was one unusual note.

"Roland, look at this."

Roland came down from unpacking their luggage.

"What?"

"Look at this note. What does that mean?"

The note on the screen stated that the roundball tournament in South York will be held tomorrow at 13:00 GMT.

"I don't know anything about a tournament. Melody, we've got to talk. Let's go outside."

They walked out to the rear of their yard, hopefully out of earshot. They noticed the Sentinels were no longer gathered around their dome.

"Melody," Roland said. "Do you think Sogan is a kind and just ruler?"

Melody looked at Roland. "During our interview with him, I wanted to believe he was a sincere and gracious person. But Roland, you were alone with him. Was his interview a show?"

"It was a show."

"I was afraid of that," said Melody. "The children were enthralled by him."

"I know."

"Roland, we should be alone. Tell me. What's happening?"

"The damned article I published has changed our lives, permanently, I might add."

"How, Roland?"

"Let's start with the Premier. You know the subject of my hypothesis. The Premier is in terrible shape. I doubt he'll live six months."

"He looked so young and virile."

Roland leaned back in his chair. "That was a computer generated picture just for you and the kids. I saw the real man, or should I say the remains of a man. Picture the most decrepit person you can think of. He's twice as bad as that."

Melody sat up in a moment of inspiration, "I know what he wants! He wants you to rebuild him in to a healthy man again. But you don't know if your process will work. If it works, change him. If it doesn't, then you can't change him. It'll be done with. He dies and we're finished with it."

"Melody, it's not that simple."

"Oh, God. There's more?"

"Yes. Much more. He's literally offering me the world. I, and my family, would almost be second in command following the Premier if I succeed in reassembling him. If I don't rebuild him, or if I can't, then…"

A Sentinel walked into their yard, his footsteps crunching on the artificial grass.

"How are you people doing?" he asked.

"Fine. Okay," answered Roland. "We're just enjoying this beautiful day."

"That's good," the Sentinel said. "Our scanners indicated you both hadn't moved for a while. I was worried you might be in trouble."

"Thank you. We appreciate your concern."

"It's our duty to protect chamberpersons." With that the Sentinel walked to the rear of the dome and stood by the rear door.

The Sentinel yelled to Roland, "I sure envy your trip to China to see the Premier. Very few citizens are allowed to talk to him much less see him."

"We're most grateful," said Roland.

The Sentinel received a level two communication call. He walked toward the front of the dome and received his call.

"Then what, Roland," asked Melody

"I don't know how to say this. I believe he has threatened me with our family's lives. And not just death but a painful death."

"Roland! He's truly a monster! Just like I feared."

"Yes, you're right," said Roland. "You know? I think in his early life he was quite benevolent but age and illness have changed him. And as they say, power corrupts."

"Roland," said Melody. "I hate this whole business. I hate this chip. I hate the chamberperson job. I am going to request to be relieved of the position."

"Just wait," said Roland. He looked around, hoping no one was within earshot. "A group is emerging. It's an underground group. They are erroneously called outlaws but they choose to be called Reformers."

"Is this what the Genome Meeting was about?" asked Melody.

"I didn't attend the Genome meeting. It was just an excuse to attend another meeting."

Melody looked around the dome to see if the Sentinel was retuning. "I knew something was up. Tell me all about it, Roland."

"If the Reformers, or outlaws as ACD wants to call them, were a legitimate organization of good people, would you consider joining them?"

"I'd trust your judgment, Roland. If you felt they were an honest group of true Reformers, I'd jump at the chance. But I'd join only if you wholeheartedly believed in them."

"I do, Melody. I do."

"What about this damn chip?"

Roland debated showing Melody his external chip. He decided this wasn't the time.

"It's no problem. They have a sure solution."

"But haven't the outlaws caused some destruction and even deaths?"

"Yes, the outlaws have as far as I know, but these people aren't the outlaws. These people call themselves Reformers. Also, the tram accident was caused by a robot malfunction, not outlaws. But these people I'm talking about are Reformers. True outlaws do exist but they are not a part of the Reformers. The outlaws are the cause of the deaths and terrorist acts."

Two older Sentinels casually walked into the back yard and approached Roland and Melody.

"How was your China trip?" asked one of the men. "Have you recovered from the time changes?"

"Yes," said Roland. "It was a fast trip."

"It sure was. We expected to be taking care of your dome for at least two weeks. We had to catalog everything in your dome so your dome in China was an exact duplicate. Was it okay?"

"It was perfect," said Melody. "The kids were thrilled and amazed."

"Good," said the Sentinel. They began looking at the artificial plants in Melody's garden.

Roland and Melody adjusted their chairs to the recline position and pretended to doze off. After about five minutes, the Sentinels left.

"Melody, do you realize there are five thousand Reformers, maybe a few more?"

"No. ACD has always proclaimed there are only one or two thousand outlaws."

"Outlaws, yes. That's what they want the world to believe. But in actuality, there are over one million outlaws. The true Reformer numbers are five thousand."

"But Roland, what about the children?"

"They can join us or be left with an ACD guardian."

"Roland!" Melody sat up. "We wouldn't leave them, ever."

"I know that but that's our choices."

"Would we have to leave York?"

Roland pulled his chair up. "Yes. We'd join other families working for the Reformers. I don't know where. They wouldn't tell me at this time. I'd be working with other scientists. We'd each be working in our own area of expertise. We could never return to York."

An older Sentinel came running up to Roland and Melody. He was holding an unusual communicating device.

"Doctor, you have message from the Premier! You must answer on the prime encoding device I have here. I must leave the area before he'll talk to you. The thought communicators are not secure enough."

Roland took the device from the Sentinel.

"Hello," he said.

"Doctor, I'm waiting until my scanners tell me the Sentinel is out of range." There was a slight pause. "Good. I see that he's gone."

"Yes, your Excellency. He's gone."

"Your wife may stay. You have three days left. "Have you made a decision yet?"

"Your Excellency, I have a question. As I told you, I need some pretty elaborate equipment. It will take several years to arrange it."

"Some of you requirements have already been met. There was another scientist who developed the same hypothesis as you earlier but he unexpectedly terminated. And as I told you, I have a limited amount of time left. I will put at your disposal unlimited resources and personnel. They will work as fast as you require or I will issue a painful ten year terminations for them!"

Roland couldn't believe his ears. Melody could hear both sides of the conversation, also. He tried to think of a good excuse to stall a few more days.

"Your Excellency, I need a day or two to see what the children want to do."

"Your children are no cause for delay. They seemed to be quite excited when I talked to them. You must expedite your decision. You know the consequences."

"Yes, your Excellency. I'll give you your answer in two days."

"Yes, I know you will." The Premier sounded perturbed.

Roland quickly walked to the front of the dome and handed the special communicator to the Sentinel.

"You talked to the Premier on my communicator!" the Sentinel said. "I've never even heard his voice. You must be a very important citizen. I am most honored I was chosen to guard you."

Roland ignored the man and rushed back to Melody.

With almost complete disregard of being overheard Roland said, "Melody, we've got to move fast if we're going to do this."

"What do we do?"

Roland remembered the message on their ACS. "My contacts are supposed to contact me tomorrow morning."

"Is that about the roundball tournament in South York?" asked Melody.

"Yes, I'm sure it is. We'll have to wait until then."

"Roland, what about the children?"

Another Sentinel startled them from behind, "You saw and talked to the Premier. That's awesome. I'm very jealous." He walked away shaking his head.

"Melody, we'll just have to see how my contacts tell me to proceed."

Risa and Brooke noisily ran to the back of the dome.

"Mom! Dad! Everyone just couldn't believe we actually saw and talked to the Premier. Even the parents were interested. It was like we were on stage. Everyone kept asking questions. We're so proud of you Dad. Thanks for taking us with you."

Roland and Melody were not able to say a word. Brooke and Risa ran into the dome, still jabbering about the Premier.

"It's going to be difficult, Roland."

"I know, but no matter what, they're going with us."

CHAPTER SIXTEEN

Morning came after a long and restless night. Roland and Melody sat by the ACS, watching every news article closely for any hints of a secret message. Nothing appeared out of the ordinary at 13:00 GMT. Roland suddenly felt he was left all alone. He was approaching panic. He didn't want to perform his experiments in China. He didn't want the experiments to be successful just to save an old tyrant. Worse yet, what if the procedure failed. He didn't want to think about failure.

One minute later, a strange message appeared. It was another message about the roundball tournament. The message said in thirty minutes, a cambri will be in front of his dome. Dr. Davidson's whole family should board the cambri. Bring nothing. It will leave immediately for the field. Dr. Davidson should invite some of the Sentinels to accompany him. This is the first and last invitation to the tournament.

It didn't make sense. Why should he invite some Sentinels? He didn't want to. He decided not to invite them. He didn't feel this was the message he was waiting for. He had hoped to hear from Lynn or Char. This didn't seem right.

"Roland. Is that the message?" asked Melody.

"I don't know. It wasn't exactly what I expected."

"Should I wake the children?"

Roland looked for any more messages. There were none.

"I don't know if we are going on a long trip or short trip or what. It said we should we pack no clothing."

Melody said, "It said this is the first and last call for the tournament. It sounds urgent."

"Yeah, it does," said Roland. "Okay. Wake the kids. Tell them to get dressed. We won't pack anything. It would seem unusual to pack some luggage just for a roundball tournament."

Roland checked the ACS for upcoming events. "Look," he said. "There is a roundball tournament all this week."

"At least Brooke will be thrilled," said Melody. "Risa will be grumpy as usual."

Roland ran upstairs with Melody. "Let's get them moving."

The family sat in the front room of the dome, waiting for the cambri. Brooke was fairly excited about seeing a Roundball Game but just not this early in the morning. Risa just sat on a couch, dozing and frowning. The children were still suffering from lack of sleep.

Thirty-one minutes later, a six passenger cambri appeared. Five Sentinels were stationed around their dome.

"Roland, I feel we are under house arrest."

"We are," said Roland. "I hope the Sentinels will let us go."

As they walked to the cambri, a Sentinel asked, "Where you folks going?"

"To a roundball tournament," said Roland. It suddenly seemed proper to invite the Sentinel. "Wanna come along?"

"Sure," he said.

Damn, thought Roland.

"He's welcome," said the driver, "but we've no room." As they climbed in, they saw Roalf sitting beside the driver. "We're full but another cambri will be along soon."

"Roalf!" Risa suddenly brightened up. "What are you doing here?"

"I like Roundball too," he said. "Let me sit in the back row with you. Brooke can sit up here in front with the driver."

Roland wasn't sure what to think. He had a premonition they'd never see York again.

Roalf said to Risa, "I didn't know you liked Roundball."

"I don't. Dad made me come. Did you know I was in China and saw the Premier?"

"Yeah, I heard. Did you know he's over one hundred and eighty years old?"

"No," said Risa. "He looked like, maybe, forty. About as old as Dad."

"Yeah, my friends tell me he's near death," said Roalf. "He's had so many transplants, he's run out of clones."

"But clones are illegal, aren't they Dad?"

Roland was glad Roalf was spreading some needed information to Risa.

"Yeah, they're illegal for us ordinary citizens, but not for the Premier."

"But he looked so good," continued Risa.

"Computer generated picture," said Roalf. "Couldn't you tell?"

Risa looked thoughtful. "Yes, come the think of it, it did look a little phony. Dad, you did see him again. Did you see him on a vision screen like us or did you see him in person?"

"Maybe we shouldn't be talking so freely," said Roland.

"It's okay," said the driver.

"Are you sure?" asked Roland.

"It's okay," said the driver again. "This vehicle is shielded."

"I saw him in person, my dear daughter," said Roland.

"How'd he look, Dr. Davidson?" said Roalf.

"Pretty bad."

Roalf added, "I hear now even some of his parts, arms and legs and stuff, don't even match."

"That's right, Roalf."

"Yuck!" said Risa. "Why'd he do that, Dad?"

Melody interjected, "He wants a very large favor of your father."

"I read your hypothesis, Dr. Davidson," said Roalf. "I bet he wants you to rebuild him, right?"

"Right again, Roalf."

"Is that why he was so nice to Brooke and me?" said Risa.

"Correct once again, kids," said Roland.

"I thought he was a little too nice," said Brooke. "That's what my friends asked, what's the Premier want of your Dad?"

Risa faked a pout, "Dad, you can tell him to go shit on himself."

"Risa!" Melody looked shocked. "Where'd you hear that word?"

"In this old book Roalf has."

Roland and Melody looked at each other and then to Roalf. Roalf looked out the window.

The cambri driver stopped at an artificial park. Plaztec green, brown, yellow and red plants were strewn about as though haphazardly planted by nature. The driver turned around and faced the group. It was Chantel Joyce.

"Chantel!" said Roland. "I'm glad to see a friendly face. I hope you're not here to take us to a roundball tournament."

"Correct, Dr. Davidson," said Chantel. "Now don't worry. There's no listening device in this cambri. Scanners are only transmitting a pause in the park. Now here is what's going to happen. I want you to know and agree to it. If you don't want to continue, then I'll take you to the tournament and another cambri will return you to your dome. The scanners will pick up your signal as though you stayed in the park."

Risa asked Roalf, "What about you, Roalf?"

Chantel answered for Roalf, "Oh, he's one hundred percent committed. He's going all the way. You four are the ones to commit."

Roland knew now was the time to tell all.

"Kids, your mother and I are going to go through with it, if you kids agree. We are going to have our chips removed."

"Dad! We'll die," said Brooke.

"Yeah, Dad. We'll die," repeated Risa.

Roland pulled down his collar around his neck. He showed Melody and the kids his taped on chip.

Melody gave a low scream. "Roland, you never told me!"

"It wasn't the right time, until now."

"You didn't die, Dad," said Brooke. "I want mine off, too."

Risa asked Roalf, "Is yours gone, Roalf?"

"Not yet, but it will soon be," he proudly stated.

"Then I'm ready," she said.

"Roland, me too," Melody said. "I just can't believe it can be so simple."

"The woman who designed the installation of the chip also designed the removal of the chip. I had mine removed while in Lower California."

"Did you know it was going to be removed in California before you left?" asked Melody.

"No, I did not."

Chantel asked again. "Are you with us so far?"

"Okay, so far," they answered in unison.

"Next," Chantel went on, "I doubt you will ever return to your dome in York nor will you even want to."

"Even tonight?" asked Melody.

"Nope," said Chantel emphatically.

"Where will we live?" asked Risa.

"You'll be living with other families, with their fathers and mothers working just as your parents will be. Yes, Mrs. Davidson, you'll be assigned a responsibility, too. But everyone will be chipless."

"Won't ACD try to find us? We'll miss our study assignments," said Brooke.

"Your removed chip will be directed to transmit your death. That will satisfy ACD. As for the moment, I left a four chip transmitter in the park. ACD thinks you are still in the park. It'll be destroyed once you give us your decision."

Melody was worried, "Where will we live? What will we eat? I have to get clothes for the children."

"You'll be living in a metropolitan community just as in York. You'll be issued credit just as before only it won't be coming from ACD and you'll have no scanner following you around. But you will be in hiding. For how long depends on a lot of things."

Melody felt the back of her neck where the chip is located. "It sounds so terrific. I've had this damned chip so long, I can't imagine living without it."

"Now, let me tell of some more downsides of joining the Reformers. We've only been able to confiscate seven robots. We've programmed them to remove chips and reverse sterilization. We have none programmed to perform other medical procedures at this time. Maybe later. We have real live human doctors and nurses for now. We have very few genetic engineers like you Dr. Davidson, to correct gene errors and we have even less lab facilities to work in. What I'm leading to is, if a gamma ray damages your chromosome, we most likely cannot correct it."

"What about fetal correction?" Roland asked.

"Can't be done. But, since only the genetically perfect adults are allowed to reproduce, most babies will be perfect. After time, though, gene imperfections will again creep into our cells and we will gradually be set back about two hundred and fifty years."

"I don't care, said Melody. "I want this chip removed."

Chantel smiled, "It's quite a feeling. Okay folks! Are you ready?"

"Yes, let's go," yelled the kids.

Roland had worried so much how to convince Risa to leave the world of ACD. Roalf did it in ten minutes. He was apprehensive about the future but felt sort of like a pioneer of old. He and his family were breaking away from the status quo. He had a reason to wake up in the morning. What would this new future bring? And, how and where are they going?

Roland, Melody and the children watched the scenery flow by the window of the cambri as they drove through the city. Each with their own thoughts about never seeing York again. Roland and Melody were apprehensive, Brooke was excited and Risa was holding Roalf's hand. In the distance they could make out the tournament crowd.

JOHN PALLO

CHAPTER SEVENTEEN

Chantel drove the cambri past the large dome where Mr. Leeger's body was examined. It seemed like an eternity ago when they were in there looking at his dead body parts. They continued on toward the river and South York Park. A large crowd of people were gathering for the morning's session of tournaments. It seemed to Roland there were at least twenty or thirty thousand people trying to get into the stadium. As usual there was no excitement displayed by the crowd. People had little to do so a free Roundball game was a chance of some entertainment. Chantel drove toward a small closed cambri door and stopped. An angry looking Sentinel came out to meet Chantel.

"Hey, black man!" he yelled at Chantel. "What do you want?"

Then he looked at Chantel and smiled. "Everybody here?" he asked.

"All here," Chantel said.

"Great," the Sentinel said. He stuck his head in and looked at everyone. "People, say goodbye to the world as you came to know it. The Premier and ACD are no longer a concern to you."

He touched a control on his belt and immediately a neatly camouflaged cargo door opened. Chantel drove in. They seemed to be driving down under the stadium floor. Above them were another fifty to sixty thousand citizens. Roland thought, how can ACD keep track of all those chips?

Roland had to ask, "ACD is tracking all these chips?"

"Yes, it is," said Chantel. "It's quite a computer. But six billion is its limit. That's why it has decreed a six billion limit to the population. But if you remember China, ACD hasn't been able to chip a lot of China's population. It just can't get them all and couldn't handle all them if it could. You were shown a happy location. They have quite a ruthless army, chipping or eliminating anyone refusing or hiding from the chippers. You may not want to hear this but over one hundred thousand people have been terminated by Sogan."

Risa said, "He seemed so nice."

Chantel said, "I know there's no Heaven or Hell, but all Hell's going to break lose when Dr. Davidson doesn't turn up on Monday with his answer. It's not going to be pretty."

"Damn, ACD is following our chips at this moment," said Roland.

"No, doctor," said Chantel. "I told you this cambri has a special roof. The last thing ACD knows is that we stopped in the park. Remember Dr. Wang? She's got the special material embedded in this roof, similar to the scarf you used in Lower California. Every one of you went out of sight as soon as I turned on the diffuser in the park. As of that moment, you all became Reformers – or outlaws if you will."

"Roland," said Melody, "Should I be scared?"

"We're all scared but ready to break out of the prison of ACD."

"Right!" said Brooke, Risa and Roalf in unison.

"Roland," asked Melody, "Is there any danger in removing the chip?"

"Yes, but it is extremely slight."

Chantel spoke, "Mrs. Davidson, it is as dangerous to remove the chip as it is to implant it."

Melody seemed somewhat relieved. "I guess I've never heard of any baby dying while the chip was being implanted."

"That's the spirit, dear. I felt no pain at all after I woke up."

"How long did it take?" she asked.

"About a half an hour."

Roland asked, "How many chip removal robots does Dr. Wang have?"

"As I said, seven," said Chantel. "We lucky to have them in Northern Americus. There are some in other countries but we just can't seem to get the people enthused about joining the Reformer movement."

Chantel approached a large cargo cambri. It had ramps leading up into the cargo area. Chantel drove the cambri onto the ramps and into the rear of the cargo vehicle.

"This is the worst part of the trip," he said. "We'll have to stay in here for about six hours. We have good ventilation, cenes and water, and rest room facilities toward the front. You can get out of this cambri but you can't get out of the cargo vehicle."

"Where are we going?" asked Roalf.

"First, we're going to a location to have your chip removed. Then we will be going to your new home."

"Where's that?" asked Melody.

"Yes," said Roland, "Where is it? I heard it's under the ocean."

Chantel looked surprised. "Under the ocean? Oh! Yes, I guess it's sort of under the ocean." He laughed.

"Well, where is it?" Roland asked again.

Chantel took on a serious look. "Let me ask you this question. If you were accosted by some Sentinels, and they asked the location of our facilities, do you think you could keep our location secret?"

"I could," said Brooke confidently.

"Even if they subjected you to their deleters, pain inducers and Sementol injections?"

"Oh, I never thought of that," he said with a little less confidence."

Chantel turned and looked at the little group of new Reformers. "There is no way any of us could hide the truth from the tools of the Sentinels. We'd blabber like babies."

"Okay," said Roland. "I can see why you can't tell us, but how about you?"

"This is very serious business, Doctor. Just as in the old days, I carry a pill. It causes immediate death if I bite into it. Only a very few, completely trusted Reformers, know certain locations. Those that know are trusted to use the pill if necessary. Do any of you want that responsibility?"

The group was dead silent.

"Throughout the history of the world, Reformers or revolters were in danger. We are all in danger now."

The cargo cambri began to move. They could feel the movement of its big soft solid tires underneath them. It made Roland think of their recent vehicle trip in China.

Since Chantel seemed to know so much, Roland asked him, "We saw a lot of poverty in China. If that's were ACD began controlling everyone, why did it seem so backward?"

"Doctor, there is still a lot of unchipped humans in the world. Not just unchipped, but unknown. There are so many remote areas in China as well as in Southern Americus and the African Colonies and even here in Northern Americus. ACD and the Premier want us to believe the world is well chipped but in truth it's not. To cover the earth, they had to spread their armies too thin. In doing so they could not locate and identify all humans. If there are five thousand Reformers, there must be one maybe two million other beings who do not know nor care at all about ACD or the Premier. Some of these numbers are maybe outlaws or just humans unaware of ACD. ACD by means of its satellites surely has sensed these people but there is just too many. China's armies lost their desire to enter some of the dangerous and remote areas of the earth. They just reported to their superiors than no humans lived in these areas. They never even looked."

"We've been told for years 99.99 per cent of the world has been chipped," said Roland. "That's all we've been told on our ALEKC."

"The Premier and ACD have told quite a few stories."

Roalf asked, "Is this cargo cambri going to be loaded onto a tram?"

"Not yet," said Chantel.

"But they check all loads and manifests of all cambris," he said. "They'll look inside the cargo cambri to check the contents. I think they'll be a little suspicious seeing a passenger cambri inside the cargo cambri."

"They won't see us," said Chantel assuredly.

"But how can they miss us when the rear door is opened?" Roalf was still worried as was Roland.

As they spoke, the vehicle stopped and the rear door of the cargo cambri opened. Several men began throwing items in and on the small cambri in the back of the cargo cambri. As they watch and heard the items hitting their cambri, they realized they were being bombarded with Roundball paraphernalia. Protective gear, shoes, dirty uniforms, face masks, smelly socks, towels and water buckets were piled high on the cambri. Anything having to do with Roundball, especially if it was smelly, was tossed in. Soon the passengers couldn't see out of their windows.

"Folks," said Chantel, "We're now the equipment cargo cambri of the first team to play today. We lost in the first round of the games and our team is mad, disgruntled, depressed and very smelly. We're going home so angry we didn't even clean ourselves down with antiseptic wipes. Six dirty and stinking Roundball players are sitting up front in the passenger section of the cargo cambri too mad to speak. The Sentinels will scan them and let the cargo cambri load on the tram."

"You think that'll work?" asked Roland.

"The tram attendant and the Sentinels are quite young," said Chantel. "They won't want to look any more thoroughly then opening the rear door and closing it. Aren't you getting a whiff of an odor now?"

As he spoke, a putrid odor was beginning to seep into the cambri.

"Yuck," said Risa. "I can't take that."

"Yes you can," said Chantel. "We'll gradually dump the stuff after we clear the city's walls. We'll have to be careful no tram attendant sees us but we'll dump it."

"How about other tram passengers?" Melody asked.

"They'll think we're just a bunch of sore losers. The average citizen of Earth is too apathetic to think about it at all."

"You're right," said Roland nodding. "They won't give it a second thought."

JOHN PALLO

CHAPTER EIGHTEEN

Since the soon-to-be Reformers had no windows in the cargo cambri, they had no idea where they were going. They could feel their tram slowing so they knew they must be uncoupling. Chantel said they'd be traveling for six hours so that would put them at or near the Mississippi River. As the tram stopped, they felt the wheel clamps release. The cargo cambri began to move slowly, driving through one tram after another until they felt it descend a loading ramp. It bounced along a bumpy road for several hours. Risa was becoming nauseous and Melody had withstood about as much smell and closeness as she could stand. The rubbish had been discarded but the odor still lingered. She needed fresh air.

Roland asked, "When do we get out of this cambri?"

"Soon," said Chantel.

Finally the cambri stopped and the rear door opened.

"We're in one of the largest caves near the Chi-Louis area. It used to be a big tourist attraction. As soon as I back this thing out of the cargo hold, you can get out of the cambri."

They had spent over seven hours in the back of the cargo

cambri. While traveling on the tram it was possible to push the remaining sports debris aside and open a door but it didn't give them too much room to stretch their legs. Seven hours in the cargo cambri turned their excitement to boredom and then to aggravation. But now, as they climbed out, the fresh air invigorated them. Their eyes focused on a few people, some equipment and roving cambris. They saw they were in an extremely large, well illuminated cavern. The walls of the cave were extremely rough and multi-colored. Many stalagmites and stalactites were in evidence. Water was dripping all around them. Two robots were located around the area and one was situated over a table. A tent-like material covered it to prevent moisture from falling on the robot. Roland knew it was the one. It was the one to remove chips.

Chantel hurried the small group over to the table.

"We have to hurry," he said. "Dr. Davidson. You have become quite a celebrity, so to speak."

"What do you mean," said Roland, trying to get the kinks out of his legs.

"It seems as if every Sentinel in the world is looking for you," said Chantel. "There's a big reward for finding you alive. Whoever catches you alive will become the Premier's right hand man, or woman, for the rest of their life."

"I hope you folks know what you're doing," Roland said.

"Believe me, Dr. Davidson," said Chantel. "We're not novices. Now let's get those chips removed so we can continue on to our final destination. Who's first?"

"Me," said Brooke.

Chantel said, "Anyone eager to watch?"

No one seemed too willing to watch except Roalf. In twenty minutes Brooke was finished. He sat up.

"Wow, I had a weird dream we weren't living on earth."

"Weird, huh?" said Chantel. "Don't be too sure."

"Don't tell me my laboratory isn't going to be on Earth?" said Roland.

"No, Doctor. I assure you all of you are heading to a location on earth."

"Shit!" said Brooke.

"Brooke," said Melody, "I don't like those slang words."

"Why? Risa says it."

"I want both of you to stop talking like that," she said.

"Who's next?"

Risa said, "Me. Roalf, stand by me."

"Okay, but I'm going to look away. I didn't like seeing it done to Brooke."

Risa's operation was completed, then Melody's and Roalf's.

Chantel turned to the group and said. "Okay. Let's head on to our city. There's been a change. We've been told to not transmit a death signal to the scanners. That would give away this location. It would have been appropriate to transmit from your home in York. But even so, a multiple signal of five deaths may have caused ACD to question the authenticity of the information."

"Do they know we left York?"

"All ACD and the Premier know is you stopped sending a moving signal when we entered the park. The Premier is frantic. I suppose I should tell you, the fifteen Sentinels protecting you have all had their lives terminated. And, it wasn't a quick termination."

Risa was visibly troubled, "He seemed so nice. I was hoping he'd get me into the food growth industry."

Chantel smiled. "What do you think you'll be doing in our city?"

"Growing stuff?" she said.

"Exactly."

"Okay. Let's get going."

They walked farther into the cavern and down a long flight of stairs. As they walked, they noticed everyone seemed to be dismantling their equipment. The occupants of the cave appeared to be packing everything in containers. Even the robots that had just performed their chip removal were being dismantled. The people were hurriedly packing their clothing and other belongings into travel bags.

"What's happening?" asked Roland.

"As I said, you are a celebrity. Our communication system has picked up word ACD's satellites followed our cambri to this cave. The trail of roundball equipment led them the Chi-Louis city and we were the only vehicle leaving the walls of Chi-Louis. Since our cambri wasn't transmitting a signal, ACD sensed something wasn't in order. And since your signal is no longer being scanned from any location, they're assuming you were in the cargo cambri. We will have to leave this cave just as we found it forty years ago. There'll be no signs of habitation when we leave. We will cause a small explosion and this rail area will be flooded. I doubt they will have divers to check under water for our rails."

Ahead of them they saw some vehicles on rails. They were not the tram rails they were use to seeing. It was two thin rails running parallel into the darkness. The vehicles had several metal wheels plainly in sight. There were only four windows on the car, one to the front, two toward the middle and one to the rear.

"What is this?" asked Roland.

"This is an underground rail system," said Chantel. "Many years ago, our country had what they called an Interstate

Highway System. They had thousands of miles of concrete highways crisscrossing the country. This one was called Interstate 40. Each person had a vehicle that traveled on these highways."

"Wasn't that wasteful?" asked Risa. "I mean if each person had their own vehicle, it would take a lot of charging equipment."

"They didn't have individual charging equipment. Each one had its own fuel burning engine in it."

Risa exclaimed, "Oh my gosh! All that smoke. That's what I was reading about on my ALEKC,"

"That's right. So now we all have forced electron engines charged by a main hot fusion generator. Fossil fuel burning is now prohibited. Of course I should add, in our underground city we have no powered vehicles at all, except for our limited trains. All travel is by foot or trike."

"What about the concrete highways?" Roalf asked.

"Sogan decreed to let them crumble. So we have made this railway underneath a vacated, four lane highway. It's the only one. No one even thinks to check underneath it."

Brooke was fascinated. "Wow! This is neat."

"How long will we be on this tram, or whatever you call it?" asked Melody.

"About twelve hours."

"Gee," said Brooke. "We're going to be a long way from home."

"Not as far as you were in China," said Roland.

"And," said Chantel, "your home is in front of you, not behind you."

"I guess so," he said.

Only one vehicle was positioned for loading. It seemed each one had its own propulsion system. About twenty people, including the five from York, were loaded on board. There were several other vehicles behind the one the Davidson group boarded. These units were being frantically loaded with the equipment from the cave. The railway vehicle was a lot more spacious than the little cambri. They could walk around and even walk to a small eating area. The passengers had their choice of cenes or old fashion earth grown foods. Roalf, Roland, Brooke and Risa carefully and cautiously ate the green and yellow foods while Melody still ate a cene.

"Try this, Mom," said Brooke. "It's good."

"Later, dear," she said. "What foods do you like and eat, Chantel?"

"I like the grown foods," he said.

"Any problems with eating only grown foods?" asked Roland.

"The only problem is nutrients. With cenes, you automatically get all vitamins needed. With grown foods, you need to know what foods give you your needed daily requirements. One food may give you this vitamin and another may give you that vitamin. You have to balance your intake with what's needed."

"I'll stick with cenes," said Melody.

The lone rail car began moving in the darkness. It was impossible to tell the speed at which it moved due to the darkness. For twelve hours it rolled along, clacking loudly as it crossed joints in the rails. They were not used to noisy rail joints since tram rails were seamless. Every so often, they would slow and then speed up. Roland expected station stops along the way but there were none.

"Is the Chi-Louis station the only one?" asked Roland.

"Yes it is," he said. "And as you saw it's being destroyed."

"Yes, on account of me," said Roland.

"Yes and no."

"Why?"

"Too much traffic. We were using it so much we were getting careless. You were the final event."

"I'm sorry," said Roland.

"No problem. We knew it would happen someday. Hopefully the explosion and consequent rubble will hide our rail system to our site."

"Are all the people at the site dedicated Reformers?" asked Melody.

"Every one," said Chantel emphatically.

A few people who were already on the train seemed friendly and greeted Roland and his family whenever they met in the aisle. Most did not wear the coveralls as the Davidson family wore. It was evident the Davidson's were new to the cause. Most people asked them where they were from and how long they had been Reformers. Everyone assured them they'd be most happy they were now members. Melody was just beginning to feel the freedom of being chipless. She kept rubbing her hand over the vacant spot on her neck. Was the chip gone? It didn't feel sore or irritated. Was it really, really gone?

She had to ask Roland, "Is my chip completely gone?"

"Yes it is, my dear."

"I just can't believe I'm not being scanned."

"We could stand outside in the sun if it weren't for the high resolution satellites of ACD. And from what I hear, their demise is coming."

The twelve hours passed slowly. Chantel had given Roland a portable and isolated ACS showing all the equipment and personnel he would have at his disposal. It detailed all the previous groundwork completed by the earlier scientist, Dr. Raul Guitarez, before he terminated himself in sight of the Premier. Knowing the conditions the Premier handed Roland, he could easily imagine why his predecessor bit his poison pill. Studying the work the man performed, Roland discovered several processes he hadn't thought of. A whole new array of ideas flooded his mind. Several impasses were dispelled by this man. If he were alive, Roland and this man most likely would solve the process in months, if not weeks. The man was brilliant. He was over 150 years old, born years before gene engineering. Roland's parents requested his IQ be established at 150, the maximum allowed by ACD. The older scientist must have been a naturally born genius. If the laboratory is arranged as shown on the ACS, Roland felt he should have his answer in less than six months.

The excitement of the past few days had finally worn off and the Davidson family was getting some needed sleep. Chantel began waking them as they neared their destination. The vehicle began slowing as the wheels squealed loudly.

"I was afraid this thing was going to break down," grumbled Brooke.

"It's very reliable," said Chantel. "Slow but reliable."

Abruptly, it stopped. Through one of the windows, a brilliant sun was shining. Roland was sure it was artificial.

"Here's your underwater home," said Chantel

CHAPTER NINETEEN

"You mean we're under the ocean?" asked Brooke.

"No, we are under a large lake in Arizona and Utah. I guess more correctly I should say it was a large lake. It's drying up quite quickly. For now it's the only way we can be sure to be unobserved by the heat seeking devices of ACD."

As they left the vehicle, they saw a complete city, similar to the underground city they visited in China but much larger. It was at least as big as a hundred Roundball fields. This city, though, had no fume exhausting vehicles. The vehicles didn't seem to be cambris, but they were evidently battery powered and all on rails. The air seemed fresh and cool. They looked toward the ceiling and realized they were in very large cavern. It wasn't a natural cave but manmade. A very large artificial sun shown brilliantly and even seemed to give off heat rays. The roof of the cavern wasn't rough like a cave roof, but smooth and blue. It was definitely an artificial ceiling. They saw many domes or housings arranged neatly in rows. Real green grass surrounded the homes. Farther off in the distance Roland saw what appeared to be fields of something growing. A flowing creek rambled around the cavern and there was even a breeze.

"What kind of ceiling is this?" asked Roland.

"It's a fiber and metal composite material. It'll flex and bend with any earthquake we may have but it will not collapse. It wasn't easy creating the cave. We had to almost hand dig a cave to make room for the first fusion generator. Once we had it set up we brought in more to operate laser rock liquefiers."

"Is there any opening to above ground?"

"Yes, we do have to have several openings. We need some fresh air every so often and of course we need entrance and exit points. We hope the above ground openings are well camouflaged."

"Okay," said Roland. "Where do we live?"

"We'll hop in the next vehicle and I'll take you there."

"There's no way to travel except by the railed vehicles?" he asked.

"Yep, or you can walk," said Chantel. "You have just been on the last run of our long distance train car. Now we'll board our local. One comes along every half hour. Just stand here and get on when it stops."

The local train was much smaller than the train they rode from the underground cave. It was a rusty brown and had a rod reaching up to a wire above it. Roland assumed it was an electrical wire that energized an electric motor in the train. It seemed to continuously hum. There were no doors but since it traveled quite slowly, none were needed. Windows were on all sides.

"How are we debited?"

"You're not. Everyone here has a job. If you're pulling your weight, there's no debiting or crediting. You can ride anywhere, eat anywhere or pick up products at any local distributing location. We've taken the electronic monetary system of ACD one step farther. It's like a family."

"What about slackers?" Melody asked.

"Again, it's just like a family. We take them aside to one of our councilmen. He discusses the problem and reminds them of the alternative."

"What's that?"

"If they refuse to comply, we'll reinstall a chip and place them somewhere in Southern Americus. We will chemically clear their mind of any of the Reformers and locations. Usually they're so confused, no one takes any of their ramblings seriously. Out of five thousand Reformers we've only had ten people leave us. We feel that's quite remarkable."

"That is remarkable," said Melody.

"And don't forget, we screen all future Reformers quite carefully, as you and your husband were. Even your children were screened although youngsters are the hardest to predict. You'll notice few teenagers are invited here. The ones you see here are home grown. They grew up from children, just as your Brooke will."

"Will Risa be okay?"

"Thanks to Roalf, Risa will be okay."

"You know," said Roland, "your world may be more perfect than ACD's."

"We would like to think so."

They approached a section of the city seemingly having a large amount of small housing units. They were not domes, but rectangular beige buildings about eleven meters by ten meters by two meters high. There was a front and rear door and a window every three meters on each side.

Risa was thrilled to see real grass on each small lawn. "Dad! Look! Is it growing?"

Chantel laughed. "Yes. She'll feel differently if you assign her the job of manicuring it."

The train car stopped near several homes. "We'll now call these living quarters 'homes.' Yours is three units down. Number 121."

"We have to walk?" asked Brooke.

"Yes," said Chantel. "You'll be doing a lot of walking now. Or you can use your trike"

"What's a trike? And how about food and clothing?" asked Melody.

Chantel handed her a map of the city. "These green marks are distributing locations. The red marks are locations of the officials. Take the train car to one of the green marks and pick out cenes or grown food, whichever you want. Clothing is also available there, too."

"How do we get it back to our dome, or home?" she asked.

"You carry it," smiled Chantel. "Take one of your family members with you and carry it. A total of seven changes of clothing are traditional for each member of a family. It might take you two or three trips. You can also use your trike. It has a large container on it to carry your things."

"You keep mentioning a trike. What is a trike?" asked Melody.

"It's a three wheeled vehicle that you propel with your feet. There are two at the rear of your home. There's a pedal for each foot. You'll figure it out quickly enough."

Roland watched and listened to the conversations and finally had to speak. "When do I begin work?"

"We'll let you rest for a day," said Chantel. "Tomorrow afternoon I'll come by for you and we'll go to your laboratory."

"You're going to pick me up?"

"No," said Chantel smiling again. "We'll ride the train car to your lab."

"Oh, "said Roland.

"You'll find we've regressed somewhat from ACD times and we've progressed somewhat from early times."

"Okay, I'll see you tomorrow."

"Last item," said Chantel. "We do not, I emphasize, do not transmit anything by electromagnetic waves. We want nothing to be transmitted in the air that may be received by someone above ground. Everything is communicated by a wire. If you call me or call anyone, a device we call a phone is connected to that person's location by a wire. That's the only way we can be sure we're not discovered. There are no wireless ACS's here other than the isolated ones. I know I don't have to tell you we cannot go above ground. The satellites would most assuredly pick up your heat signature. We do have to go out every once in a while but we are most careful. We know when the satellites pass overhead so we avoid them. I'm aware you and your family may come to feel we are somewhat primitive, but that is the way is has to be."

"We understand," said Roland.

JOHN PALLO

CHAPTER TWENTY

"Your Excellency."

"Yes, what do you want? I am in a foul mood. I hope you have good news for me."

"Yes, I understand," the attendant said. "One of our outlaw hunters in Northern Americus has made a strange discovery."

"If it has nothing to do with finding Dr. Davidson, I do not care to hear it."

"Your Excellency," the attendant said bowing continuously, "I believe it may."

"Then quickly tell me!"

"One of our outlaw hunters has made a strange discovery."

"I know! I know! You already told me that. What discovery?"

"Your Excellency," the attendant said meekly. "He has found much roundball equipment along a tram rail path. The equipment was spread along five hundred meters of tramway. He said it begins about fifty meters outside of the city of York and ends near the Toledo station."

The Premier stopped trying to move and quietly pondered his attendant's words. He glared at the attendant.

"What does this have to do with Davidson?"

"Your Excellence, there was…"

"Stop with this Excellency gibberish," yelled Sogan. "Just talk sense!"

"Yes, I, ah…there was a roundball tournament in York yesterday. According to our ACS communication records, the doctor received an anonymous message telling him a cambri would pick him up for the tournament in the morning. It stated further he should be ready to travel to the stadium with his whole family. One of our Sentinels wanted to traverse with them but the cambri was too crowded. They told him another was on the way. It never arrived."

"Didn't any of my Sentinels question this?" yelled the Premier. "He's supposed to be getting ready to travel here to prepare a laboratory for my operation. Why would he take the time to witness a roundball game? Do I have only idiots as Sentinels? I order you to have the fifteen Sentinels guarding his dome slowly and painfully terminated."

"Yes, your Excellency."

"We all understand the doctor has left York? I ask you again. Didn't his chip movement register on any of our scanners?"

"No, your Excellency." The attendant didn't want to tell the Premier about the phony four chip transmitter found in the park.

"Call the Sentinels and tram attendants at the York station. Ask them if any strange vehicle was loaded on a west bound tram."

"Yes, your Excellency."

"If you answer 'Your Excellency' one more time I'll have your head on the floor!"

"Yes, your Excellency."

Sogan screamed as in great pain. "Leave me and get my great-grandson Lo Chang."

"Yes, your Excellency."

"What is the first major tram station after the Toledo station?" asked the Premier.

"Chi-Louis, your Excellency."

"Then that is where we will start our search. Stabilize a dedicated satellite above Chi-Louis and try to catch the doctor's chip signal. Train the high resolution camera lens on the city also. I WANT HIM FOUND!"

"Yes, your Excellency."

"And I have another order," said the Premier. "Tell our York Sentinels to detain Dr. Davidson's parents and grandparents. Also detain his wife's parents. I need a method of persuasion."

JOHN PALLO

CHAPTER TWENTY-ONE

Roland's family was out exploring their new surroundings. The last he saw of his children they were jumping on a train car. He heard them saying they didn't know where it was going and they didn't care. He was glad to hear them laughing but he still had some concern about his upcoming lab experiments. And he also knew even though he had no chip, the satellite cameras could easily capture his heat signature if he ever ventured above ground. Sogan would have him and his family captured and returned to China. If his capture became inevitable, he'd request four poison pills from Chantel.

The door chime woke Roland from a nap. It was Chantel.

Roland opened his door. "Hello, Chantel," he said.

"Let's go, Doctor."

"Ready."

They left Roland's home. He left a note telling Melody where he going. Roland wrote few notes in cursive. He hoped Melody could read his handwriting. The world of ACD seldom used the written word. In the upper world everyone used their ACS or thought communicators to talk personally to anyone if they were nearby. Here underground hand written notes are the order of the day.

"Dr. Davidson," said Chantel, "I have some bad news. The Sentinels have orders to arrest your parents and grandparents."

"Damn!"

"We have them hidden for the moment. The Sentinel who met us at the roundball field had taken them to a scan shielded area for the time being. We're trying to devise a method to protect them. We've transmitted a termination signal to ACD from each of them and supplied them with a diffuser scarf. ACD thinks they are dead. A problem, though, is your mother and grandmother. They don't understand why they must wear the scarf. They keep trying to remove it."

"Yes, they have Alzheimer's."

Chantel said, "We know. We will devise something."

"I hope so."

They approached a train car station and waited for the next vehicle.

"What powers this place?" asked Roland.

"Oh, we have several central hot fusion units," he said. "We're not completely in the 2000's. And since we're in a completely closed environment, we definitely cannot burn anything. Hopefully we have enough vegetation to absorb the carbon dioxide in here."

"There's even a breeze," Roland noted.

"Yes, there are several large fans toward the ceiling. It helps the pollination process. We even have insects."

"Yes, I almost forgot how live plants reproduce," Roland said. "It's very similar to the Premier's home and underground city. It's nowhere near as advanced."

"It is?" said Chantel. "I didn't know that.'"

"He completely hypnotized my children. I was so glad the young man Roalf brought them back to reality. It was something I doubt I could have done."

"I'm glad, too."

"Roalf mentioned something about an impending explosion or destructive happening to Earth. Do you know anything about that?"

"It's a rumor. An outlaw somewhere in Southern Americus supposedly has a telescope, or should I say had a telescope. You know all permanent telescopes were deemed illegal by the Premier so when the Sentinels found it, they destroyed it. Sogan and ACD have deemed the earth as the only place beings live. According to them, space is devoid of any life."

"I know. My son had a telescope he was going to repair. Too bad we had to leave it in York."

"This outlaw insists a comet or meteor is heading toward Earth. He didn't have the precision equipment to give its exact trajectory and now he has no telescope."

"Where is this man now?" asked Roland.

"We don't know. He might have made a good candidate to be a reformer."

"Too bad."

A train car rapidly approached the pair. It stopped, its brakes squealing loudly. The two men stepped on board.

Chanted said, "It's only about twenty minutes away."

True to Chantel's word, in twenty minutes the train car stopped.

"We're here," said Chantel.

Roland was surprised to see such a small building. "This is it?" he said.

"Doctor, it's farther underground."

"Oh."

The small building didn't look too fancy, maybe even a bit shabby. Two armed men stood at the door. Roland assumed they were guards.

Chantel showed them a kind of badge but they seemed to readily recognize him. He informed them of Roland's identity and they smiled at motioned them inside. Once in the room, Roland saw it was quite plain devoid of any electronic devices. An elevator was toward the rear. Another guard stood there. He too was armed.

"Hello Chantel," said the guard. "Long time, no see. Been on top?"

"Yes sir and I got our Dr. Davidson."

"How do you do, Doctor," said the guard. "We've been waiting for you."

Roland was surprised. "What did he mean by 'We have been waiting for you'?"

"Doctor, we need you. We need to know if your hypothesis will work. I'll explain it all tonight at your house. I'll have your identification badge ready then, too. For now, I want you to see what we have already set up, and tell us what else you might need. We're not in as much a rush as the Premier, but we are in a fairly desperate situation. As I said, I'll explain it all tonight."

The two entered the elevator. Chantel pushed the only button on the console and it immediately began to descend. They didn't seem to travel too far when the elevator stopped. The door opened to a small laboratory with twenty or thirty people milling around. The lab was brightly illuminated and seemed to be well ventilated. A lot of instruments lined the walls with benches strewn about in the center of the room. The attendants seemed to be dressed quite casually and noticeably missing were the typical lab coats. They all knew

Chantel and warmly greeted him. Again, without exception, they greeted Roland and thanked him for joining their cause.

"Chantel," said Roland, "I want to find out if my hypothesis works, and I want to help your cause to…"

Chantel interrupted, "It is 'our' cause, Doctor."

"Yes, I want to help our cause to end Sogan's rule, but I don't know how my hypothesis will help you."

"Doctor, may I call you Roland?" said Chantel.

"Sure."

"Let me first show you our facilities and tonight I'll explain our needs and impediments. Our lives, and yours, are not happy in ACD's world. But first look at our equipment as set up by your predecessor Dr. Guitarez."

Roland was amazed by the thoroughness of the late Doctor. He examined the magnetic holding devices and the way the tremendous energy was harnessed. He again examined the portable ACS Chantel had given Roland displaying the Doctor's nagging barriers for atomic disassembly. Several of the problems, Roland had already solved. He noticed several incorrect assumptions he himself had made earlier. He then skimmed the equations and found several conditions that he knew he had answers to. The doctor has used an incorrect constant here and a misplaced known quantity there. Most of the figures, though, were correct. Dr. Davidson became quite exited realizing that within a month, he could possibly have the whole hypothesis completed. All that would remain is setting up the equipment and experimenting.

"This is great!" said Roland. "This man was so close. Why did the Premier terminate him?"

"Roland, you were there face-to-face with Sogan. You tell me why."

"As you know, the Premier is near death. He wants to be rebuilt into a young man again. I supposed Dr. Guitarez refused. Did the doctor have a family?"

"No. He had no relatives."

"How did the Premier get the doctor to his chambers?" asked Roland.

"Dr. Guitarez was safely here in this lab. The Premier's great grandson, Lo Chang, created a false message stating atomic disassembly, even down to quarks and string resonance theory, had been performed in the Lands of Europe by a man in Spain. The Spaniard was having difficulty holding the atoms in place while the computer formulated the reassembly of the atoms. Dr. Guitarez, being of Spanish descent, left the safety of our underground city without our knowledge. He traveled to Spain to meet this man and assist him. Since we are all without chips, and knowing the danger of being above ground, we assumed no one would attempt to leave our city. If a Sentinel would find any of us chipless, we would be assumed to be a threat and quickly terminated. Lo Chang issued a world-wide communication ordering all Sentinels to allow Dr. Guitarez to travel freely. He arrived in Spain, untouched and unchallenged. There was no Spanish scientist, just Sentinels. They took the doctor and brought him to the Premier. Since our location has not been found, we can only assume Dr. Guitarez waited until he met the Premier and then bit his pill. Of course Sogan could just be hiding the fact that he knows our location. "

"Can you be sure the Doctor didn't divulge this location?" asked Roland.

"Now I think we're safe, Roland," said Chantel. "Sogan wants you so badly that by now there would be thousands of Sentinels tearing down our doors to capture you alive. Our satellite signal intercepts display only one satellite redeployment since you disappeared. It is searching the Chi-Louis city at this time. That's as far as they have been able to track you."

Roland felt an uneasy chill down his spine. "I don't care about me, Chantel. I worry about my family."

Chantel looked at Roland and his voice took on serious tone. "My wife of one year was terminated because she would not give the Sentinels the location of my preliminary meeting place with the Reformers. They lengthened her termination to one week duration. For seven days she suffered in excruciating pain. I vowed to bring down the Premier in my lifetime. That's why I was offered a chance to be elected to a position in the Reformer movement even though I am quite young."

"I am terribly sorry," said Roland, "but are you saying there's a chain of command here?"

"Yes."

"Then you are not truly an assistant to me, are you?"

"No, not exactly."

"What is your position then?"

"Our levels are quite simple," he said. "President, Vice President, Senator, Councilmen and Sergeant. I'm a Sergeant, the bottom rung so to speak."

"Who appoints these positions?"

"We are not appointed. We are elected."

"Elected?" said Roland. "That's archaic. Who elects you?"

"The people. And unlike ancient times, everyone has to vote. No exceptions. If you don't vote, you are publicly ostracized. The ten slackers I told you about. They repeatedly 'forgot' to vote."

Roland put his hands on his hips. "This is truly an amazing place. Let me ask you another question."

"Sure doctor."

"Are the reformers here violent? Do we kill? I see your guards are armed."

"All I can say is, so far we have not had a reason to kill. Sogan has no qualms at all. Some of the Premier's Sentinels have been terminated for failing to find us but the terminations were ordered by Sogan."

"Would you kill if needed?"

"Roland, what do you think of our laboratory?" Chantel wasn't going to answer the question.

"I think I'll have an answer soon. And I think we'll be able to try a trial assembly soon, too." Roland didn't want to press for an answer to his 'kill' question.

CHAPTER TWENTY-TWO

"Roland," said Melody. "All you've talked about since you returned home is the laboratory."

"It's great. The Dr. Guitarez was so close. He was a brilliant man. He has saved me years of work."

"I think you are a brilliant man, too, dear."

"Thank you, sweetie," Roland turned serious. "Melody, do you realize what we have done?"

Melody gave her husband a hug. "I think so. What do you mean?"

"We have placed ourselves in danger. We and our children. And today I just learned my parents and grandparents have had an arrest order placed on them."

"I wondered about them, Roland," she said, "but we had no choice. Once you published your hypothesis on the ACS, the Premier was determined to have you rebuild him. You would have to be a slave to him or join the Reformers. We made the right choice."

"That damned article."

"Roland," said Melody, "Remember your old friend who had the Bible? He also had those old history books, didn't he?"

"Yeah."

"I think we are sort of like the early settlers of the United States. They revolted against the taxes of England, didn't they?"

"Yes they did, dear," said Roland. "I know where you're heading with this conversation."

"It's exciting and also dangerous."

Roland said, "Yes, exciting and dangerous, but I don't want anything to happen to you or our children."

"I didn't mean to be flippant, Roland, but once you wrote the article we had to make a choice. We could no longer stand on the sidelines and be apathetic spectators."

"I suppose you're right."

Melody was smiling, "I woke up this morning in anticipation of my assignment. I'm going to have a worthwhile job in air quality. You should see Risa. This afternoon she found out she'll be working in the planning and planting of crops. She's grinning from ear to ear."

"Yes, I'm excited too. I'm anticipating seeing Chantel this evening. He's supposed to tell me why the Reformers are interested in my hypothesis."

"Good."

"Did you know his wife was slowly terminated for not telling the Sentinels the location of a Reformer meeting?"

"Oh, that's terrible."

"Yes, again you can see how dangerous is our escapade is."

Melody motioned toward the eating area of their home. "Come on and help Risa and me fix a meal. No cenes. We're having grown foods."

Once again Roland was amazed at how pragmatic his wife could be.

The Davidson family sat around a table laughing heartily. Roland and Melody were trying to remember all the longhand symbols of the alphabet. Their children had seen very little of handwriting and they laughed at their parent's attempts to explain how to write cursive.

"That's pretty neat," said Brooke. "One letter just continues into the next letter. It's like a continuous line, only squiggly."

"I guess that's what you could call it," said Melody.

Risa said, "I bet it's faster than using the keyboard."

"I don't think so, Risa, but now we don't have ACSs all around us. It'll be a little different calling someone."

"How about calling my friends?" she asked.

"We won't have personal communicators in our pockets or thought transmitters," said Roland. "Every communication device is physically connected by a wire."

Brooke was amazed. "Neat. Now solar flares won't interfere with our communications, right?"

"Yes, I guess that's an advantage. But the main reason for wires is to prevent any radio waves to be picked up by ACD. Chantel said they want no magnetic signals to be generated, even here underground. Even wires give off some radio waves but they are quite weak."

"How about your lab, Roland?"

"It's supposed to be shielded."

The family finished their evening meal and sat in the front room waiting for Chantel.

Minutes later the visitor announcer rang its cheerful sound.

"That should be Chantel," said Roland. He opened the door.

"Good evening, folks," Chantel said. "Are you getting acclimated?"

"Yes we are," said Melody. "How are you?"

"I'm fine. Met your neighbors yet?"

"Yes, they've been most helpful."

"Pull up a seat and tell me why I'm here," said Roland. "Do you want the children to leave?"

"No, they're welcome. I want everyone to hear. There are no secrets here."

"I noticed you use Greenwich Mean Time here, too. That makes time keeping quite simple," said Roland.

"Yes. That way time keeping is truly simple."

"Okay, why am I here?"

"Roland, as I told you, there are about five thousand Reformers here in this cavern. There is another one or two million unknown and unchipped beings out there in remote parts of the Earth. Some are outlaws and some are who knows what. They seem to pose no threat to us so we have no concern about them. We're just concerned about us, the Reformers. I might also add we are seeking a new name for ourselves instead of Reformers. We are accepting suggestions, if you have any.

"We desperately need a place to live," he continued. "We can't stay underground forever."

Roland asked, "How quickly is the population growing?"

"This may seem strange but our numbers seem to have peaked. Sogan consistently tells us the six billion on Earth are happy and content. He says we have all the luxuries we want and desire no change. We know this is not true as you saw the poverty in China. I am sure poverty exists in other remote areas, too, but I fully understand why Sogan began his world domination in the United States with England, Japan, Brazil and other similar countries close behind. I hesitate to say this but most of the educated are lazy, content and completely apathetic. We know there are a few others out in other parts of the world like ourselves but communication is difficult if impossible. You and the other Reformers are exceptions to the general population. You were screened thoroughly. We were searching for inquisitive minds. We chose only those who are sincerely bored with the perfect world scenario of ACD. That's why we invited you to join us; that and your hypothesis."

"I did smile when I saw the edict 'The world is perfect'."

"True," said Chantel.

"If you are tired of living underground," said Roland, "and the Earth's surface is completely monitored, where do you want to live?"

Chantel appeared to reflect deeply. "That's the question. Either we destroy ACD, all its monitors and Sentinels and live again on the surface or…"

"Or what?" asked Roland.

"Live on a planet suitable to our requirements. The rumor you've heard repeatedly is true. There are two small cities on Mars, albeit struggling daily to stay alive. Also we feel we can soon bend space distances. We are very close to doing it now. An attempt will be made in a few months to examine the whole universe. Our scientist keeps encountering an obstacle but she feels confident she'll overcome it."

"Damn!" said Roland. "That's the most ridiculous thing I've ever heard. Our nearest star is four light years away. Have you discovered a way to travel faster than the speed of light?"

"Possibly," said Chantel.

"How? What kind of ship are you talking about? "

"We have found shortcuts through space. Did you know there is something that its effect is faster than the speed of light? As far as the vehicle, I haven't personally seen it."

Roland sat speechless and then spoke. "What does that accomplish? Are you saying we soon can travel to a solar system thousands of light years away?"

"Maybe we can," Chantel flatly stated. "If our scientist is correct, we can travel as fast as you can think of a destination."

Roland stood up and paced back and forth in the room.

"Wow!" said Brooke. "I'm ready to go."

"Oh be still Brooke," said Risa. "You're so dumb."

"Kids, let Chantel talk," said Melody.

"Roland, if we can send an unmanned vehicle in space to examine many, many possible locations for suitable environments for humans, then we may have another alternative. In five months or less this vehicle is expected to be launched. It'll bring its results after ten days of travel."

"Are you telling me in ten days it'll travel all through the universe and give its results?"

"Yes I am, Roland. Traveling one light year or a thousand light years takes only seconds of earth time. One of the current theories is the universe is a giant sphere. If we travel the circumference in a straight line, we will return to our original starting point but after eons of travel. What we theorize is that we can deform the sphere. It would be analogous to pushing your finger into a balloon until you finger touches the other side of the balloon. The other theory..., well, I'll let our scientist explain the instantaneous theory."

"Okay," said Roland, "Let's say I believe this story, why me? You still haven't told me why I'm here."

"We know it's only a matter of time until Sogan, or his great grandson, Chang, finds us. We are under Lake Powell in

Arizona and Utah. It is swiftly drying up. Soon a satellite will see the heat profile of our underground fusion generators. The water will be so shallow it won't be able to diffuse the heat silhouette. If we can only find one planet, even if it's not quite suitable for human habitation, we need to know if you can disassemble a human being and reassemble it into a being suitable to live on that planet. Let's say its atmosphere is chlorine. Could you redesign humans to breathe chlorine?"

Roland ran his hands through his hair. "But I'd have to know the complete parameters of that atmosphere, the strength of its gravity and a million other things. I'd have to program the assembly computer with all that information. I'd have to be God!"

"A perfect way to put it, Roland. Maybe the problem proves even simpler. Maybe all you have to do is improve on the oxygen transportation gene.

"And what if my hypothesis proves impossible?"

"Then we'll think of something else."

"My God!" said Roland, "And I know. There is no god."

"Any other questions, Roland?

"Yes, I am sure the disassembly and reassembly will take some time depending on how fast the computer can process a human's genome. At this time I can only guess how much time it'll take. If you have five thousand people to adapt to your new planet, it'll assuredly take a month to get everyone modified." Then Roland added, "You realize all I'm going to do first it literally take an inorganic item apart and reassemble as it was originally. I won't be able to modify it at this time. Next, I'll have to experiment with something living like a worm or bug. Replacing the genes of a chromosome at a precise locus will be extremely difficult."

"I understand. We'll cross each bridge as we get to them. As far as how we will decide who goes when, we'll have to have a lottery to choose who is to go and who is to stay. We have no choice. We will have to leave in one year."

"I won't go if my whole family doesn't get chosen."

"I know that, too," said Chantel. "We will keep families as one unit. And may I add, those of us who are leaders will be on equal footing as our citizens. We'll be chosen by the same lottery as all citizens. I myself have chosen not to be a part of the lottery. I'll stay here and join my wife in death."

"What about the Mars colony? Does it fit in to our choices?"

"As I said earlier, Mars doesn't seem like a viable choice. Several Mars Rovers of years gone by may have found signs of previous life but no hard evidence was ever produced.

"The few living there have to struggle constantly. It has no magnetic field. Therefore it cannot hold an atmosphere very well. It may have had an atmosphere at one time but Mars lost its magnetic field and solar wind literally blew away what atmosphere it had. It may also have had a molten iron core that cooled and is no longer moving thereby creating a magnetic field. We thought of basically creating an internal explosion by fusion to re-melt the core. Ironically, the same thing is happening on Earth. Our magnetic field is slowly cooling and collapsing."

"Wow," said Brooke.

"The two cities on Mars now are under a clear Plaztec dome. We're not sure how they are faring. Maybe you, Doctor, can create some vigorous plants that thrive on carbon dioxide and give off oxygen. Maybe you could give Mars an atmosphere again in spite of the solar wind. The atmospheric pressure is so low the people have to live in pressurized domes."

Roland stood with his hands on his hips. "How will you launch your space vehicle?

Chantel hesitated. "It's a highly secret location. It will most likely be launched from under the sea, near the southern border of Lower California."

"Won't ACD see it?"

"ACD will see it but it will not be able to do anything about it. ACD has very few space vehicles or satellites. Remember, it decreed space travel useless. It only has short range vehicles to refuel its moon outpost. No one lives there."

"I think there are a lot of 'ifs' in your plans, Chantel," said Roland, "but I'll begin working tomorrow. I hope I can be of use."

"I know you can, Roland. Here's your badge. Just to take some of the pressure from you, the other scientist is still working on human time travel. That is the other option."

Chantel got up to leave. Melody thanked him for her assignment and walked him to the door. After he left, Roland and Melody sat in silence contemplating all they heard. The children went off to their rooms excitedly talking about living on another planet.

JOHN PALLO

CHAPTER TWENTY-THREE

Roland caught a train car early in the artificial morning light. He knew his stop as soon as he saw the little building. The two different guards stood by and smiled at Roland as he showed his badge. Inside, standing by the elevator door the other guard smiled as he saw Roland's badge.

"Dr. Davidson, are we glad to see you. Welcome."

"Thank you," he said.

The elevator descended to its only stop. The doors opened and only a few people were visible now.

"Hello, Dr. Davidson," said an attractive woman. She was short, slightly heavy and of Spanish descent. She looked to be about forty or fifty and had long black hair and quite busty. "I'll show you to your desk," she said. "My name is Flora Montez. Chantel told me to see that you get anything you need or any assistants you may need."

"Thank you. You can call me Roland."

"Okay, Dr. Roland. Do you mind if I call you Dr. Roland?

"Fine. I don't care what you call me."

'This ACS screen is set up so you can see the previous work done by Dr. Guitarez.'

"Did you work with Dr. Guitarez?"

"Oh, yes," said Flora. "Dr. Guitarez and I worked together on this project for several years. He and I lived together, too."

"I guess you were saddened to hear of his death."

"Yes, but all of us here realize death can come at any minute."

"It seems as if all of you have faced that fact."

"Yes, Dr. Roland," said Flora. "The joke here is that death is a way of life."

"All right," said Roland, "Show me where to start."

Flora said, "As you can see here, Dr. Guitarez had these four metal plates arranged like a large box on its side."

Roland could see the plates, each about four meters square, placed at right angles.

"I think Dr. Guitarez had all the mechanical structures constructed just the way I would have. All I have to do is configure the computer, equations and power utilization."

"That's all you have to do, Doctor," said Flora.

After months of travel, the space search vehicle performed flawlessly. Chantel told Roland they picked up intercepts from ACD noting the launch but the giant computer could do nothing about it. They were trying to find out the launch location but since it was an undersea site, it couldn't determine the exact position of the site. And since it wasn't propelled by the usual combustion of fuel, it couldn't be followed by its heat trail. The Premier was his usual livid self, threatening anyone concerned with a month long, painful termination. His health was failing rapidly and he still had no word as to the whereabouts of Dr. Davidson.

Roland was almost a week away from his first experiment. The search vehicle was due to return in three days. In five days he was going to use a one celled life form, an amoeba, as the first attempt. Due to the urgent need of answers, Chantel begged Roland to begin with life forms for his first test instead of a piece of lead.

Chantel walked in Roland's office to check on the upcoming experiment. "What do you think, Roland?" he said. "Are we going to have success?"

"I hope so. I have the complete map of the amoeba entered into the computer. For our first attempt, we'll disassemble the amoeba and reassemble it exactly as it was. No changes. I still wish you'd let try a piece of wood first."

"I don't want to force you, Roland, but our time is running out."

"Okay," said Roland.

"When?" asked Chantel.

"Friday."

"What time?"

"Let's say 15:00 GMT."

"I'll be here."

Running his hands through his hair was becoming a habit and he did it once again.

"I'm going home," he told Flora. "I need to rest."

"Sure, Doctor," she said. "I'm going to check our insulation numbers again on our chamber room walls. I'll see you tomorrow."

The train stopped its usual one hundred meters from his home. Melody was at work on her home computer. She had stack of papers on her desk. She was also working on her handwriting.

"You're home early," she said. "Anything wrong? Is Mr. Amoeba ready?"

"I can't help wondering what will happen if my hypothesis proves impossible. And if it works, what use will it be to five thousand people?"

"Like Chantel said, they'll use a lottery."

"That's unacceptable," he said. "It's unacceptable and completely unfair. I hope I can find a faster way to perform the change - if it works at all. I believe the amoeba will take five to ten minutes. At that rate, five thousand humans will take approximately 35 days. But, my dear, we are not amoeba. There are over 3 billion combinations of possibilities of gene locations. Back in York we could design a perfect fetus, but we don't know what one misplaced gene could cause. If the computer made one mistake in reassembling, or if I made one mistake, we might create a monster. It may take hours, days or more for humans. I don't think the most powerful computer we have can work fast enough, mapping each person and then reconstructing each one to the new parameters required of a new planet. I've also noticed some people have dogs or cats. Taking an allotted position for an animal is out of the question."

"Couldn't you send a person together with their animal?"

"Melody, you're smarter than that," said Roland. "Can you imagine the computation required by the computer attempting to keep the atoms of the human separate from the animal? Someone already asked why not send two or three people at a time. Same answer."

"While not build two or four machines?" asked Melody.

"Don't even suggest such a thing. They barely have room and equipment for one, and we especially don't have enough power."

"Do you have a feel for how long it will take to experiment on the amoeba?"

"I don't know for sure. That little one-celled creature may take ten minutes, more or less. "

"Oh my gosh!"

"Yeah," said Roland. "Do you see what I'm up against?"

"Have you told Chantel?"

"Just what you heard me tell him, several minutes."

Melody said, "You know, I don't mind this place. The artificial sun seems to cheer me up just as easily as the real one. Do you know they have babbling brooks just like we saw in the Premier's city?"

"I'll get us out of here, one way or another." Roland didn't share Melody's feelings.

Roland requested as few spectators as possible for the test. Chantel granted him his request. Two councilmen and a senator however were present to watch. Only Flora and two of her assistants were present also. A table was placed in the middle of the four large plates. Flora placed the amoeba in its fluid in the middle of the disassembly/assembly room. A slight depression was made in the table to hold the fluid. A dish container couldn't be used because the container would confuse the computer and it would try to disassemble and reassemble the dish. Roland hoped he had properly programmed the computer to only disassemble the amoeba and not the table, depression or magnification camera. The target of the energy beam was aimed precisely at the amoeba. Flora carefully positioned it in its target area under a camera.

"Is it visible on the screen, Dr. Roland?"

"Yes, we got a good picture of Mr. Amoeba."

"Do you want me to stay in here too, Dr. Roland?" She laughed heartily.

"Get your cute, little butt out of there!"

"Cute, maybe, but it's surely not little. Hey! Can you disassemble me and rebuild me to be about twenty pounds less?"

Roland didn't laugh. He briefly thought of the Premier's command. He didn't answer Flora's request.

The entourage gathered around the computer and keyboard. It was assumed so much heat would be developed, it would be impossible to install a window. Also, electrons returning to their lower orbit give off so much light, an onlooker could be blinded. The amoeba itself shouldn't feel any heat, but everywhere around it could be extremely hot. The protons, electrons and neutrons would be magnetically held and then reinstalled according to the computer's directions.

The door was closed and secured. On Roland's signal, the power was allowed to build.

As Roland gave the signal, he began timing the event. He was hoping for no more than fifteen minutes. As the power began to increase, a slight humming was heard from the huge magnets. The magnifying vision camera was trained on the amoeba. The amoeba seemed to swim around happily unaware of what was about to happen. Everyone quickly turned their heads to watch the magnification screen. After five minutes, the amoeba suddenly disappeared. Roland entered a series of commands to the computer and waited. Was it vaporized or was it disassembled? They only had to wait approximately six seconds for the computer to analyze its code, make a map and rebuild the amoeba according to the map. Four more minutes passed. Suddenly a cheer erupted from the group. There it was; Mr. Amoeba. But the cheering immediately quieted. The amoeba's body was deformed. It had a peculiar bend in it. It had a sharp V shape. Roland assumed since moving particles at high speed creates heat, he directed Flora to introduce the cooling cycle. Slowly they opened the door while looking back at the magnifying vision screen. The amoeba was not moving. Except for its shape, it seemed complete and untouched but there was no movement.

Suddenly it quivered. It began some strange gyrations. It didn't try to swim or move any particular direction. Except for the weird 'V' shape, the creature seemed in perfect condition but it just didn't move normally. It didn't attempt to swim or ingest nourishment.

"What's wrong?" asked someone in the group. "Why does it look that way?"

Chantel asked for silence as Roland and Flora examined the amoeba.

"I don't know," said Roland.

Quickly they removed it and began an examination. Roland had to tell the onlookers to move away from the specimen. He and Flora had to examine the amoeba quickly before it began to deteriorate.

"It's dying," said Flora.

"Yes, I know," said Roland. "Why is it in that odd shape? It is just sitting there and dying. I don't know why."

The spectators began murmuring and moving away.

The councilman said, "At least it was a partial success. You did take it apart and put it somewhat back together. It just didn't bring its life with it, and it's crippled."

The group began heading for the door.

"That's okay, doctor. Just keep trying," said the senator.

"I will," said Roland quietly.

Someone said, "It lost something, maybe its brain."

No one laughed.

Finally everyone left the room. Only Chantel, Flora and the two assistants were left with Roland.

"It's like it didn't know what to do," said Saul, a young assistant. "It just sat there and didn't know what to do."

Roland didn't feel like speaking. The silence was deafening. "For one thing, I somehow I messed up its chromosome location."

A roach crawled across the floor. "Let's try this roach," said Ellen, the other assistant.

"Why not?" said Flora. "It's large enough we won't need the magnification camera."

Roland was checking a raft of numbers and formulas. "Sure, go ahead. We shouldn't have had such a large audience anyway. Let me enter its genetic code."

They anesthetized the roach and placed it in the center of the chamber. Once again they powered up the system and watched. Once again, after five minutes it disappeared. After about fifteen seconds of mapping and directing the rebuild, and an additional ten minutes, it reappeared. Another five minutes for cooling and the group entered the chamber. As the amoeba before it, the roach didn't move and it was hardly recognizable. As the anesthesia wore off the grotesque roach began to move. Its antennae quivered. It wasn't dead, but just couldn't walk. It was impossible to differentiate where its legs were, if it even had legs. It just seemed to make weird gyrations.

"It doesn't know what to do," said Saul again.

"Be still, Saul," said Flora.

Roland looked at the computer numbers and printed out several pages of data. Everything seemed to be correct. The computer mapped its code, disassembled the roach, read the map and rebuilt it. It would be nice, he thought, if Dr. Guitarez were still alive and here to help.

"I don't know what's wrong," said Roland. "I expected a possible problem with the process. I thought maybe we wouldn't be able to separate the atoms or recombine them. But the whole procedure seemed to work perfectly. The specimen was disassembled but reassembled improperly."

"Doctor," said Flora. "Let me examine the roach. Let me check and see if it is truly a roach. I'll check its DNA, molecular and atomic structure."

"Yes. That's a good idea."

Flora and an assistant took the roach and began an examination.

Ellen, said, "Let's try my apple."

Roland was getting perturbed. "Sure, let's try this chair. Let's try this jacket or your timing device. Let's try you!"

Ellen looked a little ashamed. "Doctor, I'm sorry. I thought we could try the apple and then taste it. Maybe it would give us some clue."

Roland went to her and put his hand on her shoulder. "I'm sorry, Ellen. I've been working on this hypothesis for years. I am extremely disappointed. I didn't expect this kind of problem. I imagined it just wouldn't work at all but it reassembled the sample into something grotesque. I think you have a good idea."

Roland said to Flora, "Let her try the apple."

Flora and Ellen took her apple and placed it in the target area. They closed and latched the door and began the power up cycle. Once again there was a five minute wait. The apple disappeared from the camera view. Ten seconds passed. Then twenty. After twenty-five minutes, the apple reappeared but it was purple. Nervously they waited the five minute cool down period and then opened the door. There was a slight vacuum as the door opened. Flora let Ellen get her apple.

"It feels normal and except for the color it looks okay," she said. "It doesn't feel hot. Should I take a bite?"

"Don't eat it yet," yelled Roland,

Flora said, "Let me examine a slice under the scope and do a chemical analysis."

Flora took a thin slice and looked at it. "It seems normal, almost. My quick scan shows it's not poisonous. There's a slight difference of a few gene locations. What do you think, Dr. Roland?"

"I can't think of a reason not to."

Flora cut another slice and took a bite of it.

"It tastes alright," she said. "It's slightly sweet and tangy, but something seems different. It doesn't taste bad though."

They cut more slices and each one took a piece. They all agreed. It was almost an apple.

Roland again was deep in thought. Something didn't get reassembled in the process. Something was lost. What was it?

From the back of the lab, and unheard by Roland, Flora said, "Roland, the DNA of the roach doesn't make sense. Gene location is a bit off."

Roland repeated, "This wasn't the problem I thought I'd have. I can fix gene location. It was reassembled but it lost something. Damn! What was it?"

Chantel said, "Roland, why don't you take the afternoon off. Come back tomorrow fresh."

"But you're counting on me."

"Roland, we have several options. Your way is one of them. We have other avenues."

"I think I will go home," said Roland. "Thanks for your apple idea, Ellen. That gives me something to think about."

Roland and Chantel headed to the elevator.

"I'm sorry the senator and councilmen were disappointed. We should have kept them away."

"No problem," said Chantel. "We're all so anxious to find a way out of here."

"I know. I'll keep trying."

"Roland, Dr. Volley Heitmen is in charge of our space probe. Her space research vehicle is not working properly. We still have no idea why," said Chantel. "It looks like a lot of our scientific experiments aren't working as planned."

"Oh, that's too bad. Do you think it was intercepted or just lost?"

"We have no explanation. We'll just keep waiting and hoping. Doctor, I want you to go home now and rest. Think about nothing scientific."

"That's easier said than done."

"Roland!" yelled Flora. "Look at the apple slices. They're turning brown."

JOHN PALLO

CHAPTER TWENTY-FOUR

Sogan called his great grandson, Lo Chang, to his chambers. Morgo handed the Premier a drink.

"Lo Chang, you were most wise in kidnapping Dr. Guitarez. He was caught by his sentimentality to his native countryman in Spain. That was most clever."

"Thank you most honorable great grandfather," said Chang.

"You are the next to succeed me in this throne. Your father and grandfather are too soft and lazy to succeed me. I have designated you to be my sole heir."

"Yes, great grandfather."

Hiding his emotions, Morgo was extremely disturbed by the Premier's statement.

"Now you know I am in failing health. I will live only a few more months. This Dr. Davidson can give me a good quality of life for those few months, maybe a year. I need to have him found. I will spend my remaining time training you and showing you how to govern our great world. I cannot teach you thoroughly in my current condition."

"I will find him, great grandfather. I presume they are underground. I will have our satellites search in an increasing circle using the Chi-Louis city as a center point. If they are underground, there must be ventilation openings somewhere."

"I will tell you Dr. Davidson's weakness," said Sogan. "Dr. Guitarez weakness was to his birthplace and countrymen. Dr. Davidson weakness is his family, his daughter in particular. His parents and grandparents have died, so says ACD. His daughter goes by the name of Risa. She is a headstrong but gullible young woman. Her love is the growing plant. Find a way to kidnap her and Dr. Davidson will do whatever we wish."

"I will devise a plan, great grandfather."

The Premier painfully raised his hand. "Go my trusted great grandson. I know you will do well."

Lo Chang bowed and backed away slowly.

My foolish offspring, thought the Premier. I will never relinquish my throne to him. Once I find Dr. Davidson, I will live forever.

Roland returned to his home. Melody immediately knew by his demeanor his experiment didn't work.

"Roland," she said. "It didn't work, did it?"

"No, my dear. It didn't."

"What happened?"

"The amoeba, and a stray roach, disappeared and reappeared. They were quite deformed and moved spasmodically and then nothing."

"What do you mean nothing?" she asked.

"By nothing I mean nothing. They just sat there quivering and dying."

"But they did disappear and reappear; shouldn't that be

called a significant breakthrough?"

Roland plopped himself on a cloth chair. "I suppose. I just need time to think it out."

"Was Chantel there?"

"Yeah, he and some officials and my associates."

"What did they say?" asked Melody.

"They were kind and gave me some encouragement, but I know they were disappointed."

"Roland," asked Melody, "Do you believe in a soul?"

"You mean something created by some god? You know I don't."

"Maybe your machine can reassemble a body but the soul gets lost in the transition. I don't think a being can live without a soul."

Roland angrily chided Melody. "Melody, you're an intelligent woman. I have to solve this problem with hard science, not some foolishness about a soul. I committed a familiar sin of scientists. I fell in love with my hypothesis."

Melody stopped her computer program. "Do you want some lunch?"

"Not now. Are you trying to tell me the amoeba and the cockroach has a soul? Don't be stupid."

"You should eat something," said Melody trying to change the subject.

"I want to think. I'm going to look at Dr. Guitarez's work again."

"Okay."

"You know what my problem is, Melody?"

Melody smiled, "Pride?"

"Yep. I was so proud everyone wanted my work. The Premier; the Reformers. Everyone was looking up to me as some kind of Savior."

Roland stood up and followed Melody into the dining area. "I guess I'll eat something. Is it grown food?"

"Sure is. Risa brought a bunch of things home. She's learning how to fix it. She is so proud of her work. Her hands were so dirty and she was tickled about it."

"What's her position?"

"I don't know. They are still trying to find out what she's suited for. She's dying to go up and outside the cave to see what the real sun will do."

Roland grabbed some green sticks. "What are these things?"

"Celery."

"They have no taste."

"I know but they have vitamins and fiber," Melody said.

Roland tried some green leaves. "I know what this is. It's lettuce, right?"

"Yes."

"It has no taste, either."

"I know. They put usually some sauce on it."

"It sure needs something. I'd rather have a cene."

"I have a few in the cabinet."

"Chantel told me to take the afternoon off, but I have to solve this problem. I think I'll go back to the lab this afternoon."

"Risa's food growing field is about half way to your lab. You should stop by and see how dirty she is."

"I'll do that."

Roland got off the train car at Risa's field. He stood there admiring ten to fifteen young people bending over doing something with the dirt. An elderly gentleman seemed to be supervising.

"Hello, sir," said Roland. "Do you know if a Risa Davidson is here somewhere?"

"She sure is. She's the most energetic youngster here. She's over there in the first row."

"I see her," said Roland. He walked over to her row.

Risa saw her father. "Hi Dad. Look at this." Risa's hands were dirty with a red juice on them.

"What are these?" he asked.

"They call them strawberries. Taste one."

Roland scrutinized one the fruit as he slowly raised it to his nose, sniffed it, and then took a bite. "Hey, these are good. A little tart but good."

"Yes, you put sugar on them."

"What's sugar?" he said.

"Oh Dad. You have so much to learn."

Roland thought of his failed experiment. "I sure do."

"Dad," said Risa. "I love this place, I mean this work. To me these plants are living things. They have a life, a soul. They're beautiful."

"You've been talking to your mother, haven't you?" said Roland.

"What do you mean?"

"Oh, nothing. I have to go now."

"Dad. How did your experiment go this morning?"

"Not good enough, my dear. Not nearly good enough."

"I'm sorry, but you'll figure it out. I know."

"Thanks. See you tonight."

Roland headed back to the train track and waited for the next train car. It appeared quite quickly and noisily stopped in front of him. He stepped on board and saw Flora sitting by a window. He sat beside her.

"Dr. Roland. I see you're not staying home like Chantel advised."

"I see you're on your way back too."

"Yeah, there has to be some reason for our failure," said Flora."

"It feels nice to have you accept some responsibility, too, but it's my failure not yours."

Flora answered, "Here doctor, we are family. It's our responsibility, too. We're in this together. We'll figure it out."

"Chantel hopes so." Suddenly Roland exclaimed. "I know one thing I did incorrectly. I didn't properly transfer the correct chromosome structure. That explains the deformed body of the amoeba and the extra body parts of the roach. There are too many combinations of gene locations on the helix. Some genes work independently and some work in pairs. I was in too much of a hurry and careless. I can remedy that quite quickly if I allow more time for the computer. I must speed up the computer processing."

"Roland," said Flora. "That's what I noticed with the DNA of the roach and the amoeba. There was some nonsense."

Roland and Flora sat in silence for a while as the train noisily crept along.

"Doctor, I've also been thinking about what Saul said."

"You mean our specimens didn't know what to do?"

"Sure. Maybe they needed an electrical shock."

"That's an interesting thought," said Roland. "History says eons ago our primordial soup needed a lightning bolt to start life. Maybe it's needed here, too."

"Hey! That's right. Let's try that."

"Okay but I have to also allow more time for the computer to arrange the proper DNA sequence and location."

Roland and Flora entered the lab highly exuberant, making everyone wonder what they had for lunch.

"Hey folks. We've got a new idea," said Flora.

"Great. What is it?" asked Saul.

"An electrical shock, Saul," said Roland. "You said it didn't know what to do. We'll show it what to do."

"Wow. Great. Let's do it!"

"Hey folks," said Ellen, "I thought we'd try it again. Just in case we were, I captured a mouse."

Roland said, "Okay, but I've noticed one thing, though. Gene location is quite critical. That is the first thing I was taught in my training. I was so impatient. The more complicated the subject, the longer it takes for the computer to map it and rebuild it."

"Yeah, I noticed that too," said Ellen. "The amoeba took almost nine minutes and the roach took fifteen minutes and the apple took twenty-five."

"We are taxing our computer and I must speed up the processor. Who knows how long a warm blooded animal will take," said Roland.

"Let's do it," said Saul.

Roland hesitated, looking at the mouse.

"What's a matter?" asked Flora.

"Fear of another failure. Okay. Let's do it."

They anesthetized the mouse and placed it in the target area. Roland spent several minutes reprogramming the computer. Saul attached to electrodes to the sides of the mouse and ran them to a terminal in the chamber. He then attached the outside extension of the terminals to an electric source.

"How much voltage should we use, Doctor?" he asked.

"Instead of a specific voltage, let's allow a measured amount of amperage. Let's try one hundred milliamperes."

"Gotcha," said Saul.

Flora closed and secured the door and began the process. The energy level increased and the usual humming was heard. They watched the mouse on their vision screen. It seemed to have a few spasms but no other movements. The mouse disappeared. Roland noted the computer computing furiously; the printout sheet showing an almost infinite number of chromosome characteristics and locations. Ten minutes passed, then twenty. The mouse didn't reappear.

Roland spoke his thoughts out loud, "If it takes thirty minutes for a mouse, it might take an hour for a human. This process will not work for hundreds of people. I've got to get a faster and more powerful computer."

After an additional thirty-five minutes, the mouse reappeared. It was as lifeless as the amoeba and roach but its body brought a gasp from the group. It looked almost normal except for an eye in the middle of its back. Then it began writhing.

"Damn," said Roland. "We're almost there."

"Give it the shock!" yelled Flora.

Saul gave it the small shock. The mouse jumped once.

"Do it again," said Roland.

Once again the mouse flinched. After each flinch, it returned to its befuddled state.

"The room is cool," said Flora. "Check for a heartbeat."

Ellen quickly opened the door. There was a slight vacuum again. She attached two heart monitor probes on the little creature.

"The heart beat seems erratic, now it stopped completely."

"Check for brain waves!" yelled Flora. "Hurry."

Brain wave monitors were attached to the mouse and they all rushed to the display screen. The brain waves were erratic too.

"Damn!" said Roland again. "What the hell is the problem? I've almost got the DNA correct but where is its life?"

"Roland, it's stumbling around like a baby mouse!" said Flora. "Its brain waves are decreasing in amplitude! Also, very few heart contractions!"

"Give it some food," said Ellen. "See if it eats."

Flora put some food in front of the mouse. She also placed some liquid soy near its mouth. It seemed to sniff at the food. It rolled almost by accident into the soy and put its nose in it. It sniffed at it and choked. Then it put its whole head in it.

"Damn it!" yelled Roland. "It's choking! It's drowning! Grab it!"

It was too late. The mouse drowned in the soy.

"The damn thing is too little to resuscitate."

"For goodness sake," said Flora. "It forgot how to eat or even drink. This is weird."

The group of scientists stared at the mouse completely mystified.

"What have we done?" said Roland. "What did we do?"

Flora repeated, "Roland. It acted like a baby mouse. It couldn't even walk."

Roland looked at Flora. "Are you suggesting when we rebuilt the mouse, it left behind all of its previously learned experiences? It left its instincts behind? Don't you start giving me that soul crap."

Flora started to say something but then refrained. She stared at the mouse as if she were deep in thought.

Then she said, "Maybe we should have put an adult female mouse in with it, surrogate mother so to speak."

As he had done before, Roland ran his fingers through his hair. "This doesn't make any sense. Why didn't its instincts return with the mouse? I know why the third eye appeared on its back. I know which gene that is and how to correct it but why doesn't it live?"

Saul said, "Let's try a bigger animal. Let's try a rabbit or cat."

"No way," said Roland. "This is scary enough at this point. I don't want to try any other creature or thing. I just want to think."

Flora said, "Roland, I think we've had an almost perfect success. It's just a minor glitch. We should try something else."

"I don't care, Flora. This is a big problem to me. I'm going home and staying this time. I might be back tomorrow."

"Doctor, can I do an autopsy?" said Flora.

"I said I don't care what you do, Flora."

"Sure, Doctor. Now take it easy on yourself. We'll figure this out."

"I know one thing," said Roland. "I originally theorized changing something inorganic into something else inorganic. In my enthusiasm I jumped to changing a living being into some other living being. My ego took over and I thought I could be the Savior of the Reformers. It is said, 'Pride comes before the fall.'"

"Doctor," repeated Flora, "take it easy on yourself."

Roland headed for the elevator. The train ride home took him passed the field where Risa was working. Maybe he should try working in the growth industries. He thought about his mother and grandmother. They need him to solve their mental problems. He remembered Sogan's statement saying he intervened with ACD giving his parents a few more years. Now he wondered about their safety. Roland decided to ask Chantel again about his parents and grandparents. Were they out of danger yet?

Roland got off the train car and walked slowly to his home. For the millionth time, he wished he hadn't published the article.

JOHN PALLO

CHAPTER TWENTY-FIVE

"How many of these underground cities are there?" Risa asked the farm tender.

"This is it. Our growth spurted at first but now has tapered off."

"It's beautiful, but I bet a farm above in the real sun is even more beautiful."

"It is," said the tender, "and we'll be up there someday. Say, I'd like you to meet our newest Reformer. You're not the newest member anymore."

The farm tender led Risa to a man working hard in a particularly rocky area. He was sweating profusely, straining at a stubborn rock.

"Chang," said the tender, "Meet Risa Davidson. Risa and her family were the newest members until you arrived."

"Hello," said Chang.

"Hi," said Risa.

Risa could easily see he was of Chinese descent and quite handsome. He was a well-built man about forty years old with slightly tanned skin.

"Why did you join us?" asked Risa.

"We have a similar underground city in Southern China, but the soil is so poor and our artificial sun is not nearly as bright as yours. Our farm tender arranged for me to come here to study your ways and bring them back home that we may grow plants as plentiful as you."

For a moment Risa questioned Chang's answer since the farm tender said this was the only underground city. But then she remembered the underground city of the Premier and assumed that was the city Chang was referring to.

"We were just in your underground city. We saw the Premier." It didn't occur to Risa that the city she saw in China was not a city of other Reformers.

"You saw the Premier?" asked Chang.

"Yes. He seemed so nice until we found out he wants my father to rebuild him to live forever."

"You are joking with me, are you not?"

"No," she said emphatically.

"What does your father do?"

"I'm not too sure but it has something to do with taking things apart, even people, and putting them back together again."

"Now I know you are joking with me."

"I am not joking. That's why we had to leave home and join the Reformers. He threatened our lives if my father didn't rebuild him into a healthy, young man."

"I still find this very hard to believe."

"He promised us everything and anything if my father succeeded."

"Can your father do this thing? Can he rebuild a human? Can he make a human immortal?"

"I don't know," said Risa. "He's made several attempts and they have all failed."

"Where is your home?" he asked.

"York, well, it was York. Now this is our home."

"It is beautiful here. It is fitting for an attractive woman like you to live in a beautiful city like this."

Risa blushed. "Thank you."

"So, your father is a scientist. I would like to meet your father sometime."

"Good, I know he'd like to meet you," she said.

"I would like to meet him tonight," he said. "Can you arrange it?"

"Sure, he's home now. Do you want to go now?"

"Yes, show me the way."

"Okay,"

They told the farm tender they were going home to meet Risa's father. He wondered why this Chinese man would want to meet Risa's father but he agreed to sign them off the farm. They got on the next train car and sat together making small talk about plants. Chang kept looking around at the other passengers.

"The living quarters all look the same. Which one is yours?"

"Ours is 121," said Risa.

Just before Risa's stop, the last passenger got off. Chang took a small container of fluid and sprayed Risa's face. She immediately fell asleep. He rested her head on his shoulder and they continued to ride to the end of the line. As passengers boarded and disembarked they saw a young girl, contently sleeping on her friend's shoulder. No one paid them any attention.

At the last stop, at the edge of the cavern, Chang picked up his captive and got off the train car. The train car then began its return trip to the other side of the cavern. Chang took her to a dark crevasse about fifty meters from the end of the track. He laid her down and bound her gently but securely. He then covered her and hid her from view. He made sure she could breathe freely but not shout for help. He then waited for the next train car.

At the train stop near the Davidson's home, Chang got off and walked to Roland's house. He rang Roland's visitor chime.

Melody came to the door.

"Yes," she said.

"I came to see Dr. Davidson," said Chang. "It's about his atom re-assembler."

Melody had no reason to suspect any problem so she called Roland.

Roland came downstairs from his troubled nap and greeted Chang.

"Hello," he said. "You're here about my failed experiment?"

"Yes," said Chang. "You could say that. Your daughter told me about your problems. Do you foresee solving them?"

"I don't know. Where did you talk to my daughter?"

"At the farm. I work there with her."

"Oh," said Roland. He felt slightly uneasy about this man. "She should be coming home soon."

"Great. I'd like to see her again. She's most engaging. She told me you were in China recently and met the Premier. I'm from China and never met him. He's quite old I hear."

"Yes he is," said Roland. Roland began looking toward the train car stop, hoping to see Risa smiling face.

"She said the Premier wanted you to use your new hypothesis of reconstruction on him. Would that work?"

"She told you that?"

"Yes," said Chang.

Roland felt more and more uneasy. Roland and his daughter had not discussed the Premier's desire since their talk in the cambri on their way to the roundball tournament. He wondered if he should motion to Melody to call the authorities. Chang sensed what Roland wanted to do and saw the sudden fear in Melody's eyes. "Do not call the authorities," Chang said. "Your daughter's life depends on what you do, Dr. Davidson."

Melody collapsed on a chair and Roland felt sick. He knew something was wrong. His nausea turned to anger.

"Where's Risa?" he yelled.

"Don't yell, Doctor," said Chang. "The neighbors might hear and call the authorities. That would surely be detrimental to your daughter."

Roland grabbed a chair, raised it above his head, and headed for the man.

"Doctor, look in my mouth. It's a poison pill. If I die my associates will terminate your daughter. They will terminate her quite slowly."

"How did you get in here?"

"Destroying your cavern at Chi-Louis was stupid. Our satellites noticed the heat. We examined the remains and found your train tunnel directly here. Our satellites then found your poorly hidden ventilation shafts by their heat signature. Knowing that bit of information, we have found several other heat signs. It was quite easy for me and my Sentinels to crawl down them. They're waiting for my orders."

"You bastard!"

Chang smiled, "I don't know what bastard means but I presume it to be a defamatory word."

Roland sat down next to Melody. She was sobbing quietly.

"Doctor. Let you and me be honest with each other. Does your machine work?"

"I'll never tell you."

"Oh yes you will. You must have forgotten we have your daughter. Now, does your machine work?"

"No."

"On your daughter's life, I'll believe you. Do you know the problem?"

"No, not exactly."

"Have you had any success?"

"Just limited success."

Chang looked at Melody. "Your daughter has your beauty. Of course, you picked out her genes but she must have some of your genes in her, correct?"

Melody couldn't answer.

"Who are you and what do you want?"

"I am Lo Chang, great grandson of Sogan." Then, more forcefully, he said, "What is the problem and will you solve it? What have your experiments accomplished so far?"

"We have successfully disassembled some specimens; an amoeba, a roach and a mouse. We have re-assembled these creatures but they are deformed. I suppose you could say they appear to leave all memories behind. I feel I will soon be able re-assemble without deformities but their instincts seem to be another problem. They seem to act like a newborn baby. We're not sure if instinct is the correct word but it seems that way. There! Is that what you wanted to hear?"

Chang remained silent as though in deep thought.

"What did my great grandfather ask of you?"

"You should know what he wants," said Roland.

"I know what he wants. He wants a few months of life so he can educate me how to govern weaklings like you."

"You believe that?" asked Roland.

"Why shouldn't I?"

Roland didn't know how to answer Chang. Did Chang sincerely believe his great grandfather wanted a few more months to teach or did he want immortality? Seeing the great lengths the Premier went through to live this far, it was plain to see, he wanted to live forever. Killing so many clones, so many transplants, Roland knew the answer. He was lying to his great grandson. Once he had his new body, there'd be no stopping him. Roland felt the beginnings of a desire to fail. He didn't want to succeed if it meant immortality for the Premier. Roland had to face a serious dilemma. Should he try to succeed for the Reformers or hope for failure to prevent saving Sogan? The thought of Risa brought him back to reality. He's got to save her. He decided to tell Chang the truth.

"Your great grandfather wants immortality. Look how many clones he's killed. He wants me to change him into a young man. He wants to be changed into a young man over and over again. He's promised me and my family anything we want."

Once again Chang stood in silence. He was deep in thought. Roland tried to imagine what this young man was debating. Risa's life depended on Roland making the correct decision.

"Your assumptions are not correct. My great grandfather wants me to ascend to the throne. His had designated me as the only heir. You are wrong. I am taking you to China to assist my great grandfather. When you arrive there, I'll give you the location of your daughter."

"No!" cried Melody. She ran to Chang but Roland grabbed her.

"Chang," said Roland desperately, "Think of this. He told me he wants my procedure to provide him eternal life. He's promised me and my wife and my children eternal life, too. You've seen the Premier. You've seen the grotesque transplants performed on him and the extreme measures he's gone through. You know how many clones have died because of him desiring to live forever. Does he look like a man suddenly wanting to live only a few months longer? A few moments longer to train you? He's ruthless and power mad. He'll never turn the kingdom over to you if he doesn't have to."

Chang seemed to be mulling over Roland's words. He didn't know what to believe. Roland was afraid he made his point too complicated.

Chang walked over to a chair and sat down. "My great grandfather favors me. He has told me so. He favors me."

Roland felt as if was making mental inroads to the man.

A loud bang of the door and Brooke noisily walked in. "Dad! The underground news said an island was found in the Atlantic Ocean full of dead bodies. Oh!" Brooke saw the unwanted guest.

"Brooke, go to your room," said Roland. "We're busy."

"No," said Chang. "Let the young man speak."

Brooke looked at his father and then to Chang.

In a subdued voice, he continued, "These bodies were all missing some organs. Rumor has it that they were clones for the Premier. Gosh, he looked okay to us."

Chang said, "Anything else, my young man?"

Brooke again looked at Roland.

"Go ahead, Brooke."

"Sentinels blew it up. The whole island was obliterated. The underground news guys said the Premier doesn't need it anymore."

Chang remained sitting. "Dr. Davidson, your daughter's life depends on your answer. Do you feel the Premier wants to live forever? Is he lying to me?"

"Yes I do, Chang."

"What you say makes sense. I have noticed his favorite assistant Morgo arranging many young virgins. I foolishly assumed they were for me even though I have not requested any. What you say makes sense," he repeated.

"Believe me, Chang," said Roland. "Where is my daughter?"

"She is safe. Now, let me think of my next move."

Melody pleaded, "Let me see my daughter."

"Dr. Davidson," said Chang. "Let me see you perform your experiment on an animal. Let me see it fail."

"Let my daughter go," said Melody. "Please."

"Mrs. Davidson, your daughter is the only assurance I have that I may leave here alive. I will release her unharmed when I am safely above ground."

Melody collapsed again, sobbing.

"Take me there, now," said Chang.

"Dad, where's Risa?" asked Brooke.

"She is fine," said Chang.

JOHN PALLO

CHAPTER TWENTY-SIX

Roland and Chang ran to catch a train car. They climbed on and sat together in silence. At the elevator building they jumped off and ran to the door.

"In a hurry, doctor?" said the guard.

"Yes," said Roland, "And my good friend here has an important contribution to make."

"I don't know if I can allow him to enter, Doctor. I'll have to get permission."

"Call Chantel. Quickly!"

"Okay, Doc."

Chang stood quietly while Roland paced nervously.

"Okay," said the guard. "Chantel wants to talk to you."

"Chantel, I have to take this man down below," said Roland. "Tell your guard to let him in."

"Hang on, Roland," said Chantel. "I'll be there in a minute."

"It can't wait, Chantel. Please let us through. You can come down and meet him when you get here."

"Sure. What's his name?"

Roland didn't know his complete name. "What's your name?"

"Lo Chang."

"Lo Chang," Roland said to Chantel. "I'm greatly concerned about my daughter."

Roland hoped Chantel knew Lo Chang and could understand Risa was in danger. Chantel did know Lo Chang and he could tell by Roland's voice Risa was in danger.

"Let me talk to the guard."

Roland handed the device to the guard. "Let them pass," said Chantel, "but go with them."

"Okay."

The trio entered the small building and entered the elevator.

"Why are you accompanying us?" asked Chang.

"It's common practice," said the guard. Roland knew this was not true.

They left the elevator and walked over to the chamber. Flora and her assistants were not present. Roland had to set up the experiment alone. And he had to find a specimen. He went to Flora's lab and found her animals. The smallest thing she had was a prairie dog. He grabbed it and took it to the disassembler. He then anesthetized it and placed it in the target area. He then secured the door and hoped. He hoped a larger animal wouldn't give different results. Roland was positive he had the gene location problem solved but it hadn't been tested yet. He began the power up cycle.

"It'll take about fifteen minutes."

Chang didn't say anything. He just looked at the vision screen. He jumped at the sound of the generator's humming.

Roland tried to explain the process. "The disassembler will disassemble the animal, map its genome, and rebuild it exactly as it was. My hypothesis was that it could also be altered to create a different being but that's getting way ahead of ourselves now."

Chang watched as the animal lay motionless, except for a few spasms. While watching, Chantel entered the lab and he told the guard to leave.

"Hello, Roland," said Chantel. "Is he who I think he is?"

"Chantel, can you wait a minute?"

"Sure, Roland. How's Risa?"

"She's fine for now," said Chang. "Who are you?"

"Chantel Joyce, an official."

"Good."

After five minutes, the prairie dog disappeared. Now they had to wait.

"How long?" asked Chang.

"At least twenty-five minutes."

Finally the prairie dog reappeared. It remained lifeless. A wave of relief swept Roland. He winced as he almost found himself praying. It looked normal.

"Can I see it?" said Chang.

"We have to wait five minutes for the room to cool, then you can."

The five minutes seemed to take hours. Roland tried to open the door of the chamber but it seemed to be held by something. It seemed stuck.

"Help me, Chantel," said Roland. "There seems to be a vacuum or something holding the door."

Finally the two of them managed to open the door. A slight whoosh of air rushed into the camber.

"That's strange," said Roland. "I don't know why there is a vacuum in the chamber?"

Chang went into the chamber and picked up the animal. It

was warm, as though alive, but it looked helpless. With a sudden motion it began nipping at Chang's hand. He violently threw it down.

"What's wrong with it?" asked Chang. "It seemed so tame when you placed it in your device."

"That's our problem. We don't know why it loses its senses. Everything seems correct but it acts like it doesn't know what to do. It changes."

Chang stood there looking at the crippled animal. As the other experiments it wiggled and squirmed in a nonsensical fashion. Roland put the animal out of its misery. Once again he was deep in thought.

"All my life," Chang said, "I have been taught to hate the outlaws and Reformers as you call yourselves."

"Chang, we are Reformers, not outlaws," said Roland. "We mean no one harm."

"Who is this man?" asked Chantel again. "Is he actually the Premier's offspring?"

"He," said Roland, "is the great grandson of Sogan."

"How and what is he doing here?"

"They found our ventilation tubes. He's here to take me back to China to rebuild the Premier. He and some Sentinels are holding my daughter hostage."

"What do you want me to do?" asked Chantel.

"Nothing at this moment. Let's see what he wants me to do."

"Will you go to China with him?"

"It depends," said Roland. "Melody is a complete wreck. If I have to go, please take care of her."

"I'll see to her myself."

"Thanks, Chantel."

Chang looked at Roland. "Dr. Davidson, we must go somewhere and talk."

"Let's go outside the lab."

"No. We must go up to the surface. My air vehicle is waiting for me. Mr. Chantel, you said you were an official of the city?"

"Yes, you might call me that."

"I'd like you to come with us, too. I need to think things through. I have questions."

"Will you release my daughter?" asked Roland.

"Soon. Let us go."

The three men left the lab and entered the elevator. Flora and some assistants met the trio at the door.

Roland simply said, "No questions," and motioned them to ignore them.

Chantel said, "There's no need to climb up the air vent since you now know our location. We can use our exit tunnel. It's no use hiding its entrance any longer since we've been exposed. Are you going to destroy us now that you know our location?"

Chang didn't answer.

"If you destroy the Reformers, another similar society will spring up. Discontent and boredom will surface again," said Chantel.

"Do not threaten me, sir," said Chang. "I am thinking what must be done."

The trio reached the surface from a hidden shrub. Chang's air vehicle was about a hundred meters away. He called to it from his ACD. The vehicle started up and moved to Chang. As it landed near them, Roland saw that it was unmanned. He also noted there were no Sentinels. Chang was alone.

"Where's my daughter?"

"Please restrain yourself, doctor, while I contemplate."

Even though the entrance was at the edge of the great lake, a hot and dusty wind was fiercely blowing. Large and small dust devils danced around the plains. The Reformers cavern was truly under water. Roland hadn't seen the southwest in many years. In almost every direction he could see small mountains reaching upward. The mountains to the west were clothed in a bluish haze as the sun began setting behind them. The mountains to the east glowed brightly with reds and oranges and purples with the setting sun illuminating them. Roland wondered if his daughter, and family, would ever be able to enjoy the stark beauty of this land.

Chang spoke, "Dr. Davidson, do you think you'll be able to solve your problem?"

"It's difficult to say. My assistant says the rebuilt being doesn't know what to do. My wife says I've left the soul behind, so the being dies. One of these people may be correct."

"I believe your observations are correct. My great grandfather is not looking for a few years extra life. He wants life eternal. It saddens me to think unfavorably of my great grandfather."

"I think you are right, Chang."

"Chantel," asked Chang. "Why did you want the doctor's services?"

"We want to build a civilization somewhere without ACD looking at us constantly. We are in glass houses. If we choose a world somewhere in the universe not suitable for earth beings, we hoped the doctor could rebuild us into a being that would survive a different environment."

"Are you not happy without sickness and wars and poverty?" asked Chang. "You do not have to labor or struggle to survive."

"Humans need to be challenged. People needs a reason to live," said Chantel looking at the distant mountains. "If I may say, the human needs a mountain to climb."

"I want to rule my great grandfather's world. He does not like my father and grandfather. He has placed them in what you would call 'house arrest.' The Premier calls them weak and soft. They are most unhappy. I do not like that. I believe I would like to be like my father and grandfather."

Roland added, "Don't you see? You have a challenge you want to conquer. You want to be a better ruler than your Premier."

"Don't mistake me," said Chang. "I want to rule but I also would like to be admired and honored and respected."

"Chang, please," said Roland, "Where is my daughter?"

"I will send an intercept message to be received on your wire communication system. She is bound and hidden under a shrub near the end of your train car track. I trust someone will tell your wife."

"Thank you, Chang," said Roland. "You will be a great leader."

"Now doctor," said Chang. "I have a request of you and you may think it strange."

Roland couldn't imagine what he could do for Chang. "What is it?"

"I promised my great grandfather I'd see that he got his wish if I found you and your machine. There is not enough time to take you to China and build your machine. I would like to bring him here. I would like you to rebuild him into the man of his desire."

"But Chang, you know what will happen. It's sure death."

"I do not think you will solve your problem. I do not care. I will bring my great grandfather here. I will give you thirteen days. Then he'll be transformed into the man of his dreams and then he will die. He will not die of your hands. He will die of his own lack of a soul. Without a soul, the being is no longer human. I will see to it he dies. I greatly dislike what he has done to my father and grandfather."

"Why must you bring him here to die?" asked Chantel. "Can't you simply let him die in China?"

"No. He is very suspicious and he'll question why I didn't bring Dr. Davidson to China. His aid, Morgo, is very protective and doubly suspicious. I would not be able to do away with Sogan without Morgo's co-operation. Morgo is a ruthless and power mad man but fiercely devoted to Sogan. He does not like me and seldom allows me to be alone with Sogan."

Roland knew it would take an extremely long time to disassemble and reassemble a human. The computer would have to map the being, hold the atoms in suspension and then rebuild the being according to a new map. Making a new being would require Roland to reprogram the computer to disregard the being's original mapping and use the new parameters to rebuild the new being. It would take a very long time.

"It would require a long time, Chang," said Roland. "I'd have to know what the Premier wants to look like."

"I do not care and it is a moot point." said Chang. "I'll bring a picture of a young Chinese man. If he dies while we are waiting, I will still know I was attempting to fulfill his wish. So be it."

"What do you think, Chantel?"

"Do you trust him, Roland?"

Roland asked, "How do we know we can trust you? You could be sending Sentinels to destroy our cavern city as we speak."

"All satellite information about your cavern is being transmitted only to my vehicle here. I will delete the information. You see I came alone. No one will know. No one will know where I will be taking my great grandfather except me. He and I will come alone with only four of his attendants. I will place my father in charge of the world until I return to China with the Premier's body or ashes if you have the capability. I know the wishes of my father and grandfather. They do not want the responsibility of ruling. They just want to be free."

Roland asked again, "How do we know we can trust you?"

"You cannot. I can tell you to call your wife and inquire about your daughter. You can use my communicator. Other than that, you'll have to just believe me."

Roland called his home. "Melody…"

Melody interrupted, "Roland! Risa is safe! She's home. I received a call telling me where she was. Our neighbor and I went to get her. Where are you?"

"On top. I'll be home soon. Give her my love."

"Roland, hurry."

"Good bye."

Chang asked, "Can you fulfill my request?"

"It will take time but I believe I can."

"Good, then go and prepare your machine. He'll never be able to descend this tunnel entrance. Is there another entrance?"

"Yes," said Chantel.

"Show me. Will someone meet us at the entrance to your cavern? Will you be there to escort us?"

"We'll be there, Chang," said Roland. "Chantel, give him the coordinates of our cargo entrance."

"Good," said Chang. "I'll be there mid-day, thirteen days from now. And your cavern city is safe at this time."

"Will they be safe after you are ruler, Chang?" asked Chantel.

"They will be safe," said Chang. "I too would like to see you and your outlaws on another planet. I might even assist you."

With that he got in his air vehicle and disappeared into the darkening evening sky. The two men stared into the evening.

"Do we trust him, Roland?"

"We have no choice."

"I do have some good news," said Chantel, "We've acquired quite a bit more of computer power for you."

"Great. I haven't solved my problem but I can perform my failures faster."

Chantel smiled at Roland. "As Flora said, you are too hard on yourself."

CHAPTER TWENTY-SEVEN

Roland returned to the lab after Melody assured him Risa was okay. He was still thinking about Chang's last words. Will he keep his promise? He gathered his ACS and other notes he planned to read at home. He wanted to go home and see Risa but he decided to go the lab first. Roland entered to see Flora and Ellen reading Dr. Guitarez's ACS. They were vehemently discussing something regarding Roland's hypothesis. He realized he wasn't too interested in what they were discussing and headed toward the door.

"Roland!" said Flora. "A prairie dog is missing. Do you know anything about it? And who was that man with you?"

"Chantel and I performed a little experiment. We'll explain later."

"Oh," said Flora.

"What's going on?" he said. "Have you found our problem?"

"No, not exactly," said Flora, "But we have a question."

"So, what is it?"

Flora said, "We were wondering about teleporting an object. If we could take something apart and hold it in suspension and then rebuild it, couldn't we move it from one machine to another?"

Roland smiled. It was the first time he smiled since his first failure last Friday.

"I've already thought of that possibility. There's an inherent problem with the scenario. When we take an object apart, we hold the atoms in suspension in the chamber. The computer remembers the assembly order on an electronic map. If we tried to rebuild the object somewhere else in a different machine, transmitting the electronic map would be no problem. But where would the second machine get the atoms? It would have to grab atoms from the air around it. The only atoms in air, as you know, are mainly oxygen and nitrogen. To recreate the object, the machine would have to disassemble the oxygen and nitrogen atoms and then reassemble them into the object. It would take an extremely long time and energy. And there may not be enough atoms in the area to build the object."

The women said in unison, "Oh."

Roland didn't realize it but he had the answer to his vacuum question.

"It's an interesting idea but we haven't solved the first part yet."

"Yeah," said Flora, "I know, but we were just wondering."

Chantel rushed into the lab. "Roland, they just called me. The space search vehicle returned."

"Has it found anything?" asked Roland and Flora.

"Dr. Volley Heitman said the results are somewhat confusing but it has found no suitable solar system, no sun and planets, no environment even similar to Earth." Chantel looked as disappointed as Roland when his experiment failed.

"It looks like we're stuck here," Chantel said. "We're still examining the data but preliminary information says Earth is the only planet God made for humans."

Roland ran his fingers through his hair. "There's that god person again."

Roland and Chantel walked to the side of the lab and sat at a desk.

"It seems as if we're not too successful, Chantel," said Roland.

"Roland, we do have one possible success."

"What may that be?"

"Chang. After we transform the Premier, he'll leave us alone."

"If that's true, I guess that is some good news."

Chantel looked thoughtful, "Roland, think about this. Flora examined the apple and the roach. Their chromosome structure was nearly perfect. They were closely identical to their species. There has to be something, lets say..." Chantel paused.

"What?" Roland asked.

"Something spiritual."

"Spiritual?" What are you referring to?"

"A soul," said Chantel.

"Oh, garbage!" said Roland. "Now you've been talking to my wife."

"No, I have not," said Chantel. "But think of this. Each living creature has a soul. That's what makes it what it is. The amoeba lost its soul in the transition. The roach lost its soul when transitioned."

"Chantel," said Roland vehemently, "There is no such thing as a soul. There's just one thing I'm missing in our rebuild. When we find it, we'll be successful."

"Just a thought," said Chantel.

"Think of what foolishness you're trying to tell me. If that roach has a soul why hasn't a roach written a book or composed a song or invented a cure for Alzheimer's?"

"Roland, all I'm saying is an amoeba has an amoeba soul, the roach has a roach soul and so on with the prairie dog. We humans have a human soul."

Roland threw up his hands in disgust. "I'm going to re-read Dr. Guitarez's work."

"Did you read his summary?"

"Yeah, I just skimmed it."

"Don't skim it," said Chantel. "Read it thoroughly."

"Garbage."

Roland took Dr. Guitarez's ACS home with him. He was tempted to read the summary on the train car but he resisted opening the screen. Risa met him at the train car stop and met him with a hug.

"Dad. Who was that man?"

"He, my dear, is the Premier's great grandson. Did he hurt you?"

"No Dad. He hardly touched me. I didn't know I was tied up until I awoke. He was so nice working with me in the field. I guess he put me to sleep until those people woke me up out there in the bushes."

"I think he'll be a better ruler than the current Premier. He's promised to leave us alone after we change his great grandfather."

"Change him?" she said. "Into what?"

"It's a long story. I'll explain it to you later."

"Have you had any success yet?"

"No, not yet. I've got one major hurdle and I don't know how to solve it."

"I know you, Dad. You'll solve it."

They walked hand in hand to their house.

Roland and Melody looked up at the ceiling from their bed. They could hear the train cars passing every so often in the artificial moonlight.

"Melody," said Roland. "If there is a soul, it's intangible."

"Yes, I would imagine so," she said.

"If a soul is intangible, then I can't disassemble and reassemble it."

"Yes, I believe that, too."

"Then my hypothesis is not provable. It's invalid."

"Maybe only a God can make a soul."

Roland was tempted to say 'garbage' again, but he didn't.

"Good night, Melody. Risa didn't seem too traumatized about her experience, did she?"

"No, she's pretty level headed. She knew it had something to do with your work. She said the man was so gentle with her she knew she wasn't in danger."

"She's amazing, just like you."

"Yes, she is."

"Good night, and this time I mean it."

"Good night, dear."

Roland looked up at a few new cracks in the ceiling. "Have we had any recent tremors?"

"Not that I've noticed," said Melody.

"Oh."

JOHN PALLO

CHAPTER TWENTY-EIGHT

Chantel, too, was at a loss to explain why their space search vehicle returned with no suitable planet for earth humans. Roland's experiment had failed, too. Even if they had found a suitable planet, he couldn't design a being to live on it. Roland walked into the lab and saw Chantel.

"Good morning, Chantel,"

"Hello, Doctor. We've had a run of bad luck, haven't we?"

"Yes, we have."

"I talked to Dr. Heitman this morning," said Chantel. "She is fairly sure the space search probe worked properly. There just isn't any place in the universe suitable for us fragile humans."

Roland tried to console Chantel. "Even if we had found an environment similar to ours, what could we have done? My experiment failed, too."

"I know."

"Chantel, it also bothered me that even if we found that Utopian planet, only a few could be transported. That's not right. We should try to save all of us."

"Do you think Chang would let us live in peace? Could we co-exist?"

"We couldn't be sure," said Roland. "You know what they say, power corrupts."

"God!" said Chantel. "We had such high hopes for our people."

"There's that 'god' again."

"Are you afraid there might be a god?"

"Definitely not because there isn't any. Why do you ask?"

"Because you get so agitated when anyone mentions god."

"I don't care what you believe," said Roland.

Chantel said, "People that aren't quite convinced about a belief are constantly looking for others who feel as they do. They need external support and reinforcement to quash their doubts. They are easily agitated by those who don't believe as they do."

"I have no doubts. There is no god."

"Then the next time I mention god, there'll be no need for you to tell me there is no god."

Roland was becoming visibly aggravated. "Damn it, Chantel. There is no god. There is no soul and that's that."

Chantel laughed.

"What's so funny?" asked Roland.

"You said 'damn it.' Who's to do the damning? Isn't this god the one who damns?"

Roland stormed out of the lab, slamming the door behind him.

Chantel looked upward. "If you are there God, please help us."

Roland got off the train car at Risa's plantation. He sat on a bench watching the people, young and old, laughing and sweating in their labor. Life is so simple in the fields. Why couldn't he and his family have lived three hundred years ago? Roland remembered an old artist rendering of life 300 years ago. Two boys were fishing with some kind of rods. They looked extremely happy in their tattered clothes. The green, yellow, tan and orange color of the earth and trees - not Plaztec but real trees – gave a warm and cozy feel to the picture. There were few machines then. The people did things with their hands. There was no instant communications; no instant travel, no spying satellites and no Sentinels watching your every move. The world was pure then. I think there were animals running around then, too. So we only lived seventy or sixty or even fifty years, so what? Maybe at the time they didn't seem so wonderful but looking back I can imagine them as quiet and peaceful years. If there is truly a god, why is he allowing such turmoil now?

Roland had read Dr. Guitarez's summary. The doctor had a good idea what the Premier wanted. It was eternal life. Roland could tell. In the very last paragraph Roland saw the word 'God'. The doctor wrote in large letters, *'If God has created an immortal soul, would He allow it to be disassembled and re-assembled by mere humans? I think not.'*

Roland thought, all I want to do is discover. All I want to do is solve mysteries. What makes me want to do that? Why was I bored back in York? Is there something in my makeup that makes want to have knowledge? The prairie dog's life consisted of securing nourishment and reproducing. Did I take that away? What was in the little dog's life that made it want to continue living? Was there a prairie dog soul that told it to eat? Did the soul tell it to reproduce? When the animal reappeared, it truly didn't know what to do. It had no soul to direct it. We call it instinct. What it is...is a soul. Oh my God.

Roland, just like Chantel, looked upward. "If you are there God, please help us."

"Dad!" Risa shouted. She came running across several rows of plants. "What are you doing here?"

"Just thinking and watching the people work. Are you finally content?"

"Gosh, Dad. Yes. I love this. It so much more fun than staring at ALEKC."

"I'm sure it is."

"How are things at the lab?"

"I think I've discovered something. I think I've discovered I'm a mortal trying to do something only God can do."

"Gee, Dad," said Risa. "I could have told you that but you wouldn't have listened."

"Risa, what makes you so smart?"

"You and Mom took your genes and improved them a bit and here I am."

Roland looked at the dirt on Risa's hands and knees. "You sure are dirty."

"Yep," she said smiling. "If you're not busy, why don't you come join us for a while?"

"I think I will."

Roland and his daughter joined the other farmers digging weeds and removing rocks. Roland looked at his clothes. He was completely out of place in his dress uniform but he didn't care. He and Risa spent the rest of the day weeding, seeding and tasting their crops. Roland was quickly developing a taste for earth grown foods. He realized Melody was accustomed to seeing Risa covered with dirt. Seeing him that way would be a shock.

CHAPTER TWENTY-NINE

It was near noon and Roland, Chantel and Flora waited near the cargo tunnel entrance. Roland felt he had successfully programmed the computer to rebuild the Premier to a young, healthy looking but lifeless Chinese man. With the additional computing power, he was also able to speed up the process quite a bit. There was no way to test his calculations. The test would come soon. All spectators were kept from the area. They were told nothing except that it was a very high official.

Chantel said, "I see a signal. An air vehicle is approaching."

The vehicle slowed and hovered near Chantel and Roland. Chantel had a cargo cambri sent ahead to the entrance. They would have to place the Premier in the cambri and drive it down to the cavern. The air vehicle stopped and the doors opened. Roland saw Chang and four attendants. Roland was sure one of the attendants was a woman. In their midst was a shrouded figure covered with an ornate coverlet. The Premier's face was not visible. The figure sat on a seat secured to an archaic carrying device. Two long poles extended out from each end the device allowing the four attendants to carry it. They descended from the air vehicle and Chantel directed them to the cargo cambri. It had large cargo doors and the entourage entered carefully with their ruler. Roland, Chantel and Flora entered also and the cambri began to move.

Chang asked, "Why is a woman present?"

"She's an important part of our team," said Roland.

"The Premier does not want her present," said Chang.

"I cannot work without her," said Roland. "The process is quite complicated and too intricate for an untrained assistant."

"Then she must cover her eyes. The Premier will allow no woman to see him."

"We will do that," said Chantel. "I do see that a woman accompanied Sogan."

Chang didn't answer. Roland wondered how Chang got Sogan here without Morgo. "Where's Morgo?" he asked."

"I convinced him that my father and grandfather needed him in China to watch over them."

Chang gave Roland the picture the Premier has been holding for months.

"Here's the picture of the male the Premier wants to be," said Chang.

"It took me twelve days to program a new being. I didn't have time to wait for your picture," said Roland.

"I know that," said Chang. "Just pretend to use the picture. He'll never know, is that not correct?"

"It is correct."

The cambri descended down the cargo tunnel and stopped at the small building. Chantel dismissed the two guards and several bystanders. They hadn't seen a cambri for years, especially a cargo cambri. The group entered the building and the elevator. Confined in the small elevator, a terrible stench overwhelmed the passengers. Flora was near gagging. Mercifully the descent was short lived. They opened the elevator door and the Premier's attendants carried him to the machine.

The Premier whispered something to Chang.

"The Premier has a great distrust of all outlaws," said Chang. "He wants proof the machine will work."

Flora looked at Roland who looked at Chantel.

Flora said, "I have an apple. We could use that again."

"No!" said Chantel. "You told me it turned purple, remember?"

"It's okay," said Roland. "I corrected that problem."

They placed the apple on the target area and turned the Premier's chair toward the vision screen. The Premier whispered something to Chang again.

"The Premier wants to be sure there is no trickery. He wants to see my hand visibly placing the apple on the target."

"We will do that," said Chantel.

They gave the apple to Chang. He hesitated for a moment.

"It's okay," said Roland. "The machine has not been started yet."

Chang clearly and visibly placed the apple on the target. The Premier peeked from his coverlet and watched. The stench was beginning to permeate the lab.

As before, the process commenced and the apple disappeared and reappeared. After the chamber cooled, Chang entered it and took the apple out for the Premier's inspection. Roland noticed only a slight vacuum in the chamber this time. He wondered why he is only noticing the phenomenon now. The Premier gave the apple back to Chang and commanded him to eat it. Chang looked worried and doubtful.

Roland grabbed it and cut a slice from it. He passed the slices around, each person taking a bite. Chang took his slice and gave one to the Premier. Everyone began eating their slice. The Premier's face was not visible but it was assumed he took a bite. There was a long pause and no movement from the Premier. They didn't notice the apple quickly turning brown.

Finally he whispered to Chang.

"The Premier wants one more test. He wants us to put his cat in the machine."

The Premier handed the white cat to Chang. Roland and Chantel stood frozen with fear.

Chang said, "Do it!"

Roland told Flora to anesthetize the cat and place it on the target.

"Tell the Premier we must anesthetize all living beings. The object must not move while the process is occurring."

Chang told the Premier while everyone waited to see his reaction.

"It is okay," said Chang.

Once again Chang visibly placed the cat on the target area in view of the vision screen. It was apparent the Premier was watching intently. Chang backed out of the chamber and Roland secured the door. The process began another time.

After several minutes the cat disappeared. Now they all had to wait. Chang told the Premier it may take five or six minutes before reassembly. After exactly six minutes, the cat reappeared. The Premier made a noise. Chang said the Premier is elated. He wants to hold his cat.

Chang nervously looked at Roland.

"It's okay, Chang," said Roland. "Tell him the cat is still anesthetized. He can hold the cat and feel its warmth but we must then put it in our kennels while we prepare for the Premier. He will take many minutes for his transformation."

"Okay," said Roland. "Chang. Get the cat and carefully hand it to the Premier to feel its warmth. Then we must hurry."

"Surely, I will do that," said Chang.

This time there was a greater vacuum in the chamber. It required a greater effort by Roland and Chantel to open the door. Once again a whoosh of air as the door opened.

Chang handed the cat to the Premier and everyone waited to see if their ploy fooled the Premier. He said something to Chang and handed him the cat.

"The Premier said the Doctor Davidson must sit at his right hand and be his personal attendant when he returns to China. He said to hurry with the process."

A collective sigh of relief filled the lab. Roland apologized to Flora and told her to go behind a wall and hide her eyes. Flora took the cat to the rear of the lab. There she quickly ended the cat's life before it awoke and became violent.

"No problem, doctor," she said.

The attendants moved the Premier into the chamber and removed his coverlet and scarf. Chantel hadn't seen the Premier and nearly vomited at this grotesque being. The Premier was placed between the four plates at the target sight. The vision screen was trained on the subject. They started to close the door.

The Premier yelled something.

Chang said, "He asks about the anesthesia."

"Oh, yes," said Roland. "I will do it with his permission."

Chang talked to the man and nodded approval to Roland. Roland handed an air tube to the Premier and he quickly fell asleep. Flora began the process.

Chang took the four attendants aside and began talking to them in Chinese. They all nodded. After five minutes, the Premier disappeared. Roland couldn't help feeling sorry for the man. He expected so much from Roland and he couldn't deliver the gift of eternal life to the man. It was terribly sad.

Thirty-two minutes were required to rebuild the man. Anxiously they all stared at the vision screen. The naked body of a beautiful Chinese man appeared on the target. It wasn't the man in the Premier's picture but it was a very handsome and young male. The attendants seemed to rejoice. There was no movement of the man.

Roland went to his computer and pretended to frown at some figures on his screen. He made a motion to Chang and Chantel.

"Something is wrong," he said. "Tell the attendants to go into the chamber and try to rouse the Premier."

This time the chamber door remained tightly closed. Roland quickly removed a chamber equipment cover and a great amount of air rushed in. Again Roland made a mental note to study why this was happening more often now.

Chang entered the chamber first. Roland noticed he had some sort of syringe hidden in his hand. Deftly he injected something into the Premier. It was too late. Sogan began to wake. The rebuilt Sogan looked wildly about and leaped toward Chang. He fell to the floor all the while thrashing violently with his fists. Sogan screamed and made several unintelligible sounds. Finally the injected fluid took effect and Sogan fell back to the floor. He was dead.

As the attendants tried to arouse the Premier, their glee turned to anxiety. They were mumbling to each other and to Chang.

"What should I tell them?" asked Chang.

"Tell them we were seconds too late," said Roland. "Tell them his heart failed. The stress was too much."

Roland, Chantel and Flora watched the attendant's expressions closely. After much talking, they turned and began administering to Chang. Chang was now their leader and ruler.

Chang said, "The attendants say we should cremate the Premier if you have facilities. We will bring his ashes back to China. They say I should return quickly and ascend the throne."

"Yes, we have a crematorium," said Chantel.

Chantel arranged for the body to be cremated and placed an old style urn.

"We must leave as soon as the cremation is completed," said Chang. "I will tell you this. You and your people are safe as long as you don't interfere in our world. I would hope you can leave for some place off the Earth. Go to Mars or Saturn's moons. I will give you a year to do so. After that time, I will not guarantee to restrain my Sentinels."

"Will we be allowed space vehicles for travel to a planet?" asked Chantel.

The new Premier appeared thoughtful. "Yes, but you must let me know your situation soon."

"How will we contact you?"

"I'll contact you in six months for a status report," said Chang.

The new young Premier and his attendants left for their cambri and headed to the tunnel to their air vehicle. There they will wait until the cremation is finished.

Roland and Chang would meet again.

Chantel saw Roland sitting looking completely downcast. "What's wrong?" he asked.

"My hypothesis is completely useless. It is of no use to us. Maybe I have taken the being's soul. Maybe I have sent the soul off somewhere to who knows where? I've failed again."

PART II

WHERE DO WE GO?

CHAPTER ONE

The ten scientists gathered in the small room. For the first time, Roland was to meet the president and vice president of the Reformers. The president's name was Lawrence Van Steen and the vice president was Amanda Solari There seemed to be no protocol. Everyone sat around in chairs with no particular arrangement. If Chantel hadn't pointed out the president, Roland would have never guessed the man's position. The vice president appeared equally commonplace. The twelve people in the room were made up of six men and six women. Roland wasn't sure if it was by design or by chance. Chantel and several other sergeants and councilpersons also attended but they stood at the rear of the room.

Mr. Van Steen stood up and addressed the small group.

"Welcome ladies and gentlemen. Thank you for taking the time to meet here today. We have some serious problems to address. And it seems, every time we meet we have serious problems but this is the life we chose."

The group looked at each other and nodded in agreement.

"I suppose you want to know about things above ground or, as we say, on top. As far as we know, Chang has kept his promise. No one seems to know anything about us down here so we feel he hasn't disclosed our location. We can't be sure how long he'll keep his promise. I guess he will as long as we don't threaten him. The fearful thing is we don't know if we might unknowingly threaten him. The outlaws are accelerating their destructive programs and are increasingly causing more deaths. We are hoping Chang remembers we are not part of the outlaws and that we do not advocate terror. It's been reported he has sent several Sentinel armies chasing after the outlaw groups.

"What I want to do now is get a progress report of each of you scientists. First, we'll discuss the things that didn't work. Please don't feel like this is an ALEKC schooling test. I know we have had more failures... no. Failure is not the word I want to use. I should say the realization that our theories are not attainable or even provable. After that, we'll discuss our successes. And finally, where do we want to go and how will we get there?

"Dr. Volley Heitmen, would you mind beginning?"

"Thank you, Larry." Again the lack of protocol intrigued Roland. "I am glad you chose me to speak first. I am ashamed and embarrassed to admit my failure. I want to put my failure behind me and move on. My space search vehicle was a fraud. It didn't work as I thought. I didn't actually bend space. It didn't actually search the entire universe. Yes, I thought it did at first. I didn't mean to give incorrect information to you my colleagues. After repeatedly checking my data, I found it completely confusing. My space search vehicle seems to have merely orbited Earth. Since we have no tracking devices, I didn't know until I re-examined the data. There are even more confusing data I am still evaluating. I am terrible sorry."

"Thank you, Volley," said Larry. "Volley told me this earlier but she wanted to tell you all in person. I don't think you should call your vehicle a fraud. A fraud is an intentional lie; your vehicle failure was not your intention. No one here faults you."

"Thank you, Larry." Volley sat down and kept her head bowed.

"Next, Dr. Davidson. Atomic disassembly and re-assembly."

Roland was glad Volley went first but he too hated to admit failure.

"Ladies and Gentlemen. Thank you, Larry. Volley, I too have to admit failure. My hypothesis and experiments were a complete failure as to the desired results. I disassembled an apple and reassembled it but that is not what you wanted me to do. That is not why you invited me here. You wanted me to prove the certainty of rebuilding the human body to new parameters. I couldn't do it. It seems as if I leave something vital behind. I leave the soul. I kill the being. I remember reading an old saying 'Only God can make a tree'. Only God can make a soul. I too am terribly sorry."

With that Roland sat down.

"Roland, if I may correct you, you were not invited here to prove your hypothesis. You were invited here because you and your family hated the boredom and lack of purpose of life under ACD. You were invited here because you and your family had inquiring minds. If success of all of our theories was the only reason we invited people here, most of us would have to leave. If your hypothesis is truly flawed, then we would like to use your mind and intellect to help someone else with their experiments."

"Thank you," said Roland. "I'd like that."

The rest of the scientists gave their reports. The woman working on bending of light rays was having some success. She could bend the rays around an object, making it seem almost invisible. The object wasn't transparent. The light rays simply went around the object as wind flows around a tree trunk. The woman working on time travel was having limited success. The anti-gravity scientist was able to shield a small amount of gravity lines and cause a wheel to rotate, similar to the action of a waterwheel. He also felt an object could swing through space from one planet's lines of gravity field to another with nearly no additional input of energy. This would be as one would swing from one tree vine to another. The woman working on the computer with imagination seemed to be having the most success. She laughingly accepted the challenge to have it imagine a way out of the cave. One fact kept reoccurring. No one had an answer as to where they could live in peace in the real sunlight. The group wholeheartedly agreed they did not want to live their lifetime in a cave.

Larry stood up to speak. "It seems to me we have several choices we can make. I would like each of you with theories or projects that didn't work to choose one of these people having some limited success. Work with the person now involved with them. The first choice is can we live underground the rest of our lives? Can we expand to other caves and caverns? Do we even want to live underground forever? Now that the Premier knows our location what would we have to do to not anger him?"

Larry looked at his notes. "The next choice is can we end the Premier and ACD's rule over Earth? Can we make Earth a place without Sentinels and scanners? Could we make the Earth truly free and all of us live above ground. Could we stop the implanting of chips in our bodies?

"Third. Could we make a place habitable on another planet? Is there one suitable for us to make an enclosed environment where we could live and grow nourishment? Yes, I know, other than Mars or the moons of Saturn there is none near enough to travel to in a normal lifetime. But if we can successfully bend space distances, it would be feasible to travel to it. Possibly we could build another probe.

"Finally, can we go back in time? Could we place ourselves 100, 1,000, 10,000 or more years back in time? Could we place ourselves back to the time of Adam and Eve?"

The last question genuinely piqued Roland's interest. Isn't that what I've always wanted to do, he thought? I've always wanted to be back in the time when the Earth was clean and pure. We would be like Adam and Eve. Our 25,000 chromosomes would have no defects. Without ACD we would probably live 500 or 1000 years. I am going to pursue time travel. That's going to be my goal.

Roland jumped up, "Larry, will we be able to choose our new course of endeavor?" Roland immediately felt ashamed. "I'm sorry. I didn't mean to interrupt."

"That's okay, Roland," said Larry. "Did I hit on something of interest to you?"

"Yes you did," said Roland rather shyly. "Time travel."

"If no one disagrees, I see no problem. Any objections?"

No one seemed to mind.

"Dr. Sharon DeVoy is working on time travel. Does anyone want to join Roland and Sharon in the time travel project?"

No one volunteered. "So Roland, it's yours and Sharon's. Sharon, why don't you introduce yourself to Roland?"

Sharon stood up and walked over to Roland. "Hello, Dr. Roland," she said. "Glad to have some help. I've run out of ideas so some fresh brain cells will surely help."

"Glad to meet you," said Roland. "I ran out of ideas on my atom disassembly project too."

Larry asked, "Do you want any assistants?"

"Yes sir," said Roland. "I'd like to have my atom disassembly team with me if they'd like to join me, and of course if Sharon doesn't mind."

"I don't mind since I only have one."

"That's fine. You can contact them and if they agree, they're yours. You can use your current lab for your work. It's better equipped than Sharon's."

"Yes sir, and thank you."

Larry smiled, "And Roland. We try not to be too formal here."

Roland laughed at himself and sat down. Sharon sat down next to him. She appeared quite old, Roland thought, maybe 100 to 130 years old but she stood tall and straight. She had no age spots and only a few wrinkles. She seemed quite energetic and walked briskly. Sharon possessed the most piercing blue eyes Roland had ever seen and her nearly completely gray hair made her a very attractive woman – for her age.

"It looks like I have a new project to work on," said Roland. "I hope I have better luck with time travel."

"We'll need more than luck," Sharon said. "I've been beating myself into the ground over two obstacles for the last six months. I hope you can give a new approach to the problems."

"I hope so too. You'll have to give me time to learn what you're trying to do and what you've done."

Roland and Sharon were getting so involved in the time project, they forgot Larry was still speaking about other projects.

Sharon continued, "My biggest problem is energy. I don't..."

Larry spoke up, "Dr. Davidson and Dr. DeVoy. I know you two are eager to get started but let's wait until we get others here assigned to projects."

"Oh! I'm sorry Larry," said Sharon.

"That's okay," laughed Larry. "I love to see enthusiasm, but I've got to get the others assigned to projects."

"We'll be quiet," said Roland smiling at Sharon.

The meeting ended with 'failures' being assigned different projects. The whole group was now jabbering away in little groups.

"Now folks, I know we're all excited about our new programs and assignments, but please remember, we have about one year to get answers. We don't know if the Premier will keep his promise but that's all the time he gave us. When our time is up, we have to know where we're going. Some of you can remember the mole. We don't want to end up like moles. We want to live in real sunlight again. Let's see what we can do. Thank you all for being here today."

The group rose and noisily began leaving the room. All the unfulfilled scientists were teamed up their new project leaders. No one was blaming anyone. No one was calling any lack of success in a hypothesis a failure. If a hypothesis proved unattainable, that in itself was an answer. By process of elimination the whole group felt they would eventually come upon a solution to their dilemma. The common thread keeping the group focused was, where will we live?

Roland arrived at his home about noon. Melody was engrossed in some project on her ACS. She didn't even notice Roland enter the room.

"Hi, Honey."

"Oh, Hi," she said. "How'd your meeting go?"

"Great. Really great. Everyone was very helpful and encouraging. No one placed blame on any of us that had disappointments.

"This is sure a nice group of people here, Roland. I'm so glad we left the world of ACD."

"I joined another scientist on another project. She's Dr. Sharon DeVoy and she's working on time travel."

"Why in the world did you pick that?"

"You know me. I've always talked about living in the past. I keep remembering stories my great grandmother told me about her mother. Lives were shorter and there was illness but life was simple and you could control your own destiny.

"I don't know if I'd like that. I like people and freedom from illness." Melody closed down her ACS.

"Can you imagine the city of York with no electric vehicles, no scanners, no domes and especially no electrified walls around it? We could walk out into the wilderness any time we wanted."

"I don't know if I'd like walking in the woods with tigers or dinosaurs attacking me."

Roland laughed. "I don't think tigers were ever in York. And I don't want to go back to the time of dinosaurs."

"I just can't picture it," Melody frowned.

"Think of this," said Roland stoking his chin. "If we lived in the wilderness, we'd have to be completely self-sufficient. We'd have to somehow get water, food, heat and clothing. I'd have to secure food for us and we'd have to get rid of our waste. We'd have to grow food."

"I know I wouldn't like that idea."

"We'd have our children to help us. We'd need more children."

"The first thing," said Melody as she stood up and looked Roland in the eye, "we'd have to reverse our sterilization. And second, I'd have to give birth to them. And last, I don't want to give birth. I hear it's quite painful. I like our good old birthing lab."

"You know?" said Roland, "I never thought about us being sterile."

"Keep this in mind, I'm staying sterile. If you want additional children, you better bring along some other woman for that job. I'm not doing it."

"I don't think it's an immediate worry. I'm not sure we can even find a way to travel in time." Roland sat down to eat a piece of bread. He spread some fruit material on it.

Melody took a piece too. "I do think I like these grown foods better than cenes."

"Yeah. I'm finally getting use to them. Did you check our vitamin list to see if we our getting enough of the right ones?"

Melody answered, "Sure. It doesn't seem too complicated as long as we eat some bread things, some green leafy things, fruit, beans and corn. We're supposed to drink milk but I don't know what that is. They caution us regarding animal flesh but eating fish is recommended."

"Milk? That's what you feed a baby. That's what your breasts are for."

"Oh my God. I forgot all about that. Our children were born and raised for two years in a birthing lab so I had no reason to breast feed. That sounds weird and gross."

"That's what we'll be doing if we go back in time," said Roland smiling.

"That's why you'll be going back in time alone," Melody said without smiling.

"You know, I did see some containers at the distributing location. The carton said it contained soy milk. Maybe we should get some."

"I'll get some tomorrow. You can be the first to try it."

"I will," said Roland. "But fish? Do you remember how polluted the water was in York. I'd never eat anything out of the water."

"Roland my dear, the little streams they have here are pure enough to drink. The fish will be okay to eat. I'll get some fish too."

Roland looked wistful. "I guess if I want to go back in time, I'll have to wean myself of cenes."

"Oh, just take several kilos with you."

"I don't think you are taking me seriously. If there's a way, I want to go back."

"Roland, I'm serious too. I won't go. But I think it's a moot point. I don't think it's possible."

"You're probably right but did you know about 300 years ago scientists said breaking the speed of sound was impossible?"

"Yes, I know. I have to get back to work. See you tonight." With that, Melody went back to her ACS and logged on.

Roland was not happy the direction the conversation had gone. Melody was so happy and enthused about getting away from ACD, the Premier and all the scanning. But as far as the present, she seemed quite happy to live here - underground. Roland, on the other hand, was not happy here living, as Larry said, as moles.

"Oh, by the way," said Melody. "You got a call from Chantel. It seems two women you met in Lower California were terminated by some Sentinels for no apparent reason. They were a Lynn and Char. I didn't catch their last names. Were they two of your sex partners?"

"No. They were just two helpful friends. Too bad. I always hoped to meet them here."

JOHN PALLO

CHAPTER TWO

Roland rested his head on the back of his cushioned chair, slightly dozing. He was thinking about the first time he met Lynn and Char. The landline communicator rudely announced a call.

"Hello," said Roland.

"Hi Roland. This is Flora. I just heard the great news. We have a new project. Dr. DeVoy just called me and she's on her way over."

"Great. I'll be right there." Now there's enthusiasm he thought. Roland's mood improved greatly.

"Bye," he yelled to Melody but she never heard. He left for the train.

Roland reached the elevator just as Dr. DeVoy arrived.

"Hi," she said.

"Hello Sharon," said Roland. "I see you want to get started right away."

"You bet. I can't wait to pick your brain."

"I hope you find something of use in there."

"I know I will, Roland."

They reached the lab level and left the elevator. Flora, Saul and Ellen met them at the door.

"Hi guys," said Roland. "Here is our new leader with our new assignment. Dr. Sharon DeVoy."

"Hello, and there's no leader here. We're all on one project and all of our opinions and ideas have equal weight. Glad to meet you."

Roland pointed to each of his assistants as he spoke. "This Spanish beauty is Flora Montez, and this tall, blond drink of water is Saul Pardo and the woman half his height is Ellen Wolfe."

Sharon said, "I had met Flora once before. My assistant, Rene Hendrickson will be here tomorrow. I want to see what equipment you have here and what I have that would complement yours. You sure have a big lab here. I see why Larry suggested I work here. I just didn't have enough of an energy source in my lab. This looks great."

"Thanks," said Roland, "but a lot of credit goes to my predecessor, Dr. Guitarez, or should I say, my late predecessor."

"Yes, I knew him," said Sharon. "He was a good friend of yours, wasn't he Flora?"

"The best," said Flora, "but life goes on, albeit painfully."

Sharon said, "That's a good attitude, Flora. I was told my husband was eliminated thirty years ago by ACD which may or may not be true. He allegedly gave some assistance to some outlaws. He actually didn't but ACD didn't like his independent thinking. He spoke too vocally against the use of Sentinels."

"I'm sorry," said Roland.

"Okay," she said. "When do we have our first meeting to see where we stand?"

"Dr. DeVoy, we're joining your team. You tell us."

"Or," said Sharon, "we could say we are joining your team."

"I guess we could argue over leadership all day but seriously Sharon I think we should work with your progress so far and see what impediments you've had. After I see what you've done, it might give me some ideas. You could see if any ideas I have come to the problem from a different direction. I would like you to be the group leader, though. I have so much to learn about time travel."

"Okay, but please don't be so polite that you hesitate to state an opposing opinion."

"Great, Doctor," said Roland. "Let's begin."

The group gathered some chairs and sat in a loose semicircle. Sharon brought her notes and her ACS.

Dr. DeVoy began. "One of my problems seems to have solved by your energy source. My lab was just too small to get a large energy generator dispenser in it. I have been trying for months to solve the problem of time travel by Einstein and Rosen's wormholes. Have any of you heard of those men and their hypothesis?"

"Yes, I have," said Flora.

"I have, just vaguely," said Roland.

"So here's what it means," said Sharon, "It means going into a wormhole here in 12206 N and coming out in, let's say 12306 N in the future. To put it more succinctly, a space-time tube acts as a bridge or tube connecting distant places. In effect, traversing a wormhole would be faster than the speed of light. It would be analogous to gravity; it has no speed limit. We still don't understand gravity but its effect is instantaneous. I feel if I could get four large metal panels two or more meters square and place an extremely large electrical charge on them at the proper frequency, I could open up a wormhole to the future. The problem is I don't know where the other end of the wormhole would be. Where in time would we be? And I just don't have enough computer power. Finally, I'd have to hold the wormhole open for an undetermined amount of time."

"We have plenty of electrical and computing power. But are you trying to go to the future or in the past?" asked Flora.

"Either way, I just don't know where we'd end up." said Sharon. "It seems it would be like standing on a rotating surface and throwing something into the dark. Where would it land?"

"Sharon, we've been performing our experiments with metal plates like you mentioned in our assembly/disassembly procedures, without the desired results," said Roland.

"I see that," said Sharon.

"Wouldn't we have to have four identical metal panels somewhere else to complete the wormhole?" asked Flora.

"I don't think so," said Sharon. "I believe our panels here would be the beginning and the end of the wormhole. There would be a distance between the beginning and the end but it wouldn't seem that way. If you looked down the hole, you'd see the end off at a great distance. One step would be required to get through the hole but looking back, you'd see the beginning off at a great distance. Do you understand what I'm trying to say?"

"I guess time doesn't take up any physical space," said Saul.

"Yes, kinda like that."

"Will that be our first experiment?" asked Roland. "We'd have to reconfigure our computers."

"I think so," said Sharon, "but let me tell you of the other problems. Have any of you heard of the Granny Paradox?"

"No," said Flora. The others agreed.

"Here's how it goes. If you could go back in time and let's say, just for discussion's sake, you kill your grandmother. What would happen to you? You would have never been born. Would you suddenly disappear? Would anything you've done also disappear? Would your children disappear? See what I mean?"

Roland ran his fingers through his hair. "Wow, that's a weird thought."

"Okay that brings us to the next hypothesis; the parallel universe hypothesis."

Roland said, "Maybe I should have stayed with my disassembly work."

"Here's what the parallel universe hypothesis is. If you killed your grandmother, then you would jump to a parallel path, a path where your grandmother never gave birth to your mother who never gave birth to you and you never had children. Maybe you'd pop up somewhere else in this other path but we don't know."

Everyone was silent, deep in their thoughts.

"Picture this," continued Sharon. "Picture a tree with many branches. Let's say you cut off a branch – kill your grandmother. That branch is gone but there are many other branches to jump on to. A different branch continues to grow. We'd have to assume the tree has an infinite number of branches. You can see this conundrum would appear in any time travel whether you travel through a wormhole or the next hypothesis."

"Okay," said Roland, "What's the next hypothesis?"

"It's purely mental; a state of mind. Let's say time was created just for humankind. Let's say there is no such thing as time. Everything is in the present. There is no past or future, just here and now. Just as sure as we are sitting here, so are all the people who lived in the past and all the people who will ever live in the future. They are all here but we can't see them. We can't because they are in a different time element or dimension. Maybe our time machine will let us see over into the next time element. Maybe it would even let us physically jump over into the next time element. We could program our machine to see the happenings of 11,990 N or 1990 AD as they used to say or even the future 13,300 N."

"Dr. DeVoy," said Roland, "These are questions we'll never be able to answer until we do it, however we do it."

"That's right, Roland."

"Do you honestly think it can be done?" asked Ellen.

"I wouldn't dare say it can't. History has taught us that fact."

"I've got a question, or should I say, a thought," said Roland. "If we can assume humankind will eventually solve this problem – that's saying we don't – why hasn't anyone from the future come back to see us. Why haven't they stopped by and said 'Hello'?"

Sharon and the group chuckled. "That's a good perception, Roland. Who's to say a wormhole doesn't open up right here next to me and a human from 400 years in the future steps out and says 'Hi.' I don't know. Maybe they are going back in time but just never happened to hit 12206 N. That's one of the arguments against the feasibility of time travel. Why is there no place in recorded history where a future being dropped in and said 'Hi. Let me help you build those pyramids' or whatever."

"What are your impediments at this time?" asked Flora bringing the group back to relevancy.

Roland was surprised and intrigued by Flora's genuine interest in the time travel phenomenon. She's wholeheartedly getting into this, he thought.

"At this moment," said Sharon, "I need much more power that I have available. From what I've seen and heard, you seem to have it right here. With your power, I just might be able to open up a wormhole right here in your lab."

Roland suddenly had a frightful thought. "Sharon! You talk about power. We have been using tremendous power for our disassemble experiments. What if I was unknowingly transmitting things – people – into another time? Not just their body but their intellect or mind or soul or whatever you want to call it, too. Or what if I was shooting their body and mind through time but holding their mindless copy here? That might explain why the creature we saw here had no instinct."

"My God!" said Flora. "That's weird."

Sharon was speechless.

"What if we immediately reversed the process?" asked Roland.

"I don't know what to say," Sharon finally found her voice.

"We never tried to reverse the process," Flora said.

The six scientists sat in utter silence contemplating the last few words. No one moved. No one looked at anyone; they just looked down deep in thought.

Flora broke the silence. "My first reaction, Roland, is to quick try it on our amoeba. But we have to clearly think about what we're doing and what are the possible results? If we reversed the process we might then have a copy and the original being in our machine."

She looked at Roland. "God! We don't want to return Sogan."

Roland shook his head. "Right, but I know I can prevent that."

Sharon didn't understand Flora's statement. "What do you mean return the Premier?"

Roland answered, "I'll explain later. Sharon, we have to think of the conceivable possibilities of what we have done. We don't know if this being we returned kept its instinct or intellect. How could it live? How would it move? There are so many difficult questions. We do know the copy doesn't live long."

Ellen stood up. "We've got to try it. We've got to try something."

Sharon asked, "Is your lab still set up for disassembling?"

"Yes," said Flora.

There was so much tension and anticipation in the air, no one could sit still. They wanted to try it immediately.

"I can't believe this, Roland," said Sharon. "You're telling me you may have been sending people into another time period all along while making a copy here?"

"I don't know if I want to say that yet, but I think we may have been sending the original being somewhere. But then, was the being we saw reappearing here in our lab a true copy? We may have sent the deformed body of Sogan into the future, or past, and built a new body from scratch out of thin air. That may explain the vacuum."

"What's next?" asked Saul.

"What do you think, Sharon," said Roland. "How about we all separate until tomorrow and each of us think of different ways to test our hypothesis. I don't want to take the show out of your hands but do you have any ideas?"

"Don't worry about my show, Roland," said Sharon. "I think it would be fantastic if you were on the verge of the answer all along. Let's sleep on it – if we can – and come back tomorrow with a bunch of notions and concepts."

"Great," said Flora. "Let's go."

Everyone quickly rose and ran for the elevator. It barely held the six scientists. They almost ran out of the elevator and rushed for the first train car. The guard stood at the door clearly befuddled by the quiet excitement of the people.

Each of the scientists got off at their stop, so deep in their thought, they didn't even say goodbye to the others. Roland's stop was the last of the group, and he almost ran to his home.

JOHN PALLO

CHAPTER THREE

Roland rushed in his home grinning from ear to ear. He went to the ACS and found Melody using it. Back in York, six or seven persons could use one ACS with no problem. Down here it could handle only one at a time.

"Melody!" he said in a louder than usual voice. "I need to use the ACS. How much longer are you going to be on it?"

"I've got a lot of work to do, Roland. Why do you need it? You usually do your stuff at the lab."

"We've stumbled on a new direction on our time travel problem. I've got to come up with trial tests to do tomorrow."

Melody kept working on the ACS. "I don't know why you're still working on that ridiculous hypothesis. Nobody is going to want to go back in time anyway. It's a pure waste."

"You don't know that, Melody," said Roland. "A lot of us want to get out of the damned cave."

"I do know that I sure don't want to, Roland. Only a fool would want to go back in time, or even the future. Things are so good here. I wish you'd work on something worthwhile."

"You just don't comprehend, do you Melody?"

"I comprehend perfectly and if you don't stop this foolishness I…"

"You'll what?" asked Roland.

"Oh nothing. Listen, I'm very busy. Go get something to eat. I'll be here until late tonight."

"I need the ACS, Melody."

Melody acted like she didn't hear Roland. "Oh, and tomorrow I'm leaving early for an air cleanliness meeting. Now please leave me alone."

Roland stood there not believing his ears. Who is this woman? He didn't recognize her. Was this the same woman worried about being a chamberperson? Wasn't she worried about the duties changing her? His wife who once said she couldn't live without him was changing right before his eyes.

Roland grabbed a couple of cenes and stepped outside. The artificial sun was slowly setting in the make believe west. His earlier excitement was suddenly trampled by his wife. What's happening to her? Roland was wondering if he was wrong in wanting to get out of this cavern. Brooke was happy with his mechanical training. Risa was happy farming. Melody was happy at her air cleanliness position. Why wasn't he happy? Roland sat on a chair and tried to think who in his family was wrong. His conclusion; he was wrong. Why would anyone in their right mind want to go back to archaic times? His answer; Dr. Roland Davidson wants to go back, maybe without Melody. The thought surprised him. Melody never came to bed that night.

The morning found the lab sextet all gathered around in a loose circle. Each had some notes and their ACS in their lap.

Sharon spoke first. "We all look-bright eyed today. Who wants to go first?"

"Let's go alphabetically," said Ellen.

"Ellen Wolfe," said Roland. "That means you go last."

"I know. I'm happy with that," she said.

"Okay. That means you, Roland, are first," said Sharon.

"I guess someone has to be first," said Roland. "Okay. Here goes. I believe I can work out a way to reverse the process without making a copy. I thought about placing another amoeba in the chamber. We then disassemble it and as soon as it disappears, I reverse the process instead of rebuilding the amoeba. I know we always get a reassembled creature but I just wonder what we'd get when the process is reversed. Since it wouldn't be a copy it may act normally. It could be alive and well. The results of that experiment would determine our next move."

"Sounds good, Roland," said Sharon. "Do we try it now or wait until we hear from the others?"

"No Sharon," said Flora. "You're next. Why don't you tell us what you want to do?"

"My idea is quite simple; maybe too simple," said Sharon. "I'd like to get a precision recorder, like a Dexmon vision recorder. Now don't laugh, please."

"No one here will laugh," said Roland. "Nothing is too simple at this stage."

"All right," continued Sharon. "We get this Dexmon recorder. I don't think the next time dimension is too far away. We place the recorder in the chamber, turn it on, wait a period of time and reverse the process. Then we look at the vision recorder and hope to see something."

"I don't see anything wrong with that," said Flora. "It sounds like a safe way to look in the wormhole, if we actually have a wormhole."

"Who's next?" asked Sharon.

"I guess I am," said Rene. "My thought is even simpler than yours, Sharon. I thought we could just turn on the process and do nothing. Maybe a passing bird or bug or whatever might just be passing by in flit into our wormhole."

"Or a passing dinosaur," said Sharon.

Rene laughed, "Yes, we'd have to keep the door closed."

Ellen said, "We don't know, though, if we are looking forward or backward in time. We might see some futuristic animal."

"True. You're next, Flora," said Roland.

"I'm a little more adventurous. I say let's put a live animal in it. We could put a rope around it so we could get it back."

"I see nothing wrong with that," said Sharon.

"Let's get a large animal and put a rope on it and tie the recorder on it too," said Saul.

Roland spoke up, "Yeah, like killing two ideas at once."

Flora laughed and gave Roland a friendly shove, "A tiny little amoeba isn't going to come back and tell us anything."

"You're right, you're right," said Roland, giving Flora a gentle shove in return.

"Saul, what do you think?" asked Ellen.

"After hearing all of your thoughts, I don't think I have anything better," he said.

Roland ruffled young Saul's blond hair, "Here in this place, no idea is too simple or ridiculous. If you have any input, let's hear it."

"My idea is very much like yours, Flora. Let's put an animal in it but just keep on longer. Instead of setting the computer to start reassembling the animal immediately, let's wait a few minutes and then have the computer reverse its procedure."

"Okay, we'll do that too."

"Ellen," said Sharon. "You're on."

"Here are my thoughts," she said. "After looking at our computer programs, I think our computer is making a copy instead of reassembling the real thing. Our computer looks at the structure of the object we put in the chamber, disassembles it and then builds a copy. Where the real item goes, I don't know. Maybe it goes to another time. Since the copy isn't the real thing, it just lies there and dies. I personally believe in a soul. I think the soul went with the real being. The copy doesn't have its soul. The real item, wherever it is, took the soul with it."

"I have reservations about this soul stuff but your idea does deserve some thought," said Roland.

After a short pause, Sharon said, "Ellen, why did you want to be last? That's an amazing concept. What do you think, Roland?"

"Although I don't believe in a soul you may be on to a novel idea." said Roland standing. "That's what my formula and program does. I was just making copies of the original item. And I'll say it again, if the original item still exists, where does it go? Sharon, do you think it's truly possible I've accidentally opened up a wormhole into the future – or the past?"

"I don't see why not, Roland."

"At first I wasn't taking any of this wormhole stuff seriously, but what if...?" Roland paused, "Maybe if I reversed the process, I'd have both the copy and the original sitting in our machine. I'll have to formulate a program that doesn't make a copy but just sends the thing into the future."

"Can you do that?" asked Flora.

"I believe so."

Sharon stood up too. "Let's take a break and then decide our next step. I think the time is drawing near for some action."

Sharon pulled Roland aside and asked him, "Roland. What's this about returning the Premier? What did Flora mean?"

Roland motioned Flora to join Sharon and him. "You don't know this. I don't know how long you've been underground but the old, original Premier died and his great grandson, Lo Chang, has taken over."

"Yes," said Sharon. "I heard that."

Roland continued, "Lo Chang quite easily snuck in here. Under a threat to do harm to my daughter, the young Premier commanded I rebuild Sogan's failing, 180-year-old body into a young, handsome, 40-year-old Chinese man. He was in terrible shape; a motley mixture of mismatched transplanted arms, legs, organs; you name it. He was running out of clones and dying. He told his great grandson, Lo Chang, he wanted to live just a year longer to give him time to instruct him how to run the world. Chang believed him at first but after seeing what my hypothesis was supposed to do, he realized the old Premier wanted life eternal and Lo Chang would never ascend to the throne. The old Premier had a picture of a young Chinaman that he wanted to be made into. I told Lo Chang our process didn't work. He didn't care. He fooled the old Premier into thinking our process worked and let me change him. So, I changed him into a young man, but it was a lifeless young man. We, and Lo Chang, assumed the old Premier is dead. I hate to think the old Premier is alive in another time and place."

"My God," said Sharon.

"If he is somewhere out there in time and space, either he is in the same terrible shape he was when I transported him or he's in the shape of the handsome Chinaman. I don't know what shape he could be in."

"How did you get him into your lab?" asked Sharon.

"Chantel, Flora and I smuggled him in here."

"You mean the new Premier, his great grandson, knows our location?" asked Sharon.

Roland looked at Flora, "Yes but he was grateful for us assuring he ascended to the throne. He promised he wouldn't reveal our location for at least a year. Hence, the hurry to find out if we can travel in time. Traveling in space seems impossible for now."

"Do you trust him?"

"We have no choice."

"No, I guess not."

Roland said, "We don't know if Sogan is out there in the body of a healthy young man or a dying old man. Also, we don't even know if we'll go to the same time and place the Premier is. And, if we do happen to meet him, he may just like it where he is or he may be livid with anger. We just don't know."

"Roland, have you heard some of the underground rumors were hearing?" asked Sharon.

"What do you mean?" asked Roland.

"It seems as if there is some discontent above. The Premier, I guess the new Premier, has been relaxing some of the restrictions and ordinances. The old Sentinels want nothing to do with the new rules. They like the old harsh rules. There's talk of revolt."

Roland looked surprised. "I guess Lo Chang is trying to soften the firm hand the old Premier had. I can see the old Sentinels resisting. If Lo Chang's rule collapses I can see our safety threatened."

"That's a good reason for urgency in our endeavor," said Flora. "Gosh, I'd love to go back in time."

Roland looked surprised. "You mean you'd go back to diseases and growing food and just plain hard work?"

"In a second," said Flora.

"Even childbirth?"

"In a second," Flora repeated. "Raul - Dr. Guitarez - and I were planning to have a child. I had my sterilization reversed and he was going to also. He never lived long enough." Flora took on a somber mood, thinking about the doctor.

Roland went over to Flora and put his arm around her. "I would too. My favorite time would be about 1870 AD, just after the great Civil War in the United States. I loved reading about the people and challenges they faced then."

Sharon brought the two back to harsh reality. "Okay you two. Break's over. What do we do?"

"Let's vote," said Saul.

"Good idea," said Sharon, "Only let's do it by secret ballot. We'll write our choice."

"I can't write," said Saul.

Sharon smiled. "Write a number. You can do that, can't you Saul?"

Saul laughed, "Oh yeah. I can do some of the numbers."

"Okay, here goes. One will be Roland's plan; two, mine; three, Rene's; four, Flora's; five, Saul's; six, Ellen's."

Flora handed out a piece of paper and a writing means to each.

"Sharon," said Rene, "How do you make a two?"

"My goodness, I'll write one here on the board."

"Not that I'm going to write a two. I just wanted to know," she said.

The group silently sat contemplating their choices. After several minutes, all seemed to have made a choice.

"I hope there are no ties," said Roland.

Roland walked over to the door of the chamber. "You know what I just thought of? We've always assumed there was a tremendous amount of heat around the specimen, but not on the specimen itself. I'd like to place several thermocouples around the chamber to see what kind of heat is developed. If someone is going to eventually go somewhere in time, we have to know if they can withstand the heat."

"Good point," said Flora. "Maybe we should place more visions transmitters around the target area."

"Yes! Yes!" said Roland. "We want to see in every direction. Maybe we'll see a tunnel or wormhole. We never had a look straight into the opening. We were always looking down at our specimen."

Flora pulled Roland aside. "Roland, I hate to be the devil's advocate but I have a question."

"Go ahead," said Roland.

"If we send an animal in the chamber with a recorder attached to it, what's to prevent the computer mixing up the atoms of the recorder with the creature?"

"I've thought about that and I have a solution. Two live beings would be a problem if I was disassembling them. But I'm not disassembling anything now. I'm just transporting them – I hope."

"Oh, good," she said.

The group immediately got busy placing heat sensors and vision transmitters around the area.

Sharon said, "Let's not count our votes now. Let's go home and rest and see our results tomorrow."

"Fine with me but I got to stay here and work on my formulas," said Roland.

"Why don't you just go home and relax," said Sharon. "You can work on your formulas on your home ACS."

"No I can't. Melody's using the ACS full time. I'll just work here."

"Okay, but don't you dare do any trials without the rest of us here. We do this together."

"Sure. I promise."

"I'm staying too," said Flora. "Do you mind, Roland?"

"Fine. No problem. But first I want to try our new process on the amoeba. If I am truly just sending it forward or back in time, it shouldn't be deformed in any way. If it's a copy, it might show some defects."

"Right," said Flora. "Let's try it."

Quickly Roland and Flora tried the amoeba. After waiting several minutes, the amoeba returned in good health.

"Great," said Roland. "It went somewhere and came back okay. Tomorrow we'll hopefully see where it went."

Sharon and the other lab assistants cheered. "Okay! We're on the right track. We'll see you guys in the morning."

The group left, talking excitedly about their ideas.

CHAPTER FOUR

Roland sat at his ACS and began re-computing his program to run without the reassembly equations. Besides disassembly of an object, it seemed as if Roland was unknowingly opening up a door to the past or future. What he had to do is set up the computer to just open up a door but not disassemble the specimen. He needed to know just where the door ends up. He'd want the door to open up somewhere up above the ground.

"You seem perplexed, Roland," said Flora. "What's the problem?"

"Just this. If we open up a door to the future, it can open up right here in this cave, because the cave was built in its past. But if we open up to the past, this cave didn't exist in the past. We'd be opening up a door to solid rock. This cave wasn't built too long ago. It's only been here about ten years."

"Yes, I see what you mean."

"We've got too many variables. We have to be able to program a certain time and location."

"Do you have any ideas?" she asked.

"Yeah, but think of this. If we were accidentally going to an extremely early Earth, even before any life existed, we may have caused life to begin. We sent an amoeba, a roach, a mouse, an apple, a prairie dog and a cat. We also sent a man. Who knows what we may have done. We may have played God again. The first life on earth may have come from the future, not from some primordial soup and a lightning bolt."

"Kind of like which came first, the chicken or the egg?"

"Exactly," said Roland. "But then again, something had to come first. This going back in time stuff can get complicated. I think it's like Sharon said, I don't want to go back and kill my great grandmother. I would disappear."

"Oh, I wouldn't like that," said Flora. "I'm just getting used to you."

"Was I that difficult?"

"No, but I feel as you do; I think I would like the past better than the future."

"Melody sure doesn't like the past or future. She likes it right here."

"As Larry said, I don't like living as a mole," said Flora. "Even the Utah desert above us is better than living down here."

"I agree, but we have to think seriously about what we might be doing. We can't change history – or at least I think we can't, or I think we shouldn't. I believe a Violation of Causality comes into play. The principle holds that if you go back in time and save your grandfather from a fatal accident while he was a child, there's no problem. He may remember some young person saved his life, never realizing it was you sixty years later. You would still be born. But if you pushed him into a fatal accident, you would never have been born. What would happen to you here and now? Would you suddenly disappear? The Violation of Causality theory suggests that the wormhole through which you went to the past would close up. It would be pinched shut, preventing you from changing the past in a way that would affect the future. If somebody went back in time and showed the Egyptians how to build the pyramids—no problem. They're here. But if somebody went back and attempted to destroy the pyramids, the wormhole would close. It would prevent you from changing the future. It's only a theory. Maybe it's true and maybe not."

"Roland," said Flora looking Roland straight in the eyes, "Let's just jump in. Let's see what happens firsthand."

Roland smiled, "Don't tempt me. But I'll say this, if it proves to be the past, and if there's a way we don't mess up history…"

"You know what I was thinking Roland?"

"I've no idea," said Roland leaning back in his chair.

"We have perfect chromosomes. We were born with no chromosome damage or missing genes or extra genes. We wouldn't have to worry about ancient diseases. We'd be able to fend off viruses. We could have perfect children. Oh! I'm sorry. What am I saying?"

"I know what you mean. Until cosmic rays eventually damaged our genes, we'd be perfectly healthy. Our children would be healthy too although after time, mutations would show up."

"You know another plausible problem, Roland," said Flora.

"What's that?"

"You brought up viruses. We all currently have the same gene structure, albeit perfect."

"Yes," said Roland.

"If a virus mutated and infiltrated into our bodies, we'd all die. It'd be like a world-wide plague. Unless someone had a mutation in their genetic structure unaffected by this virus, the whole Earth would perish."

Roland looked at Flora, "I know. I've thought about that off and on. At this moment we could be on the brink of extinction."

"Maybe God knew what He was doing by giving all of us a different gene structure."

Roland nudged Flora. "Why do all of you keep bringing up this god?"

"Don't worry about it, Roland. Someday…" She picked up her notes. "Anyway, I bet childbirth wouldn't be so bad. My mother had an easy time so I should have it fairly easy too."

Roland stood up, "Damn! I wish we knew what we were doing! Can you imagine a scientist saying that?"

"I imagine a lot of scientists say that," said Flora.

"I'm getting hungry. Let's call it a day."

"Good idea," said Flora.

Roland shut down the computers. "Melody's busy with some stuff at home. Is there any place around here where someone can get some cenes or something to eat?"

"Probably the only place to get something ready to eat is a distributing station," said Flora, "or you could just come by my home. I've always got something to eat if you like grown food. I don't care for cenes at all anymore."

"Yes, if you don't mind, I think I'll take you up on the offer. But I might add, I'm a little cautious about eating foods out of the dirt."

"Oh, don't think of the foods like that. Just think of them as grown foods not from dirt but minerals converted by the leaves and our artificial sun into sugars."

"I'll try," said Roland. "I'm pretty hungry so I might just eat anything."

"Fine. Let's go. We've got to stop thinking about work for a while."

Roland and Flora rode the elevator to the entrance level. The guard wished them a good evening. Roland headed for the train stop.

"We don't need the train," said Flora. "I live only a few blocks away. We need the exercise."

"Right. I haven't got much exercise lately."

"Me either. I've put on a little too much weight. Even with perfect genes, if you eat too much, you gain weight. It's that simple."

Roland and Flora casually walked toward the housing area. For a while, both seemed to be deep in thought. Roland wasn't thinking about their upcoming time travel experiment. He was thinking about something else.

"Tell me Flora, about this giving birth thing. Weren't you sterilized at birth?"

"Yes, but I had the sterilization reversed when they removed my chip."

"You mean they can do that here, too?"

"You remember good old Dr. Wang? She does it. If you live here underground you're expected to help propagate our world wherever it may end up. You'll be expected to help populate the earth or this cave or wherever."

"That's amazing," said Roland. "And if you went back in the past, you'd have children?"

"In a second. You and Melody should think about it. If our time machine actually works – and you go back in time – you will be expected to have children."

"No, Melody won't do it." Roland mood changed. "I guess she's so happy with a meaningful job – and no chip. She flatly stated she won't go back, or forward. I don't know about my children."

"I suppose it's a moot point until we know if we can be successful," said Flora.

"I suppose," said Roland.

They reached Flora's home as the artificial sun was setting. Roland noticed Flora's home was furnished in an unusual motif. He was not familiar with the style.

"What kind of furnishings are these?" he asked.

"I'm Spanish in case you haven't noticed my big breasts and thick waist. This is Spanish décor."

"It's quite colorful," said Roland, "and I see nothing to complain about with your breasts and waist."

"Are you being polite or are you serious?"

"About your colors or breasts?"

Flora's dark complexion didn't hide a slight blush.

"My colors, you silly man."

"I like them. Melody is going to decorate our home with some simple colors and few decorations, like she did in York. Or should I say, she was going to decorate. She's gotten so involved with her job assignment her decorating has gone by the wayside."

"Keeping the air healthful is quite a problem down here. I can see where it would be time consuming," said Flora.

"Yes and I suppose my experiments were very time consuming on my part too. But her work sure has changed her. She was so worried about her appointment as chamberperson changing our relationship. Now she doesn't give it a second thought about how our life has changed.

Flora opened her cooling cabinet. "Here are the things I have to eat. If you see any grown foods in there that you want to take a chance on I'll fix them."

Roland picked up strange looking reddish item. "What's this?"

"That, my dear sir, is fish, or more correctly, salmon."

"Gee, I don't think I could eat it."

"Have you ever eaten fish?"

"No."

"Then I think you should. The way I season it, you'll love it."

Roland sat at the table. "Okay then, but if I get sick, you'll have to nurse me back to health."

After Flora baked the fish, Roland cautiously took his first bite. He was surprised. It was good. The whole meal was good. He was getting accustomed to earth grown foods even to the point of using utensils. Flora said she didn't eat animal flesh. It just didn't seem appealing, and Roland agreed.

After their meal, Roland helped clean up the dining table. They talked about their upcoming experiments and then agreed to stop talking work. Flora said she had a word game they could play on her ACS. After several rounds, Roland was ahead quite a bit.

"Are you letting me win?" he asked.

"No way. I'm too competitive for that. You're good at words but if we play enough, I'll find your weaknesses."

"My weaknesses are quite apparent. You'll find them."

"I don't think you have any. You seem like a straightforward, honest man. I like that."

"Thank you. You seem pretty straightforward too."

"Roland, maybe I shouldn't ask this, but do you have to go home tonight?" asked Flora.

"You know? I actually don't."

"Would you want to spend the night with me?" Flora asked rather shyly.

"Yes, I'd consider it a privilege."

"My gosh. I'm no privilege, but I've had no one since Raul died. I haven't met anyone I respected or admired. I respect and admire you."

"Wow, we sure heap the admirations on each other."

"I mean them, Roland."

"I do too."

"So what's on your mind?"

"I'd love to spend the night with you, Flora."

The two scientists spent a comfortable, enjoyable and intimate night together.

CHAPTER FIVE

The morning found the laboratory full of highly enthused personnel. Everyone seemed ready to start their trials.

"Hey!" said Sharon addressing Roland and Flora. "I saw you two walking to the lab as I rode by on the train. Doing some overnight experimenting?"

Roland ignored Sharon but Flora had to answer, "There was no experimenting if you please."

"Good," said Sharon. "I'm glad somebody thought about something else besides work. I couldn't sleep a bit thinking about today."

The scientists again sat down in their semicircle with Sharon at the center.

"Here are the results of our voting. The Dexmon vision recorder attached to a large animal seems to be the winner. So Flora and I will get to do our idea, unless anyone objects."

"No, it sounds like the way to go, but some of us didn't even vote for their own idea."

"I didn't like my idea," said Ellen.

"I think eventually we'll try them all," said Flora.

"Then it's settled," said Sharon.

"When do we start?" asked Saul.

"How about now?" said Roland.

"Agreed," several said in unison.

"Roland, can you program the computer to not make a copy but just open up the door for our object?" asked Sharon.

"I've already done that,"

"Great. Let's get our animal. Do we have a Dexmon vision recorder here?"

"Yes we do," said Saul.

"Do we want to tie it or tape it to our animal or just focus it on the animal?" asked Ellen.

"I think the best is to focus it on the animal. If the animal runs away into its new world, we'll lose our Dexmon."

"Here we go," said Flora.

The group nosily scurried about setting up the experiment. They took a rabbit from Ellen's menagerie and placed it in the chamber. They sedated it slightly and then focused the Dexmon on it.

"Gosh, I can't wait," said Flora animatedly.

"Relax, lady," said Roland.

"Okay, I'll try." She grabbed Roland's hand.

Sharon asked Roland, "Do you have any variables to enter that might change when or where or subjects may go?"

"Yes I do, but with no reference I don't know what variables do what. It'd be nice if when we entered, a calendar just happened to be in our view."

"I see what you mean. So we just go and do it. We should be able to tell if we're in the future or past."

"Yes, but don't forget," said Roland. "It can't be the past. The cave wasn't here in the past."

"If we see pure rock," said Flora, "we'll know it is the past."

"That's right," said Sharon.

"Roland," said Flora, "I feel strongly it will work. I want it to work."

Roland looked at Flora. He wanted it to work too but was unable - or hesitant - to express why. He unexpectedly had a strong desire to have his sterilization reversed.

"I do too," he said.

They closed the chamber door. As the usual humming began, they all watched the vision screens. This time a second vision transmitter was placed in a position to look lengthwise into the plate area. The Dexmon vision recorder could record events and also transmit what was being recorded. They had three vision screens to observe. For the first five minutes each screen displayed the expected insides of the plate areas and chamber walls. The rabbit remained sedated.

Melody had been trying to contact Roland most of the night and this morning. She and a small crew had to sneak up and out of the cavern to do an air quality test of the atmosphere. They had to do a comparison of air samples at night and during the daylight. She wanted to tell Roland she wouldn't be home. She wondered where he could have been.

She called home about noon.

Brooke answered. "Hi Mom. Where are you and Dad?"

"I don't know where your father is. I'm working with my air quality crew. We had to go up above ground for air samples. Is there any messages from your father?"

"No. Nothing here."

"Did he come home last night?"

"I don't think so."

"Where's Risa?"

"She stayed over at Roalf's"

"We've got so much to do I won't be home tonight too. Can you and Risa get something to eat at the distributing center?"

"We're fine, Mom," said Brooke. "We've got plenty to eat. Risa brought some stuff home last night before she left and we ate it. It was pretty good."

"How's your schooling coming?"

"Great. I really like being taught by a live person. It's a lot more interesting when the whole class gets into a discussion. The old ALEKC allowed very little time for group discussions. The neat part is that we get to actually put our hands on something. I got to touch things called nuts, bolts and bearings. It's amazing that a nut and a bolt can hold something together."

"Okay. Sounds like fun. I'll see you when we're finished."

"Should I try to call Dad at the lab?"

"No. The damn fool has probably jumped into the past."

"What do you mean?"

"Oh, never mind. He's so excited about ancient times. He wants to go there."

"You mean time travel?"

"Yes. It's so stupid with wars, diseases and the elements to fight. I just don't understand him."

"I kinda like it here," said Brooke.

"Me too. Talk to you later."

CHAPTER SIX

The rabbit and the Dexmon vision recorder disappeared. The group of scientists quickly turned to the screen displaying the transmissions of the Dexmon. Nothing appeared on the screen. Before the recorder disappeared, the screen displayed the rabbit and the other side of the chamber. Once it disappeared, vision display only produced a white screen. Nothing else showed up.

"Okay folks, let's don't make too much of this. I didn't think we could receive any transmissions from wherever we sent it. I just hope that we can get it back from wherever."

"I hoped we could get something visual," said Flora. "I wanted to see green trees and plants and beautiful birds."

"I think you are a dreamer," said Roland.

"I am," she said.

"Roland," said Sharon. "I think it's time to reverse our process, don't you?"

"Yes. I'll start the reversal now."

Roland entered a holographic quartz film sleeve with a new set of numbers and started the process. The new entries didn't have information to make a copy, just entries for a complete reversal.

They waited for what seemed an eternity. Finally the Dexmon recorder reappeared. It was soaking wet. Some water even ran out onto the floor. They scientists gave out a victory yell. There was, however, no rabbit.

"I'll be damned," said Flora. "Is the reversal complete Roland?"

"Yep. It's finished."

"How about inside temperature?" asked Ellen.

"Look! It's room temperature. We always thought it'd be hot in there."

Roland shouted, "Quick! Open the chamber door and get the Dexmon."

"God. I can't wait," Sharon said anxiously.

The chamber door opened easily.

"There was no vacuum problem this time. I wonder what that means?"

"I've got an idea what it means," said Roland. "But first we got to see what's in the Dexmon. It's a good thing it's waterproof."

They connected it up to a screen viewer and gathered around it. Magically a picture appeared.

"My God," said Roland. "What is that?"

"It's just dark brown. It looks like dirty water. The Dexmon was under water. Every so often you can see bubbles." Sharon was in awe. "I'm guessing we went into the future and Utah is under water."

Roland stood in disbelief. "No. Do you think so?"

"What else could it be?" said Flora.

"Yeah," said Ellen. "We know the world is getting warmer. I bet all the ice caps at the poles have melted."

Saul had to make a wisecrack. "We should have sent an inflatable boat."

"Be still, Saul."

Sharon stared at the screen. "You know what? We could have also gone to the past."

Roland groaned. "I've got to figure a way to know if we've gone into the future or past."

"We can't be going into the past or else we'd just see rock. This location, this cavern, wasn't here even ten years ago."

"Look at this," yelled Ellen. "The Dexmon is just completely drenched.

"Quick!" Sharon shouted. "Analyze the water. See if it's salt water or fresh. Look for any organisms in it. That should give us a clue."

"Right," said Roland.

Chantel walked into the melee. "What's happening folks?"

Nobody answered. They were all too busy and excited.

Roland finally noticed Chantel. "We've gone somewhere but we just don't know where or when. Our Dexmon has been under water."

"That seems simple to me," Chantel said. "This cavern was built only a few years ago so it has to be in the future. Pumps are constantly pumping water out of here or else we'd be flooded. And it would have to be dark. No light gets in here. Also it would have to be fresh water."

"He's right," said Sharon. "It can't be the past. It should be the future and pitch black with water."

Roland showed Chantel the vision screen.

"It's certainly not dark. I see light. You should have had your Dexmon pointing upward."

Flora called Roland. "It's fresh water!"

"Damn. Now what does that mean?"

"And Roland," she continued, "There are no signs of life in it. And there seems to be an extreme quantity of ash in it. It's similar to volcanic ash. The water is quite murky and just plain dirty."

"Poor rabbit," said Saul. "We drowned it."

"Saul," said Flora. "Can't you be serious?"

"We drowned several animals and the Premier," said Roland. "The amoeba may have lived."

"But what about the re-assembled creatures you had here, Roland?" asked Chantel.

"Those were copies. I thought I was rebuilding the object but I was just making copies. I'm only guessing the original beings went into the future and under water. I also believe that is why a vacuum was created in the chamber. The computer had to make the copies out of something. It grabbed the oxygen and nitrogen atoms in the chamber to make the copy. The original is out there somewhere. If we just send a being into the future and not make copies, there will be no vacuum."

"How come the water didn't come rushing into the chamber?" asked Saul.

"Saul," said Flora. "You asked the damndest questions."

"How come?" he asked again.

"I don't know," said Roland. "There's a lot here we don't know."

Sharon motioned to the group. "I think we'd better stop guessing and have a little discussion about what we did and what our next step should be."

"Good idea," said Roland. "Let's just see what we've done."

"What exactly did you change in your formulas, Roland," asked Chantel.

Roland picked up his notes. "I took the instructions for

disassembling and reassembling an object and revised them. Instead of focusing on an object, I let the computer concentrate on the area between the plates. It radiates the area with a high electric field at an extremely high frequency. I let the computer dictate what would be radiated and what the frequency would be. It constantly monitors the charge between the plates to prevent an arc. I used the vibrating string hypothesis and let the computer decide how to implement it."

Sharon interjected, "Let's don't forget the main thing. We've had a kind of success here. We've definitely gone somewhere. I believe like Chantel we've gone into the future. For some reason, this cavern area is under water. Either it has been – I forgot, it's the future - either it will be flooded or the cavern roof will fail."

"It could be the melting of the ice caps," said Ellen. "That event is supposed to be in our future."

Roland reminded Ellen, "We'd have salt water if so. And that was proved to be cyclical, Ellen. Remember, the Earth in on a 26,000 year wobble cycle. We were in a hot cycle in the early 2000's or as we say now 32,000 N. We've burned nothing for over 100 years and the carbon dioxide in the air hasn't changed one bit. As our wobble warmed the earth, the Greenhouse effect actually cooled us. It was an even tradeoff."

"And," added Sharon, "place ice cubes in a glass full of water to the brim. As the ice melts, the water will not overflow. So if the icecaps completely melted, the oceans would rise almost unnoticeably.

"Roland!" yelled Flora. "If we could see the North Star, we could tell approximately where we are in time!"

"You're right! Get me a star chart."

Saul turned on his ACS and brought up the star charts. "Here it is!"

"Read it to me," said Flora.

"Okay. We are on a 26,000 year cycle. In 2,000 BC, that's before Christ as they used to say, Thuban was our North Star. That would have been 8,200 N. Currently 12206 N, or as they used to say 2,206 AD, it is Polaris. In 17,200 N, it will be near Aldermin. In 27,200 N it will be Vega. And in 34,200 N, it will be Thuban again. That completes our cycle."

"If we can identify the North Star, we'll have an approximate idea where in time we are, at least within 5000 years. I think knowing the location of other stars we'll be able to get a more accurate date."

Roland looked at Saul's ACS. "That's easier said than done. We'll have to get above the water and look at the sky. We can identify the stars but how will we know which one is above the North Pole."

The group grew silent.

Sharon spoke up. "I remember how to use an old sextant. I can find our longitude and latitude coordinates of our cavern entrance point. If you can get me to the surface near our entrance, I can tell you what star is over the North Pole."

"Yeah, we're still under water," said Flora. "We'd have to get to the surface directly above our time machine exit. We don't even know how deep we are."

"We can't be too deep," said Ellen. "We see light and don't forget, the water is very murky."

"I think the hard part is solved. We have a calendar in the sky. All we have to do is get someone to the surface, look at the sky and bring the information back to us."

Sharon looked at Roland, "You think I'm too old to be that someone, Roland?"

"You tell me," said Roland.

"Gosh, you're blunt."

"I don't mean to be cruel, Sharon, but we need someone young and possibly foolish to do this."

"Why is everyone looking at me?" asked Saul. "I can't swim."

"Nobody is looking at you," said Flora, "but you are the most young and most foolish."

"I don't mean to insult you, Sharon," said Roland, "but you are too valuable to us. I would hope you could give me a crash course on star navigation."

"You!" yelled Flora. "No, not you. I should be the one. I was an expert swimmer. We can get some old SCUBA gear and I'll be the one."

"I happen to be a very good swimmer and SCUBA diver too," said Roland.

"Anybody else here a good swimmer?" asked Sharon.

"I'm a fair swimmer," said Chantel.

No one else raised their hand.

"There you are," said Roland. "It looks like Flora and I are the ones."

Flora looked at Chantel. Their eye contact distinctly spoke words.

"I like that combination," said Flora. "Sharon, teach us quickly how to use your sextant."

Sharon hesitated. "It's at my home. I'll bring it tomorrow. It'll take some time. It's not like operating an ACS."

"Where can we get some underwater gear, Chantel?" asked Flora.

"You won't need any old SCUBA gear," said Chantel. "We have some pretty good equipment for our guys in water pump maintenance. You can stay underwater for four to five hours with no problem. The equipment actually converts water into breathable oxygen as needed."

Sharon said, "They'll need more than five hours. We don't know if they will be up there in the daytime or nighttime. If there looking at the morning sun, they'll have to wait until dark to see the stars."

"We can arrange for up to 36 hours of oxygen."

"How about temperature?"

"It maintains body heat, too," said Chantel. "It quite light too since no air tank is needed."

"Good. Can you bring it in tomorrow?"

"Wait a minute, Roland," said Sharon. "Just how fast do you think you're going to learn to use a sextant?"

"I was designed by my parents to have a 150 IQ," said Roland.

"It takes a little more than brains," smiled Sharon. "It'll take some common sense too."

"Okay. Okay. We'll learn to use the sextant first and then plan our ascent to the surface."

"You're going to need a lot of equipment. I think you should also take four or five hundred meters of a light weight rope with some kind of anchor. That way you can locate the entrance to the tunnel on your return."

"Fine."

"You'll also need eatables, water, a timepiece – oh, and an inflatable raft of some kind."

"Gosh, we'll be taking enough for a weekend camping trip."

"And, you will need a Dexmon vision recorder. And don't forget to constantly enter your findings into the recorder."

Roland laughed. "Will there be room in the chamber for Flora and me?"

"We'll stuff you and everything in there."

"Sharon," said Roland. "I think we should test a few things first. Let's put the Dexmon in there facing upward. Then let's put a depth gauge and a temperature gauge in there. We could be too deep for Chantel's equipment. We could be crushed."

"I agree," said Flora.

"Okay. We'll do that tomorrow."

Sharon stood up and stretched. "Then it's decided. Roland and Flora are our explorers. Tomorrow is study day and test day. Then we'll decide our day of ascension."

"Sounds good to me," said Flora.

"Me too," said Roland.

"Okay with me," said Chantel again looking at Flora.

The lab people stood up too and headed for the exit. Sharon gathered her notes and Roland's and walked over to Roland. "I want to study your notes at home tonight?"

"That reminds me, I better check on things there. I'll call home."

Roland called his home on the land line phone. Brooke answered, "Hi dad. Where are you?"

"I'm at the lab. Is your mother there?"

"No. She's working. She said she'll be there all night. Will you be coming home tonight?"

"No. I'll be staying at Flora's. You kids have something to eat?"

"Yeah, Dad. We're fine."

"Okay. I'll see you later."

"Bye," said Brooke.

"So, you're staying at Flora's?" said Flora.

Roland turned to see Flora smiling.

"I'm sorry. I guess I was a little presumptuous."

"No you weren't. I was hoping I'd see you again tonight."

"Yeah, we got some planning to do."

"Roland," asked Flora in a serious tone. "Would you mind seeing Dr. Wang tonight?"

"Why?"

"To get your sterilization reversed."

"Oh."

"Roland, whether we get back or not, I'd like to think we might have a child started. It's foolish and highly improbable I know but…"

"I don't know what to say but I'm flattered. You mean Dr. Wang works this late in the day?"

"She will if I ask her. We can go to her lab now. Do you care if I call her?"

"No, I guess not. Do you think our adventure to the surface will be successful? I'm wondering if we're rushing things."

"I don't think so, Roland. I get the feeling things are going badly on top. The new Premier is having his problems. We may be visited by Sentinels soon."

"I heard that rumor too. I suppose there is a sense of urgency to find a way out of this cavern."

"My I call the doctor?"

"Sure."

Flora and Roland entered her home after the short walk from the lab.

"Make yourself comfortable while I call the doctor." She went into the back room and placed the call. After a few minutes she returned.

"She said we should come over right now. She was just leaving but she'll wait for us."

"Is she very far away?" asked Roland.

"We'll have to take the train."

Flora and Roland left the home and ran to catch an oncoming train.

"Why me?" asked Roland.

"Like I said, you're the second man I've ever admired or respected. After Raul died, I didn't think there'd be another. I have always wanted a child. I don't want to come between you and Melody, but if we don't make it…" Flora stopped. "When we do return, I'll be extremely proud to carry your child. I'd never tell anyone though."

"Flora, I'm extremely interested in returning to the past and I think you are too. If it turns out there is a way to do it, I'm going for it. I don't know why but Melody wants no part of it and I'm prepared to leave her. It'd be great to have you come too."

"You know I would, Roland," said Flora. Whether Roland would admit it or not, Flora could see he still had feelings for his wife.

"And if it is impossible, I suppose I'll have to return to Melody."

Roland seemed to become a little pensive. "I wonder what we'll find at the water's surface. Whatever it is, we'll be together."

"I know that."

Flora held Roland's hand tightly as they rode the train. She wondered how angry he'll become when he finds out she and Saul are the ones going into the water. Together they reached Dr. Wang's lab. The doctor prepared Roland for the operation. Dr. Wang had her robot ready for the procedure.

"We only have six robots left with that function," said Dr. Wang. "We don't have any repair robots left so as one of our surgery robots fail we have to discard it."

"Will this be painful?" asked Roland.

"Not at all, Roland. It'll take ten minutes."

"Okay."

"Breathe from this tube."

"I have to be sedated?"

"Just a precaution," said the Dr.

Roland took the tube and drew in a deep breath. He immediately fell into a deep sleep.

CHAPTER SEVEN

"Roland will be extremely angry," said Sharon.

"I know," said Flora. "But he's much too valuable to be the first to experiment. Do you have the programs properly entered?"

"Yes. How long will Roland be anesthetized?"

"Dr. Wang said about one more day."

"And you and Chantel feel you can handle the sextant? It was an awfully brief lesson."

"We can do it, right Chantel?"

"I'm confident, Flora."

"Here's our location," said Sharon. "We're N 37.02 and W 111.47. And here's a time piece and star chart. They're waterproof."

"Sharon, I hope you can explain to Roland why Chantel and I have to be the ones to try the time tunnel. Chantel and I lost our loved ones and if the experiment fails, we want to join our lovers. His family needs him. If we don't make it, give him this note. If we do, destroy it."

"I doubt he'll understand at first but in time he will. And I feel sure you two will return and you can tell him personally."

Chantel looked at the test results. "It looks like the water temperature is sixteen degrees Centigrade and the depth is about a hundred meters. Our diving suits will work fine."

Chantel had some doubts about the gauge readings. The dark, gritty water appeared to have infiltrated the gauge sensors. He wondered if the water would interfere with the water to oxygen generators on their diving suits.

"Now let me repeat our procedure," said Sharon. "It seems as if only one door opens at a time. You enter here at our lab. I start the process and the door to the present closes. After five minutes the door to the future – or past – opens. That, my dear Saul, is why no water rushes into our chamber."

"Oh," said Saul.

"Now, I want you two to just stay there; don't move for three minutes. After three minutes I will reverse the process and we will check on you two to see if you are okay and want to proceed. Do you think three minutes is too long?"

"No. Just right," said Flora.

"If you give me a thumbs up we'll reverse again and let you go out into the water. You can decide if you want to inflate you raft. After five minutes, I will reopen the door. If you don't get back in the chamber, I'll assume you're heading to the surface. I will reopen the door every five minutes for an hour. That way if problems arise at the surface, you can follow your tether back to the location of the chamber. You have your stun equipment in case of a large fish or shark attack. We just don't know what will be in the water with you even if it is quite contaminated. After the first hour, I will open the door every hour on the hour. The longest it should take to be in darkness should be twelve to thirteen hours at this latitude."

Chantel rechecked his diving suit. "I think you've covered everything except the unknown."

"That's a great way to put it, Chantel," said Flora. "I hope Roland understands."

"I think he will," said Sharon. "Okay, are you ready?"

"Do it."

Flora and Chantel entered the chamber and stood next to their equipment. There wasn't much room for anything else. They held hands and looked straight ahead. Sharon gave both of them a hug and closed the chamber door. She quickly scanned her notes and had Ellen recheck a few items. Saul and Rene positioned the view screen to a better location.

"Good bye, Flora," said Saul. "You know I've always been in love with you."

"Yeah, yeah," said Flora through the voice monitor. "You've always loved my big boobs."

Sharon began the process. Again sound of the humming of the large magnets and the power supply filled the lab. After the usual five minutes, the chamber was empty.

"Mark the time," said Sharon.

After another three minutes, Sharon reopened the time tunnel door. No one appeared. Neither did any of the equipment.

"My God," said Sharon. "Where are they?"

JOHN PALLO

CHAPTER EIGHT

"God damn it! God damn it! God damn it!" yelled Roland. "Whose God damn idea was it?" Roland was furious, pacing back and forth.

"It was Flora's idea from the start. She and Chantel suffered great personal losses. They were ready to be martyrs. Here's her note to you, Roland."

"I don't want to read a goddam note." Roland was so angry, he was near tears. He grabbed the note but didn't open it.

"God damn it," he said in a much quieter voice. He looked at Sharon. "How long have they been gone?"

"Twenty three hours," said Saul. "They can last thirty six hours under water but if the atmosphere is breathable they can last a lot longer."

"Great, that's just great," said Roland putting his head in his hands. "I'm going home. "You are still opening the door every hour, aren't you?"

"Yes I am. And yes, I think that would be best for you to go home, Roland," said Sharon. "I'll call you if anything happens."

Roland headed for the lab door. "I think it's already happened."

"Don't give up yet, Roland," said Sharon.

Roland waited for the train. He had a lot to think about. Did he truly want to leave Melody and the kids for the future or past? A more serious problem though was what went wrong? That was his main purpose. Had he actually stumbled onto time travel? Where are Flora and Chantel? He had to put his personal feelings aside and use his expertise to understand where they went? Did he kill them just as surely as he killed the old Premier and the prairie dog and everything else they put in his time machine? He decided they were in too much in a rush. They should have configured some kind of robot for the venture into the unknown. "That's what should have been done," he said almost out loud. "Not they! Me! I should have done it. It's my fault." The train arrived and he climbed aboard.

As it passed Risa's work site he quickly jumped and got off the train. He hoped he'd see Risa somewhere. She was nowhere in sight. Roland sat on a bench overlooking the whole plantation.

God damn it, he thought. He then laughed at himself. Why do I keep asking this god to damn something if I don't believe in him?

Okay God, he thought. If you truly exist, tell me this. Is this hypothesis not provable? Is time travel impossible? Is bending space impossible? Is it impossible to travel faster than the speed of light? What did I do to those people? Did I plain and simply kill them? Answer me that?

Risa ran up behind him and grabbed him around the neck.

"Dad," she said. "Where have you been? Mom's worried sick about you."

"Oh, I've been working on another failed experiment. I haven't solved anything since I've been here. I am completely useless and I may have killed Chantel and Flora."

"Oh Dad. I'm sure you didn't. Why don't you come home? Mom's there. She needs to see you."

"Are you sure?"

"Yeah. She's kinda down too. You guys could console each other. Things didn't go smoothly for her at the air cleanliness meeting."

"Okay. Let's get the next train."

"Good!" Risa exclaimed in the exuberance of youth. Her moods raced from peaks to valleys as fast as any healthy teenager's.

Father and daughter waited hand in hand for the next train.

"Roland!" said Melody. "Am I glad to see you."

"I'm glad to see you, too. I think I may have caused the death of two of my associates. I hear you've had a bad day too."

"Gosh yes," she said as she hugged him. "But who died?"

"Chantel and Flora. I'll explain when I understand it better."

"But you stayed at Flora's home the other night, didn't you? Is it because I didn't want to time travel with you?"

"Yes, I guess so," Roland said as he plopped himself on the couch. "She wants to go back in time and she also wants to have a child."

Melody sat beside him. "Roland, we had to go to the surface for our air comparisons charts. It was beautiful up there. I could see the blue lake and the distant mountains. It was a little hot and windy and there were little white caps on the water. But then I focused my eyes on the hills off in the distance and it was very relaxing. I just stood there until one of my assistants asked if I was okay."

"It can be quite comforting and consoling looking at the mountains."

"We then had to get back underground because it was time for a satellite to pass overhead." Melody put her head on Roland's shoulder. "I got scared, Roland."

"Of what?"

"Of getting too wrapped up in my work. I never realized the world is so beautiful on top. It's not so nice down here. Then I got scared of losing you. You were gone for almost three days."

"I got scared, too, Melody. I even thought of running off with Flora. She wants a child so bad I pictured the two of us as a modern day Adam and Eve."

"Roland, I'll go with you, backward or forward or right here in the present. I'm afraid to go through childbirth though."

"I can't tell you a thing about childbirth. I hear most of the problems of years ago were because of imperfect genes. There were miscarriages, deformations and cesarean births. These have all been eliminated but I can't tell you it's easy. I'm a man, and how would I know? We have two beautiful children so we don't need more."

"I may change my mind. We'd have to get our sterilizations reversed."

"It can be done quite easily but let's just wait and see what happens. I don't think my time travel machine works."

"Have you tried it?"

"Yes, and it may have killed Chantel and Flora."

"Oh my God. It surely wasn't intentional."

"I know. I should have planned more testing. I was careless and rushed. I was upset with you. It was quite unprofessional of me."

"Please don't say you killed them. They died doing what they like to do. They like to experiment, just as you do. They knew the risks and they accepted them."

"I know," said Roland.

"Roland, do you know what Brooke wants to do?"

"I have no idea."

"You know, up in York, we had robots to do and fix everything. They don't have repair robots down here. Brooke wants to learn how to fix things, with his hands. He wants to be able to use tools. Can you imagine how practical that would be? If our heating unit fails he could fix it. Isn't that amazing?"

"That's interesting. He'd have to procure tools and other equipment. I watched Saul fix an illumination unit in the lab. It took him only five minutes. That's faster than robots fixed things back in York."

"And you know what I've done?"

"No. Tell me."

"I've requested a transfer to the farm. Risa and I will be working together. If we go to the past or future, I'm sure we'll have to know how to grow things."

"I can't believe all I'm hearing. Melody, do you believe in a god?"

"Roland, as a scientist, isn't there a lot of things you just don't understand? Aren't there things that completely baffle you and you just can't figure out?"

"Gosh Melody, there's a million things I can't figure out."

"You're pretty smart. But if a smart man like you can't figure them out, then somebody a whole lot smarter than you must have invented them. I call that someone God. Another person might call that someone intelligent creator or great designer or whatever."

"It just such a foreign thought for me to admit I – or any scientist – can't solve every mystery in the world."

Melody smiled, "It's that old pride thing again."

"Am I that proud?"

"It's occurred to me every so often."

"Hmmm."

"If you want, why don't you tell me what happened in the lab for the last several days."

"I think I will."

Roland went through the whole scene at the lab, at least what he knew. He had been sedated for almost two days so he missed most of the preparations and the failed results. It's been thirty-six hours since Chantel and Flora had been seen. They surely are dead – almost surely.

Melody listened intently. She wasn't upset about Roland staying with Flora for now she knew the reason. She was extremely happy to have him back with her again.

"Let's look at a simple success," she said. "You did bring some water back from the future. That shows your system is working, doesn't it?"

"Yeah, I guess so."

"You know what I think, Roland?" she asked.

"What."

"I think there is no such thing as time. Everything is in the present and we just don't know it. I think time is just a spot; an instant. Everything happens right now, the past, the present and the future is just a spot. Now, this creator which I call God created time just for us mortals. He stretched this spot out to about 15 or 20 billion years just so we'd have some reference. He did this so we'd have some way to measure our achievements and failures. We can look back and see what we did well and not so well. We can look forward and say this is what we will do better and this is what we will avoid."

Roland frowned. He thought about Lynn and Char. "Someone once told me I had a very intelligent wife."

"Who was that?"

"Lynn and Char, the ones you told me that were terminated. I met them at that Genome Conference. Wow. That seems like eons ago. Anyway, that person was absolutely correct. That is a brilliant observation."

"Gosh."

"Melody, I have to go back to the lab, but I will definitely be back by dinner time. You have given me a tremendous idea. Your thought has given me a new tack. Gotta go. Love you. Oh! Please call Sharon and have her meet me at the lab."

"Sure. Good bye. What did I say?" Roland kissed Melody and rushed out the door.

"We're having spaghetti tonight."

"Great. I'll be here. What is it? Never mind."

Off he ran for the train.

CHAPTER NINE

Roland reached the lab just as Sharon was arriving.

"Sharon, believe it or not, Melody has given me a tremendous idea. Listen to this. Maybe, just maybe, we can find Chantel and Flora."

"Roland, can't you wait until we get into the lab?"

"No. Listen. What if there is no such thing as time? Everything is instantaneous. Time was created for us just to give us measuring points along the way. Melody put it perfectly. This instant, the present, is just a spot. Now, we stretch this spot, this instant out for 15 billion years. We live at different points along this stretched out string if you will. It was created by some being just for us humans. It gives us a way to measure our achievements and failures."

The elevator descended to the lab level. Saul and Ellen were already there. Rene followed behind Roland and Sharon.

"Roland's on fire with a new idea," said Sharon.

Roland continued, "If time is merely a string, then we are all on it at different positions. Sharon, you came along on the string before me, and Ellen and Saul came on after me. We are all on the same string. I believe I can position us at different points along the string. I can manipulate our placements."

"You can do that?" asked Ellen.

"Yes, I believe I can but I won't know until I try, and the first thing I'm going to do is try to locate exactly where Chantel and Flora are. God! It's so simple. And yes, I think there is a God."

Roland began feverishly working at his computer. The others gathered around him and watched as he entered computation after computation. He worked so quickly they soon lost track of his programming.

"Here it is!" he yelled. "I placed Flora and Chantel in..." Roland was still calculating, "in 12301 N! That's only 95 years from now! I did it! I did it! Thanks to my sweet wife, I did it!"

Everyone broke into laughter. Someone even cheered.

Then the mood got somber. They thought about Flora and Chantel.

"Where are Flora and Chantel?" said Roland.

"Roland, does everything point to successful time travel?" asked Saul.

"Yes, it all seems to," said Roland. "We've retrieved water unfamiliar to us so it's definitely not from the present."

"Let's put a Dexmon in the chamber attached to a robot. If we can hit the exact same time, or later, the robot should see their tether rope and the Dexmon can record the event for us. It may take a few tries but the robot should be able to grab the rope. Set the Dexmon to focus left, right and up and down. It should see their rope. Then the robot should be able to get its robotic arm to grab it and pull it into the chamber."

"Good. Let's do it," said Sharon.

"Otherwise," said Saul, "I'm going to jump in there and grab the rope myself."

"No you're not. Not yet," said Roland. "Get a simple robotic arm from distribution."

"I'll get one right now," said Rene. She rushed out of the lab to procure an arm.

"We'll have to pre-program its actions. We can't manipulate it from here."

"No problem," said Saul. "I can have the arm grab the rope and then program a rotating action. That way it will wind the rope around its arm"

"Make sure you program enough revolutions to get all the rope."

"I'll add some extra revolutions," said Saul.

Roland got thoughtful again. "What happened to Flora and Chantel?"

"I can't explain it," said Sharon. "I told them explicitly to wait in the chamber for three minutes and I'd reopen the door. I waited and reversed the machine and nothing. They were gone."

"Was all the equipment gone too?" he asked.

"Yes, everything."

"Was there water? Was the chamber wet?"

"Yes."

"Sharon. Let's think about the possibilities. We know positively we went into the future. We are almost positive our opening here is in the exact same place our opening is in the future. That's why we can't go back more than ten years because the cavern wasn't built yet. We would open up a hole into pure rock. Okay so far?"

"Yes, I follow you," she said.

"Now, we found fresh water but highly contaminated with volcanic ash. We also saw light. That should mean the oceans haven't reached Utah but the water did enter the cavern. We saw light too. That means the roof of the cavern is gone. What are the possibilities?"

The two scientists sat quietly for several minutes.

"Okay, Roland. Here's what I think. The volcanic ash must have come from some gigantic volcanic eruption. Either it was a medium sized eruption nearby or a tremendous eruption somewhere else in the world, spreading contamination everywhere. That doesn't bode well for travel to the future."

"I agree so far," said Roland.

"Now. As for the light in our cavern, that means the roof is gone. Something removed or tore off our cavern ceiling."

"True. And since the water is filled with ash, the roof was gone before the volcanic eruption. A dirty Lake Powell has drained into our cavern."

"And Roland, that means in the very near future, something is going to destroy our cavern ceiling."

"And a volcano is going to erupt after the roof is gone. Wow! What a thought."

Once again the scientists sat in silence.

"Rene's back," said Ellen breaking the silence.

Ellen entered the lab with a tall, thin woman about 40 years old. She had fair skin and long, blond hair tied in a ponytail. Her rimless glasses seemed out of place in this age of eye corrections, but it made her look very professional.

"Roland," said Rene. "This is Lea Noster. She is…ah…she is going to help us…ah…help us like Chantel did."

"Oh," said Roland. "Hi Lea. Glad to have you here. I guess Rene is trying to say you're Chantel's replacement."

"Yes, Doctor Davidson. I will attempt to replace him. He was a great man and his greatness wasn't appreciated until his wife was terminated. Then he most assuredly came to the forefront."

"Yes, he became a good friend of us all. I remember when I first met him."

"I hope I can help," Lea said. "We have your mobile robot. It doesn't have any of the advance features of our other robots but it can do short maneuvers."

"Good. We want to get started as soon as possible."

"Doctor, may I call you Roland?"

"Definitely."

"Roland I have two messages for you from above ground."

"Oh?"

"They're not good."

"I'm ready."

"First, Chang has sent a message for you. It was cleverly coded. He said some of the Sentinels are not cooperating with him. The old Sentinels have teamed up with the outlaws. They don't like Chang's rule. They don't like his method of ruling with compassion. He's afraid his rule and his life will be short. He said your location is no longer safe if they overpower his guards and torture the truth out of him."

Roland looked at Sharon.

Lea continued, "He feels they will soon take over and they know there are Reformers hiding somewhere in the Northern Americus lands. Our location will soon be exposed."

"Sharon, maybe we know what will happen."

"There's more, Roland. He would never disclose our location but as we know, they have ways to make even the strongest talk. He is prepared to die if need be but he's not sure he'll have enough time or advance notice."

"Poor man," said Sharon.

"Chang would like to join us," said Lea, "But he knows it's impossible. If we have discovered a way, we should leave the planet. He says good bye to us all."

"We've got to tell Larry," said Saul.

"He's already been informed," said Lea. "Here's the second message. Roland, I am sorry to say your parents and grandparents have been terminated."

"Damn," said Roland. "Was it a lengthy termination?"

"I don't know. It just says they were terminated."

"Christ Almighty." Roland then thought about his choice of words. "It's amazing how bad times can make you religious."

Sharon put her arm around Roland. "Do you want to go home?"

"Yeah, but please don't try Saul's robot idea until I come back tomorrow?"

"We won't," said Sharon. "I think we should all go home and relax."

"Agreed," said Ellen. "It's late."

Like attendants at a wake, the group dispersed.

CHAPTER TEN

This time Melody gave Roland a hug as he entered the house. They sat down together on the couch.

"What's a matter, Roland?" she asked.

"Mom and Dad and my grandparents have been terminated."

"Oh Roland."

"We have a replacement for Chantel and she gave me the news."

"Any idea what brought it on?"

"No, but Chang notified me too, that his reign is in jeopardy. The old Sentinels and some of the outlaws have joined forces. He also said he can't guarantee our location will be kept secret."

"Roland! That means we will have to leave here."

"The man said he wished he could join us but it's pretty much impossible."

"What do we do?"

"I don't know yet, but I do have some good news."

"Yes, tell me some good news."

"Your idea about time; it was right on target. I was able to find out exactly where I sent Flora and Chantel."

"Are they okay?"

"I doubt it. Melody, it looks like the future of this cavern is very short. With our analysis of the water and Chang's message, the cavern will be destroyed in the next fifty to one hundred years."

"That means going to the future is not an option."

"I believe so," said Roland. "At least not the immediate future."

"Then you may just get you wish. We go to the past."

"There's a problem there, too."

"Why?"

"The cavern was built about ten years ago. If we go back any farther than that, our time window looks into pure rock. There was no cavern then."

"Can't you change the location of the exit of the chamber?"

"I don't know yet. I'm working on that. If I can, we may have a window to the past and some location away from the cavern."

"I can tell you this; I and the kids will go wherever you go."

Roland held Melody a little tighter. "That's very comforting to know. If I ever find a place to go, I'll discuss it with you thoroughly. I won't take us to the old wild west of the 1800's."

Melody played with a curl in Roland's hair. "You've said we should have a better time of it since our genes are defect free. The diseases of those days shouldn't affect us too easily."

Roland said, "We will have to look at some old history books and choose a time and place. They have a building here they call a reference room. It's sorta like the library extension we had on ALEKC. I think we can get some information there."

"It seems so hard to find a perfect, peaceful place here. I guess God doesn't want us to find Heaven here on Earth."

"You and your god," said Roland. "It seems like the only time I use the name god is when I'm cursing something."

"It's a start, sweetie."

"I wonder if Flora and Chantel met this god guy."

"I'm sure they have. Now, are you ready to try some spaghetti?"

"It sounds terrible. What is it?"

"It's a long, thin bread type thing that's boiled in water. It's quite soft. There's some red tomato sauce to pour over it. It looks good."

"What's a tomato?"

"Oh Roland. Come into the eating room while I boil the water. Don't be so fussy."

"Mom use to say that."

The two walked arm in arm into the eating room.

Today was a designated rain day. Every Thursday, the sprinkler nozzles on the ceiling of the cavern were turned on to produce a shower of water. The artificial sun was dimmed somewhat to simulate a cloudy day. It was most realistic.

Sharon covered her head with her notebook as she ran from the train to the lab entrance.

The guard greeted her cheerfully on this cloudy day. "Morning Sharon. Roland, Ellen, and Rene are already here. Seems like you have big plans for the day. You people seem pretty chatty."

"We sure do. Pray we have some success today. It's been pretty dismal lately."

"I know. I liked Flora and Chantel. Maybe they'll turn up some day."

"I don't have much hope of that but who knows?"

Sharon entered the lab elevator. In the lab, Roland was already hard at work.

"Any new ideas today, Roland?" she said.

"Just one. I'm working on it now."

Saul and Lea entered the lab together.

"Roland," asked Saul. "What if we went back two weeks and told Flora and Chantel to not enter the time tunnel? Couldn't we save their lives?"

"Saul," said Roland. "That's exactly the thing I'm afraid of. We shouldn't do that. I don't know why but it is interfering with time and events. I know it sounds cruel and heartless but it just can't be done, or should I say, it shouldn't be done. Don't ask me why."

Saul looked perplexed. "I still don't see why not."

"You'll see someday. I'll try to explain it to you later, if I can. It's called violation of causality. Now, you and Lea set up your robot in the chamber – and be sure to try it out first," Roland said in a louder voice."

"I know, I know," said Saul mimicking Roland's voice.

"Sharon, I'd like your input on my idea. I'm trying to see if I can make our chamber exit at some other coordinates rather than in this cavern."

"I believe that will be our last hurdle, Roland."

"I hope so," he said. "But then comes the task of determining who will be the first to try it. We'll have to see what Saul's idea produces."

"First we have to try to get the rope. Have you left it

programmed to exit just at the other end of the chamber?"

"Yeah." Saul and Lea set up their robot outside the chamber for its test. Saul programmed it to visually search for a rope hanging vertically down from above. Then it should grab it and rotate, winding the rope around its arm. He dangled a rope in front of the robot's visual receivers.

"It's sighted the rope," Lea yelled.

"Okay, make it grab it."

The robot grabbed Saul's dangling rope. "Done."

"Now it should begin the rotation," said Lea.

"Working like a charm. Okay, take that rope off of it and let's shove it in the chamber. Close the chamber door and get the okay from Roland to execute our maneuver."

"Okay."

"Roland! Sharon! We're ready," shouted Saul. "We've tested it and it's ready."

Roland and Sharon came over to the vision screen and watched as the computer powered up. After five minutes, the robot disappeared.

"I hope the robot doesn't lose its mind," said Lea. "How long should it take to grab the rope and wind it up around its arm?"

"I programmed twenty minutes. Then I gave it five minutes to reverse itself into the chamber again."

"It should be enough."

The robot was placed in the chamber. Every one breathlessly watched their time indicators.

"Twenty minutes," shouted Saul.

They stood without breathing hoping the reversal process would work properly. On the vision screen the robot appeared. It looked completely drenched. Wrapped around its arm was the rope. A cheer rose from the group.

"Damn," said Roland. "This could be our first definite contact with the future."

As they waited to open the chamber door, they noticed a water container attached to the end of the rope.

"Roland! Look at that. It looks like an empty water container tied to the end of the rope. We didn't do that. Flora or Chantel had to have done it. They must be alive!"

As they entered the chamber, they could see the clear container had been tied to the end of the rope. Inside they saw a note.

"My God Roland! A note," yelled Ellen.

It was near bedlam as they untied the container and brought it to a desk. Ellen's hands were shaking as she opened the container. All six heads tried to read the note at once.

"Back up folks," said Roland. "Let Sharon read it."

Sharon read the note out loud. *"Sorry,"* it says. *"Water so dirty, foul. Ruined our water-to-oxygen converter almost immediately. Can't breathe. Had to inflate raft to get to surface to breathe. Couldn't wait three minutes for you. Air on surface even worse. It's raining. So foul, dim light, no wind, can't see sun. Severe choking. Flora is dying, I will soon. I see rubble on shore. Looks like cavern ceiling destroyed. Ceiling material all around on shore. Believe foul air caused by recent volcanic eruption. Hope you get this note. See no life on shore. No birds. Don't come here! The rain is burning our skin. Good bye. Glad to give my life to serve others. -Chantel Joyce."*

Sharon's eyes were wet. Roland looked away from the others. They all sat in silence, deep in their own thoughts. Ellen began quietly sobbing.

"I kept thinking there might be a chance," said Roland. "They're dead because of my impatience and carelessness."

"Roland, stop it!" Sharon said through her tears, "Don't

you dare take any of the blame. You joined my team. Time travel was my responsibility. We were all too eager. It's no one's blame. Chantel and Flora were determined to go."

"Right," said Saul. "How could we know the future would bring a volcanic eruption? How could we know the cavern would somehow be destroyed?"

"Yes, Roland," said Ellen. "Think of this. If there had been no volcano, there would have been no ash in the water; no ash in the air. Flora and Chantel would be on the surface laughing and coaxing us to join them."

"I guess you guys are right," said Roland. "We have no control over nature, now or in the future. God does that."

Sharon dried her eyes. "Let's move on. What are our choices now? They only went approximately 95 years into the future. Eventually the ash will settle. Maybe a thousand years or five thousand years the Earth will be clear again. It's happened before in Earth's history, it'll happen again."

"Sometimes I just want to be a farmer like my wife and daughter."

"Roland," said Sharon, "Remember, in 95 years or less this cavern will be destroyed. If Chantel would have seen your bones on the beach, he'd know you didn't get out of here soon enough. Think of your family."

"Yes, I've got to think of my family. Does anyone else here have a family?"

"No, Roland," said Sharon. "You're the only one."

"I want to save my children," said Roland. "And my wife. I don't care about myself."

"I believe once before we talked about how and who to save," Sharon said. "Whether we were going into the future or a distant planet, we were going to use a lottery."

"That's archaic," said Roland.

"It's the only way, Roland. We could never send five thousand people through our time machine."

The land wire communicator sounded its chime. Ellen answered it. "It's for you, Lea."

Lea went to the phone. Her face showed shock. She hung up the phone.

"Roland, Chang has been terminated. The new Premier is Morgo. I don't know him."

"I never formally met him but I saw him in China," said Roland.

"Roland," said Sharon, "Do you think he gave away our location?"

"We'll never know until it's too late," he said.

"Do you have the formulas to determine where in time you can send people?"

"Yes."

"I don't think we have time to try different periods to see if they're hospitable, though, do we Roland?" asked Sharon.

"We don't know when this place will be destroyed Sharon. It could be today or 95 years from now."

"And we can't tell the citizens or there would be pure panic," said Saul.

"Let's just go by who has lived here in the city the longest," said Roland. "The first arriving occupants here go first to whatever time period they desire. Then we go to the next and so on."

"Hell no!" said Sharon. "You just got here, Roland. If we went by that, you and your family would be last. I should go. I'm old. Let the old be last."

"No," said Rene. "You've got the brains. People like you and Roland should go first."

"I'll never leave my family behind."

"Ladies and gentlemen," said Sharon in a voice of authority. "It can only be a lottery. That's the only fair way. And we keep families together. The last one turns off the lights."

There was a reserved laughter through the group.

"If we're lucky," she said. "We'll all make it."

Roland brought up a point, "How can we have a lottery without the citizens questioning our actions?"

"I don't know," said Sharon. "I just know I'm going to be last. Roland, you said you can pick a time in the future. Did you figure out a way to change the exit location of the chamber exit too?"

"I believe so, but it's got to be tested."

"We don't have time," Sharon said emphatically.

"I know but look what happened before. I was worried about the ash in the water but kept silent."

"Pick a spot a thousand years from now and locate it on solid earth," said Sharon ignoring his argument. "Put the Dexmon on a robot and have it stick its nose out there and look around. Then bring it back. Let's quit this bickering."

"Okay," said Saul. He immediately grabbed the Dexmon and began mounting it on the robot. "It'll be ready in five minutes."

Roland shuffled slowly to his computer's terminal. "Sharon, sometimes you make decisions so easily."

"At least I'm good at something," she said.

"Yeah," he said.

Roland set up the new parameters and entered them into the computer. "Okay, I'm set but it looks like I can only locate the exit about 100 to 200 meters from our entrance. Anything farther I get an error message."

Saul motioned that he was ready. "Let's roll it into the chamber."

Saul and Ellen rolled the robot toward the chamber. "It'll go out about one meter, scan every direction and return. Total time, five minutes."

"I'm set," said Roland. "Here goes."

They all waited for what seemed an eternity. After five minutes, the robot disappeared. Roland waited for another ten minutes and reversed the machine. Once again the robot appeared. It was covered with frost.

"Crap!" said Roland.

"What does that mean?" asked Ellen.

"It's a word my kids use when things don't go well. It looks like we went into a deep freeze."

They brought the robot into the lab. It was ice coated from top to bottom.

"We don't even have to look at the recordings. They did anyway. The vision screen showed what appeared to be a dead frozen world. There was absolutely no wind. The temperature was ninety below zero Centigrade, if the thermocouple was working properly. It could have been on the surface of Mars except for the frozen moisture.

"So, we don't go forward a thousand years," said Sharon, "But we at least proved we can change our exit point. Where did you place the exit, Roland?"

"About 100 kilometers north of here."

"It looks like the best of time on Earth was in the early 1800's," said Saul. "That's where I want to go."

"I'm with you, Saul," said Roland. "Now I just have to convince my family."

"I'd like to try 30,000 years from now," said Ellen. "Maybe

the Earth will warm up again by then."

"Hurry Roland," said Sharon. "We've got to know our options."

"Is the robot thawed enough?" Roland asked Saul.

"It's ready but the vision lens has a little frost still on it. I'm cleaning it now."

"As soon as you're ready."

After a few minutes Saul said the robot and Dexmon were ready.

"Here we go."

Once again they rolled the robot and vision recorded into the chamber. Roland set the time advance for 42,206 N; thirty thousand years into the future. He was also able to locate the exit an additional 100 meters farther away. Once again the familiar hum. After five minutes the robot disappeared. They all waited patiently this time, leaning on the outer chamber wall. After ten more minutes, Roland reversed the process. The robot appeared. It looked perfectly dry; no frost or dust. They opened the chamber door and connected it to the vision screen.

"Roland," said Sharon. "It's beautiful. Look how green and lush the plant life is. And look at the lake. It's gorgeous. I wonder if it's Lake Powell?"

"Look!" shouted Ellen. "Wasn't that a bird?"

"I don't know. It was too quick."

"Back it up," said Sharon. "Go in slower motion."

Even in slow motion it was hard to be sure but it did appear to be a bird or some flying object. They were ecstatic.

"Thirty thousand years in the future is my place in time," said Ellen.

"You'd take a chance on that?" asked Saul.

"Oh yes," she said. "When I get my lottery number, I'm

going for the 30,000 mark."

"We've got to meet with Larry," said Lea.

"She's right," said Sharon. "We've got some hellish decisions for Amanda and him to make."

"Lea," said Roland. "Set up a meeting with Larry as soon as possible."

"Okay Roland." Lea went to the land line communicator.

Roland headed for the door of the lab. "I want to go home and talk to my family. Give me a call when Larry can meet with us."

"Okay Roland."

CHAPTER ELEVEN

Roland left the elevator and headed for the train. At the plantation, he got off and looked for Risa and Melody. He saw them at the far end of the field. The Thursday rain had just ended but the women were thoroughly soaked. He walked through the mud to reach them.

"Hi Dad!" yelled Risa. "What are you doing here?"

"Hello ladies. Having fun?"

"We sure are," said Melody. "What's up?"

"I think we should go home. We've got some serious decisions to make. Can we get Brooke too?"

"Yes, I can call him," said Melody. "You look so somber. What's wrong?"

"I'll tell you when we get home."

"Okay."

They women checked out with the farm supervisor and headed for the train, after a good cleaning of the mud.

"I got a hold of Brooke," said Melody. "He'll meet us at home."

Not much else was spoken on the short ride home. They noticed a lot of scurrying of people all heading to their homes.

"What's going on?" asked Melody.

"I guess the word has gotten out. I'll explain when we get home."

At home, the women cleaned up a little more and changed clothes.

Brooke rushed in, "Hi. What's happening?" His hands seemed to have some blackish material on them. "I just learned how to lubricate a wheel on a train. It's really neat. You just squirt this black stuff on the axle. And we have to memorized things, too."

"What's an axle?" asked Risa.

"Kids," said Roland. "We've got some important decisions to make."

The family sat around the eating table. "Anybody want anything to drink?" asked Melody.

"Yeah, I do," said Brooke.

"Please go clean your hands first," said Melody.

Finally everyone was seated and had their drink.

Roland began. "I hope I can trust you with some very serious information. It cannot be shared with anyone yet, although it seems to spreading already. I have to trust you won't panic. We're working on solutions now and we'll be meeting with Larry Van Steen soon."

"My God, Roland. What is it?" asked Melody.

"Is everybody in agreement?" asked Roland.

"Yeah Dad. Give it to us straight," said Brooke.

"Okay. Anytime from this instant to 95 years from now, this cavern will be destroyed. We don't have any better information than that. I will be eventually running some time events backward from 95 years to the point where I see no damage."

"Wow," said Brooke.

"What it gets down to is, where do we as a family want to go?"

"Gee," said Risa.

Roland jumped up. "I'm going to call Sharon right now and have her start trying different dates to get to the point where she sees no damage. That will tell us when the destruction starts."

The land line phone startled the family. Risa answered it.

"It's for you, Dad. It's Sharon."

Roland grabbed the phone. "Sharon, I was just going to call you."

"Roland," she said excitedly. "Let me start entering different dates from now on to see where the destruction starts. I think…"

Roland interrupted her, 'That's exactly why I was going to call you."

"Can I go ahead?"

"Do it! Then call me. I'll be here with my family."

Sharon hung up.

"That's great," Roland said. "We will then know the date of the end of our cavern."

"What do we do, Dad," asked Risa.

"We have to decide, as a family, when in the past or future do we want to go. We may even want to choose the present if Chang is alive and can regain control - and the Earth isn't destroyed. It's that simple. Where we can go is even simpler. I can only place us up to 200 meters from here. I'm working on getting the exit a little farther from our entrance."

The family sat quietly drinking their flavored soy. Each had their own thoughts.

"I can tell you this much," said Roland. "At 12300 the Earth is completely inhospitable. At 13,206 N, Earth is a frozen waste land. In 42,206 N, it is quite beautiful as far as we can tell. We did seem to see a bird but we don't know what other kind of animals exist."

Again there was complete silence.

Roland spoke, "I shouldn't rush you until we know how much time is left. There may be no rush at all. Sharon will let us know."

The land line rang again. It was Lea.

"Roland, Larry says he'll meet with us tomorrow morning. He doesn't feel anything will happen that quickly."

"I hope he's right." Roland explained to Lea what Sharon was doing.

"Great. I'll wait to hear from you."

"Good bye."

Roland turned to his family. "Any questions you want to ask?"

"What about diseases, Dad?" said Risa. "I hear in the past they had all kinds of epidemics and plagues and stuff."

"Yes, they did, but the populace at that time had imperfect genes. They had few immune defenses. We, on the other hand, have perfect genes. Our RNA transmits its information perfectly in replicating cells. If we go to the past, our bodies will be able to fight off diseases. Due to cosmic ray damage, though, our children and grandchildren will eventually have chromosome imperfections but that will be years off. Gene mutations will occur. Another problem is viruses mutate too. If they mutate into some form that we have no defense against, it could wipe us out. The odds, though, are against that happening."

"But Dad," she continued, "We're sterile. We can't have children."

"We will get that reversed."

Brooke asked, "What about the future? Tell me more about it."

"We know less about that," Roland said. "If we have time before this place is destroyed, we can examine it more carefully."

Melody looked at Roland. "What about people? Did you see any people in the future?"

"We only saw what looked like a bird. We couldn't tell even in slow motion exactly what it was."

Again a silence.

Brooke broke the silence. "Let's do a quick, non-binding vote right now."

"Brooke," said Risa, "You are so weird."

"I don't care," said Melody. "Let's vote now with the information we have."

"Sure," said Roland. "You want to go first Brooke?"

"Yeah, I vote for the future."

"Risa?"

"Yeah, me too. I vote for the future."

"Melody?"

"I'm scared of childbirth but until I know more about the future, I vote for the past."

"Okay, that leaves me," said Roland. "I vote for the past. Since I know the world will last long after my death, I would like to go back. If I go for the future, the very next day after I arrive, there could be another volcano eruption killing all life again."

"Another eruption?" asked Melody.

"Yes, we do know right after the destruction of the cavern, there was a great volcanic eruption. It seems to have killed all life on Earth including Chantel and Flora."

"Wow," said Brooke. "I'm not changing my vote."

No one wanted to change their vote.

The land line rang again. It was Sharon.

"Okay Roland," said Sharon. "Here's what I have so far. We have almost six months. At six months, everything seems to be completely flooded. It's uncanny but the time tunnel exit looks like it is still in the chamber in the lab but it seems to be halfway underwater. So, I guess if we have all left this place, the time tunnel entrance was still here. The last person to leave must have preprogrammed it to transport them wherever and just left the machine here. I'm sure it is ruined. This is so hard to comprehend, this future thinking stuff."

"I know," said Roland.

"At thirteen months the whole place seems to be flooded. There's blue water and it looks like clear air at the surface. That means the cavern roof has been destroyed sometime after six months but still no volcano. At 12300, there's tons of ash everywhere and it's not much different at 13206."

"Okay."

"I will narrow it down farther to see when the cavern was destroyed but I figured you should at least know what I have at this time."

"Thanks, Sharon. We'll at least have some information to give Larry. See you tomorrow."

"Bye."

"Okay, guys," said Roland. "We have at least five months maximum."

"Great," said Brooke. "At least we'll have time to eat."

Risa shook her head and walked away.

"Remember Risa," said Roland. "We can't say anything until Larry makes an announcement."

"I think we should leave Brooke here," she said.

"Now Risa," said Melody. "Surely you don't mean that?"

Risa went to her room. On her bed she began softly sobbing. Her dreams farming a small piece of land with Roalf at her side seemed to be in jeopardy. Risa had read about wars and violence in years past. She just wanted to raise a family. She wanted to raise earth grown food. She pictured the future Earth clean and fresh. There would be no pollution or disease. She pictured Roalf and her making love.

CHAPTER TWELVE

Friday morning found all the scientists gathered in the President's small auditorium. Larry and Amanda were seated at the front of the room. Roland and Sharon were also sitting at the front. Roland was quite ill at ease having so much attention placed upon him. Sharon, on the other hand, was cool and collected. Roland had asked her to do most of the speaking.

Besides the scientists, all the other leaders were present. The senators, councilmen and councilwomen and sergeants sat around loosely mingled with the scientists. As before, Roland was amazed at the lack of formality.

"Okay folks, let's start the meeting," said Larry. "Roland and Sharon have some information for us. You've heard a bunch of rumors by now and as usual most rumors are true. I must ask you all to be extremely discrete in whom you disseminate the information you are going to hear. I don't want to tell you to keep it secret or to lie about it. Our government here doesn't work that way. Use common sense."

He motioned to Roland. "Do you want to begin, Roland?"

"Ah, I think Sharon wants to start."

"Okay. Sharon?"

Sharon stood up and faced the audience.

"Ladies and gentlemen. We, or should I say Roland and I, have discovered his atom disassembly program cannot work the way he originally hoped. Making a copy of a being reassembles the object without life. But what it does do is transmit the being into the future - or past. We can time travel. We can go forward or back in time. It's not a fast process but it does work."

There was some spontaneous applause and cheers.

Sharon went on. "That's the end of the good news. The bad news the cavern roof will be destroyed, at the earliest, six and a half months – or to be more exact, any time after 195 days from now."

The faces of the gathering suddenly became solemn. There were no smiles now.

"Roland, do you want to explain how we did it?"

Roland slowly stood up. He nervously loosened his collar and walked to the podium.

"Ladies and gentlemen, I finally discovered a way to see the future and actually go there. Most of you know I lost Chantel Joyce and Flora Montez with a botched experiment. I sent them…"

Sharon interrupted Roland, "Pardon me Roland but I was the one who sent them. Chantel and Flora volunteered and I let them go. Roland was sedated, right Dr. Wang?"

Dr. Wang nodded. "We felt Roland was too valuable to volunteer. I sedated him for three days."

A murmur went through the audience.

"I'm sorry I interrupted, Roland. I had to correct you." Sharon sat back down.

"Okay, anyway, we lost them. We sent them forward 95

years. They found the cavern was full of murky water. It meant the pumping systems had been shut down or destroyed. Some light filtered down so they knew the roof of the cavern was gone. Lake Powell above us had flooded our underground city. The water was so contaminated it immediately fouled their breathing apparatus. They were suffocating. They pulled the inflatable raft cord and rose quickly to the surface, hoping for pure air. The air at the surface was even worse. Chantel saw our ceiling material scattered on the banks of the lake confirming his suspicion that the roof was gone, probably blasted away. He couldn't see the sky. It was nearly dark with a muddy dust mixed with rain and volcanic ash. Coincidentally, there must have been a recent cataclysmic volcano eruption spewing ash throughout the world. This must have happened soon after our cave was destroyed. The air was too polluted to breathe. Within minutes, it killed them. They barely had enough time to write a note."

Everyone's eyes were riveted on Roland. His apprehension to speak to the gathering had vanished.

"Taking more time and care, we sent a robot with a Dexmon vision recorded attached to it. Why we didn't do this earlier I don't know. I guess we were in too much of a hurry. Now, Sharon has made a quantity of robot trips and we know with some assurance when the events took place."

"I'd like to interrupt again, Roland, if I may?" said Sharon. "We had no way of knowing the cavern would be destroyed nor did we ever think a major volcano would erupt. If none of these things would have happened, Flora and Chantel would be here talking to you in person."

"I could argue that point with you, Dr. DeVoy, but that's not why we're here. We're here to discuss our alternatives."

"You're right, Roland. I'll be quiet."

"I didn't mean to chastise you, Sharon. I guess I was too emotionally connected to Chantel and Flora."

"I understand."

"Okay. Here are the choices. We have to tell the public something. So, of course, we tell them the truth. We have six and a half months for each person to decide. Do they want to go forward or back in time? How far forward or back do they want to go? Do they even want to go? They could stay here in the present but leave the cavern and take their chances with the new Premier and the volcano. We did get a message about the new premier, Morgo. To be honest, he doesn't sound too benevolent. We'll have to let each person decide. And do they want their sterilization reversed?"

"Those are valid questions, Roland," said Volley. "But what I want to know, what are the mechanics of this time travel? How long does it take and how many people at a time can go? And, most important, can you dictate where the exit of the time tunnel is?"

"That's my next point. In answer to your last question, at this time I can locate the exit no more than one hundred to two hundred meters from the chamber entrance. We won't be dumping people out into the bottom of the lake as we did to Chantel and Flora. I think I have devised a way to locate the exit a kilometer or two away from the current exit, and it just may be possible to locate the exit anywhere in the universe but that will take me quite a while to confidently say that. As to quantity, about five or six people can fit in the chamber at a time. It takes about twenty minutes turnaround time. If my calculations are correct, and our population is five thousand and twelve, it would take about 1,003 trips in the machine. If we operated twelve hours a day, it would take about twenty-eight days. That's assuming we always have a group of five that all desire the same exit and point in time. And maybe some would just decide to leave the cavern and live above ground in the present. We're not sure if the volcano was a worldwide catastrophe or just a local event. Either way, we seem to have plenty of time to make a decision."

The audience leaned back in their chairs and seemed to relax a little.

Larry spoke, "We will most likely have a lottery to decide who goes first. And we'll definitely keep families and sweethearts together."

A kind of reserved laughter passed through the group.

Someone asked, "What happened to the cavern?"

"We don't know for sure," said Roland. "The roof of the cavern seems to have been blasted off due to the rubble Chantel mentioned in his note. Judging by the robot visions, no damage appears to have occurred before the six and a half month period from the present. During that time, we see the inside of the cavern seemingly filling with clear water from Lake Powell. After 95 years or so, the water appears extremely murky. We assume that to be caused by the volcanic ash content. Granted, it's a lot of conjecture."

Amanda spoke, "Since we have a fair amount of time, I believe the lottery is the only way to go. We can instigate the lottery as soon as possible. We'll publish the contents of this meeting in our periodical. If a person or family is not ready, they can request to be moved back a number until they're ready. What do you think, Larry?"

Larry appeared to be contemplating. "Roland, what did the outside world look like before the cavern destruction?"

"I don't know. Sharon, did you have the robot look around at the surroundings at the six months' time interval? Did the world look any different?"

"It looked normal as far as I could tell in terms of plant life," she said, "but I still saw no signs of animal life. That doesn't mean anything though because there's not a lot of life running around the desert this time of day. I did note one thing, though. Lake Powell seemed to be extremely low. I assume the flooding I saw in our cavern was the lake somehow draining into it."

"Sharon," said Roland. "That means the lake was draining into the cavern even before the cavern roof was destroyed."

"Wow! I wonder what caused that?"

Larry stood up. "I think we should have our secretary, George, publish everything we've said here today. Then we should immediately construct our lottery. Every person or head of a household will then draw from the lottery. They can come here to this building to draw their number. Any other ideas?"

No one spoke.

"Roland, do you believe 30,000 from now is the best time to travel to?"

"It seems the best but I will send a robot with a Dexmon to further examine the area. I'll have it look for signs of life. I might add, though, ironically Sharon said the world seems the same 30,000 years in the past, just as lush and green as 30,000 years in the future."

"Okay, for now we'll say the 30,000 year mark is the best time in the future. We'll leave that as our tentative date. Travel to the past will be up to each individual. They can study ancient history in our library."

Everyone sat in silence. The Reformers knew their life underground would have to end someday but not like this and so quickly.

"Fortunately," said Larry, "most of us have not acquired much in the way of personal possessions. From what I've seen of the chamber, it's not big enough for a large amount of property."

"Six months may seem like a lot of time," said Sharon, "but the future and even the past assuredly harbors many unknowns. Each of us should be very careful what we choose."

George's periodical will be on everyone's doorstep Monday morning.

Monday morning was surprisingly quiet. Larry and Amanda expected in avalanche of landline phone calls. The citizens were amazingly calm and the phone conversations were extremely civil. It seems as if everyone knew the end would come some day and that day was here.

A few already stated their intention to stay in the present and move up to the Utah desert. They all felt they could move away from the area before the volcano erupted. They were all quite willing to take their chances with the new Premier.

Most, though, were anxious to get their lottery number. A majority of people wanting to go to the past asked permission to take an ancient weapon of some kind. A large store of rifles and guns were stored in a warehouse near the pumping station. Larry assured anyone wanting a weapon would be issued one. They would also be allowed a fair quantity of ammunition. Most library pictures of the populace in Old West Magazines showed the people wearing weapons. The citizens requesting travel to the future didn't seem to be concerned about weapons.

Several of the council people were assigned the task of designing a lottery. The first step was to find out how many people wanted to get a number. Since families or couples would want to go together, just one person of the unit would draw a number. To make it a fair system, they devised a completely non-electronic procedure. They printed up a quantity of numbers and placed them in envelopes. These envelopes were then placed in a rotating barrel. Roland was impressed with this highly non-technical scheme.

After a week, the resulting amount of numbers needed was 2,104. Larry was pleased with the requests since it gave them plenty of time to fulfill their task. Larry decided to wait one more week to be sure no one wanted to change their requests. The following Monday the drawing would start. The people were instructed to drop by the president's office and draw their number. The actual time travel procedures would start one month from Monday. Due to the lack of immediacy, there was no panic or even fear. Everyone was busy deciding what they would take and where they would go. The library was fairly busy as the rearward travelers searched for a time of peace. The most difficult part was the parting of friends with one going into the future and the other going to the past.

CHAPTER THIRTEEN

The Davidson family sat down for their evening meal. It was time for the family to have another meeting.

"Dad," said Risa. "I want to go where Roalf goes."

"That's no big surprise, Sweetie," said Roland. "Where does he want to go?"

"We, ah, he doesn't know yet but he definitely doesn't want to stay here. He feels sure the world is going to be destroyed somehow. He says we have to go to the future or get off of this planet."

"Oh Honey," said Melody. "The world is going crazy, I agree, but the Earth will be okay. The leadership of the new Premier may be a catastrophe but the world will survive."

"Dad, where will we be safe? Where's the best place to go? Where is everyone going?

Roland said, "I don't think even we ourselves know the best place. One thing we must keep in mind, unless I discover how to change the exit location, whether we go to the future or past we can only locate ourselves about 200 meters from the location of the time tunnel. That means we will be just north of what used to be Page, Arizona. Travel any farther will have to be by foot. We don't know if there will be trams like we have now. I doubt it."

Lake Powell is so low Larry is afraid the infrared seeking satellites will soon be able to spot the heat outline from our fusion generators. The drought and the increased leaking around the porous walls of the dam have made it almost impossible to retain water in the lake. Since the lake has so little volume, the volcano will easily pollute it. We also don't know if Chang gave away the location before he died."

"Dad, isn't the Lake Powell area all desert?" said Brooke.

"I see you've studied your geography. Yes, it is hot, dry and dusty now but from what we see, in 30,000 years it is green and lush but the same can't be said for 30,000 years ago. It is a manmade lake. I might add, though, 1,000 years from now it is a frozen waste land. If the volcano was an epic event, the whole Earth might be tainted causing an extreme drop in sunlight reaching the ground. If the volcano was only a local event, something else may have caused the temperature drop. Either way, the world is green again in 30,000 years."

Risa asked, "Have you looked at 100,000 years in the future?"

"No, we haven't. I admit it might be quite interesting. Flora did jump up to 1,000,000 years and got an error reading. She exited the program for the time being. She said we could check it out later."

"Wow," said Brooke. "One million years."

Risa wistfully looked out the window at the fading artificial sun as it set in the western sky. "Dad, can Roalf go with us if we all agree on the same point in time?"

"Yes, six can go at once," he said. "But we won't be able to take many belongings with us."

Brooke asked, "Can't we make two or three trips?"

"Theoretically yes, Brooke. The only problem is I can't be sure I can repeat the same exact time point and location repeatedly. You might get there at this instant in time and your underwear may not arrive until three or four days later – or earlier. It may even arrive one meter from your exit point or 100 meters from your exit."

"No problem for me, Dad," he said.

"Since we have a fair amount of time," Roland said, "I should be able to solve the time problem. I would like to see you in clean clothes."

"Me too," said Risa.

"Should we do another preliminary vote?"

"Roland," asked Melody. "Can't you show your Dexmon vision scenes to us? It would be nice to see a picture of the choices we have."

"That's a good idea, not just for us but for all the people. They might be more comfortable seeing their choices. I'm going to suggest it to Larry."

"Roland, won't a lot of people want to go the past to get rich? What's to keep someone from going to California before the gold rush era? They'd know there was gold and where to find it. I know gold is worthless now but back then in the 1800's people fought for it."

"That's an interesting thought," mused Roland. "The same is true for oil fields and even for scientific breakthroughs. I remember reading about the first computer discoveries and communication devices. Wow! If someone else discovered the phone instead of Mr. Bell, all history books would be incorrect."

"I think it is safer to go forward," said Melody. "Don't you?"

"I guess I just picture us in a little cabin in the northwest raising our crops. I just thought we'd blend in to the era and not do anything spectacular. It might be hard not to interfere with history."

"This is weird, Dad," said Brooke. "I know all about changing illumination devices now. I couldn't say anything about them. I think that's why I still want to go to the future."

Risa agreed. "I still vote for the future."

"I better bring up these points with Larry. We've may be opening up a great disaster."

Roland walked into Larry's office Tuesday morning.

"Good morning, Roland," he said. "What's got you so concerned?"

"Here it is," Roland said as he sat down. "It's called the grandmother paradox. Sharon and I have talked about this before. Let's say someone goes back in time. Let's say this someone has an argument with your great grandmother and kills her. What happens to you?"

"Yes, we've talked about that before."

"Here's another point. What if someone wants to go back to the gold rush days, you know, when gold was a valuable commodity? Or someone chooses to discover the computer, or chooses to buy land over an oil field. Oil used to be a very lucrative business to be in. It not so much that this person will become very rich, but what if somehow that person changed history. The resulting chain of events could be catastrophic."

"Why can't things be simple?" said Larry. "I see what you mean. Out of the approximately 2,000 inhabitants desiring to go back in time, someone is bound to cause a change in history. We've studied a lot of history. We could forecast all sorts of catastrophes."

"Exactly," said Roland.

Amanda had been sitting silently, listening to the two men. "You know what I think? I think no one will listen to these fortune tellers. Did they listen to the warnings about Pearl Harbor? Did they listen regarding the 911 attack in York, or New York as it was called then? Nobody believed Georges Lemaitre that the Big Bang, or as now believed, the Big Bounce ever happened or Columbus that he could sail to India by sailing west. They even said fusion would require more energy input then resulting output. I think our time travelers will not influence history one bit. The people of those times will just call us crackpots."

"You could be right, Amanda," said Larry, "But how are we to know? All it takes one careless mistake. And don't forget our genetic structure. Without ACD dictating our life span, we'll live 200 years or more. Don't you think that will raise eyebrows?"

"Maybe they'll just think we're aliens from outer space," said Roland.

Larry wasn't amused. "Seriously Roland, I think we may have jumped too quickly on this. We didn't think it through."

"You're right, Larry," said Roland. "I didn't mean to be flippant."

Suddenly the ground began to shake. It was a slow rolling shake. It was an earthquake.

"My God," said Larry. "Let's get out of here and check our ceiling."

The three left the office and looked up at their artificial ceiling. True to predictions it seemed to be holding firmly. There was no dust or debris falling from their blue roof. A second more powerful quake hit. It was almost impossible to stand upright without grabbing onto something. After eight seconds it quit. Still no dust or debris fell on them.

"Wow!" said Larry. "I wonder if that is it? Roland, maybe you could check on our immediate future."

"As I said, everything is still here for the next six months."

Larry breathed a sigh. "I guess I feel relieved."

After several aftershocks they retreated back into Larry's office.

"What do we do, Larry?" asked Roland.

"Roland," asked Amanda. "If I made up a vision disc of the choices, both of the future and past, could you make up a kind of show of the different time periods? Our assembly room will handle a little over a thousand people at a time. We can show the citizens their choices. They can actually see what their future holds for them."

"Yes, I can do that. It would take me a couple of days to set it up but if you get me the disc, it can be done. What do you think, Larry?"

"Fine. I'll have George put it in our next periodical. We can divide the city into quarters and have one quarter attend at a time. We can have five showings. That should get anybody that missed the four other showings."

"Sharon and I will get started on it now. We'll have it ready by Thursday morning."

"Okay. George will get the extra periodical out as soon as possible. I know a lot of people may want to change their choices but their lottery number will still be the same."

As Roland got up to leave the room, a man ran into the room.

"Larry!" he said. "The dam is collapsing. The earthquake weakened the dam. It's failing. Lake Powell is draining into our cavern and we'll soon be flooded if the pumps can't keep up."

"Damn!" said Larry. "There goes our cover. The satellites will be able to see the heat signature of our fusion generator. It won't take long for them to decipher our hiding place."

"How often does a satellite pass over us?"

"A little over two hours," said Amanda. "It may take them a while to understand what they're seeing. ACD isn't exactly looking for anything like this. I don't know how long we have. I doubt Chang gave our location away."

"We've sure had a run of bad luck lately," said Larry. "First we have little time for decisions, then we have six months, and now we may have only two hours. I better send some observers up and watch for any activity. They can tell me how fast the lake is draining."

"I'm going to the lab but I'm going to talk to my family first."

"I'm going home," said Larry.

"Me too," said Amanda. "I want to be with my family."

Larry dispatched an observer to each ventilation opening and several to the exits. He started to gather some papers but thought better of it. They all left, looking up at their artificial sky.

JOHN PALLO

CHAPTER FOURTEEN

Roland jumped off the train and trotted to his home. He found his family huddled around the eating table.

"Is the roof going to collapse?" asked Risa.

"No, it's fine. The problem is the dam. It's failing. The lake is draining and we'll soon be exposed to the heat sensors of ACD's satellites. The pumps will keep the water level from rising in here, but we've got to move fast."

"Move to where?" asked Risa.

"I don't know. Where do we want to go?"

"The future," said Risa and Brooke.

"Melody, how about you?"

"I don't care," she said. "Just some place safe."

"Do you children want your sterilization reversed?" asked Roland.

"I do," said Risa. "Roalf does too."

"Then call him and get him over here."

Risa went to the land line and called Roalf.

Melody asked, "Roland, what are we going to do?"

"I'm not sure but I'm formulating a plan for us. Sentinels

will soon be rushing in here and terminating us. Or they may just blast our cavern."

"Yes, but you said you saw it here six months in our future."

"Yeah, that's right. Maybe they just rush in here and terminate everyone but leave the cavern alone. I wish I knew."

Risa came back into the room. "Roalf's on his way over. I told him to bring any small valuables."

"I guess you have an idea what we're going to do, Risa."

"Yes I do, Dad," she said. "I'm getting my stuff ready now."

"Me too," said Brooke.

"You better do the same." Roland told Melody. "I'm going to call Dr. Wang. I hope she's there. Then I'm calling Sharon."

Roland called Dr. Wang. "Doctor, can you perform a sterilization reversal on my children now?"

"Yes. Why the hurry? Is it because of the earthquake?"

"Not exactly. I feel we are in eminent danger of being discovered by Sentinels. I want my family out of here. I don't know where we're going but we're going."

"What's causing the rush to be reversed?" she asked.

"The earthquake damaged the dam. The lake is draining and that will leave us exposed the ACD's satellites. The Sentinels will be here soon and wherever we go we want to be able to reproduce."

"I understand. The young must survive. Get here as quickly as possible. Once everyone else realizes what is happening, I can expect a big rush. I have no assistants."

Roland then called Sharon. She wasn't at home so the called the lab.

Sharon answered. "Hello."

"Sharon, this is Roland. I'm bringing my family over. I'm

taking them to 42,206 N. Can you be ready for us? We're going to Dr. Wang's first."

"I'll be ready," she said. "Larry just called. He told me what happened in the earthquake. He'll be here soon too. Amanda and her family are going with Larry. There'll be quite a rush as word gets out."

"I know and I feel very selfish. I've got to save my family."

"Don't worry about it," said Sharon. "I always said I'd be last to leave and it looks like I'll get my wish."

"I'll see you soon, Sharon."

"Bye."

As soon as Roalf arrived, they all headed for the train to Dr. Wang's office.

Dr. Wang ushered Risa into one room to a waiting robot. She put Roalf in another room.

"I was just able to get two more robots after I heard the news about the end of our cavern. I didn't think I'd be in this rush so soon."

"I see," said Roland.

"Do you or your wife want a reversal too?" she asked.

Roland looked at Melody. "I don't know."

As soon as Risa and Roalf were completed, she told Brooke to get on the table.

Melody walked into the other room and climbed on the table.

"I'm ready Doctor," she said smiling at Roland.

"Then I'm ready too, Doctor," said Roland.

"You're already reversed."

"When?"

"Remember that long sleep Flora had me put you in? I did it then."

"Oh my gosh."

"I knew you'd want to be reversed sooner or later," said Dr. Wang.

After thirty minutes, the group left Dr. Wang's office. The doctor refused Roland's offer of coming to the lab. "I've got to stay here. There will be others needed my help."

"Good bye Doctor." said Roland.

They ran for another train and headed to the lab. The train traveled a little more slowly and even hesitated every so often but they eventually made it to the lab. They jumped off the train and headed for the lab door. The guard waved the family into the lab entrance.

"Look Dad," said Brooke. "The sun is dimming."

"I know. The pumps are putting quite a strain on the generators."

Roland squeezed his family and Roalf into the small elevator.

"I haven't received any word yet of Sentinels entering the cavern," said the guard, "But if they do, I'll hold them off as long as I can."

"Thanks," said Roland.

Unseen by the guard and Roland, twenty or thirty Sentinels had already entered the cavern by means of the air vents. Many more were entering through the entrances.

Roland and his family packed themselves into the elevator and descended down to the lab. Sharon was waiting for them. As they walked toward the time tunnel, they heard loud explosions. They knew these rumbles were not additional earthquakes. These were destruction bombs. Roland knew the cavern wouldn't be destroyed yet. According to the pictures he had of the future, it had to happen in six months. The explosions just didn't make sense.

"Quick, gather your things and get in the chamber," said Sharon.

Roland and his family along with Roalf entered the chamber. They didn't have time to get many personal items. They all fit comfortably in the time tunnel. Roland wished he had time to gather his papers and vision disks of his work.

Sharon yelled in, "Okay, where to?"

Roland looked at the group huddled together.

"Future, Dad," said Risa.

"How about you, Melody?"

"I think the future is the best, don't you?"

"I suppose I'm outnumbered," he said. "Okay, Sharon. Give us the year 42,206 N. That's 30,000 years from now."

Sharon closed the door of the chamber. Roland leaned back and held Melody. The children all held hands. As the door closed, it became pitch black. There was no light in the tunnel.

"Will it hurt, Dad?" asked Brooke.

"I don't think so but I don't know for sure."

"I'm scared, Roland," said Melody.

"Me too."

They could feel the vibration and humming of the generating equipment. Gradually the humming stopped. Now they heard nothing and could see nothing.

"Shouldn't we see something?" asked Melody.

"I don't know," said Roland. "It's too dark to see anything. I'm afraid to step out and feel for the chamber door. I don't want to be separated from you if the system would suddenly transport. I'd be left behind."

The door to the chamber opened. Two Sentinels with weapons were standing at the entrance.

"Why are you hiding in here?" asked the older Sentinel.

Roland saw Sharon being held by a Sentinel. They hadn't gone anywhere. Apparently the Sentinels stopped the process before they had left the present. They were still in the lab. It was still 12206 N.

"I'm sorry Roland," said Sharon. "They got to me before I could start."

Melody and Risa began sobbing. They were all captives of the new Premier, Morgo.

"What happened?" asked Roalf.

"We didn't make it," said Roland

"What is this thing?" asked one of the younger Sentinels.

"It's a machine to clean your clothing," Roland said sarcastically.

"Why are you still wearing your clothing while it's being cleaned?"

"That's the advantage," Roland said hiding a smile. "You don't have to take your clothes off to be cleaned."

"Oh," said the Sentinel.

"For some reason, our great Premier wants to see it. He'll be here in three days. In the meanwhile you are all free to move about your cave until he arrives. The exits, however, are blocked."

The younger Sentinel asked the elder, "Why would our Premier want to see a clothes cleaning machine?"

"I don't know but we just follow orders."

Another Sentinel saw Sharon's half eaten plate of salad. "I don't understand how you people can eat things grown out of dirt. It's not healthy."

Five Sentinels made themselves comfortable in the lab.

"We'll stay here until the Premier, Morgo, arrives. You may all relax but don't touch any equipment."

Another Sentinel kept running a scanner over the occupants of the lab.

"There's no signal," he said. "I don't understand. If any of our robots were here, these people would all be terminated."

"I don't understand either," answered another Sentinel. "This is a strange place. Why would anybody want to live underground?"

"Can we go to our homes?" asked Roland.

"Yes, but we'll stay here," said a young Sentinel. "I'm sure when the Premier arrives, he'll want you to return and explain this clothing machine."

"We'll come back," said Roland.

As Roland headed for the lab door, the land line phone rang.

It was Larry. "Roland, are they there?"

"Yeah, we'll have to return here when the Premier gets here in three days."

"I don't know if the pumps can keep up for three days. What's the Premier want?"

"I don't know but I bet he thinks we're still set up for disassemble and reassembly instead of time travel."

Roland then spoke in a more guarded, quiet voice. "I facetiously told the Sentinels this is a clothes cleaning machine. They believed me."

"I think our time on earth is limited, Roland."

"I heard a lot of explosions. Is there a lot of damage?"

"No," answered Larry. "I think they were just trying to impress us with their weapon power."

"We're going to our home. Melody and the kids are quite depressed. We almost made it."

Larry said, "We all would have made it if that damned earthquake hadn't exposed us."

"We'll just have to think of something else. I'll talk to you later."

Roland and his family left the lab and headed for the train stop.

Sharon caught up with the family at the stop. "Roland, do you mind if I go home with you? I have no reason to go to my home."

"Sure. How about Ellen and Saul?"

"I'll go back to the lab and call them. I'll have them meet us at your home."

"Fine. We'll meet you there."

As a train car approached, Roland saw some minor damage on the front of it. It still seemed to operate properly.

The Davidson family was in a quite somber mood upon entering their home. Risa and Roalf cuddled on a coach. Melody still sobbed quietly.

Roland tried to think of something to console his wife. "We'll figure something out."

"We can't, Roland. We'll all be terminated. I just know it."

"Let's don't give up yet. They haven't terminated anybody yet."

The visitor chime rang. It was Sharon and the lab crew.

"Come on in folks," said Roland.

A somber silence permeated the home. For three days, no one left the home. And for three days the water level in the cavern crept up ever so slowly.

CHAPTER FIFTEEN

A loud thumping on the door woke Roland from a deep sleep. Melody awoke too.

"What is it?" she asked.

"I'll go see." His time piece denoted the time at 8:00 GMT. "Who can it be this early in the morning? Morgo must have arrived."

At the front door, Roland saw several Sentinels. Roland opened the door.

"Yes?" he asked.

"The Premier is here now," said a Sentinel. "Come with us."

"Doesn't Morgo sleep?" protested Roland.

The Sentinels didn't seem to understand. "Come with us now!"

"Let me get dressed."

"You knew the Premier was coming," shouted a Sentinel. "Why weren't you dressed? Hurry!"

"I'll be there."

Roland grabbed some clothes. Sharon was sleeping in a back room.

"Sharon," said Roland. "The Premier is here. I have to go now. You better come with me."

It took Sharon a second or two to comprehend. Once awake, she jumped up and quickly got dressed.

"I'm ready. Let's go," she said.

"I have to go," Roland yelled to Melody. "I'll call you later."

Roland, Sharon and several Sentinels boarded a train and headed for the lab. The Sentinels were fascinated with the train. To them it seemed so antiquated. One of the axles squealed nosily. Roland thought of Brooke and how proud he was knowing how to lubricate an axle. Finally they reached the lab. Roland noticed the lab guard was no longer standing at his post. They entered the elevator.

As they left the elevator in the lab, Roland saw Morgo and several attendants. The attendants were not armed as were the Sentinels. The last time Roland saw Morgo was in China. He was the man handing Roland the picture of the man the old Premier wanted to be.

"Hello," Morgo said in perfect English. "What's this nonsense about this being a machine to clean clothes?"

"I was teasing your Sentinels," answered Roland.

"They can be quite simple. I know exactly what it does. The Premier repeatedly explained it in great detail to me. It's too bad his heart failed or he'd be here today leading us to greater glories."

"What happened to Chang?" asked Roland.

"He was too soft. He didn't know how to rule. I had to discharge him and rule the way the old Premier did."

"Has Chang been terminated?"

"No. He's in hiding somewhere. I don't care. I'll worry about Chang at a later time. He's powerless and of no concern to me."

"Can't your scanners or satellites locate him?"

The Premier laughed. "Scanners? Satellites? Hah! But what I need is your machine to put me in perfect health."

Roland wasn't sure what Morgo meant by that. Since the lab was at a lower level than the floor of the cavern, Roland looked for signs of water. There were none.

"What do you want of me, may I ask? You seem to be in perfect health."

Morgo turned to the Sentinels. "You will leave us now."

Immediately the Sentinels left the lab but the four attendants stayed.

He turned to Sharon. "You must leave, too, woman."

"She's my assistant," said Roland. "I need her."

"She must leave," Morgo said adamantly.

Sharon looked at Roland.

"You should leave, Sharon," said Roland. "I'll call you if I need you."

"I repeat, you won't need her," said Morgo.

Roland, Morgo and his attendants were now alone. Once again one of the attendants was a woman. Roland mused as to why he too seemed to distrust Sharon, just as Sogan did.

Morgo looked at Roland. "You say I look healthy. In truth, I am not. I know what your machine can do. I heard the old Premier tell me many times. It can rebuild me to be in perfect health. If you rebuild me, I'll allow you to live wherever you desire. If you do not, I will order you and your family to receive a slow and painful termination."

"What is wrong with you?" asked Roland.

"My medical technicians tell me I have an immune deficiency problem. A careless wench most assuredly caused me to have this illness. She is in the fourth day of a painful termination."

A thousand ideas raced through Roland's mind. Could this be a chance to rid the world of Morgo? Would another even more ruthless ruler take his place? Most assuredly Morgo would want to see a test. How could he accomplish a successful test?

"Don't you have perfect genes?" asked Roland.

"We were not quite as advanced as your country when I was born. Even now my doctors are not able to correct my immune system. They have given me six to seven months to live. You must rebuild me before I begin showing signs of weakness. There are several waiting to take my place if I die."

"You know the old Premier died even after I rebuilt him."

"Yes, he waited too long," said Morgo. "I will not make that mistake. Your family's lives are at stake Doctor."

"I am fully aware of that," said Roland. "But it will take me several days to reprogram the computer for rebuilding a human being."

"Then begin now."

"It will be much faster if you allow me to have my woman assistant."

Morgo seemed to be considering Roland's request. "If word of my illness reaches anyone before I am healed, your family will be severely punished."

"I know that. My assistant is most trustworthy."

"Then call her. I will be waiting your call above ground. Do you know your cave is filling with water? I don't understand how you can live underground like worms."

"It was the only way to escape ACD," said Roland.

"ACD?" said Morgo. "You haven't heard?"

"No. What?"

"A rogue band of renegades, or outlaws as you call them, sent an unmanned missile to the Moon. It destroyed ACD. It was pure chance that it hit ACD. All scanners are inoperative."

"I didn't know."

"I like it better anyway," smiled Morgo. "Now I am in complete control. I didn't like having a machine control me. The outlaws saved me the necessity of having to destroy ACD."

"Are humans still being chipped?"

"No. I don't care if they are chipped or not as long as they know I am their ruler. I have armed all my Sentinels, at least those I can trust."

Morgo headed for the door of the lab. "Enough talk! Do as I tell you. I will expect your call soon. Call me on this communicator." Morgo handed Roland a small wireless device.

Roland ascended the elevator with Morgo. Waiting at the entrance was Sharon. The Premier ignored her completely and gave some orders to his Sentinels. They then positioned themselves around the entrance to the elevator. Roland was glad they were not going to be down in the lab. Sharon and he had some serious problems to discuss.

"Let's go back down to the lab, Sharon. We've got some work to do."

"Okay," said Sharon. Together they descended back down to the lab.

Once inside the lab, Roland explained their predicament. "Sharon, my family's life depends on secrecy."

"You can count on me, Roland, but you know we can't rebuild Morgo. What are we going to do?"

"I don't know for sure but I've got a lot of ideas. I found

out Chang is still alive somewhere and ACD has been destroyed."

"No more scanning?"

"Yes. I'm glad we've had our chips removed anyway."

"Okay. Let's make a plan."

Roland sat at his desk. "Morgo has given me about three days to reconfigure the computer. It will only take me three minutes to do it but I wanted to buy us some time."

"Let's send the beast to the same death as Flora and Chantel."

"I've thought of that but I don't know how his attendants and Sentinels will react."

"From what you've told me, it seems as if Chang might be a better ruler."

"I believe so. He kept his promise. He never disclosed our location. The earthquake did that."

"That reminds me," said Sharon. "Larry told me to tell you the pumps are having a hard time keeping the water out of the cavern. The river is flowing in as fast as the pumps take it out. There's no margin for pump failure. And since we are lower than the floor level, we will be flooded first."

"What else can go wrong? Also, I'm sure Morgo will want a test of some kind. How can we pull that off?"

"That's easy," said Sharon. "Since it only takes minutes to reprogram from time travel to disassembly mode, we can test whatever Morgo wants us to test. We'll just send the item, or being, one second to the future. We'll tell him it was disassembled and reassembled. He'll never know the thing was never disassembled. We'll then show him the copy."

"Right. Then we can send Morgo to somewhere in the future. But then there is still the same problem, what do we tell the attendants and Sentinels when they see the copy dying?"

Sharon thought a moment. "If we could only feel them out as to their feeling towards the Premier..."

"The Sentinels don't seem to have the ability of having an original thought, but the attendants seem capable of thinking on their own. They are so close to the Premier. I'm sure they have seen his ruthlessness."

"Did the attendants seem to have a leader?"

"Yes, a short woman seemed to be calling the shots. She even told a Sentinel what to do. I never heard her name."

"There must be a way to sound out their feelings toward the Premier," said Sharon. "Where are they now?"

"They went up and out of the cavern. Morgo doesn't like being underground."

"Could you go up under some pretense of checking him or something? Take this wave meter and act like you're testing his atoms. He won't know the difference. If you can talk to an attendant, they might give you a hint of their feelings."

"It might work. He gave me a personal communicator. I guess I should see if it works."

As Roland was preparing to call Morgo, the land line phone rang. It was Larry.

"Roland," he said, "Did Sharon tell you about the pumps?"

"Yes, how are they holding up?"

"Okay so far. But now I've got a new problem to tell you. The Sentinels are implanting explosive devices all around the roof of the cavern. They tell me they have orders to destroy the cave as soon as Morgo leaves."

"We wondered how the future picture of the cavern's destruction was going to develop. Now we know. But it is still supposed to be in six months from now."

"What does Morgo want of you?"

417

"I can't tell you, Larry," said Roland. "He's holding my family's lives over me. Just trust me. Sharon and I are working on a plan. Pray that it works."

"You don't believe in God. To whom should I pray?"

Roland emitted a slightly forced laugh. "Larry, my firm belief in not believing is starting to whither. It would be nice to have someone or some being to lean on."

"How soon will we know what's going on?"

"Three days at the most."

"Good luck."

"Thanks."

Roland now called Morgo.

A voice answered, "Yes?" It wasn't Morgo's voice.

"I'm calling Morgo."

"Is this the doctor?"

"Yes."

There was a short silence.

Morgo spoke, "Are you ready now?"

"No, I just wanted to confirm some readings and perform some tests on you."

"That's not true," Morgo said. "You're just delaying my operation. Don't you know I have the ability to ascertain when a human is lying?"

Roland was fairly certain the Premier was bluffing. "I have many parameters and calculations to make concerning your body."

Roland heard Morgo talking to someone. The discussion was fairly spirited.

Morgo then spoke, "You must not be aware one of my attendants was present when you rebuilt the old Premier. What if I ask her what the procedure was at that time?"

My God, thought Roland. I did notice a woman attendant here at that time.

"Then ask her," said Roland feigning confidence.

Again there was a discussion.

"She says you are lying. There was no test on the Premier. You only performed your test examples on an apple and his cat. What do you say now?"

Roland began to sweat. Has his bluff put his family in danger? Should he continue his game or admit to a lie? He only had one option. If he admits to a lie, his family will surely suffer. His only chance is to continue.

"Morgo, I need to perform these tests. I respectfully submit to you your attendant may have forgotten the complete procedure."

"Hah! I was testing you," said Morgo. "My attendant said she was not able to see the whole process. I will send some Sentinels to bring you up to me."

Roland hoped Morgo didn't hear his sigh of relief. So far, so good.

After about twenty minutes, a cambri met Roland at the lab exit. They drove down the sidewalk, driving over shrubs and plants people had planted. They then drove to an exit and up to the entrance to the cavern. The entrance was clearly exposed now as there was no need to hide anything anymore. Roland saw a large entourage of cambris and cargo cambris stationed around the cavern entrance. They stopped at a large, highly decorated cargo cambri. Roland was ushered inside and directed to Morgo. The cambri had a cooling system preventing the desert heat from entering.

Roland felt a little foolish holding a simple wave meter. He had to pretend he was doing something scientific. Hopefully no one knew what a wave meter was. As he moved the meter over Morgo's body, Roland tried to see the attendants. One was definitely a woman.

"Were you one of the attendants for the old Premier when he was here?" Roland said to the woman. She made no answer.

"I admired Chang," Roland continued hoping to get a response from her.

"Why do you admire a weakling like Chang?" roared Morgo. "He was weak and soft."

"I meant the way he tried to save his father and grandfather. He showed great respect for his elders." Roland hoped he hadn't angered the Premier.

"It's in all Asians to respect their elders. Unfortunately his father and grandfather taught only sympathy and compassion to Chang; useless emotions. Old Sogan knew how to rule. Ruling must be consummated without any showing of weakness."

Again hoping to get some response, Roland cautiously persisted, "He went through great pains to bring the dying Premier to our cavern. The outlaws would have surely attempted to kill him had they known he was here."

"Hurry up," shouted Morgo. "You're wasting my time. Get on with your tests and call me."

Roland felt as if he was losing any chance to talk to the woman attendant. Finally he could stall no more. He had to cease running the fake tool over Morgo's body.

Morgo uttered, "I think when I return to China I will seek Chang and have him slowly terminated. He may rise up again and challenge me. It is a sure sign of weakness to let an enemy live."

Roland was sure he saw the woman attendant momentarily freeze. Then she continued her movement.

"Take him back to his lab," Morgo yelled to some Sentinels. Then he went to the rear of the cargo cambri. "Bring me some liquid refreshment."

As Roland walked to the cambri, the woman attendant called out to one of the Sentinels, "Have the doctor show me his instrument readings. I want to see for myself."

Now it was Roland's turn to freeze. He had nothing to show her. The meter indicator would display nothing. A Sentinel brought Roland to the attendant.

The woman roughly grabbed the meter and spoke loudly, "Show me your results." Then in a soft voice she said, "Can you cure Morgo?"

Roland hoped this was not another test, "I cannot be sure I will be successful in rebuilding Morgo."

"Can you assure me that the rebuild will not be successful?" she asked.

This was the moment of truth. If he told her the rebuild would definitely send Morgo somewhere in time or even kill the Premier, would she be overjoyed or angry? If the attendant told Morgo the truth, then he would be eliminated. Roland would have to make a decision. He would have to kill his family to prevent Morgo from sending them to a long and painful death. Roland decided to believe she wanted Morgo dead.

Roland's decision was confirmed when she said, "The wench that Morgo is slowly terminating is my daughter. He doesn't know it."

Morgo screamed, "Raya, come here!"

"He will die," Roland said.

"I want him to die slowly and painfully."

Raya left him quickly and went into the cargo cambri. She turned and gave him a hint of a smile.

Now Roland knew her name. It is Raya. He was overjoyed. If he can get rid of Morgo, Raya may be able to help Chang return to power.

CHAPTER SIXTEEN

After three days of constant harassment by Morgo, Roland was prepared to call him. It seemed as if Morgo called every hour to check on Roland. Finally it was time.

Sharon and Roland rehearsed their scheme. Roland would call the Premier to the lab. They were sure Morgo would want to see some kind of test. They'd use a rabbit first. They would send the rabbit one second into the future and immediately return it. They would tell the Premier it was disassembled and reassembled. Surely he'd want to send a human next. They would do the same. The human would be sent one second into the future and returned. The plan seemed foolproof.

Once again the voice answered the communicator. "Yes?" It wasn't the voice of Raya.

"Tell Morgo I am ready," said Roland.

"Good," said the voice. "We will be there in thirty minutes.

Roland and Sharon waited nervously for the Premier's entourage. Finally they heard the elevator descending to the lab. Morgo, four attendants and three Sentinels proceeded to walk from the elevator. Raya was in the lead.

"I said no woman should be here!" shouted Morgo to Sharon.

"But your Excellency," said Roland, "I assumed since your female attendant would be here, surely my female assistant could be here."

'She is only here to accompany me on my journey. She will go with me. We will both go into your machine and be rebuilt."

Roland was near panic. This was the unexpected Roland and Sharon feared.

"But Morgo," said Roland in the calmest voice he could muster, "I haven't had time to analyze her as I did you. I don't have her genetic code mapped into the computer. She would end up either dead or a grotesque creature. There may even be confusion. The computer may mix your code with your attendant's. The computer wouldn't know how to separate the information."

Morgo seemed to be weighing Roland's words. "Do you think I'd be foolish enough to let you put me in your machine alone?"

"Morgo, let me do a demonstration on one of your attendants after I gather their genetic code. Then I can give the computer their genetic code. It would take another three days to enter your attendant's code." Roland was hoping for a miracle. A miracle, he thought. Okay God. Once again, if you're there, help me.

Raya spoke, "Your Excellency, I saw the Premier's new body. He was most handsome and strong. We carried him out of the room. His skin was most smooth and warm. We were so close to success had his heart not failed."

"You did not wait three days to rebuild the Premier," Morgo said. "Why not?"

"We were building an entirely new being," said Roland. "Chang gave me a picture of the desired result the Premier wanted. In three days I conjured up a being to look like the picture. I made up a genetic code to match the picture."

Roland hoped his nervousness wasn't too apparent. But it was.

"Why are you so nervous?" asked Morgo.

"I am always nervous when performing my operation on persons of your importance. I was very nervous working with the old Premier. I can't help it."

"This is true, your Excellency," said Raya.

Morgo kept coming up with more questions, "I was told you performed a test on the Premier's cat. You didn't wait three days for that, did you?"

Roland had no quick answer but Sharon spoke up. "Your Excellency, we had already performed the rebuilding process on a cat of our own. We already had a genetic code of a cat. The cat didn't actually turn out to be the exact same color but the Premier didn't notice. The cat remained in the chamber under sedation."

Again Morgo stood in silence. Then he spoke, "I will wait your three days. Then I will watch as you demonstrate." Morgo paused, "You will demonstrate on your assistant. I believe you call her Sharon."

Oh my God, thought Roland. Won't he ever give up?

"That is fine with me," said Sharon immediately. "We don't need three days. Roland already has my genetic code entered. We can proceed immediately."

Roland wondered how long the charade could be continued. He looked at Sharon. He couldn't say a word without displaying doubt.

"Let's do it," said Sharon. "While you're at it, make me a young blond, about twenty years old." Then, as if having second thoughts, she said, "No, you'd have to enter new parameters and that would take two or three days. No, just rebuild me as is."

Roland brushed by Sharon and squeezed her hand.

Without further conversation, Sharon entered the chamber. Morgo watched intently.

"You can watch on the vision screen," said Roland. "She will disappear and then reappear."

"How do I know it isn't trickery?" asked Morgo.

"Raya," asked Roland. "Would you go into the chamber so Morgo can see you next to Sharon on the vision screen?"

Morgo shouted, "You don't give orders to my attendants!"

Then Morgo looked at Raya. "Do as he says."

Raya entered the chamber at stood next to Sharon. Morgo seemed satisfied. Then he slammed the chamber door. "Start the process now with the two of them in there."

"Morgo," said Roland, "I don't have Raya's code. I can't."

Morgo laughed, "I was just testing you again. I have always found liars to be inconsistent."

Roland opened the chamber door and guided Raya out. She avoided Roland's eyes.

The sound of the generator's hum told Sharon the process was beginning. Roland had programmed the computer to take Sharon one second into the future. Roland hoped the only thing that would be wrong would be Sharon's time piece. Sharon would have one second added to her life.

After five minutes, Sharon disappeared. Finally she reappeared. Roland quickly opened the chamber door. Roland noted the fact there was no vacuum. Sharon seemed fine. Roland wanted to grab her and hold her and ask how she felt but he could not display any surprise or shock. Sharon was okay.

"There you go, Morgo," said Sharon. "I've been rebuilt and I feel fine."

"You must address me as your Excellency."

"Your Excellency," she repeated.

Morgo sat down and seemed to contemplate. "Why," he asked, "Do I get such a feeling of anticipation and anxiousness?"

"You are the ruler of the Earth, your Excellency. I want to finish our business and get back to my family."

"Have you discussed with your family where they would desire to live?" asked Morgo.

Roland knew he had to show confidence. "Yes, your Excellency. On the new colony on Mars. We want to continue cultivating vegetation to help the planet manufacture oxygen."

Again, the Premier contemplated for what seemed an eternity. It amazed Roland how the mightiest of rulers become so childlike when a life and death decision must be made regarding their own life.

Finally he spoke, "Proceed." Then he said, "Wait! I want to be six centimeters taller."

Roland brought Morgo back from the chamber entrance. "Your Excellency. Maybe we should wait to perform your rebuilding. Tell me any features you desire and I'll incorporate them into your code. After three days, I'll have the new parameters entered."

"No. Proceed," he said. "I was just testing you again."

Roland hid his exasperation. "Yes your Excellency."

Roland led Morgo to the chamber. He told him to sit on the floor and to move as little as possible. Morgo obeyed almost in a childlike manner. Roland closed the chamber door.

Roland asked Raya, "Do you want to watch?"

"I do not want to watch." The other attendants and Sentinels, however, were glued to the vision screen.

Roland and Sharon had to reprogram the computer from time travel to rebuilding. It would take several minutes. He would be sent to who knows where.

"Hurry up," came the Premier's voice over the chamber communicator.

Finally the hum of the generator. After five minutes, Morgo disappeared. Roland heard the Sentinels murmuring among themselves. Two of the attendants also whispered to each other but Raya remained silent. Ten more minutes elapsed and the Premier reappeared. As expected, it was a lifeless body. It was a copy of Morgo. The real Morgo was somewhere in the future.

Once again it took two men to open the door, fighting the vacuum. Raya and the other attendants rushed into the chamber.

Raya shouted, "He is without life!" Roland prayed he had done the right thing.

The Sentinels now rushed into the chamber. Roland and Sharon knew they had to show concern also but there was no room for them to enter the chamber. They watched at the door.

Raya asked, "What is wrong?"

"I don't know," said Roland avoiding Raya's eyes.

Clumsily the body of Morgo began to move and fell off the table. It let out an unearthly scream. Its right arm swung wildly outward and hit the edge of the table. Another scream and blood began gushing from a cut on the arm. As in the actions of previous creatures, Morgo jumped in spasms and wild gestures.

The attendants rushed to the door of the chamber but jumped back when the man banged itself against a wall.

Raya said, "He seems to have gone wild."

"I don't know why," lied Roland.

The wild creature swung around violently banging its head on the door. Suddenly Morgo's copy fell motionless to the floor, bleeding profusely. The head wound seemed to be fatal.

Raya shouted, "He's dying!" Roland pretended he had done the right thing.

"He had no weakness," she said sternly. "Just one minor illness. You were supposed to cure him. Now he's dead. I expect you to explain what went wrong."

Raya then motioned to the Sentinels to leave. "Go and give the announcement that Morgo has died. I will announce our new leader soon."

Roland was amazed at the power this woman seemed to have.

After the Sentinels left, Raya turned to Roland. "I know where Chang is hiding. I will communicate to him now. He can return to power. He has much work to do. There are many unruly and unfit Sentinels to deal with. The older Sentinels didn't approve of Chang's commencing a dialogue with some of the outlaws.

Raya told the attendants to have several Sentinels help remove Morgo's body. "Do you have facilities for cremation?" she asked.

"Yes," said Roland.

"Thank you. We will then take him home to be buried in China," she told Roland.

"What happens now?" asked Roland.

"We all are leaving. Chang will discuss with you your options. There is no need to explain to me what went wrong with Morgo. Good bye."

The entourage waited several hours at the crematory. They neither accepted nor requested any food or drink. After cremation, Raya and her attendants left with four Sentinels carrying Morgo's ashes. Sharon and Roland sat near the crematory in utter astonishment.

Later that afternoon, Sharon asked, "Can you explain to me just what happened today?"

"Not in a million years," said Roland. "But I think we are going to live a while longer.

"Sharon," said Roland. "Let's go back to my home. Did you notice the water creeping up at the rear of our lab?"

"Yes."

CHAPTER SEVENTEEN

Roland and his family sat around the eating table along with Roalf and Sharon.

"Once again we are here trying to decide what to do," he said. "I guess the way to start is to ask each one of us, what do we honestly want to do?"

"I know what Roalf and I want to do, Dad," said Risa. "We want to grow foods from the ground. We don't care where, do we Roalf?"

"No," said Roalf.

"How about you, Brooke?"

"I want to fix things," he said. "I want to have my own set of tools and fix things for people."

"Melody?" asked Roland.

"I'll be perfectly happy wherever you are, Roland," she said, "but I'd like to work with Risa and Roalf on their plantation."

"Sharon?" asked Roland.

"I'd like to go back to Chi-Louis. My husband isn't dead. He's somewhere in hiding. After I left to come here, ACD was determined to hold him hostage until I returned. They told me he was dead but I'm sure he's hiding. I think I know where."

"I didn't know, Sharon," said Roland.

"Yes, we were married fifty years ago and I sure he's hiding in the area where we were married."

"I feel confident Chang will allow you to do that, but what about the volcano?"

"I feel it is just a local event."

"Okay," said Roland shaking his head.

"So Roland," asked Melody, "What about you? What's your great desire?"

"I'd rather not say," he said.

"No. You have to tell us," said Risa.

"You won't laugh?"

"No Dad. We won't laugh," said Brooke.

"I'm a scientist but I have great questions about this God person. I want to study all the religions of the world, past and present. I want to find out what makes humans need to believe in a supreme creator or an intelligent designer. It may be because we scientists keep bumping up against questions that don't seem to have an answer. I may even become a religious leader."

No one laughed.

"That's neat, Dad," said Risa. "I think you'll be great."

"Then the last question is, where?"

"Roland," said Sharon. "I don't think anyone should dare go to the past. No matter when in the past they would go, I feel it would completely destroy history. It is like the 'butterfly flaps its wings' analogy. The butterfly flaps its wings in China resulting in a hurricane in Northern Americus. We might only pick a flower in 1800 and it could cause a great historic event to change. Or farther back, what if we taught a caveman to use tools before history noted it. It'd be catastrophic."

"That's a valid concern, Sharon," said Roland.

"And I don't like the future, Roland," said Melody. "I think we should let the future come to us instead of us rushing to it."

"That doesn't leave many options, does it?" he said.

"It leaves only one, Dad," said Brooke. "Mars. They need people to fix things and they need people to grow things."

"Do they need a religious person?" asked Roland smiling.

"They most definitely do, Roland," said Melody. "Let's take the next supply ship to Mars."

"Do we want to do that? What about York? Doesn't anybody want to go back to York?"

"No," they said in unison.

Risa added, "And I know about a hundred people from the plantation that want to go to the Mars plantation too."

"Interesting," said Roland. "So, let's hold that thought until Chang contacts me. We'll see what he says."

"Great!" said Brooke. "Now, let's eat."

CHAPTER EIGHTEEN

Chang's return to power was extremely dynamic. Each and every Sentinel was examined by brain wave analysis to determine their deepest thoughts. Any hint of hostility or belligerency was noted and that person was relieved of duty. All scanners were dismantled as were the satellite observers. If so desired anyone wanting their chip removed was given a place and time for the operation. Since ACD was inoperative, cambri operation was in the hands of the driver. Citizens had to relearn how to drive.

Chang had several seismic scientists set up operations in Southern California. They were to monitor any minor quake or plate shifts in the area. The most recent quake continued to have minor aftershocks.

Chang paid Roland a visit. "That's interesting, Dr. Davidson," said Chang. "You say all you saw in 12301 N was a dark sky, full of ash."

"I didn't see it personally but that's what was in the note from our assistants," said Roland. "The water was extremely muddy. It almost immediately shut down their water to air devices."

"Was there any way to tell if the whole Earth was ash covered or just in this area?"

"No. Our method of future travel could only locate our exit about 200 meters from the tunnel. A Dexmon could survey the area to the right, left, up and down. That's as far as we could tell."

"And this will happen six and a half months from now?" Chang asked.

"We seem to be able to tell the cavern will be destroyed six and a half months from now but the volcano seems to be occurring about ninety or so years from now."

"Does it cover the whole Earth?" asked Chang again.

"We don't know nor do we have any way to tell," answered Roland, "since we can only enter into the future a short distance from the time tunnel exit."

"My personal feeling is all life on earth isn't destroyed by the volcano. I have no fears of remaining on Earth."

"We still want to go to Mars, Chang," said Roland.

"I will arrange it when you desire."

Roland added, "And I'm somewhat ambivalent if we should even offer time travel as an option."

"I agree." Chang added thoughtfully, "I wonder what someone will think ninety years from now; they find two bodies in the old Lake Powell area."

"I hope nothing," said Roland.

"Roland, I believe your time machine should be destroyed for the Earth's protection. I think time travel could be a curse."

Roland didn't answer.

Chang looked at the console of the time chamber. "Did you ever think about the fact that no one from the future ever came back to visit us?"

"Yes we have."

"On the other hand, maybe all of our brilliant discoveries were due to someone returning to the past. Maybe someone gave Einstein his formula? Maybe a future being taught the cave man how to use tools?"

"Maybe," said Roland, "someone gave Dr. Roland Davidson the hypothesis of how to rearrange molecules?"

Chang smiled. "It's quite a conundrum."

"I firmly believe you are right," said Roland. "We should destroy the time chamber. If humans ever interfere with history, I don't want to be the one that made it possible."

"Maybe that's why I will decide to destroy this cavern six months from now."

"I'd hope you'd wait until all inhabitants have left."

"You know I would, Roland."

"How would we get to Mars?"

"We have five ships in China and Russia has six. I caution you, though; they are all one-way trips. We can't bring you back. Morgo had all other ships destroyed. You would have to construct your own Earth bound ships on Mars. Mars' gravity is about one third that of Earth so it would be easier to reach escape velocity."

"Our president, Larry Van Steen, is on his way over here. We'll have to impress on him our feelings."

"Good, I want to meet him."

Changing the subject, Roland said, "I see you brought Raya with you. She saved our lives."

"She is a good woman and very strong. I'm sorry I couldn't save her daughter. She died before I returned to power. I will soon take Raya as my wife."

"Do you think you'll be able to maintain control?"

"Yes, I've eliminated all the older Sentinels. I feel I have a loyal population now. In the meantime I suggest you and your family study your future home. Mars does not contain a human friendly environment."

"My children are doing that as we speak."

"I believe your skills as a geneticist will much more useful on Mars than your experiments in atom disassembly or time travel. You'll need to create plants that will grow quickly in the carbon dioxide atmosphere of Mars. There's only a minimum of oxygen."

"I know that. I'll have plenty to do."

"As the population of the planet grows, you will have to discover a method to move out from under the protection of the clear Plaztec domes."

"I am fully aware of my task." Roland didn't want to mention his other ambitions; that of a reverend and that he was still very interested in time travel.

Roland and Chang drank a green drink and waited for Larry to arrive. Soon Larry, Amanda and Sharon walked into the lab.

"I still get nervous seeing all those Sentinels milling about here," said Sharon.

"They are all dedicated to me," said Chang. "And did you notice most are not armed?"

"Yes I did," said Larry. "And your attendant Raya is most cordial."

"Yes, she is."

"Chang, we are here to hear what our choices are? What should we do and where can we live?"

Chang answered, "I understand, Larry Van Steen. Your first concern should be the water. I see it has reached your lab. This will be first place to flood. Second, I believe we are not ready for a time machine. I want it destroyed. Your scientist, Roland, concurs with me, do you not?"

"Chang, a scientist never wants his work destroyed but you and I have already gone through the scenarios of damage and confusion time travel may cause. Then again, I am not a ruler or leader. I can't make that decision."

"I feel it should be ended, but what do we tell our citizens?" said Larry.

Chang volunteered, "I will take the blame if it will help. Tell your people I demanded the program be terminated."

"Yes, but Chang, don't you want the populace to believe you are a caring leader?"

"This is true," said Chang. "Do your citizens know they must soon leave this cavern?"

"Yes they do," said Larry. "They know the cavern roof will be blasted away in six and a half months."

Roland said, "The pumps are taking so much power now that there isn't much left to operate the time tunnel? How are we doing now, Larry?"

"As I said, if one of our six pumps should fail, we start flooding. I think we are already losing the battle."

"Does your time chamber require much power?"

"Yes, quite a bit," said Roland.

"How many people so far want to go to Mars?" asked Chang.

"About one thousand."

"And the rest want to travel forward or backward in time?"

"No, not everybody," said Larry. "Another one thousand want to take their chances with the volcano, and if I may say so, with you as the Premier."

"With me?" asked Chang.

"Yes, they're not sure what kind of leader you'll be but they will chance it."

"I can understand."

Larry added, "The remaining three thousand have expressed interest in traveling in time. We couldn't destroy the tunnel until all interested people were sent to their destination whether it would be Mars or somewhere in time."

"I know," said Chang.

"Chang," said Roland, "How many can we take to Mars in the available rocket ships?"

"Each ship can carry approximately two hundred, which means the thousand that want to relocate on Mars can do so. There will be a housing shortage for a while as more homes are being built but the ships can carry quite a bit of cargo."

"I never thought about housing."

"Yes," said Chang. "And I will direct the robots to build more transport ships for space travel, but they can only build one ship a month."

"We would only need the ships if we can convince the people wanting to time travel to change their minds and go to Mars."

Roland paced the floor, "Chang, what about the rest of the world's population? We've only been discussing possibilities for our Reformer populace. Have the citizens been informed of a possible volcanic catastrophe?"

"I'm sad to say they don't seem too concerned. I don't know what to do about them."

Larry paced the floor with Roland. "Roland, what you and Sharon have to do is find out how encompassing the volcano is. You have got to get some kind of vehicle into the near future to see how extensive the damage is. If it's a local volcano, we can all rest easy. If not, then it's fair to say we can all panic."

"Nicely put," said Sharon.

"How big of a vehicle can you place in your time chamber?"

"It's about eight cubic meters."

Chang called his advisor on his ACS, "Find out what kind of robot is available for programmable travel. It can't be remotely operated. We must be able to program its functions. It can be no bigger than two meters on a side."

"He will call me back."

"Let's just tell our people the truth," said Amanda. "Let's tell them time travel is too dangerous. Going to the past will most assuredly create an historic catastrophe. Going forward contains too many unknowns. The people would have no way to travel, no eatables, no shelter or protection from animals or humankind. They would have no way to sustain their lives."

"That might work," said Roland, "And, it's the truth."

Larry pondered the thought. "Okay, the only people we have to deal with are our own here in the cavern, right Chang?"

"Correct. From what I've been able to ascertain, the world population seems unconcerned about Reformers. They call you outlaws and want nothing to do with you. I might add they are very apathetic and lazy. They are happy doing nothing. They are not happy with the thought of having to work to survive."

"Sharon, why don't you start right now and find out exactly when the volcano ash began appearing?"

"Roland," said Larry. "Don't forget. We have to conserve power. Every time you run your time tunnel, we lose pumping ability."

"You're right," said Roland, "but we have to do it."

"I'm on it," she said. "I'll give you results as I get them."

Sharon went to work checking the future conditions in ten year intervals starting one year from the present.

Chang's ACS announced a call. "Yes?"

Chang listened intently to his advisor. "Thank you," he said.

"Here's what we can get you. We have a programmable robot in the old country of Europe. It will fit in your chamber but it will take two days to get it here. I've started it on its way."

"I guess now we just wait," said Amanda.

Every time Sharon sent the Dexmon into a future time, the water rose ten centimeters. The Colorado River was taking over the cavern.

CHAPTER NINETEEN

"Here's what I have so far, Dad," said Risa. "A day on Mars is 24 hours, 39 minutes and 35.260726 seconds. A year is 686.98 earth days. Mars only has two tiny moons, probably captured asteroids. They circle the planet two or three times a day so months are non-existent. Gravity is one third that of Earth. Its distance from the sun varies from 207 million kilometers to 249 million kilometers. Since Earth varies from 147 million kilometers to 152 million kilometers I guess the sun will appear a little smaller."

"Interesting," said Roland. "You've done quite a bit of research. How about temperatures?"

"It ranges from minus 133C to plus 27C. The atmosphere is 95% carbon dioxide. There are other gases too, but oxygen is only 0.15%. The density of its atmosphere is only 1% that of earth which is why we'll have to continue to live in pressurized domes. I guess that's why we'll be living in the domes until you get the plants manufacturing oxygen and create as atmosphere. But even then, a problem remains. Mars seems to have lost its magnetic field which is why it has no atmosphere. The solar wind literally blew it away. You know, maybe at one time it was a lush and green planet."

"Maybe," said Roland. "We may not be able to create an atmosphere without a magnetic field. It seems I've got to do in years what took God eons to do."

"Gosh, Dad. You mentioned God."

"I know. Amazing, isn't it?"

Roland's land line phone announced a call. "Yes?" he answered.

"Okay, I'll be right there." He hung up the phone.

"What is it, Roland?" asked Melody.

"The robot will be here later today. I don't know how Chang got it so fast but he did."

Roland rushed to the lab. Larry, Amanda, Sharon and Chang were already there as were Saul, Lea and Ellen.

"Let's see when the sky falls on us," said Larry.

"Here's what I have set up if everyone agrees," said Sharon. "We'll go to 42,303 N, 43,206 N, 43,256 N and 43,306 N."

The land line rang. "Hello," said Roland. "It's for you, Larry."

Larry took the phone. "What? Okay. Our bad luck just seems to keep on coming. We'll start evacuating now."

"What is it?" asked Roland.

"The pumps are failing. The cavern is filling with water. I'm not sure how long we have, maybe a couple of days at the most. I told the officers to start sending everyone to the exits. Our whole meeting here is for naught. The cave is history."

"Crap!" said Roland. "All our equipment will be damaged beyond repair. Can't we save any of it?"

Chang shouted, "No! The lab is flooding. Let's get ourselves out of here!"

"I've told the sergeants to announced evacuation on the public speakers. I imagine there'll be some panic."

"I'm going home to get my family," said Roland. "And I'm leaving my papers, formulas and equations here. I want them destroyed."

Roland immediately had second thoughts. Lagging behind the others, he grabbed his papers and shoved them inside his shirt. The scientists quickly left the lab. The elevator slowly and begrudgingly brought them to the surface. The artificial sun was half its normal brilliance. An announcement was echoing throughout the cavern as Roland stood at the lab elevator door. The trains were not running.

To the left of the lab elevator entrance Roland saw an abandoned cargo cambri. Its battery showed full charge. Once again he thought about his work and the time tunnel. He jumped in the cambri and drove it to his home.

The address system blared, "The fusion generating system will begin an automated shutdown in 5 hours! This will prevent the water from causing an explosion of steam and water. Please move to an exit or vent tunnel as quickly as possible."

As Roland approached his front door, he saw the artificial creeks overflowing their banks. His family met him at the door.

"Roland," said Melody.

"Don't talk. Just follow me. Get in this cambri!"

Melody, Risa, Roalf and Brooke got into the cargo cambri.

"Where are we going, Dad?" asked Brooke.

'We're going back to the lab. I want you all to help me load something into the cambri."

"What?" Melody asked.

Roland looked around. The people were all heading toward the nearest exit or ventilator shaft. They hardly questioned the cambri heading in the opposite direction of exits.

He herded his family to the elevator at the lab.

"I need you to help me load this equipment into the cambri."

"What is it?" asked Melody.

He quietly said, "Just some equipment I may need on Mars. It might help me get plant growth started on Mars." This statement wasn't exactly true.

The water was 15 centimeters deep as Roland and his family sloshed around gathering equipment. The elevator was inoperative so they had to use the stairs. After loading the cambri, Roland drove it and his family up the exit and out on the desert floor.

Five thousand scared citizens began running toward an exit tunnel. There was little panic but everyone wasted no time. There was a lot of urgency in their steps. They all carried as much of their belongings as possible. Fortunately the exits were on higher ground. The lower levels were already underwater. There was the smell of something electrical burning and the wind fans slowed to a stop. The light continued to dim.

The two exits and fifteen vent holes in the desert above the cavern began spewing a constant stream of people. It looked like an ant hill disgorging its inhabitants. They could easily see the river emptying its entire contents into a giant hole. No water would flow downriver until the cavern was completely inundated.

Roland and his family stood in silent awe at the spectacle. Hundreds of former Reformers stood around the desert. They were all speechless. Above the crowd, Roland saw an air vehicle circling the area. It was Chang's vehicle.

From the vehicle, Chang was making an announcement. "Please remain calm where you are. I have a sufficient amount of cargo cambris on their way. They will have water, eatables and sanitation facilities for all and will arrive in two hours. Stay calm or the heat will dehydrate you. Sentinels will circulate through the area. Inform them as to your desired location and they will furnish you with the required documentation for tram travel. Do not be concerned that you have no chip. ACD is no longer operational."

A spontaneous cheer arose from the crowd.

"Dr. Roland Davidson!" he continued. "I am trying to locate you. Try to get my attention."

Roland immediately grabbed Risa's red jacket, stood on top of the cambri and began waving it in the air. After several passes over the crowd, Chang saw Roland. He circled and the people cleared for his landing.

After landing he walked over to Roland. "How are you doing?"

"We're all here."

"Good. Bring your family over to my vehicle."

"I've got an operational cargo cambri here," said Roland. "We'll use it. Are the trams still running?"

"Yes. I've got several trams bringing the supplies to the town of Page. I also have several cargo cambris arriving here soon. The cambris will be able to transport the eatables and water here soon after they arrive. I'm glad all are in good health"

"Yeah, we all have healthy genes," Roland said in a laugh. "I guess we've solved the time travel dilemma. Now that the equipment is destroyed, there are only two choices. Stay on Earth or go to Mars."

Roland felt a twinge of guilt. He still had his time travel documents, and the time machine, with him. He wondered if he'd have the opportunity or need to use the time travel equipment on Mars.

"I believe you are right," said Chang.

"Wow!" Brooke shouted. "When do we go?"

"We will have to wait until Mars is closer to Earth. We'll have plenty time to get ready."

Larry found the group. "I'm staying here for certain," he said.

"I've been thinking," said Chang. "Since we can only send a few hundred people to Mars at a time, we'll have to set up a system of sequence as to who goes when."

Larry said, "We're way ahead of you. "We worked out a lottery for our people. We were going to use it to decide the order of who goes when to the future."

"That's interesting.'

"I guess we'll have to find a place to live until we're ready to go," said Melody.

"You can come with me to China," said Chang, "until your ship is supplied and we have a proper launching window."

"We've made some friends here, Chang. We'd like to see what their intentions are before we leave."

"That's fine. The offer is still open."

"Thank you," said Roland. "And you still have no qualms about the volcano?"

"No, I'll take my chances. I don't think it'll be a worldwide event. This old Earth is pretty tough. I believe it can handle a lot of catastrophes. It's worked fine so far."

"I suppose you're right," said Larry.

"Risa," asked Roland, "Have figured out how long a trip to Mars would take?"

"Kinda. It depends when we would go. The distance varies so much. Its closest distance is 55 million kilometers and the farthest is about 400 million kilometers. I guess it could take from a half year to forever."

"Your daughter has done some detailed study on Mars," said Chang.

"Yeah," said Roland. "She's eager to go."

"We'll let our space engineers figure the best time for you to go. Since you're the one needed to design plants that need little oxygen and water, I've designated you to be our priority space traveler – you and your family that is. Give me a list of scientific apparatus you'll need. I'll try to get it on the next available ship."

"I've got some needed equipment for plant development in this cambri," said Roland. "I'll need it on Mars. I'll also need several fusion generators."

"I'll see that as much as possible gets loaded with you on this trip and the rest on the next ship," said Chang.

Roland had some doubt if there would be enough power to operate the time tunnel but, Mars is quite inhospitable and he had to think of his family. They may need a way off Mars if living becomes impossible.

"That's great. We appreciate your consideration. I just feel bad for our people from the cavern. I guess the Reformer's cause is ended."

"Not exactly," said Chang. "I like your idea of mandatory voting. I don't want to give up being the Earth's ruler but I like people voting for their leaders."

"I can understand the feeling of power and control."

"I will try to be fair. Maybe I'll let the people vote for their immediate leaders and I'll just oversee everything."

"That's an intriguing concept. I hope it works," said Roland."

"Your United States didn't let the people vote directly for their leaders. They did that in case the populace voted for the wrong person. I would do the same."

"Yes, I can see that," said Roland. "Who governs on Mars?"

"I don't know what they have set up as a ruling class. You can decide for yourselves. I want no part of ruling another world."

"We are starting from scratch."

"You'll have quite a few challenges. Not many natural resources have been discovered yet. They just recently found water under the surface. Until you can start an atmosphere, you'll have a hard time getting it."

"We're still excited," said Roland.

"I will have supply ships sent to you as often as I can."

"Send us all the fusion generators you can. I guess all decisions have been made except when do we go?"

"I'll let you know as soon as I find out," said Chang. "Now. Where do you want to live until your ship is ready?"

"How about our old home in York? And Chang, I feel we must leave before the volcano erupts."

"I'll try."

Chang escorted the Davidson family at a tram station. He gave clearance for their travel to York.

In York, Roland and his family including Roalf, found their dome just as they left it. Chang assured them when their space travel arrangements were made, he'd contact Sharon, Saul, Ellen and Rene and ascertain their wishes regarding Mars.

Two days later Chang called Roland. "Two ships will be able to leave in six months."

"Great," said Roland.

"Do you think the world will be shut down by the volcano?" asked Chang.

"I do, Chang. Why don't you get on one of those ships?"

"I can't leave my people," he said. "They'll need me however violent the eruption turns out to be."

"Sometimes you show the qualities of a good leader," said Roland, "and I mean that most seriously."

"One thing bothers me," said Chang. "An old outlaw insists it's a meteor not a volcano that causes the disaster on Earth. Have you heard anything about a meteor?"

"Yes, but we all assumed it was a rumor by a crackpot. There are no telescopes left to confirm or deny it."

"Whatever happens, happens. Thank you, friend. And I never thought we'd become friends."

"Me either," said Roland. "Be sure to see us before we leave."

"I will."

This time Roland and Chang would not meet again.

CHAPTER TWENTY

The Davidson Family watched in awe as their ship was being loaded. Chang had the family and their equipment transported to the Chinese launch pad. He remarked in regards to the amount of lab apparatus Roland was taking. It was unbelievable that a vehicle traveling only on the magnetic fields of adjacent planets could carry so many tons of equipment and two hundred people. Several extra fusion generators were being sent, as electrical power was in short supply in the two cities of Mars. It was critical that Roland create and cultivate plants that would survive and propagate outside of the protective domes. Ironically, he had to create a greenhouse atmosphere. Also, Roland had a secret agenda.

Their lift-off day was fast approaching. The volcano eruption was also supposed to happen in approximately three weeks. Chang had the cavern roof destroyed the previous week. The Colorado River was once again flowing since the cavern was now completely inundated. Larry believed all the Reformers had successfully escaped but no one was completely positive. A lot of scientific equipment and laboratories were ruined but there was no time to save anything but the citizens. Life in the cavern of the Reformers seemed like eons ago.

Chang told the Davidson's the trip to their new home will take approximately six months. They tried to think of anything and everything they might need, even the cute little trikes they used in the cavern. There are no cambris for transportation. The current population on the planet is 213 meaning this ship will double the population. A lot of temporary housing is being built for the influx of people.

During the days of ACD and Morgo, communication to Mars was prohibited. Now transmissions occur regularly. The inhabitants of the first Martian city named it Genesis since it was supposed to be another beginning of life. The town hadn't had a supply ship for several years. They were quite thrilled to hear that supply ships will begin regular runs to their planet. It was also a great relief to no longer be thought of as outlaws. They were free to create their own government, free of Chang's rule.

It still isn't known exactly what kind of natural resources lie underground on Mars. Only a minimal amount of excavation equipment has been transported so far but more machinery will be on the next shipment leaving in a week. No factories have been built yet but the only machine shop is kept very busy. Water was available underground but very limited. The seasons are unequal as compared to Earth.

Melody, Risa and Roalf will work in the plantations under the huge domes. Even though Brooke just turned eleven, he will be working with the construction crews. There is a big shortage of mechanics. Roland has his assignment; inventing new plants.

Finally the Davidson's were boarding their spaceship. All of Roland's lab assistants choose to stay on Earth. When it came time to make the decision, most of Earth's inhabitants were fearful of traveling in space and even more afraid of living on Mars. The family of the Davidsons, and Roalf, would know no one on Mars. Since they make friends easily, they weren't the least bit concerned.

"Dad," asked Risa. "Is it really happening?"

"I believe so, daughter," he said. "Any doubts?"

"None," she said.

"Anyone here have second thoughts?"

"Not a bit," they said.

"In one hour we'll be heading to Mars."

A ship attendant handed Roland a note. It was from Chang. It read:

Sorry I couldn't see you on your way. There are serious rumblings in southern California. A minor earthquake has commenced. Southern cities have been damaged but the cause of the earthquake isn't the volcano. Since our concentration has been earthward lately, it seems we haven't been watching the skies. A very large meteor has Earth in its sights; Southern California to be exact. The time of impact seems to be in four days. I believe its great gravitational force is causing the earthquake,

I'm sending the second ship ten minutes after you lift off and seven more at one-hour intervals. I hope I'll have someone left on Earth to rule. Good luck. I hope you find your God. -Lo Chang.

"What does it say, Roland?" asked Melody.

"It's from Chang. It isn't a volcano causing the problems.

It's a meteor. Southern California is the suspected impact site. I've always felt it would be a volcano darkening the Earth and assumed it would cause the ash and temperature drop. Chang feels he'll have no one to rule, that is if he lives."

"Poor man."

"Dad," asked Brooke. "Will we get to see the meteor when we take off?"

"I doubt it. It'll be on the other side of the Earth."

The ship announcement system blared a message. "Attention all passengers. The launch time has been moved up. We are going to launch as soon as everyone is secured. Please hurry to your launch couch immediately! As soon as the attendants verify everyone is secured, we will launch. The second ship will launch immediately following our launch."

"I'm scared Dad," said Risa.

"Hold Roalf's hand and you'll be fine," he said.

"Hold my hand, Roland," said Melody.

"Got it," said Roland. "How about you Brooke?"

"Fine, I don't need to hold anybody's hand."

"Good ol' steady Brooke," he said.

A sudden violent rumble shook and rocked the ship. It sounded like a gradual explosion. The travelers were plastered into their seats.

"Dad!" yelled Risa. "Roalf and I want to get married!"

"Fine but I can't do much about it for the moment," yelled Roland.

"I know," the vibrations creating a warble in Risa's voice. "Can the Captain of the ship do it?"

"I'll ask," Roland's voice warbling too. "Can you wait until we escape Earth's gravity?"

"Yeah."

"Okay then."

For the next five minutes the passengers were unable to move. Just as suddenly, they were free of Earth's bounds.

Another announcement. "Please remain in your couch until we energize our artificial gravity. You may then move about."

"Wow, that was neat," said Brooke grinning from ear to ear.

"Yeah," said Roland.

"I'm going to be sick," said Melody.

After three weeks in space, an attendant called Roland to the captain's quarters. "Dr. Davidson?" he said.

"Yes."

"I just received a transmission from the Premier."

"It's for me?"

"Yes. I will repeat it for you. He said,

The meteor hit with a tremendous amount of force. I'm being told it slightly changed the Earth's orbit. You were right. It looks like the human species will go the way of the dinosaur. The sun is completely obscured, temperature down to 10 C and falling. Every living creature on Earth is dying. Good bye my friend. Chang'."

The year is 12218 N. It's been 12 years since the Davidson family left Earth. Every day is a struggle to live although there have been some small triumphs. Several edible plants seem to be growing outside the protective dome but show no signs of propagating. Without insects, it's nearly impossible to pollinate the plants. Supply ships have ceased arriving from Earth. It's been over eleven years since they have received any word from Chang or anyone from Earth. The new Martian inhabitants have resigned themselves to the verity that Earth is dead.

Roland still wonders if writing the article saved his family from freezing to death on Earth or caused them to fight for lives on this barren planet. He finally had the time tunnel rebuilt but he was somewhat fearful of testing it. His calculations kept repeating the fact that the exit was still only two hundred meters from the entrance. It seems as though no matter where in the universe the tunnel entrance would be placed, the exit would be exactly the same distance from the time tunnel entrance. If he used it here, their exit would still be on Mars. What purpose would it serve to be dumped out on this dead planet? There was no need for it now but the day may be fast approaching. He must configure a program for the exit to be a great distance from the entrance.

Roland was also still struggling to understand religions. He was on the verge of admitting there were things he could never understand. The odds of evolution, random mutation and natural selection were just too great to have all that happen take place in just 15 billion years. There were things he had to give credit to an intelligent creator. There were marvels in the world he would never be able to comprehend. One of those marvels came running up to him now.

"Grandpa," yelled a miniature Roland. "Look what grandma and I grew. A carrot."

The boy's carrot was the size of his little finger. He was the first genetically perfect human born on Mars. He was given the name 'Chantel'.

PART III

WE ARE HOME

CHAPTER ONE

Aerial Vance became the acting ruler of the Martian village Genesis. She had more or less adopted Roland as her second in command. She called him to a meeting.

"Roland. We have to face a fact."

Roland sat next to the clear transparent wall of the protective dome. Outside to his left he could see his twentieth attempt at growing plants drying up and withering. There just wasn't enough water and the slight atmosphere the plants created kept whiffing off into space. It seemed as if no living thing would ever be able to live outside the protective domes. Off to the west he could see another tremendous dust storm approaching.

"I think I know what the fact is," he said.

"We're dying," she said. "Our attempt to live here is failing. We would have to build the domes over the entire planet. Four hundred and sixty people here in Genesis and one hundred and seventy in our western city of Paradise are going to die soon. Our scientists have told us to survive and reproduce successfully, we need to have a population of at least 2000. It also seems as if our domes have a life span of ten to twenty years more. If we only had some way to build or repair our domes, we'd have some hope. Transportation is still a big problem."

"Yeah, I know."

"Oh," she added. "Do you remember the meteor that hit Paradise last month? They're not sure it can be repaired."

Roland pushed his hair back. "I wonder what else can happen? If Mars still had a dynamic molten iron core like Earth it would develop a magnetic field. It would deflect the Sun's solar wind and Mars could maintain an atmosphere."

"I know, I know. Maybe it did at one time. I guess I knew it was hopeless."

"You haven't spent too much time over in Paradise have you?" she said.

"No, I've only been over there once. I hear it's a very inappropriate name. Its dome keeps leaking oxygen. Why do you ask?"

Aerial added, "Just curious. I feel our name Genesis is inappropriate too."

"I don't like getting out in the sun if at all possible," said Roland. "I'm afraid of gene mutation by solar rays. But why are you asking?"

"Do you think you or Melody or your children have had any gene mutation?"

"I don't think so but I haven't examined our chromosomes lately. Aerial, what's on your mind?"

Aerial stood up and looked at the failing crops. "Would you perform a chromosome analysis on yourself and your family as soon as possible?"

"Why?" asked Roland.

"Okay, I'll tell you, but I don't think you'll like my reason." She walked toward Roland and sat near him. "Do you remember Dr. Volley Heitmen?"

"Yes. She was one of the doctors working on space travel back in our reformer days."

"That's right. She lives in Paradise, here on Mars."

"Volley Heitman?"

"Yes. She happens to be here in the next room."

Aerial walked over to the door and asked Volley to come in.

"Hi, Roland," Volley said. "I came here on the last ship from Earth. I heard you were here and meant to visit you many times but never got around to it."

"I'll be darned," said Roland as he gave her a hug. "You look tired. Are you okay?"

"No, I'm not well. Paradise isn't as well protected from the sun as you are here in Genesis. It seems as if my once perfect genes were bombarded by enough cosmic rays to cause some damage. I have acquired skin cancer and as you know, we don't have injectable cancer nano-machines here on Mars. And we can't seem to find out why we keep losing our oxygen. We're checking but we think the meteor hitting the edge our dome is the cause or it's the fact the soil around us is so porous. We just don't know."

"Oh. I'm sorry."

"Roland," said Aerial. "We are starving to death. Paradise is a lot worse off than we are but it's inevitable, unless we find some larger quantities of water, we'll soon die. We have to find a way to build domes or move underground."

"I know," said Roland. "It seems as if I've failed again. I can't get food plants to grow here. This planet is just meant to be lifeless."

"You might just be correct," said Volley.

"But what's this got to do with my children and me?" asked Roland.

"You tell him, Volley."

"Roland, remember the space probe I sent out to search for a habitable planet?"

"Yes," said Roland. "It came back without finding a planet suitable for life."

"That wasn't entirely true."

"What do you mean?" asked Roland.

"It was programmed to search for a planet with temperatures tolerable for humans and an atmosphere suitable for human reproduction. Do you know the only thing that travels faster than the speed of light?"

"No."

"Gravity. Its effect is immediate."

"I never thought of that," said Roland.

Volley looked quite downcast. "That's the source I was attempting to use."

"Go on," said Roland.

"It was a partial success."

"It was? You mean there are other planets similar to Earth?"

"Let me finish," said Volley, "It seems as if my probe didn't attain the gravitational effect I had hoped for. My ship wasn't traveling around the whole universe faster than the speed of light. It was only traveling 27,419 kilometers per hour – the escape velocity to leave Earth. I didn't program my computer properly. I found out what I did incorrectly. I made the changes but never had the time to fly my probe. The earthquake put a stop to my work. I never had a chance to try my new program."

"My God," said Roland.

"Before I realized my mistake I proudly proclaimed I found two suitable planets. I saw it discovered two planets but instead of traveling the universe it only traveled around our solar system. Roland, one of the planets was Earth but it was Earth about 31,000 years in the past. I thought I designed the probe to search ninety percent or more of the universe. It was supposed to be programmed to travel through wormholes. It successfully traversed wormholes but it didn't travel great distances, it only warped time. The sad part is that, instead of traveling across the universe, it traveled back in time. It never left our solar system. I didn't know it but it found an ancient Earth."

"What about the other planet?"

"Since the big one was the closest planet I ignored the other planet since it was so small. I didn't bother to ascertain the time period of the second planet. I thought it was too far away. I was so shocked by seeing this beautiful planet. I stupidly thought it's just like our Earth. Foolish me. It was Earth. This planet seemed so desirable I focused on it alone. It looked so welcome but it was Earth at 31,000 BC."

"That's unbelievable."

"It came back to a planet that was lush and green; pure and blue. Also, my date of 31,000 BC is only an educated guess. It's more like plus or minus 1,000 years. I can't narrow it down any closer. Anyway, it was – it is a beautiful Earth."

"I know. I can imagine what it's like. Sharon and I went 30,000 years ahead and about 30,000 back in time with our little time tunnel. Either direction it is truly beautiful."

"I know," said Volley. "For the last five years I've been sitting on this knowledge afraid to tell anybody. I didn't know what to do with the knowledge. The revelations came to me so quickly I didn't know how to react. Then Aerial told me last week she couldn't avoid facing the fact that life on Mars is failing."

"But why, Volley, did you wait so long to say anything?" asked Roland.

"I guess because of my pride. When I left Earth, I had my lab and my space probe shipped up here with me with the hope I could comprehend what happened. That is when I discovered why my results made no sense. It found two earthlike planets and I just didn't believe my data. One of them was our Earth. I never told anyone due to a slight problem. I was ashamed. I kept praying my little craft wouldn't be needed."

"What's the problem?"

"Capacity. We can only send seven or eight people in my small probe. I'm fairly sure with confidence I can send anyone or anything back in time or even to present day Earth. It will get to Earth but I just don't know precisely what time period. I can program the probe for 31,000 BC or the present. Also it's a one way shot. We can send eight people and that's all. I kept thinking we could always build more if needed. But there are no facilities on Mars capable of building more probes."

"Damn," said Roland. "Can you program any other date other than 31,000 years ago?"

"No. It has to be approximately 31,000 or the present. Actually Roland, I'm not even sure of the times at all.

"On these eight people will rest the fate of humankind. They will have to populate whatever planet they go to. I feel the Earth is a good choice. Also, I am greatly concerned. Not only can't I get a precise time, I can't get an exact landing location."

"You mean it could land in the ocean."

Volley didn't answer.

"You want to send me and my family back, possibly to an early Earth or Earth as it is now?" he asked Aerial. "Isn't Earth still in a clouded shroud of dust?"

"No," said Aerial. "The meteor hit twelve years ago. I would think the dust has fairly settled."

"I doubt it. I don't like to gamble with my family's lives."

"It would be with your consent and approval. You could choose whether you wanted to go back in time or take a chance on the present. Your children are adults now. They could help make your decision. You could also choose to stay here on Mars."

"My first reaction is a vehement no. But then I don't want my children to die here. I feel we can last here on Mars a few more years. How long do you feel we have?"

"We seem to agree we can live here about one or two more years. We will then slowly starve or suffocate one by one, that is unless we can find a way to build many more domes."

"This God I am trying to believe in doesn't give us easy choices," said Roland.

"No, She doesn't."

Roland had to smile at Aerial's choice of God's gender. He hadn't smiled much lately.

Aerial continued, "What I was tentatively trying to do was find several humans to save. Volley gave me a place to send them. I chose, for no particular reason, you and your children first. There's no rush to make a decision. Just think about it."

"Sometimes I want to just throw up my hands and all of us take a poison pill."

"I know you don't mean that, Roland," said Aerial, "but just think it over."

Roland stood in silence.

"How old are Risa, Roalf and Brooke?" asked Aerial.

In almost a whisper, Roland said, "Risa's twenty-seven, Roalf is twenty-nine and Brooke is twenty-three and his intended mate is eighteen. Chantel is twelve."

"Why don't you go home, Roland," said Aerial. "Don't mention this to your children until you and Melody talk it over."

"Volley," asked Roland. "If you found an ancient Earth, what was the other planet?"

"Mars."

"Did you check it out?"

"Yes. I was just as dry and desolate as you see outside our window now."

"Thanks." Roland slowly walked home. For years, Roland thought, I've studied as many religions as I could and I still have no answer why life is such a challenge. If there were no pain, sadness and death we would have Nirvana here on Earth – I mean Mars. Maybe this God is keeping track of our good and bad decisions. Roland reached his home quite somber and trying to think how to pray.

CHAPTER TWO

For the millionth time Roland thought about his time travel equipment he had secretly brought with him from Earth. He constructed it in his spare time not completely sure he'd even use it. If he did use it, where would he go? They'd probably still be on Mars except they would be in the future or past. He didn't care for that idea since it seems Mars always was and always will be a lifeless planet. He thought of using it as an escape module many times if he could only perfect his wish to locate the exit in an ancient and beautiful Earth. Volley's probe, as haphazard as it is, may accomplish it.

With no protective atmosphere meteors played havoc on the surface. In any second the dome could be hit, causing a slow death to its inhabitants. He hadn't told anyone about the time travel equipment, not even Melody. If Volley's ship worked, he'd then tell Aerial about it. They could use it as they saw fit. Volley's statement that its timing is very chaotic bothered him and he didn't like the idea of not being able to choose a landing place.

Melody immediately noticed his mood. "What's wrong," she asked.

"Melody, our life here on Mars is ending. We can't sustain ourselves. We aren't surviving."

"Roland, I've known that for years. I could tell. It's impossible to get an atmosphere here. I could tell you were having no success with the plants and I could see our plantations failing. There's not enough moisture on this planet."

"Yes, I guess it was pretty apparent."

"What did Aerial want? Anything regarding our future?"

"Most assuredly. She and a Dr. Heitmen have a way to save eight people. The rest will die."

"Oh, Roland."

"Those eight will be the ones to continue the human race."

"Roland, come pray with me."

"Pray? I still have problems with that."

"Just sit here with me. I'll show you."

Together Roland and Melody sat holding hands.

"Roland, just think of this super being, existing somewhere all around us. Think of this being knowing exactly what we're going through. Think of the being, this creator of all you can understand and all you can't understand, knowing full well what our problems are. See if it's possible for this kind being to give us an answer. Hopefully we'll be smart enough to see the answer. It would be contradictory for this being to create us and then let us die with no purpose served. I feel an answer will be apparent soon. This, Roland, is what I feel a prayer is. Do you follow me?"

"I don't know if I follow you completely but it is sure relaxing and comforting to put your problems in someone else's hands."

"That's the idea. Now, how will they pick the eight humans?"

"They already have. It's you, me and our children."

Melody screamed, "No! No! No! Wait. What am I saying?"

"Don't think of us. Think of our children. They'd live, Melody. Would you want them to starve to death or die due to lack of an atmosphere?"

Melody sat down again. "I don't want them to starve. I don't want little Chantel to die. How? Where?"

"Ironically, back to Earth, now or in the past."

"Roland," was all Melody could say.

Melody gathered her thoughts, "Isn't Earth now cluttered with the dead remains of every creature that lived."

"I suppose so."

"I don't like that. How would we get there?"

"Dr. Heitmen has one small vehicle. It can hold eight and it's a one way trip. It seems Volley found the function and true results of her space probe. She thinks she has made the necessary corrections."

"How long can we survive on Mars?"

"One or two more years if the domes last."

"I guess I'd do anything to save our children and Chantel, and us too. But is there no other way? I want to see my grandchildren grow up. I want to play games with them. I want to teach them about the Earth we knew."

"I know, Melody, but now we'd be there to show them in person."

"A dead Earth. It sounds horrible. The past sounds even more frightful."

"I know," said Roland.

"Would we ever be able to see our friends on Mars again?"

"No."

"Would we be able to communicate with them?"

"No, but Melody, remember we will all soon die here on Mars."

Suddenly Melody screamed, "God, I know you're there! Help us!" She sat down crying.

"Roland," she sobbed, "I don't think my belief in this god is as strong as I thought. Who am I to preach to you?"

"You, my dear, are an intelligent being. Let's sleep on it and see what tomorrow brings. We've got a lot of time to think about it."

As Melody cuddled in Roland's arms he thought about his time tunnel. She gradually stopped sobbing.

Roland went to his small lab and performed a gene analysis of himself and his family. His tests proved their chromosomes to be undamaged.

CHAPTER THREE

Their communicator announced a call.

"Roland, this is Volley. We've got an emergency. The meteor that hit Paradise, it's created quite a catastrophe. The people only have few electric vehicles that operate. The inhabitants are rioting and fighting to use them to get over here to safety. The oxygen will be exhausted in Paradise in about two hours. I doubt if any will make it here. Hopefully my space probe is already on the way here."

"Damn."

"Bring everyone over here to Aerial's office."

"We'll be right there."

"Have you told your children about our plan yet?"

"No," said Roland.

The family almost ran the whole way to Aerial's office. The children still had no idea what was about to be presented to them but their parent's apprehension was contagious. They rushed into Aerial's office out of breath, even in the light gravity of Mars.

"Sit down," Aerial said. Dr. Volley Heitmen wasn't smiling.

Volley began. "Do your children know what this is all about?"

"No," said Roland. "Just Melody."

"Okay. Here goes. Kids, Paradise was hit with a meteor. The people are rioting and I'm afraid the panic will kill them all. There aren't enough vehicles. We are certain Mars can't and never will be able to support life. There's no way to sustain life here. We've tried and so far failed. This village will last about one or two more years and Paradise is already being destroyed. And we have no facilities for building any more giant domes."

The children's smiles quickly vanished.

"But we've chosen one select family to return to Earth. We can send eight people to Earth at 30,000 years ago or Earth at present time. The Davidson family is our choice. We have a space vehicle on its way here from Paradise that can handle all of you; Roland, Melody, Risa, Roalf, Chantel, Brooke and his intended, Nadia."

The children sat in silence.

"Dad," said Risa. "Weren't you trying to accomplish time travel many years ago on Earth? Weren't you telling us we could go to the future or past?"

"Yes, I thought we could do it but the cavern was flooding and nearly destroyed my time tunnel. We did see the Earth as it was 30,000 years ago it was quite beautiful."

"Do you think present day Earth will be safe?" asked Roalf. "We don't know what we will find there. And won't the Earth be full of rotting bodies, even after twelve years?"

"Yes Roalf. There will be decomposed bodies all around us. But if we stay on Mars, we will soon be decomposed bodies ourselves. And I don't think death on Mars will be kind."

"Oh."

Aerial said, "You children would be like Adam and Eve. You and your children would have to mate but incest would be no problem since you all have perfect genes. As we said many times over, Adam and Eve's children had to mate. There were no other beings around."

Melody spoke, "I feel guilty living while everyone here on Mars dies. Is there no other way?"

"We already chose once to leave present day Earth and again when we thought a volcano was going to destroy everything," said Roland. "I felt some guilt then because only a few could live while six billion died. There was nothing we could do about it. We were chosen to survive then just as we are chosen to survive again."

"All those dead beings all around us," said Melody. "Do you think there could be diseases or scavengers running rampant? Maybe the future would be a better choice."

Roland said, "I'm sure by now germs, viruses and animals have been killed by the ash and extreme cold. Even in the present or future I'm concerned if there will be anything to eat. Will there be any edible plants? How will we keep warm?"

"It just sounds terrible," said Melody.

"How long will it take us to get to Earth?" asked Roland.

"It will appear to be about one week, or longer," said Volley.

"Okay, is there a problem?" asked Roland.

"Yes," said Aerial. "Supplies. Volley has been able to slightly enlarge the volume of the sphere if we bring an extra fusion generator from the city of Paradise to help the at the launch site. You could cut down on supplies but there is no way to bring a fusion generator with you. You'll have to figure out how to get food and shelter quickly. You'll have to walk.

There'll be no cambris, trikes or even a fusion generator. You'll have a few tools and weapons and you'll have to be quite ingenious and frugal but we think you can do it."

"Dad," said Risa, "I'm pregnant."

"Travel will be no problem," said Volley. "You'll feel no acceleration at all. Birthing will be up to you and your mother. You had no problem with Chantel's birth in the one-third gravity here on Mars; giving birth on Earth should be just as easy. You'll have to be somewhat careful in moving around. Your bones will take a while to strengthen and get used to the increase in gravity."

"Are you saying all here in Genesis are going to die?" asked Brooke.

"I'm afraid it's very possible, Brooke, but not certain. We can't help it. We had a quick consultation and decided the Davidson entourage should be the lucky group. And who knows, maybe our polar exploration group will discover a way to get water to us and we may discover a way to build sturdier domes. There's even talk of building a city underground. But you people will be the ones to repopulate the Earth again."

"Gosh," said Risa, "I'm excited, scared and sad."

"We understand," said Volley, "but someone has to carry on and you're it. Will you all do it? Can you do the task at hand?"

"Can we ever come back?" asked Melody.

"No and there will be no way to communicate. If someday your descendants become advanced enough you can build a ship to visit Mars. You could see if our Mars citizens survived."

The silence was deafening.

"Now," said Volley. "Here's the problem. In checking my calculations, I realize I can't accurately control where you will land."

"That's the part I don't like," said Roland. "That's not good. No matter which choice we choose, I feel we could possibly land in an extremely remote or a cold area with no means of building a shelter. We can't even be assured we'd land on dry land. Volley, we've got to take a fusion generator and some kind of shelter. And your ship sounds a little haphazard to me."

Volley lowered her head. "I know, Roland."

"When do we do this, if we agree?" asked Melody.

"In approximately one month," answered Aerial.

Roland asked, "I have to ask this question again Volley, but you couldn't assure me we'd land on dry land. Can you even be sure we'd land on Earth?"

"I can't," said Volley with a noticeable hesitation.

"We're for it," said Brooke and Nadia together. "It's better than staying here. If things go bad on the trip, it would be a quick death. Staying here will be pure torture."

"Good ol' steady Brooke," said Roland.

"Okay here," said Roalf.

Roland again wanted to mention his completed time tunnel, but didn't. He still couldn't determine where his machine would place them.

"I guess we're agreed too," said Melody.

"Then it's settled. Get organized and decide in what time period you want and what you want to take. There's little room and you'll have to be extremely careful to take only things you will definitely need. We'll tell you how much equipment you can take."

In contrast to their hurried rush to Aerial's office, the Davidson family slowly walked home, conversing in low voices. Roland was quite reserved about the whole operation. He didn't like the vagueness of the voyage. He knew his time tunnel was tremendously more accurate—except where the exit would be. Who's to say? His own time machine might land them in the ocean or at the North Pole. They could end up on an Earth dying because of a meteor.

As the Davidson family entered their home, the dome over Volley's home in Paradise collapsed. Her space probe and all of its computer controls were destroyed just inside of Paradise's air lock. Roland's concern about using Volley's ship became a moot point. Roland's time tunnel became their only means of escape.

CHAPTER FOUR

The news of Volley's space ship seemed to completely deflate Roland's family. The up and down events had his family confused, bewildered and depressed. Roland decided now was the time to act. Roland brought his family to his lab.

"Look," he said to them. "Do you recognize this?"

"Yeah, Dad. It looks like that square thing we got into on Earth, just when Morgo's Sentinels stopped us."

"That's it exactly," said Roland. "I've been rebuilding it for the last several years just in case it became necessary."

"You never told me. Does it work?" asked Melody.

"You bet. I have full confidence in it, or should I say I have 99 percent confidence. The only problem is where the exit will be."

"The good news is we would be getting out of here," said Roalf

Roland said, "I can program it for 30,000 years ago and I think we'll end up on Earth. All we have to do it get in. We don't have time to debate. Now is the time. Let's grab our equipment and get in. Wherever we end up, I'll need to test the atmosphere to see if it is breathable. All plants will have to be tested to see if they are edible. I want to take as much test equipment as possible. Pick up some warmware, too. I don't know it it'll be cold or hot."

"Will other people be able to use the generator and time tunnel?" asked Brooke.

"I doubt it. This fusion generator has only enough fuel to last another one or two days, enough to get us out of here. They'll have to obtain another one and understand my papers."

"Roland," said Melody. "Every time we're ready to leave others to a certain death, I feel guilty."

"I know. I do too. And we don't know if we are doing the right thing either. Are there any other options?"

"No, I guess not."

Roland said, "I'm grateful Aerial and Volley thought of me and my family but we've got to go."

"But Roland," said Melody, "On Earth I thought you could only locate the exit point a few hundred meters from the cube exit? Won't your tunnel keep us here on Mars?"

"I surely hope not. 30,000 years ago Mars was still a barren planet. We certainly don't want to end up here. I believe the computer will still place us at the same point on Earth, near the old exit point on the Colorado River. That's the only exit I was able to program into the computer. The Colorado River hadn't been dammed yet so we won't be placed in Lake Powell. I also don't believe Arizona or Utah was a barren desert 30,000 years ago. My only unknown is how long it will take."

"I don't know what to think anymore," she said.

"Then the third time is a charm. Is everyone ready?"

"Yeah Dad," said Brooke. "Let's do it before a meteor or something hits us."

"Then here we go."

Roland's family hurriedly stepped into the cube. They quickly gathered as much equipment, water and eatables as possible. Roland wished he could load aboard a fusion generator but there wasn't enough room but he did take his test apparatus. He wanted to be sure the atmosphere of the exit point was not noxious.

"Come on kids," Roland yelled. "We got to move. I hear yelling outside. I think they suspect something."

He turned on the computer and entered his special program. His hands were shaking but he was determined to save his family. He then attempted to dial up the date of 30,000 years in the past on Earth. His computer seemed balky and moved slowly. He entered the figures and nothing was displayed on his screen.

"Oh my God," he said for the second time in his life. "If you are there, please help me save my family."

The computer seemed to move in a snail's pace. He entered the figures once again and then a third time. Finally it seemed to be accepting his key strokes. Now he paced back and forth waiting for the word "Complete." His confidence in his time machine was thoroughly shaken.

"I've got to save my family!" he cried. "What's changed? Everything looks different. I don't seem to know what I'm doing."

He hurriedly entered the time mark again not completely sure of the date. The screen would not verify the time or location of exit. Finally the screen displayed "Complete."

"Move over folks. Here I come."

After a dreamlike period the Davidson family heard the humming cease. Carefully Roland pushed one of the plates aside. They were all enthralled immediately by the lush and green beauty. It had just rained and the air was fresh and moist. While not unpleasant, it did have an unusual odor.

"Dad," said Risa. "Earth is beautiful!"

They saw flying birds and heard their strange songs. A stream babbled nearby with greenish but clear water. An odd looking rabbit type animal was drinking. It and a different animal scampered by. Their color was unusual and their fur seemed to sparkle in the distant sun. The sun! However beautiful, it seemed smaller. The smaller, distant sun told Roland they were not on Earth. It was pleasantly warm but fairly breezy. The horizon seemed so close and the sky was a pinkish blue. He expected the two-third increase of Earth's gravity to be a shock after years on Mars but there was no increase.

A sudden realization hit Roland. They weren't on Earth 30,000 years ago. They weren't on Mars 30,000 years ago either. They were still on Mars just as Melody had remarked but it was a Mars many, many years in the past. He didn't know exactly the date but possibly many millions of years earlier. He quickly tested the oxygen content of the atmosphere. It contained slightly more oxygen than Earth and somewhat less nitrogen but the atmospheric pressure was less. They were not experiencing any ill feelings or light-headedness. Their exit was still two meters from the time machine entrance. Suddenly it disappeared.

But Mars was not a dead planet. It was alive and beautiful. Surveying the lush growth around him, Roland felt confident he and his family would survive. They would test carefully the fruits surrounding them. There was an abundance of material nearby to construct a shelter.

Roland lamented that he had no literature available to study the religions of the world but maybe he'd be able to see God in his beautiful surroundings. However, the Davidson family was home. The Martians were home.

THE BEGINNING, AGAIN

ABOUT THE AUTHOR

John retired as a district sales manager in 2000 after nearly 29 years with the same employer. He has always wanted to write and now in his retirement years he has the time to pursue his interest. John has traveled all fifty states and most Canadian provinces gathering material for stories.

His hobbies include model trains, guitar and piano, singing in the church choir, and helping family and friends with home improvement projects. His younger years included running eight marathons and belonging to two tennis leagues.

John lives in Iowa with his wife Clara.